LUST (

Caroline glared at Lucian as she shrugged the coat from her shoulders. Beneath it she was all but naked. She wore just a thin white camisole that reached to her waist with matching stockings and suspenders. The points of her nipples and the circles of her areolae were plainly visible through the flimsy top. The pale dome of her belly and the strip of honey-coloured curls at the junction of her thighs were framed by the suspender straps. To Lucian's eye she had never looked more ravishing.

'I hope you're satisfied,' she said bitterly.

'Not yet,' he replied, 'but I intend to be ...'

Also available from Headline Delta

Lust on
the Line

Noel Amos

First published in 1996
by HEADLINE BOOK PUBLISHING

A HEADLINE DELTA paperback

10 9 8 7 6 5 4 3 2 1

ISBN 0 7472 5323 4

Typeset by Keyboard Services, Luton, Beds

Printed and bound in Great Britain by
Cox & Wyman Ltd, Reading, Berks

HEADLINE BOOK PUBLISHING
A division of Hodder Headline PLC
338 Euston Road
London NW1 3BH

Lust on
the Line

One

BLUE DESIRE

1

'So tell me, Lucian,' said Miranda Lynch, newly appointed Chief Executive of once-grand book publishers, The Whimsical Press, 'where do you stand on Erotica?'

Lucian Swan, editor, opened his mouth. 'Er...' he said. It was expected of him to say something. Miranda's grey eyes, as threatening as a stormy sea, were demanding a response.

But what did she mean by 'Erotica'? Was it an island in the Pacific? A Greek philosopher? Or some small academic publisher he'd never heard of?

'Well...' he said, aware he was about to plunge into the unknown and sound like a fool.

Luckily for him she misunderstood his hesitation.

'It may be a shock to one of your rarefied sensibilities, Lucian, but we've got to turn this company round somehow. And if that means churning out a line of smutty novels then so be it. Obviously I need an editor. Where do you stand?'

For once Lucian said nothing. So that was what she meant by Erotica. Jerk-off books. Mucky novels for hand-shandy merchants. Pornography. Well, he didn't have anything against it in principle though he knew nothing about it in practice.

Lucian found himself nodding. It was one of his problems, he always agreed with his boss – whoever that happened to be at the time. And right now it was the meanest woman in publishing, imported by their new German owners to knock the flagging business into shape.

Despite her immaculate blonde beauty and ever-ready smile, Miranda had a reputation as a hatchet woman and so far that morning nine members of staff had been chopped. Until this moment Lucian had expected to take the number into double figures. Now it seemed he was reprieved. At a price.

'Exactly how many books were you thinking of?' he asked, pushing a dark lock of hair out of his eyes with a languid flick.

'Three a month,' said Miranda. 'Starting in April.'

Lucian gulped. 'I can't do it. I've got a full programme of Whimsical Walks to publish,' he protested.

'No, you haven't. I'm dropping the series.'

'What!'

This was a bombshell. Whimsical Walks of the World had been the cornerstone of the firm's publishing programme since the war – a quirky, lovingly compiled sequence of rambles all over the globe which now comprised some 120 titles in print and a defunct backlist of 500. Lucian had edited the series for five years, ever since he had been appointed by the previous Chief Executive – or Managing Director as he was then styled – Basil Swan. Lucian's uncle.

'But,' Lucian protested, 'that's madness. That's our bestselling line. That *is* The Whimsical Press.'

'Quite. And The Whimsical Press made a loss of two point four million pounds last year on a turnover of fifteen. As for bestsellers, what's your fastest-selling new title?'

'Well...' Lucian was caught on the hop. This kind of conversation about sales figures was his least favourite. '*Barnacle*, I suppose.'

'OK.' Miranda's fingers were already tapping at her computer keyboard. 'Here we are, that great bestseller *Whimsical Walks in Barnacle Country*. A hundred and thirty copies have moved in the last six months. A hundred of which appear to have gone to one customer.'

'The author. He sells them at his lectures.'

'I see.' Miranda narrowed her eyes and an out-of-place furrow appeared on her perfect brow. 'It seems he hasn't paid for them yet. In the same period fifteen hundred copies were returned.'

'Oh.'

'That's not much of a bestseller, is it now?'

'It got terrific reviews in the area. And it won a prize from the local ramblers' association. Mind you, the author is a former president of the association, so ...'

Miranda's eyes drank in every nuance of Lucian's discomfort as the words died on his lips.

'You take my point?' she said. 'I'm sure you understand that you would be better employed on books that actually make some money.'

'Can I still do my literary novels as well?'

Miranda's strawberry-pink, unpainted mouth turned down.

'Such as?'

'Quentin Constant. He's on the point of a breakthrough, I'm sure. I bet you lunch at Grimaldi's he wins the Baxendale Prize next time.' Lucian was conscious that this show of bravado was possibly pushing it but someone had to stand up for Literature now the barbarians had taken over.

The barbarian in front of him reached once more for the computer keyboard. A thin gold chain encircled the pale stem of her neck and the honey-blonde helmet of her gleaming hair brushed the collar of her cream silk blouse. For a barbarian, Lucian reflected, her appearance was seductively civilised.

'What was his last novel?'

'*Lambent Peonies* but there's no need to look up the figures—' Her slender, unadorned fingers paused. '—I know it was only moderately successful but there was a cock-up on the jacket. The first "e" in Peonies got lost – the designer thought it was a children's book.' The fingers resumed their clicking. 'It was only spotted at the last minute so we didn't have a jacket for the sell-in. It was nobody's fault really, just bad luck—'

Miranda made a small hissing noise through clenched teeth as she stared at the screen in front of her. The sound of executive frustration silenced Lucian's babble as effectively as a punch in the throat.

'It's sold three hundred and twenty copies to date,' she said in a voice of ice. 'If that's one of your moderate titles I'd be curious to see the performance of a bad one. No, please, Lucian—' Lucian bit back the urge to interrupt '—spare me any more of your past successes. Let's discuss the future.'

'Fine,' said Lucian, sitting up and trying to appear more upbeat than he felt.

'That's if you think you have one with this company.'

'Oh.' Lucian slumped like a punctured balloon. 'Haven't I?'

'Let me be frank with you. You're not the most productive editor on the staff. You edit fewer than a dozen books a year and their sales, as far as I can tell, are negligible. Your expenses exceed five hundred pounds a month and you currently owe the company nearly two thousand pounds—'

'But that's an authorised float for legitimate expenditure—'

'—authorised by your uncle who is no longer employed here. To continue my assessment, you talk too much and listen too little. You are poorly acquainted with the financial implications of your day-to-day efforts. You are a pushover for any manipulative literary agent, which means all of them. And you have no idea of the prospective market for any of the books you produce. In short, you are a garrulous dilettante out of touch with the demands of the modern publishing industry. Now, am I being unfair?'

Lucian thought for a moment. 'Sometimes I ask the agents to pay for lunch,' he said.

Miranda laughed, a disconcerting barking noise at odds with her feminine appearance.

'And I love books. It's in the blood,' he added, playing the family card.

'So when did you last read one?'

'I've just finished Quentin's new synopsis and I've got some interesting pages from a freelance journalist.'

'That's not what I mean, Lucian. When did you last go to a bookshop, buy a book published by another firm and read it all the way through?'

'Oh.' Lucian thought. A few years back he'd bought a bestseller about the history of time by some genius. He'd only got a far as page three though, so that didn't count.

'You see?' Miranda's face was triumphant. 'Editors like you aren't in touch with the book-buying experience. I bet, for example, you've never even looked at these.' And she produced a bundle of paperbacks from a drawer and spread them across the desk top.

'Erotica,' she announced with zeal in her voice. 'This is what's selling these days. Call yourself an editor – get me some of this. I want a list of prospective titles from you by next Monday or there's another interesting page you'll be reading.'

Lucian didn't want to ask but he knew he had to.

'What's that?'

'Your P45.'

2

From behind the curtain of his first-floor study, Montgomery Hastings watched his wife as she unlocked her scarlet Mercedes convertible. Karen Hastings was an open-faced beauty with gleaming black hair that fell like a dark waterfall onto the olive-brown skin of her shoulders. On this hot summer's day she wore a flowered frock that looked a rag when on a hanger and a million dollars on her slender, graceful frame. It had indeed cost a few bob – as had most things to do with Karen and Monty Hastings.

Karen even looked good as she bent to climb into the low-slung car, her bronzed legs flashing as her dress rode up her thighs. Then the car door clicked shut, the motor fired and the costly machine purred down the leafy driveway out of sight.

Monty Hastings grinned and stepped from his hiding place. He was pleased to see his wife out of the way. He was no longer inspired by her beauty and elegance. He took it for granted, as he did everything he possessed. If his Rolex were to tell the wrong time or his swimming pool spring a leak, then he would be perturbed. Likewise, if his wife went around looking like a bag lady, he would be distinctly put out. The point of owning expensive things was that they performed their functions impressively. And Karen's function was to look impressive on his arm at book launches and first nights. In that respect she was a worthwhile investment.

At the moment, however, Monty was not thinking of possessions or investments. This was his favourite time of the day and he was going to make the most of it.

He took the stairs down to the kitchen two at a time and quickly ground some coffee beans. While the kettle boiled he laid a tray with two cups, a small jug of cream and a plate of fresh croissants. If Karen had seen him she would have been amazed, she was not aware he even knew how to use the coffee-grinder.

Two minutes later, Monty was pushing open a door on the second floor which gave onto a large sunlit room running the whole length of the house. He set the tray on a small wicker table in front of a battered but comfy chesterfield and announced, above the tap of fingers on a keyboard, 'Room service.'

The tapping ceased and a woman seated in front of a computer terminal swivelled in her chair and gazed at him through the windows of her outsize tortoiseshell spectacles.

'Mmm, I just love the aroma of fresh coffee,' she said in a low and husky tone. When Monty had first heard that voice he had been forced to suppress a giggle, it had sounded like deliberate affectation. Now when he listened to it the blood rushed to his cock. Bestselling novelist Montgomery Hastings and Harriet Pugh, secretary, researcher and handmaiden to his muse, were in lust.

'Has she gone then?' said Harriet, standing to take the cup Monty offered her and biting into a croissant.

'Yes,' said Monty from the depths of the sofa. Harriet stood just in front of him. She wore a pink vest cut off below the bust and white denim jeans, the creamy plain of her bare belly peeping in between. Monty gazed with absorption at the dark whorl of her navel, like an inverted thimble, just begging for the insertion of his fingertip.

'I wonder where she goes every morning?' she said, chewing hungrily. Monty's eyes flicked upwards to the movement of her full

9

red lips. A flake of pastry fell downwards onto the shelf of her bosom thrusting out in unfettered provocation.

'To the shops and the gym, I think. I don't really know,' he said. He didn't care either, just so long as she was out of the way when he felt the urge to avail himself of his assistant's personal services. Like he did now. He restrained his itching fingers as Harriet took a gulp of coffee and reached for another croissant.

'Maybe she's having an affair,' she said.

'Come off it. She's not interested in sex.'

'You mean she's not interested in you, darling.'

'No. She's dead below the waist. Believe me, you've got more fire, more passion, more outright sensuality in your little finger than she has in her entire body.'

As he spoke these words, Monty placed his hands on the violin curve of her hips and pulled her close. He nuzzled her bare midriff. Harriet licked her fingers free of crumbs and laid them on his thatch of luxuriant dark hair.

'You're only saying that because you want to fuck me,' she said, wriggling against him as his hot breath played over her skin.

'That's not the reason but, yes, I do want to fuck you. Right now.' And he found the zip of her jeans with his teeth and began to tug.

'I've got work to do,' she gurgled. 'What would my boss say?'

He had her zip down and was sliding the denim over her hips.

'He'd tell you to take your big tits out and give him a mouthful.'

Harriet laughed, a throaty rattle of a sound. 'For a literary man and a Baxendale prize-winner, you do have a coarse way of putting things, Monty.'

Nevertheless, she pulled the vest up to her shoulders so that the material pressed down on the bare globes of her breasts in a thin restraining line, emphasising their pouting pear-shaped perfection.

From Monty's position, looking upwards at the twin peaks looming above him, they appeared huge, the swollen gourds like ripe cantaloupes.

'Is that satisfactory, O Master,' she said as she fed a fat raspberry nipple between his lips.

He savoured the hard bud in his mouth before replying. 'I have only one complaint,' he said.

'What's that?' Her jeans were round her ankles, her panties too.

'I've never won the Baxendale.'

'You poor darling. Better luck next time.'

'If there is a next time.' He had his hands on the cheeks of her bottom, the soft flesh overflowing his fingers. The bush of her pussy was in his face now, filling his nostrils with a heady fragrance.

'There *will* be a next time,' said Harriet, 'I promise you.'

Monty would have laughed, not out of merriment but out of bitterness and cynicism and blighted hope. But he couldn't, not with his tongue deep in the honied recess of his devoted assistant's cunt.

At the same time as Monty was indulging in elevenses with Harriet, Karen was pulling into a garage ten miles down the road.

'Is Barry around?' she said to the big man in overalls who ambled over with a smirk on his face.

'What do you want 'im for, Mrs?' he said. 'I can change your oil just as good.'

Karen smiled good-naturedly at him. 'I'm sure you can,' she said. There was a pleasant Welsh lilt to her voice. 'But Barry knows the car, you see. I really need to speak to him.'

The big man might have prevaricated further but a tall blond youth had appeared at his side. He was stripped to the waist and his smooth hairless chest glowed bronze in the hot sun.

'Hello, Mrs Hastings, looking for me?'

'There's a funny noise in third, Barry. Have you time to hop in and listen?'

The words were scarcely out of her mouth when the boy had vaulted into the passenger seat and Karen was gunning the motor.

'Lucky little bleeder,' muttered the big man as they roared out of sight.

Neither spoke as they drove. Karen turned off the A road through farmland and then into some woods. She took a track to the left that was not obviously visible and came to a halt a hundred yards on when it became rutted and overgrown. She got out and walked into the forest. She did not look back – she knew the boy was following her. She stepped up to a big horse chestnut and leaned her back against it. Barry stood in front of her and placed his hands on the trunk on either side of her head.

'Well,' he said. 'That's a very troublesome motor you've got there.'

She grinned and her dark eyes flashed. She was blushing.

'It needs regular servicing, doesn't it, Mrs H?'

'Call me Karen.'

'Want me to look at your gearbox, do you?'

'Please—'

'Like me to grease your axle?'

'Oh God—'

'You can't get enough of my cock, can you, Mrs H?'

'Don't be crude, Barry.'

'Why not? This is the third time in ten days, isn't it?'

'I'm not counting. I just felt like seeing you. You didn't have to come.'

'But *you* did, didn't you? You're dying for it. I bet your cunt's running like a tap.'

'Barry!'

'Show me then. Go on. Show me your pussy, you cock-happy nympho.'

Karen shut her eyes. The smile was gone. Her face was taut with anguish. But she reached for the hem of her dress and pulled it quickly to her hips. She was leaning back against the tree and her legs were braced apart. At the junction of her thighs was a thin vertical strip of coal-black hair. Below it the nude mouth of her pussy gaped, the outer lips swollen and wet. She wore no underwear.

Barry stared at this exposed intimacy of flesh, the tough-boy words stillborn in his throat.

'Go on,' she prompted him. 'Don't stop.'

'But, Karen, you're so gorgeous, I—'

'*Barry.*' There was a warning in her voice and her eyes were open, fixed on his.

He took a deep breath and said, 'Get my dick out, bitch.'

Karen moaned and fumbled for his fly with her free hand.

'Hurry up!' he ordered as the zip stuck. But then her fingers were in and his cock was out, thick and crimson-tipped, hairless like his chest, obscene in her slim hand. She ran her fingers from base to tip and back, squeezing and rubbing, testing the steel-hard rigidity of the youthful flesh.

He was panting now, the script wiped from his mind. Her fingers delved further and eased his balls out of his jeans. She dandled the full orbs in her palm. He crushed his lips to hers and she pulled her mouth away.

'Put it in,' he commanded, suddenly remembering. The rest of it was easy. 'Put my cock up your wet snatch, you little tart.'

But she was ahead of him, for her pelvis was tilted forward and the swollen plum of his glans was in the fork of her thighs. She stood higher than him on the roots of the tree – as if she had selected the spot for the very purpose – and now she bore down on him, pushing the fat tip of his penis into her nook and slithering along his sturdy length.

'Oh God, yes!' she cried, all pretence gone, and they clung to each other in a quaking, shivering clinch as his tool thrust and drove into the hungry centre of her. Despite the awkward position it didn't last long and, as the silver spray gushed in a deluge from his twitching cock, his knees buckled and the pair of them slumped to the earth.

They did not speak on the drive back either but, before he got out of the car, she allowed him a long and tender kiss.

She sang to herself as she set off, at last, to the shops.

3

That evening Lucian stayed late at the office. The painful interview with Miranda had plainly laid his future on the line. Lucian could take a hint – especially when it was delivered with the subtlety of an executioner's axe. So now he sat in his scruffy basement office, surrounded by the piles of paperbacks he had hastily acquired from the top shelf of the local newsagents.

It was nearly nine and everyone else had long gone, he assumed. But there wasn't much point in heading home himself, not now Caroline had left him. He sighed indulgently as he poured a glass of lukewarm plonk, then picked a book from the pile in front of him. It was one of life's ironies that the day after he had foresworn sex for good, he was ordered to steep himself in sexually explicit material.

Reluctantly he began to read.

'Your time has come, Selwyn,' breathed Edwina Justice as she rose from behind the glistening rosewood desk, the horsewhip clasped in her fist. 'Prepare to suffer!'

'Spare me, mistress,' blurted the distraught youth.

'Never!' cried his implacable tormentor as she strode towards him, her emerald eyes flashing like lightening bursts, the thrusting mounds of her magnificent breasts tumbling from her bodice, the erect nipples cleaving the air like juddering drill bits . . .

'Bloody hell,' whispered Lucian, a vision of his own tormentor,

Miranda Lynch, taking shape in his mind. He recalled those smooth pink cheeks flushed with missionary zeal as she spoke of the commercial appeal of sex-book publishing, the glint in those wide turbulent eyes and the silky thrust of her pert bosom.

'Bloody hell,' he repeated, easing his stiff cock into a position of comfort within his underpants. Perhaps there was something to be said for this erotica stuff after all.

The sound of a cough made him jerk his hand suddenly from his trousers. His colleague Lorna Prentice was standing in the doorway. For a moment he was worried that she had noticed him fiddling with his tool then, as she took an unsteady pace into his office, he realised she probably wasn't up to noticing much.

'So this is where you're hiding, Lucian,' she said. 'We're all at the Running Rat drowning our sorrows.'

'I didn't know,' said Lucian. 'I'd have come too.'

'We couldn't find you. Never mind, I've found you now. I've come to say goodbye.'

'See you tomorrow then.'

'No, Lucian,' said Lorna, 'this is a real goodbye. I've been sacked, I'm not coming back.' And she slumped into the chair on the other side of his desk, her long coltish legs sprawling apart. Now Lucian could see the misery in the swirling depths of her green eyes and in the downturn of her pretty mouth.

'I don't believe it,' he said.

'It's true. Miranda said she had to make editorial cuts and it was last in, first out. That means me. I've only been here eight months.'

'But that's stupid,' said Lucian, outraged. 'You're brilliant, you're going to be a star!' He was on his feet, he hadn't felt so animated all day. 'I'm going to talk to Miranda. She doesn't realise what she's doing.'

'Thanks, Lucian, but it won't do any good now. I've left already – I just came back to get my things.'

'Why so soon? Wouldn't she give you time to look around for another job?'

'Not after I told her to shove it up her bum – though I doubt she's got a hole there. I bet she never takes a crap, the shit just stays in her system and spews out of her mouth.'

'Good God, you didn't tell her that, did you?'

'I nearly did when she stopped on her way out to wish me luck. Hypocritical bitch. I'm going to get a brilliant job somewhere else and show her, I swear.' And she laid her hennaed mop of hair on her arms and burst into tears on Lucian's desk.

Lucian watched the rise and fall of her thin shoulders beneath the cotton of her summer dress. It was funny how someone else's troubles put your own into perspective. He produced a box of paper tissues from a drawer.

After a moment Lorna sat up and blew her nose loudly. She dabbed at her eyes and took a deep breath. Lucian handed her wine in a paper cup. As she drank she noticed for the first time the pile of lurid paperbacks that littered the desk. She laughed.

'Lucian, what are you doing with all these mucky books?'

'Research.'

She snorted in disbelief and her full lips spread into a grin.

'That's better,' said Lucian, 'now you look like your normal gorgeous self.'

'Don't try and change the subject. You were playing with yourself when I came in, weren't you? Did I catch you at it?'

'*No*. This is research, honest. I too have had a review of my job prospects with the merciless Miranda. She wants me to drop everything else and produce a list of books like these.'

'So, it's farewell Whimsical Walks—'

'Quite.'

'—and hello Whimsical Wanks.'

'Very funny.'

Giggling, she picked up a book and scanned the page. An explosion of mirth followed. She chucked the book aside and took another. This time the merriment faded and she read for a full minute before turning her eyes to Lucian.

'Wow!' she breathed. 'Are you sure you're up to this?'

'I'd better be. There's no Uncle Basil to protect me now.'

'Uncle Basil treated you like shit. I don't know how you put up with it.'

'Ah,' said Lucian, pouring them both another drink, 'I'm a put-up-with-it kind of person. Things happen to me, I don't happen to them.'

Lorna nodded. 'You're all languid and floppy, Lucian, that's true enough. But Caroline has happened to you, so don't knock it.'

'Caroline left last week.'

'Oh no! Why?'

'She said I was too laid-back – and she wanted to be laid elsewhere.'

'So that's why you're hanging around the office getting smashed.'

'I suppose so.' He sighed.

'We're a pair of real sad sacks, aren't we?' she said.

'Orphans in a storm.' He picked up the bottle but it was empty.

'This is pathetic,' said Lorna, getting to her feet. 'There's something I've always wanted to do and now's my last chance – will you help me?'

'Do what?'

'Shut up and follow me.'

The boardroom was on the first floor. Through the high windows the ornately moulded ceilings and glass-fronted bookshelves, lined with the output of The Whimsical Press, were dimly lit by the orange glow of a streetlamp. Down the middle of the long room the mahogany surface of the boardroom table gleamed faintly. Here was where the regular business meetings took place, where editors pitched their projects, publicists plotted strategy and salesmen cursed missed targets – in short, where the daily round of publishing ground on. It smelt of sweat, stale coffee and furniture polish. And boredom.

Lorna's eyes gleamed in the half-light as she closed the door behind them. She kicked off her shoes and turned her back to Lucian.

'Undo my buttons.'

'What?'

'The buttons of my dress. Come on!'

Lucian's fingers fumbled as, nothing loth, he rushed to do her bidding. 'What are you up to?' he asked, baring the nape of her neck.

'I'm going to dance naked on that table. It's one of my fantasies.'

Beneath the dress was a thin white half-slip. There was no sign of a bra.

'I've sat here in meeting after meeting,' she said as the dress slithered over her slim hips to the floor, 'just dying to do something really rude and wave two fingers at the system.'

Lucian chuckled. 'And I thought you were all business.'

'Oh I am. It's just that I've got a wide range of business interests.'

She was facing him now, her hands on the hem of the tiny camisole. She pulled it over her head and the wild cascade of her hair and threw it over her shoulder in triumph. She drew her knickers down her thighs and tossed them, too, into the gloom.

'Help me up,' she said and Lucian steadied her narrow back as she climbed onto the table. Then she began to move.

It wasn't a conventional dance in any sense, just a combination of graceful bending and swaying as she undulated her long lean body up and down the length of the table. Lucian was mesmerised. He couldn't tear his eyes from the nut-brown nipples on the gentle curves of her breasts and the black vee of hair at the junction of her thighs.

She stood above him and, suddenly, belly-bumped her pelvis like a stripper.

'Of course,' she said, 'that's only the beginning of my fantasy. In the next bit I need a man.' She tossed her head and the dark mane shimmered across her slim shoulders and the little bowls of her breasts quivered. 'Take your clothes off, Lucian.'

'But—'

'Don't you dare let me down,' she said as she jumped off the table top. 'What's the matter? Don't you want me?'

It would sound feeble to explain that, after Caroline, he had vowed to give up sex. In any case, Lucian thought as he took off his shirt, this wasn't sex *per se*. It was a symbolic act of vengeance by a wronged woman. He was simply a means to her end – or his cock was.

Lorna's hands closed around it at once.

'Is that in your fantasy?' he asked, seizing her by the hips.

'Oh yes,' she said, 'except the one I was thinking of was bigger.'

Lucian pinched an apple-cheeked buttock. 'Bitch.'

Lorna giggled. 'What's the point of a fantasy if it doesn't improve on life?'

Lucian kissed her hot little mouth and kneaded her bottom. Her nipples were burning into his chest and her fingers were sliding up and down his tool. If she kept that up her fantasy might come to a premature conclusion.

'What happens next?' he muttered between kisses.

'You fuck me on this table.'

'It won't be very comfortable.'

'Who cares?'

She led him to the top of the table and sat herself on the edge.

'This is Miranda's place, isn't it?'

'Yes.'

'Let's do it here, then.'

She opened her legs and he stood in the fork of her thighs, her cunt almost on a level with his throbbing cock.

He combed his fingers through her bush, the hair softer than he had expected. The flesh beneath was soft too, her pussy mound plump and sticky and perfumed like a ripe peach. He found the little pip of her clitoris and she squealed.

'Put that thing in me now,' she hissed and he obeyed.

It was weird, fucking in the meeting room where he had yawned and fidgeted and suffered on so many occasions. Now this tall girl with the pretty mouth and big dark nipples was stretched out backwards, her mane of hair fanned out across the wood, her legs round his waist, engulfing his raging cock.

'This is fantastic,' Lorna said. 'I feel like I'm fucking the whole rotten firm.'

'You're fucking me,' said Lucian, bending to kiss those curved and luscious lips.

But they were set in a hard thin line and Lorna's eyes were closed as she whipped her head from side to side, muttering and cursing, 'You bitch, you bitch, Miranda Lynch! I swear I'll fucking fix you – OH!'

Her orgasm overtook her in a rush and Lucian was almost a spectator as she thrashed beneath him. By contrast his culminating twitch and gush seemed a poor and feeble thing.

Lorna looked up at him squiffily as his limp member slipped from the hairy nook between her legs.

'Will you come home with me?' said Lucian, thinking suddenly of his empty flat.

Lorna shook her head. 'Sorry. Charlie's expecting me. He'll kill me if he finds out about this.'

'I shan't tell a soul.'

She sat up and hugged him. Her kiss was sweet as she patted his cock.

'Lucian,' she said, 'I want you to know that when it counted you weren't floppy at all.'

4

As a rule, dinner in the Hastings house was not a jolly affair – not these days. Tonight was no exception. Monty made himself a ham sandwich and washed it down with a bottle of designer lager. Then, grabbing the last piece of apple pie, he retired to his study to work on his current masterpiece.

Later, Karen assumed, he would set off for the village local to mix with 'some real people', as he put it. She had often heard him say how important it was for a 'historian of the imagination', i.e. a novelist such as himself, not to lose touch with 'the sons of toil and soil'. Monty's cronies at The Turnip Clamp included a stockbroker, a Harley Street proctologist, a public relations consultant and the owner of a chain of video rentals. At closing time these sons of toil would repair to Ray the video man's bachelor cottage where, Karen assumed, they would catch the latest addition to his ever-expanding blue movie collection. In the not-too-distant past Monty would have returned in the small hours and given Karen the benefit of his hard-on. No longer, not now they had separate bedrooms.

Karen's disillusion with her illustrious husband had begun as a small crack in the façade of their unity. Now the fissure ran from top to bottom. The issue that had first divided them was children: Karen longed for them, Monty said he did too – but not yet. Six years after their marriage, the position had not changed, except that he had met with literary success and, wonder of wonders, was fast becoming rich.

Some eighteen months previously a lucrative commission had

beckoned from Hollywood. Karen had decreed that this was the time to procreate and Monty had turned green and run off to Los Angeles. There he earned obscene sums of money for work destined never to be seen and performed obscene acts with a lot of actresses. Whether it was the running away or the actresses that started the rot in their marriage, Karen couldn't decide. Not that it mattered, it was the babies he was denying her that were important.

Somehow they had stayed together. No word of their difficulties had got out. They were still seen as a happy, glamorous, perfect couple. But, to Karen, the new start with the new money in the new house in the Oxfordshire countryside was a sham. She was married to a phony. And, damn soon, she was going to make sure everybody knew it.

After Monty had gone to his study she made straight for her own bedroom. She locked the door behind her and then, with a key taken from her bedside drawer, she opened her walk-in closet. The space had been specially created for her when they had refurbished the old house and was designed to accommodate an extensive wardrobe. Karen had easily been able to make room at the rear to house a desk and a personal computer.

While the machine was booting up, Karen drew the bedroom curtains and flung off her clothes. The only problem with working in her closet was the heat. On summer nights like this her naked body would swim in perspiration. The sweat ran from her forehead to her chin to the tips of her breasts then down her domed belly to pool in the black strip of hair between her legs. There it would mingle with the thick juices which welled from her vagina as she fell under the spell of her own words. Karen was writing a sex book. If Monty discovered what she was up to he would have a shit-fit. That thought, more than anything, really turned her on.

Tonight Karen reviewed her encounter with Barry, the blond mechanic. The boy was a hunk, no doubt about it, and she loved the way just the sight of her body drove him to distraction. Unfortunately, his mind didn't measure up to his cock. 'Same old story,' she muttered to herself. No matter how often she instructed him to treat her mean in their lovemaking, to threaten and humiliate her as he bore down on her with his angry red-tipped cudgel, it wasn't in him. In reality, Barry was just an adoring puppy who wanted to lick her all over and bask in her approval. Unfortunately for him, Karen was not turned on by puppies. She wanted thrills, excitement, danger – her book would be all the better for it. Perhaps she should look elsewhere for inspiration.

Karen considered her progress so far. She had completed a hefty chunk of manuscript, nearly 200 pages of A4, neatly word-processed and laser-jet printed. It looked most professional. And she wasn't finished yet.

Her story was about the infidelities of a childless couple whose relationship survived in name only. Though the wife's indiscretions were based on her own firsthand experience, for the husband's she had had to be more ingenious. Of course, any resemblance to persons living or dead was entirely coincidental.

In a drawer below the printer lay the source material for the husband's story. There were a few documents: a copy of a decree nisi naming Montgomery Hastings as co-respondent in the separation of Madeleine Bennett and Professor Hieronymus Bennett, accompanied by a newspaper cutting ('Double-First Student Steals Prof's Wife'); an affidavit drawn up by Marvin B. Flugle, public notary, of Orange County, California, on behalf of Brenda de la Costa, actress, detailing Monty's relationship with her and her friends during a fifteen-week period less than two years ago; and hard copy of an indiscreet e-mail correspondence between Monty and a fan in northwest London which Karen had managed to lift off his computer in the days before Harriet Pugh, when she herself had acted as Monty's handmaiden of the keyboard.

This was a role she had performed for Monty from the very beginning of their relationship. After the Hollywood episode she had found it hard to sustain. Converting his precious 300-word a day output from fountain pen to disk had become a chore she could no longer bear. Particularly the 'analysis' he required of his secretary, i.e. the fawning post mortems of his genius which she had given so generously in the days when she revered him as a writer, BLA – Before Los Angeles. Now Harriet provided those commentaries on the sensitivity of his observation, on the brilliance of his perception, on the wit of his *mots justes* – and so on.

And Harriet also provided other services for Monty that were almost as precious to him. Karen knew all about the cosy relationship between Monty and Harriet, far more than she really wanted to know. In fact she had it taped – on the dozens of audiocassettes that lay in her drawer on top of those incriminating papers. Every evening, when Monty was out of the way, she would remove the tape from the concealed recorder in the office and replace it with a new one. So far, Karen had ten weeks' worth of material. If the Hastings' marital disillusion should ever reach the lawyers, Monty wouldn't have a leg, or any other pelvic appendage, to stand on.

The tape-recorder ran on a timer. At the beginning, Karen had experimented and discovered, unsurprisingly, that Monty was more likely to incriminate himself if she was not around. As a consequence she had developed a routine: every day she left the house on the dot of eleven. A quarter of an hour later the machine switched itself on and, for the next hour, recorded every sigh, whisper and indelicate comment uttered in the room. Concealed in the base of a large table lamp, Karen had no doubt that this piece of technological cunning would remain undetected for as long as required.

It had not been Karen who had fixed it up, of course. For that she had had to obtain the services of Benjie Allsop, a shy lanky youth who worked at the electrical goods store in Long Swivenham. Benjie, not long out of school and in awe of the female sex, had not needed much persuading once Karen had lured him into the house and poured a couple of Monty's favourite malt whiskies down his throat.

In the event, by way of payment, she had relieved him of his virginity on the desk in the study where Harriet Pugh toiled daily. And she had been so impressed with his work, both technical and personal, that she had secured his services on a retainer. Once a month now he would drop by and Karen would entertain him royally in her bedroom. She told him that if he ever breathed a word about the recorder or their lovemaking he would never have the pleasure of her company again. She did not tell him that their liaison also formed the basis of the third chapter of her novel. 'There was nothing,' she wrote in the persona of her heroine, Evangelista, 'nothing quite like the silken smooth, rapid, eager and volcanically eruptive action of an unschooled virgin cock . . .'

Just wait till you read my book, Monty Hastings, she thought as she slipped her index finger into the mouth of her slick vagina. *You're not going to rob me of* this *baby*.

5

It was late when Lucian returned home. The thrill of the encounter with Lorna had worn off and his thoughts were all of Caroline as he stumped up to his attic bedroom. Some of her clothes still hung in the wardrobe and her perfume lingered. The tussle with Lorna had awoken his sexual desire but not assuaged it. He knew even before he took off his jacket that, despite all his vows to forsake carnal thoughts, he would have to masturbate – and masturbate with Caroline in mind. He pulled off all his clothes and looked at his prick. It was thick, half hard and salivating. It smelt of Lorna's juices and his own. It was a red and bestial organ whose throbbing needs could not be ignored.

With a pounding pulse he took from the bedside drawer two objects that were fast becoming a fetish to him. First was a pair of Caroline's pink cotton panties, an unremarkable undergarment to all but the lovelorn. He had found them beneath the bed the night she left and he imagined they still smelt of her. The other item was a Polaroid photograph. It showed Caroline kneeling, half naked, one hand holding her blonde hair off her face so the camera could capture her pretty pouting lips ringing an erect penis. Her eyes were closed and her cheeks were hollow with the force of her sucking – and the cock in her mouth did not belong to Lucian.

He had no idea who it did belong to. Maybe it was someone he knew, maybe not. The thought tormented him. He had found the photo on Caroline's dresser just a week ago. The row had been predictable and so had been the result. She had planned it, he had no doubt, for she already had a bag packed. After one phone call – to a lover he assumed – she had disappeared into a black Jaguar which purred along the street ten minutes later, leaving him with a broken heart and these pathetic mementos. He knew he should destroy them. He couldn't.

He wrapped the panties round his cock and groaned with unhappy lust. This worthless piece of fabric had once encircled his lover's fabulous arse – how he himself longed to do so again! He held the Polaroid close to his face so he could drink in every detail – the bead of sweat on her lip, the curve of her graceful neck, the flawless skin of her cheek stretched to receive the hideous organ of her brutish lover ... '*Caro*,' he moaned aloud as his hand rubbed the panties up and down the shaft of his cock. His body trembled as passion shook him and the photo slipped from his fingers and fluttered to the floor.

It broke the spell and disrupted his rhythm. He looked for the photo but it had vanished. Maybe it had fallen behind the bed. He stepped forward, squeezing behind the bedside table to reach down. It was an awkward position, for the attic ceiling sloped and there was an angled skylight over the bed which had been left open. For a second he looked out through the window and then froze. In that spot, half bent, his gaze aimed obliquely through the glass, he could see directly into the top bedroom of a house diagonally across the street. And what he saw, in the fickle way of lust and prurience, drove faithless Caroline from his thoughts.

He saw a woman taking off her clothes. Her thick chestnut ringlets obscured her face as she bent to unzip her skirt and slide it down her legs. Lucian was instantly entranced as she slowly began to unbutton her blouse. It slipped from her shoulders and joined the skirt on the floor. The white cups of her brassiere gleamed against the bronze hue of her skin and the dark shadow of her pubic bush was clearly visible through the thin cotton of her panties. Her hips were rounded and her legs as long and spectacular as a showgirl's.

Wearily, it seemed, the woman bent to pick up her clothes and moved out of sight – to hang them up, Lucian presumed. By now he had worked out who this vision was: Nicole, the wife of his neighbour and occasional tennis partner, Hugh Sessions. He'd always thought she was a looker but had never realised quite how fabulous she really was.

Nicole returned and sat in front of the dressing-table. Her upper half was still visible. As Lucian watched, his pulse racing, she reached behind her and unhooked the white bra. She tossed it aside and reached for her hairbrush, shaking her dark tresses. Her golden breasts shook too. They were big and round and heavy and the breath hissed from Lucian's throat as he imagined burying his face in their bounty. She brushed her hair vigorously, working the bristles through the thick curls, every pull of her arm echoed in the shifting of her full bosom.

Lucian was so entranced by the flow of her brush and the lift and sway of her flesh that it was a moment before he realised that she was talking to someone in the mirror in front of her. She shrugged and pulled a face. Her eyes flashed. Lucian thought she was delightful.

Lucian recognised Hugh at once, of course. His naked body was familiar to him from the tennis club changing-room – though he had never before seen him with an erection. It was an impressive sight, he had to admit. Hugh was an athletic fellow, shorter than Lucian but more compact, with a deep chest and thick muscular thighs. The hair on his head was fair but on his belly it grew reddish brown and, from this thicket, thrust the bulging barrel of his tool.

He stepped behind the seated figure of his wife and slipped his hands around her body to still those trembling breasts. Lucian could imagine his yearning penis pressing into the warm skin of her back.

She stopped her brushing and allowed Hugh to cup and stroke her tits. He had one in each hand and the flesh overflowed his fingers. He pinched her nipples and her mouth opened in an O of pleasure – or pain, Lucian couldn't tell. Hugh pulled down on the soft globes, then pressed them close together to create a dark line of cleavage in between. There was a tight, humourless grin on his face as he gazed at the work of his hands in the mirror. Lucian wondered if this was a nightly ritual – and what would happen next.

He didn't have long to wait. Hugh suddenly released Nicole's bosom and yanked her to her feet. He pulled the chair she had been sitting on out of the way and then bent her over the dressing-table. Obediently she supported herself on her arms and thrust her bottom back towards him. She looked straight ahead into the mirror and Lucian tried to read her expression. Was that lust or disgust in her eyes? He was too far away to tell.

Not too far, though, to see Hugh working her panties off her proffered posterior and gazing intently at the exposed and out-thrust cheeks. If only, Lucian thought, he could see what Hugh could see but, regrettably, Nicole's naked bottom was hidden from his view. He had no doubt, however, that it was as glorious as the rest of her.

Hugh obviously thought so, for his cock was straining upwards from his belly. He spat into his hand and worked the spittle into the crimson plum of his knob and down the shaft. He spat again and pushed the wet fingers between her legs. She stiffened and then pushed back as he closed on her. Lucian could imagine the bend of his knees, the positioning of his tool, the aligning of pelvis to crotch. And then he was in her. She seemed to slump forward as he thrust but he pulled her up again by the hair. Her head went back and her slender throat gleamed whitely in Lucian's vision and, below that, her extravagant bosom danced as Hugh pumped into her, making her whole frame shudder.

It didn't last long, not the way Hugh went at it. And, with a final lunge that sent her sprawling face down among her make-up and perfume bottles, he shuddered to halt. For a moment they were still, locked in position like statues. Then he backed away from her and disappeared from sight.

Nicole slowly stood up and, for a moment, Lucian saw her naked to mid-thigh. As he had thought, her pussy mound was thickly forested, with hair a shade darker than on her head. Below, on the perfect curve of her inner thighs, the evidence of their coupling gleamed.

Nicole took a handful of paper tissues from a box on the table and wedged them between her legs. Then she sat down and picked up her hairbrush. As she resumed her rhythmic brushing, her big beautiful breasts once more began to sway.

Lucian became aware of a stabbing pain in his neck. So mesmerised had he been, he had no idea how long he had been standing in a such a twisted crouch. Nor did he remember reaching his own climax. Yet, when he looked down, he saw his cock had dwindled between his thighs and, in his hand, Caroline's panties were dripping with spunk.

6

Karen felt the sales assistant's eyes upon her as she stood in the bookshop. Maybe it was because she had been browsing too long or, more likely, it was the nature of the books she held in her hand. Whatever it was, the girl's gaze followed her everywhere.

Karen was used to being stared at. Her beauty had won her admiring glances ever since she was a little girl. Only recently had she been able to hold her head high under these looks of admiration, envy and – the most frequent of all – lust. Not too long ago she would have resented this stranger's curiosity. Now, since she had embarked on her secret research project, she had come to welcome such appraisals. So far they had proved most fruitful.

She took her selections to the till and laid them face up on the counter. They were paperback erotic novels from the New Threshold range. The assistant's hazel eyes met hers and Karen read something in them that set her blood singing in a familiar way. But not that familiar. She had never slept with another woman. It was an aspect of her research she had not yet come to terms with.

On impulse she said, 'Are these any good?'

The girl seemed taken aback. 'They're very popular,' she said after a moment's thought.

'Have you read any?'

The assistant blushed. She was taller than Karen and very slim.

Her fair brown hair was fastened with a wooden barrette, showing off her oval face and long slender neck. Karen could imagine her lying naked on a bed in a Modigliani painting. She wore no make-up and her pale complexion was as unlined as an egg. Karen guessed, however, that she was not as inexperienced as she looked.

'I've dipped into this one,' she said and tapped the top book on Karen's pile: *Love or Chains* – 'One woman's erotic odyssey', said a line on the cover. 'It's about a student who fucks her way through college.' The obscenity seemed incongruous emerging from that schoolgirlish mouth. 'Some of it's pretty horny, actually, though it depends on your taste.'

The way the girl looked at her made Karen's throat go dry. 'What's *your* taste?' she heard herself say.

The assistant chuckled, a naughty little sound. 'I don't think I should say. You're the customer.'

'That's why you should tell me.'

The girl grinned. 'I thought the scenes with the philosophy tutor were really rude. The female philosophy tutor,' she added, challenging Karen with those hazel eyes.

'I'll take it then,' said Karen.

As the girl gave Karen her change it seemed to leap from her hand. Both of them bent to retrieve the scattered coins, their heads close together as they crouched.

'My name's Adele,' said the girl, her breath like a scented breeze in Karen's face, her eyes now fixed on the beckoning slope of Karen's breast revealed in the neck of her white summer cardigan.

Karen took the coins, returning the squeeze from the girl's long fingers.

'I've done enough shopping, Adele. Where can I go to get a cup of coffee?'

Twenty minutes later the girl from the bookshop appeared at Karen's table in the chintzy café across the street. She didn't sit down.

'Let's go,' she said. 'I told them I've got an emergency dental appointment. I've got two hours.'

She led Karen to a car park behind the shops and unlocked an ancient mini. Inside, squashed together, she seized Karen's face in her hands and pressed her sugar-pink lips to her mouth. She plunged in her tongue and kissed Karen fiercely.

Karen let her do what she wanted, her stomach bubbling and fluttering, telling herself all the time that she must remember every sensation so she could record it. Oh how Monty would hate her for this!

Adele drove for ten minutes until they reached a row of whitewashed terraced houses in a part of Long Swivenham that Karen did not know. Inside the tiny hallway she was surprised to see a man's jacket on the newel post and a large pair of muddy trainers sitting by a bag of golf clubs. Adele caught her glance.

'Don't worry,' she said, 'my boyfriend's at work.'

There were more signs of the boyfriend in the bedroom but Karen wasn't bothered about the boxer shorts on the floor or the pile of motor-racing magazines. She was more interested in Adele's hot mouth whispering in her ear and her long fingers unzipping her skirt.

However catholic her tastes, Adele knew how to strip a woman. Within seconds, it seemed, Karen was naked but for her knickers and Adele's lips were on her breasts.

'My God,' whispered the girl as she slipped to her knees and lowered Karen's panties. 'You are just gorgeous.' Her fingers were now in Karen's exposed muff of black hair and then she was pressing kisses to the soft skin of her inner thigh. As the tip of her tongue flicked like a snake between the frill of her labia, Karen's knees gave way and she toppled onto the bed.

'Are you all right, darling?' asked Adele as she lay on the mattress beside her.

'Oh yes. You just took me by surprise.'

'Am I going too fast for you?'

'It's OK. You've not got much time, you said.'

The girl grinned and squeezed Karen's breast till the nipple stood up, scarlet with blood and excitement. 'Actually, I think my toothache's getting worse. I might have to spend the rest of the day in bed.'

A mass of thoughts filled Karen's head as Adele went to work between her legs, sending her racing to the quickest climax she could remember. She thought of the new promiscuous purpose to her life; of Monty and Harriet doubtless screwing without thought of her at this very moment; of the funny creaking bed that she found herself in, which must creak even louder when the owner of the trainers downstairs was in occupation. And she thought of the unknown girl whose innocent-seeming mouth was breathing such heavenly sensations onto her sensitive flesh.

She'd always imagined that women were more languorous and less bull-at-a-gate than men. Evidently this was not always the case. Adele had been as eager to bed her as any over-juiced teenage lad. But Adele was better at pleasing her, that was certain.

Karen stroked the dark head bobbing at the junction of her thighs and wondered how it would be when it was her turn to press her lips and tongue to the other girl's sex. She didn't feel repulsed at the thought of it. Kissing the girl's mouth had been different to kissing a man, softer and sweeter – and just as sexy in a sly sort of way. To taste the other mouth between her legs might be even more exciting. There was only one way to find out.

Karen pulled Adele from between her legs and wrapped her arms around her. The schoolgirlish mouth was now red and sticky. Karen kissed it and tasted herself.

'My turn,' she breathed.

Adele did not protest, her cheeks were flushed and her eyes were wild. She helped Karen unbutton her grey-and-white check frock with trembling fingers to reveal a broad but shallow bosom with candy-pink nipples. Karen bussed them quickly with her lips as she pulled the long skirt to the girl's waist. Her legs were lean and her belly was flat. Her navy blue panties were dark with her juices, plastered to the hair of her prominent mound. A musky, flowery, woman smell filled Karen's nostrils as, without thinking, she closed her mouth over Adele's vagina and began to suck her through her knickers.

'Oh God!' yelled Adele.

Karen lifted her head. 'Am I doing it wrong?' she asked.

'Please, please . . .' muttered the girl, almost incoherent as she pushed Karen back into her crotch and began to rub her pussy against her face. It seemed to Karen, as she tugged the sodden panty gusset to one side and slid her tongue between Adele's swollen labia, that she didn't have to do much at all. The girl was so excited that the merest whisper of breath upon her quim was enough to send her over the edge. And over the edge she went.

Afterwards, lying back on the rumpled bedspread, with Adele's hands gently exploring her breasts, Karen said, 'Is it always over so fast?'

'What do you mean?'

'Girls making love. I thought it was meant to be a more subtle process than with men.'

Adele stiffened, her fingers ceased toying with Karen's engorged nipples.

'Haven't you slept with a woman before?'

'No. You've just taken my second virginity.'

'I wish I'd known, I wouldn't have been so piggish. Are you about to get up and flounce out of the door?'

'Actually, I was about to ask you if we could try a few things.'

Adele relaxed and her fingers resumed their dalliance. 'What things?'

'I was wondering what it was like to do a sixty-nine with another woman ...'

Twenty minutes later Karen had found out. It was far superior experience to doing it with a man, there was no doubt.

'It's a much better fit,' she enthused. 'A man's cock gets stuck at the wrong angle half the time.'

'And it's impossible to come off together,' said Adele. 'Not to mention getting a mouthful of spunk. Yuk.'

'Don't knock it. I love it when I'm with the right man.'

'There's never a right man.'

'What about your boyfriend, Adele?'

The girl pulled away from Karen and folded her arms across her slender chest. 'Will's my fiancé. We're getting married in the spring.'

'Does he know you like girls?'

'You must be joking. He's rather straight.'

Karen looked at the downward tug of Adele's pretty mouth and resisted the urge to kiss it.

'So what would Will do if he turned up right now and found us in bed together?'

'He'd die. Correction, he'd kill me first then he'd die.'

'So you won't have any more ... toothaches after you get married then?'

Adele turned her big hazel eyes on Karen full beam. 'Why are you asking? You're not exactly faithful yourself, are you, Mrs Hastings?'

Karen said nothing.

'You're married to Monty Hastings,' Adele continued. 'He's been in our shop for signing sessions. I've seen you there too.'

Karen shrugged, there was no point in denying it. But she wasn't to be deflected from her own line of enquiry. 'If you prefer women, Adele, why are you getting married?'

'I like Will. I really do. He doesn't make me do things I don't fancy in bed.'

'But marriage is for keeps, Adele.' *In theory*, she added for her own benefit.

'I know. The truth is, a woman can't give me what I really want. I want children and so does Will – don't you understand?'

Karen didn't reply, she understood only too well. She folded the girl into her arms and hugged her.

After a moment the hug turned into something more significant. Karen ran an exploratory finger the length of Adele's pussy crack – it was a long, delicious journey. She mustn't get sidetracked by this girl's personal dilemmas, she thought. However, Adele's situation was not without further possibilities. An idea was forming in her head.

'Ooh!' squealed Adele as Karen fingered her clit. 'I've seen you in the shop lots, Karen. Each time I've wanted to put my head up your skirt and lick your cunny. And now I have – I still can't believe my luck.'

'Before you get married, Adele, you've got to tell Will you like girls.'

'I can't!'

'Would you like me to help you?'

'What do you mean?'

'A threesome.'

'What!'

'Think about it. I bet he'd love to watch us making love.'

'Oh.'

'And he could join in. He could be included in your dirty little secret.'

'But how could it be done?'

Karen laughed. 'Don't worry about that. Leave it to me. In return I need a favour.'

'What's that?'

'I've never felt a vibrator on my pussy. You wouldn't happen to have one, would you?'

Adele's eyes gleamed as she rummaged in her bedside drawer. Karen watched her with the glow of past and future satisfaction singing in her loins. She'd always wondered why authors said they enjoyed the research more than the writing. Now she knew.

7

So far Lucian had had a frustrating day. For the first time in his publishing life he was faced with a challenge – to kill off Whimsical Walks as painlessly as possible and to set in motion the new erotic series. By mid-afternoon this double-headed test of his ability had left him looking down the barrel of failure. Double-barrelled failure at that.

As far as Walks went, it was a question of pulling the plug on any project due for publication after the end of the year – and for ditching those in that period that hadn't yet been delivered.

'But it's about to go in the post to you this morning,' squealed author Nancy Bollard.

'Sorry, Nancy, but you've been saying that to me for the past three months. You're beyond your deadline and I've got to cancel. I've got no leeway.'

'I'll sue, you beastly little Nazi! This would never have happened in your uncle's day.'

That was true enough, reflected Lucian as he replaced the phone, shaken by the third abusive conversation in a row with people whom he had once counted as friends. Though that, he knew, was his fault rather than theirs. 'Never confuse good author relations with true friendship' had been one of Uncle Basil's sayings. On second thoughts, the old bastard would have had no compunction about dumping some of these deadbeats.

As for the erotica, Lucian had a killing schedule. He had nine months in which to find, commission and process a launch list of three titles, to be followed by three more each month after that. As yet the series had no name, no cover style, no market profile and, most serious of all, no authors. Lucian picked up the phone and dialled some literary agents.

'I've got a librarian in Basingstoke who churns them out,' said Bill Dougherty, 'but Pervertimento have her tied up for the next five years. Not literally of course though, off the record, I don't think she'd object.'

'Oh God, not you too,' said Francesca Fry. 'My writers are legitimate professionals but all you publishers want these days is smut. I've got plenty of self-help authors and craft specialists. On second thoughts, Iris Maynard could do you a fabulous *Knit Your Own Dildo* if the money was good enough.'

But the most depressing response came from Marilyn Savage, the well-known literary piranha who, at publishing lunches, was rumoured to devour the editor as well as the entrée. 'For God's sake, Lucian, what's the point?' she screamed. 'You'll offer me peanuts and my writers aren't monkeys, even if some of them behave as if they're in a zoo. Anyway you're too late, New Threshold and Pervertimento have the market sewn up. Don't bother, darling, that's my advice. Now, what's the latest on your wicked Uncle Basil?'

Lucian finally got Marilyn off the phone and surveyed the sheet of paper on his desk. He had headed it 'Launch list April 3rd' but beneath that the empty space mocked him. He considered heading for the Rat where he could at least get pissed with the Art Department.

The phone rang and he snatched it up. It was Samantha the receptionist. 'I've a Miss Pilgrim here to see you.'

Lucian bit back the curse that sprang to mind. It was not politic to be rude to Samantha.

'I'm not expecting anyone,' he said, 'and I'm just about to leave for a lunch appointment.' With the Art Department – he had definitely made up his mind.

'She wants to deliver her manuscript to you in person. You commissioned it, she says.'

'What's her name again?'

'Tania Pilgrim.'

Lucian remembered now. *Whimsical Walks in West Marimba* by T. Pilgrim had been in the limbo file for some time, the author having failed to deliver and vanishing, it seemed, off the face of the earth. Lucian gave vent to a heavy sigh. For this feckless writer and her redundant offering to turn up today of all days was about the last straw.

'Get rid of her, Samantha. Tell her to leave the book and I'll write to her.'

'I don't think you want to do that,' replied the receptionist *sotto voce*.

'I bloody well do.'

'Lucian,' she continued, 'if you don't see her I shall tell Ms Lynch about the stains on the boardroom carpet.'

'Oh Christ,' moaned Lucian and put his head in his hands.

That was the position in which Tania Pilgrim discovered him two minutes later.

'Shit a brick,' she said in a broad Australian accent as he looked up from the desk, 'either you've had an operation or you're not the Mr Swan I met last time.'

Lucian stumbled to his feet, dazed by the sun-tanned bubble-blonde in cut-off denim shorts and pneumatically filled lemon T-shirt who stood before him like an answer to a lonely man's prayer. *Samantha*, he thought, *you're more than a mother to me*.

'You probably met Basil Swan,' he said. 'I'm his nephew, Lucian.'

She looked at him closely and grinned, her small gleaming teeth a brilliant white in her bronzed face. 'That's right. He commissioned my book. I'm afraid I'm delivering a little late.'

'Too late for Uncle Basil, certainly. He left the firm a few weeks ago.'

T. Pilgrim seemed unfazed. 'Too bad,' she said, 'but nothing's going to spoil this moment. I've been looking forward to it.' And, from a battle-scarred rucksack, she produced with a flourish a thick brick of close-typed A4 paper. 'Here's *Whimsical Walks in West Marimba*, Mr Publisher, I'm sorry it's three years overdue.'

After that it seemed churlish for Lucian to pour cold water on her triumph by revealing that her efforts would never see the light of day. So he said as little as possible while she chattered about travelling, writing, the thrill of being back in England and what a hell of a time she had had in Marimba. As she spoke, Lucian admired the cute rash of freckles on her nose, the eyes as blue as a tropical sea and the points of her nipples thrusting like thimbles against the fabric of her tight top.

She uncrossed her sturdy bronze thighs – thighs that had propelled her athletic frame half the length of a continent, Lucian reflected – and reached once more for her rucksack.

'I'm sorry I'm running off at the mouth,' she said, delving into a canvas compartment, 'but I only arrived yesterday morning. I kind of get off on just talking, you know? Say, do you mind if I smoke?'

She held up a lumpy white tube of paper, obviously some kind of hand-rolled cigarette.

'I'm sorry,' said Lucian, 'but there's a ban on tobacco in the building.'

Tania grinned like a slice of melon. 'That's OK then, 'cos this ain't tobacco, it's finest Marimba weed.' She lit up and smoke as thick as an allotment bonfire swirled around the room.

Lucian closed the door and opened the window. He didn't have any objection in principle to marijuana but refused the spliff when she offered it to him. Two years of his life had been lost to dope, passing in a haze of moody guitar solos and pizza-and-chocolate binges and wee-hour hysteria. Somewhere between picking up a bog-standard degree in Eng Lit and his mother imploring him to shape up and take the job Uncle Basil had laid on for him, Lucian had quit. He'd not smoked since.

'Hey, come on, man, don't look so down.'

Lucian gave Tania a wan smile. Her euphoric good humour and the sunshine of her presence suddenly flooded him with self-pity. Here he was, with a broken heart and his job on the line, faced with the prospect of telling this bouncing breath of fresh air that the three years she had spent fulfilling his firm's commission had been a total waste of time. He held out his hand for the joint.

'Way to go, Lucian,' said Tania as she handed it over. 'This is the best grass you've ever tasted, I swear.'

Lucian groaned inside. As far as he could remember that was what dopeheads always said. He took a hit and the smoke scorched the back of his throat like breeze from a barbecue, hot and pungent.

He handed the joint back to her and after a moment she handed it back to him. As it went back and forth she said, 'Lucian, there's something about my book I've got to explain.'

'Uh-huh.' He had the stinking cigarette between his lips again. It didn't seem to have got any smaller.

'Don't get me wrong,' she said, 'I'm very happy with it. In my opinion it's a fresh approach to travel-writing. But, I've got to admit, it's not exactly typical of your Whimsical Walks series. It's much more – er – personal.'

'Really?' Lucian tried to sound interested but, in the circumstances, it didn't really matter about the book – he wouldn't be publishing it anyway.

'I mean,' she went on, leafing through the typescript and pulling out a page, 'there's stuff like this.' She passed it across the desk.

'This morning on the beach,' he read, 'opposite Oyster Island, I met Jim the fisherman who offered to row me across. As I stepped into the dinghy he threw in a large plaid rug and I wondered why. As he rowed me over the waves, the muscles rippling in those great shoulders and his long hair rippling in the wind, I had a very naughty idea. Then I realised the naughty idea wasn't all mine as I noticed the way he was staring at my bikini. As he had his eyes on my chest anyway I thought I might as well give him his money's worth and I took off my top. I thought he was going to drop an oar. Not that it would have mattered – from where I was sitting it looked like he had a spare in his pants.'

'I see what you mean,' said Lucian. 'It's certainly different. As you say, a fresh voice.'

'It gets a lot fresher than that, I can tell you. Wait till you get to the bit where the fishing crew kidnap me for a fortnight.'

'What?'

'Well, it wasn't a kidnap to be honest. I stowed away on the trip to be with Jim and things got out of hand. Christ, I shouldn't be telling you this, we only just met. But, as my editor, I guess you're kind of like my doctor, aren't you? I mean, it's in the book, anyway.'

Lucian grabbed the typescript and began to flick through the pages. As he did so it became clear why the project had taken so long to complete. What Tania had been up to in Marimba had not left her with the time or the energy to write.

'Would you be prepared,' he said, inspiration striking, 'to put in more of this kind of stuff?'

'More?'

'Yes, lots more, make it up if you have to.'

'Oh, there's no need to make it up – I mean, that's why the book is so late, I kind of got sidetracked.'

'Sidetracked?' said Lucian, his head in a marijuana muddle. 'Do you mean you followed the track on the side of the road going the same way? Or was the track on the side going in another direction?'

'No, no,' she said. 'It's just that the tracks on the side had guys on them and I had to go down those tracks to ...'

'To what?'

'What?'

'To do what on the tracks with the guys?'

'Get laid, of course.'

'Of course. How fantastic.'

'It was.'

'I bet.'

'I'm very stoned.'

'So am I.'

'We must sound like idiots.'

'Who cares? Can I kiss you?'

'Of course, that's why I'm here – to deliver my book and my body. Are they acceptable?'

'I have to examine them, I'm afraid.'

'Well, look at my body first, for crying out loud ...'

In the smoky fuggy haze of his office it seemed to take Lucian an age to cross the short distance to Tania's chair, to fall on his knees between those outstretched bronzed thighs and press his oh-so-dry lips to a plush curling mouth that opened to suck him in like some exotic sea creature. The phone was ringing as he kissed her and when it stopped he could hear traffic outside in the street and then muffled voices from the corridor – all alien sounds echoing from a distant place. In his hands was the only reality, the golden globes of her full round breasts, tanned like the rest of her, the dark crinkle of her nipples abrading his lips as she stroked his hair and held his face to her bosom.

Her eyes were closed as he rose to his feet in slow motion and pulled his cock from his trousers. Yet her hand found his upstanding spike and pressed it to her tits in one movement, as if she were expecting to perform just this intimacy with a man she had met barely half an hour earlier.

'Mmm,' she said and dipped her head to lick the crimson head of his tool. 'Yes, do it to me there.' She was working his penis with her fingers, pressing it into the deep valley between her breasts and in the state he was in, his cock stoned-sensitive from the joint, his mind completely blown by the glorious bronzed expanse of her, it didn't take more than a minute.

'Oh *yes*!' she breathed as he inundated her big brown globes with his seed. 'Spunk off on my tits, Lucian, just like your Uncle Basil.'

It was only later, sprawling between her legs, his hands full of her beach-ball-firm buttocks and his tongue deep in the sweet and sticky folds of her honeypot, that the implications of her words sank in. There was no doubt that he still had a lot to learn if he were to be as successful a publisher as his distinguished uncle.

8

For nearly a quarter of a century, from the early fifties to the mid-seventies, Monty Hastings' rambling manor-house had been home to a boys' preparatory school. And though many alterations to the building had been made by successive owners since then, not least by Monty and Karen themselves, various features of the school remained. One of them was the ugly black external staircase, erected as a fire escape, that disfigured the rear of the building. Karen hated it, imagining it not so much a way out in an emergency as an invitation to prowlers, burglars and rapists to come on in.

This morning, however, she was thankful for its existence. She had left home as usual at eleven, driving out of the gate certain that Monty's eyes were following the progress of her car. Since he had spent the previous three days at a symposium in Edinburgh debating 'The Semi-Colon as Ideology', she knew he would be keen to resume his normal work schedule with Harriet Pugh.

She had parked five minutes down the road and returned through the woods that bordered one side of the house. It was a simple matter to cross the back lawn and tiptoe quietly up the fire escape until she reached the small landing on the second floor. She was careful not to drop the video camcorder she held in her hand. The door now facing her opened onto the large office room where, at about this time, Monty and Harriet were to be found beavering away at his latest creation.

The door was of solid steel but with a small window at head

48

height. Across the window was a curtain held in place at top and bottom by elastic threaded through the hem. The previous night Karen had adjusted the curtain in preparation for this moment. The chinks on either side would give her just enough space to aim the camcorder and record what was going on within.

As she placed her eye to the crack, trepidation was mixed in equal part with anticipation. This was simply another facet of her research. Along with gangbangs, buggery and three-way orgies, she had not yet experienced voyeurism. She had every expectation of bridging that gap in her knowledge.

At first she was disappointed – if that was the right word to describe the sight of her husband sitting on the sofa with a pad of paper on his lap and a pen in his hand. Could it be that, for once, the rat was actually at work? And where the hell was that tramp, Harriet?

The mystery was solved a moment later as the door to the office bathroom opened and Harriet appeared. But this was not the Harriet of T-shirt and jeans that Karen was accustomed to. She was transformed.

In a crimson satin basque trimmed with black, cinched tight at the waist, the half-cups of the bodice revealing the slope of her breasts down to the pigment of her areolae and the straps of her suspenders cutting into the soft white flesh of her thighs, Harriet Pugh was a spectacular sight. Her stockings were sheer, her heels were high and her strawberry-blonde hair hung loose to her creamy shoulders. In the pit of Karen's stomach the disappointment was gone, replaced by jealousy, hurt and, she had to admit it, a burning coal of excitement. She thumbed the On button on the camcorder and lifted it to the crack in the curtain.

Harriet was putting on a display for Monty. Up and down she walked on her precarious heels, showing off her provocative front and then her incredible rear. Karen watched through the camera lens as Monty's personal assistant stripped off her black lace panties and wiggled her bottom, inches from her employer's face. She turned to face him, fluffing up the brown thatch of hair in the fork of her thighs and revealing the long pink lips of her pussy. Harriet Pugh was behaving like a complete slut. In a funny kind of way, Karen thought, she was magnificent. It would never have occurred to her to perform like this to keep Monty happy.

And Monty *was* happy. The writing pad had been set aside and the pen was lost on the floor. There was a glazed look on his face that Karen used to know well. Her faithless husband was now in the grip of desperate lust and needed release quickly. And Monty, Karen recollected, had never been one to wait for his satisfaction.

But Harriet made him wait, Karen was amazed to see. That is, she took her turn first, seizing his head and pushing it into her open crotch as she stood over him. And from the way she moved her hips and squirmed her big round buttocks in his burrowing hands, Karen could tell she was taking her pleasure in earnest.

As she watched her husband's hands at work on another woman's naked bottom and heard the moans and sighs of approaching orgasm filter through the fire-escape door, Karen forced herself to consider the point of her self-inflicted ordeal. She had no doubt she could portray the scene before her to telling effect, just as she had described all the other erotic experiences which had come her way. Those hot and horny scenes, vividly transposed sometimes just minutes after the events which had inspired them, now comprised two-thirds of a book. It was quite enough material to submit to a publisher. She had decided to call it *The Novelist's Wife*. Maybe it would be deemed unpublishable, in which case the research had undoubtedly enriched her life – for better or worse. On the other hand, Karen was sure that what she had written was good enough to accomplish her real purpose – to embarrass the hell out of her fraud of a husband.

Through the camcorder lens Karen observed Harriet Pugh's big pink buttocks quivering like jelly as she reached her orgasm with a full-blooded scream. The noise was so long and loud that Karen was insulted all over again. How could the bitch behave like that in *her* house with *her* husband? Just what did the woman think of her? Of course Karen knew the answer to that already. Harriet thought Karen didn't count. She'd find out she was wrong, Karen reflected, when she saw the full details of her indiscretions described in print.

The thought brought Karen back to the dilemma of her book: just who should she approach? It would be easier if it was someone she already knew. Maybe Eric Goldwin, Monty's first publisher. Eric was a one-man band who had supported Monty out of his own pocket for two years while he wrote *The Waning Moon*, the novel that had made Monty's name. Nowadays Eric hated Monty – with good reason, for Monty had jumped ship after *Moon* and signed up elsewhere for the kind of advance that Eric couldn't match. But Karen knew that Eric was not the right man for *The Novelist's Wife*. He was old-fashioned and prudish, certainly far too much of a gent to make the most of such sensational material to Monty's detriment.

Karen considered Driftwood & Denton, the firm who had stolen Monty from Goldwin House. They loathed Monty too, these days, after he had accused them of being cheapskates for not coming up with three-quarters of a million for a new contract. He had written to the books supplement of the *Sunday Blizzard* complaining about their mistreatment of authors in general and their short-sighted parsimony to him in particular. This was after GrabCo Worldwide had coughed up an incredible million-pound agreement for a novel, a collection of short stories and the first volume (God help us) of Monty's autobiography.

The action on the other side of the fire-escape door was continuing. Harriet had now had her fill of Monty's mouth between her legs and the pair were going at it on the sofa in the regular fashion. Monty's bare bum – still lean and desirable, Karen had to concede – was thrusting in purposeful rhythm between Harriet's legs as she lay on her back along the cushions. Karen watched in fascination as Harriet pried open Monty's arse crack and began to circle his anus with a blood-red fingernail. Was it something he particularly liked? she wondered. If so, he'd never asked her to do it.

All that was academic now, Karen reflected. Even though she enjoyed her liberal clothes allowance, her fancy new car and the rest of the bounty spread on Monty's table, the crumbs stuck in her throat. She had seen through the great author now and, in her opinion, his writing wasn't good enough to publish on toilet paper. On second thoughts, she wouldn't approach a publisher directly. She needed a different kind of helping hand to make the most of the intriguing possibilities of her literary revenge – a cool professional who knew all the angles.

On the sofa, matters were coming to a conclusion. From the pink flush on Harriet's neck and bosom Karen guessed that she was approaching yet another earth-shattering climax. As the grunts and yells built once more to a crescendo, Karen watched the red fingernail cease its circular journey and plunge down and in, deep between Monty's buttocks to the second joint. A shout of a different pitch rent the air and Monty spasmed, his whole body rigid, his loins glued to the pliant cushion of flesh beneath him, his arse pierced to the core by the witch who now monopolised his affections.

As she lowered the camcorder from her eye, Karen allowed herself a small dry laugh. She'd stick more than a finger up Monty's arse with her book. She'd expose his entire greedy, self-indulgent, cheating, fraudulent life to the world and she knew now just who was going to help her do it. Someone who loathed Monty as much as she did. Someone who knew every move on the publishing chessboard. Someone with iced water in her veins and no mercy in her heart.

A literary agent called Marilyn Savage.

* * *

'No strings, eh?'

'No strings. You live your life, I live mine. You let me stay here till I've done the work on the book and I pay you rent.'

'OK.'

It was the morning after the night after the afternoon of the drug-inspired orgy with Tania and Lucian was feeling fragile. The clock by the bed told him it was almost noon but his limbs were like lead and only the fumes from the coffee Tania had made him were keeping him awake.

She, on the other hand, seemed as fresh as a daisy. Her hair was damp from the shower, tied back off her head in a purple scrunchy that showed off the smooth sweep of her neck and the little blonde curls on the nape that Lucian remembered exploring with his fingers last night as she—

This was no good. Yesterday had been an aberration. His extensive carnal investigation of this admittedly gorgeous woman had been brought on solely by drugs. He struggled to get his mind back to their conversation.

It seemed that while he had been sleeping she had explored his apartment and discovered the study with the spare bed and PC. Evidently she was in need of both those articles and he had agreed to make them available to her. The fact that her towel was slipping down her chest was an irrelevance.

'I've given up sex,' he heard himself say.

She had the grace not to laugh. 'You could have fooled me.'

'You were . . . this was . . . er, exceptional. You seduced me from my resolve. I promise it won't happen again.'

She narrowed her eyes. 'Is there a reason?'

'I've just broken up with someone. I need time to recover emotionally.'

'Oh right. You're a tender flower who's all bashed up.'

'Exactly. It's not that you weren't, aren't, wonderful and I haven't enjoyed every moment—'

'OK, I get it, Lucian. I don't mind being past tense already. Whatever suits you, it's your place. There's just one thing.'

'Yes?'

'This is a business arrangement, right?'

'Sure.'

She leaned across and removed the empty mug from his hand. As she did so the towel gave up its struggle to conceal her sumptuous bosom.

'That puts me in a bit of a spot.'

'Oh?'

He couldn't take his eyes from her breasts as they swayed with her movements. They were so thrusting and firm. They made his parched mouth water.

'You see, Lucian, until I collect the delivery advance on my book I haven't got any money to pay the rent.'

'You can owe me, Tania. I trust you.'

How pretty her nipples were, nut-brown and snub-nosed. He couldn't banish the thought of them last night, erect and sharp, rubbing against his chest . . .

'I've a better idea. In Marimba they don't have much money – so they barter.'

'Really?'

'Yes. Petrol for beer. Spark plugs for a chicken.'

'Fascinating.'

'It is. I've got used to the Marimba way of doing things. Why don't we barter?'

Lucian blinked at her. He knew he must seem dense. He also knew she was somehow making it easier for him to agree to something he shouldn't.

'Think about it,' she went on, tugging at the bedsheet and exposing the abused, pink – and fully upstanding – penis twitching on his belly. 'You are the spark plug and I am the chicken.'

She wrapped her fingers round the barrel of his tool and

squeezed. His glans peeped from his foreskin, purple with desire.

'A business arrangement with no strings?' he said.

'Precisely that,' she replied and slipped his cock into her mouth.

Lucian didn't have to do a thing. He just lay back and thought of Marimba.

9

The sound of the doorbell took Lucian by surprise. He was even more surprised to see Caroline Fitzjohn on the doorstep, carrying a suitcase.

'Hello, darling,' she said and sailed past him up the stairs. She stopped halfway up the first flight and turned, the pose showing off her slim bare legs below the hem of her pleated grey skirt. She looked familiar yet somehow changed, as if the few days in which she had been gone had altered his perception of her. Her fine blonde hair was swept back off her brow and silver-set pearl earrings glinted in the lobes of her ears. Beneath her navy blue blazer she wore a plain white scoop-necked T-shirt that left bare the smoothness of her throat and the upper slopes of her summer-brown chest. Caroline always dressed smartly, in conservative styles that somehow seemed to show off her body more thoroughly than a wardrobe of tarty gear.

'I've come to pick up some of my things, I hope you don't mind.'

'You could have rung me, Caro,' he complained as he climbed after her, knowing he sounded wimpish even as he spoke. That was one of the problems with relationships, he thought, you ended up seeing your least attractive traits through your partner's eyes.

'Sorry, darling, I never got round to it. Life was just *too* hectic. Don't tell me I'm interrupting something exciting like a slide lecture for your perambulating authors. Mind you—' She stopped again, halfway up the second flight. '—these days, I gather, it might be an orgy for your sexy writers.'

'How did you hear about that?' he said.

Her face, inches above his, dimpled with merriment. 'So it's true then? You're editing a porno series. I hope you won't find it too taxing.'

She turned away with a smirk and took the last couple of steps to the door to his flat. Lucian put down the case which he had carried unbidden and pushed back the door for her to enter.

'It's meant to be a secret, Caro. Where did you hear about it?'

'I can't remember, darling. I've been talking to so many people recently.'

Caroline worked on the diary page of the *Daily Dog* so she could have picked it up from almost anybody in the know.

'I hope you aren't going to write about it in your rag,' Lucian said.

'Oh come off it. Our readers aren't interested in publishing pond life. Though I suppose I could dress it up a little. "How the mighty have fallen – once-proud British publishing house The Whimsical Press has been cancelling contracts with some of the country's most respected authors in order to commission a series of pornographic novels. Editing this tide of filth is Lucian Swan, nephew of the firm's former owner Basil Swan. 'I know I am betraying my uncle's literary legacy,' he sobbed, 'but the Germans own us now and I'm only obeying orders.'"'

'*Caro!*' Lucian was apoplectic. 'Don't you *dare!*' He found himself gripping her by the shoulders and shaking her in fury. The sound of her high tinkling laughter brought him to his senses.

'I'm sorry, sweetie,' she said, her pale blue eyes gleaming with triumph. 'I still know how to get you going, don't I?' And she stood on tiptoe to plant a conciliatory kiss on his cheek.

Lucian turned his mouth and shifted his grip to fold this infuriating and exquisite woman into a lover's embrace as of old. But she was gone, slipping from his grasp and leaving him stupidly clutching at the empty air.

'Bring my case up, would you, darling?' she called over her

shoulder as she took the stairs to the attic bedroom. Lucian did as he was told. He found her surveying the fitted wardrobe which ran down one wall. Most of the hanging space was taken up with her clothes.

'Gosh,' she said, 'there's a lot of my stuff, isn't there?'

Lucian did not reply. The amount of space her things took up was an old bone of contention and he wasn't about to disinter it.

'Remember this?' she said.

It was a black evening gown with a deep décolletage which she had worn to a gala at Covent Garden in the first week of their romance. Lucian remembered it very well. He particularly remembered slipping his hand into the high split in the skirt and fondling the soft bare skin of her inner thigh during a selection of Puccini arias. At the time, his hand had been far from frozen.

'Or what about these?'

'These' were a minuscule pair of fuchsia-pink Lycra cycling shorts – not that Caroline would ever dream of climbing on a bicycle. She had used them to provoke Lucian, squeezing her fleshy little bottom into them and strutting around the place of an evening to rouse him into a rutting frenzy.

She turned the immodest garment over in her hand. 'I bet I couldn't even get into them these days, my bum's got so big.'

'Oh for God's sake,' sighed Lucian, this also being a familiar topic of discord. Like ninety-nine per cent of women, in Lucian's experience, Caroline was obsessed by her weight. In reality she was a small woman, a slender five foot three with fine bones and a nicely distributed set of curves.

However, if there was one area of her anatomy that was possibly out of proportion, it was her rear end. And Lucian adored it for that very reason. Her bum was broad and bulging and provocative. When her panties rode up into her crack, the exaggerated cheeks of her buttocks were like swollen teardrops joined by a tiny strip of cotton. He worshipped that bottom. During their stormy affair it had been the rock of flesh that he had clung to in the most turbulent of seas. In bed at night now, his cock stiff and eager between his legs, it was with the image of Caroline's perky out-thrust posterior in mind that he spunked off again and again. If there was one thing above all that he missed about Caroline Fitzjohn, it was her smooth, juicy, porcelain white, simply *beautiful* bottom.

So he watched with disbelief and excitement as she turned away from him to hitch up her skirt and yank down her knickers. Then she began to pull the tight pink stretchy material up her slim legs.

'Caro, what are you doing?' he said unnecessarily.

No words came from her lips, they would have been superfluous – her arse was doing all the talking. Lucian drooled as she tugged the shorts to the top of her thighs and began to wriggle her glistening buttock flesh into the constricting band of pink. The shorts squeezed and her bum billowed, overflowing the waistband. Caro pushed out and bore down, her cheeks flaring and broadening, exposing for a moment the thrilling fissure inbetween, whose delights Lucian knew so well.

'I think it's got tangled up,' she said, looking at him over her shoulder. 'Help me, Lucian.'

He fell to his knees in a trance. He could see no impediment to the garment's progress but nevertheless he reached out a hand to touch the magical flesh of his lost lover.

'Hey, Lucian, do you want a beer?' the voice shattered the intimacy of the moment. Lucian snapped his head round to see Tania standing in the doorway, gazing at the pair of them in astonishment.

'Gee, I'm sorry,' she said, stepping back out of sight. The sound of her footsteps could be heard descending the stairs.

Caroline had whirled away from Lucian at the interruption. The grey skirt now concealed her loins and she was already sliding the pink shorts back down her legs as she hissed at him, 'You bastard.'

'That's Tania,' he said feebly, still on his knees.

'You little shit,' she said, retrieving her knickers and pulling them on, her face a mask of rage.

'She must have come back while we were up here.'

'It didn't take you long, did it? I've only been gone a week and you've got some scrubber in here.'

'She's my lodger, Caro. She needed somewhere to stay. She's sleeping in the spare room, I swear.'

But Caroline didn't appear to be listening. She was pulling dresses and trousers off their hangers and bundling them into her suitcase. The silence was ominous as her nimble fingers went to work.

She glanced at the remainder of her clothes still hanging in the wardrobe. 'You can send those on in a few days. I'll let you know where.' Her voice was full of frost. It began to soften, however, as she continued.

'Let me get to the point, Lucian, then I'll leave you and your little girlfriend in peace.'

'What point?' said Lucian, thankful she no longer looked as if she were going to castrate him.

'I need some money.'

Lucian sighed. How many times had he heard these words from her lips? It was a mystery to him how a woman who earned twice what he did was always broke. At least this time he would have no hesitation in refusing her. Even in the depths of his recent lovelorn misery he had taken comfort from the fact that she could no longer make demands on his pocket.

'It's not what you think,' she said. 'I'm not asking for another loan and I haven't forgotten the others.'

'Well, I have,' he said. 'There's no need to pay me back, Caro, just don't ask me for any more. I haven't got it.'

She smiled at him and his heart at once began to soften. He knew it and loathed himself for it.

'Here,' she said and gave him a sheaf of papers she had taken from the zipped compartment of her suitcase.

'What is it?'

'It's a submission for your new list. You can commission me to write an erotic novel.'

Lucian was struck dumb.

'What's the matter? Aren't you looking for books?'

'Yes, desperately, but ...'

'But what? Don't you think I can write? I'm a professional journalist, don't forget. I can hammer out three or four thousand words a day, no problem. Give me six weeks and you'll have a red-hot rude read sitting on your desk, I guarantee. I haven't got an agent at the moment but I'm sure you'll give me the best possible deal you can. For old time's sake, eh darling?'

She laid her palm upon his cheek and kissed his lips.

'But I can't just give you a contract,' protested Lucian. 'I've got to evaluate the project and discuss it with my colleagues and—'

'Come off it, Lucian. All you've got to do is read ten pages, then you'll see how brilliant it is. If you don't buy it, I'll hawk it round to *Pervertimento and* I'll run that piece about you in *Dog's Diary.*'

'Caro – no! You wouldn't surely?'

'Just joking, darling. Ring me at the paper ASAP. I need a cheque *soon.*'

After she'd gone, Lucian slumped at the kitchen table and got the whisky out.

A moment later Tania emerged from her room. 'Is the coast clear?' she said.

'That was Caroline,' said Lucian, reaching for another glass.

'I figured as much. I'm really sorry I barged in like that. I guess I screwed it up for you.'

Lucian poured her a large one. 'Who knows? You probably saved me from myself.'

'You've still got the hots for her, haven't you? You looked like you were about to snog her arse when I came in.'

Lucian gave a wry grin. 'You have a very direct turn of phrase,

Miss Pilgrim. How did Uncle Basil ever imagine your style was suitable for Whimsical Walks?'

'He didn't. I had to persuade him. The same way I suggest you get Caroline with the big bum to persuade you.'

'You mean—'

'Sure. I told you I had to get down on my knees for your Uncle Basil and suck his cock till he was convinced I had the skill to write the book. You could do the same with her.'

Lucian couldn't help smiling, the thought was so delicious. 'You mean, put Caroline through the same rigorous editorial selection procedure that you went through?'

'Absolutely. And if I were you, considering how that snooty bitch has trampled all over you, I'd make it extra rigorous. You want to stand up for yourself, Lucian. Next time it's her turn to kiss *your* butt!'

10

'I hope you've made progress with the erotica, Lucian,' said Miranda Lynch, 'we haven't got much time.' Her grey eyes surveyed him critically. The day of judgement was at hand.

Lucian tried to look confident. A couple of plums had fallen into his lap and all he had to do was tell Miranda how juicy they were. He had decided his best strategy was to let her taste the fruit herself.

'Actually, I reckon I've got a couple of possibles for the launch list. Take a look at this.' He handed across the desk two pages of Caroline's proposal and Miranda took it without a word.

Lucian watched her intently as she began to read. Her gleaming blonde helmet of hair hung in immaculate precision and her small picture-perfect features were rapt in concentration – as if she were absorbing a board report or assessing a computer print-out. But she wasn't. She was reading this:

Marietta surveyed the artist's studio with dismay. She saw an unmade bed, paint and canvasses strewn around, bare boards and piles of dusty books. Everywhere she looked, grime and squalor filled her sight. It was worse than she had expected.

Bruno appraised her with a wolfish grin. 'Take off your clothes, Contessa Strepponi.'

'What!'

'I can tell from the sneer on your beautiful face that you fear contamination from the unpretentious nature of my humble home. So take off your expensive designer gown, my dear, so it will not spoil.'

She laughed nervously.

'Remove it at once,' he said, his voice soft and sinister, 'or I will rip it from your exquisitely beautiful back.'

With a sob of despair, Marietta obeyed. She fumbled as she unfastened the tiny pearl buttons on the bodice and her fingers shook as she slipped the embroidered silk down her slender legs. He took the flimsy garment from her and folded it with mock ceremony over a broken-legged chair.

'And the rest,' he commanded.

'No!' she cried, hugging her arms to her chest, one hand fanning over the bulge revealed beneath the slender protection of her gossamer-thin knickers.

'Oh yes,' he said, implacable. 'How else am I going to paint you if not naked?'

Marietta was frozen with despair. Yet the blood was singing in her veins as she allowed him to divest her of the last vestiges of modesty. Her camisole was pulled over her head, her shoes were plucked from her feet and her drawers were tugged down her thighs. Then the Contessa Marietta Strepponi stood as utterly nude as she had been at her moment of birth.

'*Bella, bella,*' muttered Bruno beneath his breath, blinded by the exquisite perfection of her beauty. 'Maybe,' he breathed, 'you are the one I have been looking for. Get on the bed.'

'But—'

'On the bed, my lady, and spread those pretty legs.'

'I hate you!' cried Marietta even as she allowed him to position her limbs. And when his cool strong fingers touched her burning flesh a flame leapt in the pit of her belly, as if he had lit a fire within her. 'Oh!' she moaned, unable to contain herself, helpless with need and dripping with want.

'And now, Contessa,' he said, sitting opposite her with a

sketchpad in his hand, 'I want you to show me just how much of a woman you really are. Touch yourself between the legs.'

'No!'

'Why so coy? You are spread before me, wet and naked. Show me how you give yourself pleasure and together we will make great art.'

'You brute!' she cried but her fingers were there, among the folds, teasing her petals, releasing the river of desire that flowed – at last – from the very core of her sensuality.

'Yes!' he cried in triumph as his pencil flew across the paper, capturing the flush of ecstasy in her eyes as she yielded to her deepest darkest urges.

And the hand between her legs moved in a blur as the river of her desire burst its banks ...

'Is this all there is?' said Miranda, a note of regret in her voice.

'No, there's another ten pages and a synopsis. You see, the Contessa's a bored and beautiful socialite who falls for a wild and brutal artist who shows her the depravity of real life. She's always lived within a pampered and protected circle and she's never been able to really feel—'

'You mean she can't have an orgasm?'

'Well, yes, but her inability to respond is indicative of the paucity of her shallow existence. Bruno the artist is a force of nature, a symbol of a brutal world where the reality of sensation—'

'Spare me the symbolism, Lucian, for goodness sake. Just tell me, is there a lot of fucking in it?'

Lucian gulped. 'Er, yes, according to the synopsis. Anyhow the author will bung in as much as we want.'

'Good.' Miranda leaned back, a smile of satisfaction on her lips. 'Tell the author we want lots. Who is it, by the way?'

'A journalist on the *Daily Dog*. Caroline Fitzjohn, though I doubt if we can use her real name.'

The pink lips pursed. 'Pity. When can she deliver?'

'In six weeks, so she says, but she's never written a book before.'

'Give her two months then and keep a close eye on her. Try her on two grand.'

'Really?'

'Of course really. Pay her a bit more if you have to, just get it in on time and make sure it's full of filth.'

Lucian couldn't believe his ears. Normally The Whimsical Press spent weeks deliberating over the most insignificant acquisitions. That was obviously not Miranda's style.

'Next?' she said and before he knew it she had agreed to transfer Tania's book out of limbo and onto the new list.

'We're calling it Blue Desire,' she said.

'I think,' said Lucian, 'the author's rather keen on *A Walk on the Wild Side*. It started off as a walking book, you see, and—'

'I'm talking about the imprint name, Lucian. Blue Desire Books. I'm sure you'll like it when your brain catches up. I've briefed the Art Department and they're working on cover styles. All you've got to do is get more books. Off you go.'

Lucian was dismissed. The meeting had lasted just five minutes – but he still had his job.

He rang Caroline at once.

'OK, Caro, you're on. We'll pay you two thousand pounds advance against royalties.'

'God, darling, can't you do better that?'

'I thought you needed money?'

'I don't call two grand money, I call it an insult.'

Lucian sighed. Nothing was ever easy with Caroline – he'd thought she would be pleased.

'I suppose I could find you a bit more.'

'How much?'

'Five hundred. But you've got to deliver eighty thousand words within two months – and come to a weekly editorial review of progress.'

'What does that mean?'

'You and I meet up to see how you're getting on. You show me what you've written and I make sure you're on the right lines.'

She gave a sigh of exasperation. 'All right then, I'll do it. I suppose I can stand a weekly lunch at Grimaldi's.'

'No lunches, Caro. An evening session at my place every Tuesday night. If you want that delivery cheque.'

'For God's sake, Lucian, when did you learn to be such a bully?'

When I read your book proposal, thought Lucian, *and found out what really turns you on.*

Lucian was in a mood for celebration when he burst into Tania's room after work. She was sitting in front of the computer screen in her bra and pants with a fan blowing in her face full blast. She looked up in surprise to see him brandishing a champagne bottle.

'Party time?' she said.

'You bet,' he said and popped the cork in an eruption of fizz. 'Here's to you, Ms Pilgrim, author of the very first Blue Desire book. My Führer has sanctioned the publication of your masturbatory masterpiece.'

'Hey – erotic literature if you don't mind and I'm just in the middle of a particularly erotic bit.'

'Excellent,' said Lucian and hooked his finger in the webbing between the cups of her bra and pulled upwards, baring her big brown breasts. She shrieked as he splashed champagne on her chest but there was a gleam in her eye as he bent to lick the wine from her nipples.

'Can I assume,' she said, 'that you're in the mood to give me some editorial guidance?'

'You bet,' he said and pushed her backwards towards the bed.

She sat on it and unbuckled his trouser belt.

'What happened about Miss Snooty?' she said and uncovered his raging erection. There was no doubt that all of him was in the mood for celebration.

'Don't be rude about your fellow author.'

'So you're going to publish her kinky rubbish?'

'Erotic literature, Tania. As you yourself said.'

She had both hands on his cock and balls now and was wanking him slyly. His shaft seemed vast in her hand, bigger than he'd ever seen it. As he stood there with his trousers round his ankles and his penis twitching in her face, his self-satisfaction was palpable.

'Has Caroline agreed to your terms?' said Tania as he pushed her flat on the bed and pulled her panties over her hips.

'She has.'

'She's agreed to your hands-on editing?'

'She's got no choice.'

He bent his head and insinuated his tongue into the lightly furred groove of her pussy. His finger found her clit.

Tania chuckled. 'No wonder you're looking so bloody smug then. I hope you don't back off when it comes to the crunch.'

'No chance.'

He moved over her body till the fat head of his cock was at her entrance, nosing between her labia. Fortunately her literary efforts of the afternoon had ensured that she was already well lubricated.

'Just think,' she said as he plunged his tool all the way home, 'you'll soon have Caroline at your mercy—'

'Yes!'

He was thrusting hard already . . .

.'Stark-naked for your pleasure—'

'Yes!'

Driving and butting and poking . . .

'Her mouth open and her legs spread—'

'Yes! Yes!'

Plunging and jabbing and squirming . . .

'That juicy little arse bent over just for you—'

'Yes! Oh God – OH!'

. . . Both of them out of control.

They lay in a sticky heap, glued together by sweat, the whirr of the fan suddenly loud in their ears.

'Thanks, Lucian,' said Tania at last, 'that's just the kind of editorial input I need!'

Two

TO THE HILT

11

Percy Carmichael gazed on the shimmering calm of the Mediterranean as he sipped his third beer of the morning. For the first time since leaving home the previous day with his wife and three children he felt he really was on holiday. Felicity was having a sailing lesson, the kids had been packed off to the children's activity clubs that were the chief selling-point (to Percy's mind) of the holiday package and he was getting gently smashed in the beach bar. This was more bloody like it.

He watched the whizz and dip of the wind-surfers and the scud of the small sailboats out in the bay. The sand was dotted with eager sunbathers, pink and white blobs straight off the plane from England now sweltering beneath a layer of Factor 15. Some of them were young, nubile and almost naked. This *was* the life. Percy was practically inspired.

It occurred to him, as the bronzed barman set beer number four in front of him with a wink, that after a few days of this he might be able to think of writing seriously again. Not the advertising brochures and dreary company histories that were the mainstay of his existence as a freelance writer but a creation to stir the soul and stimulate the intellect. He could taste it already – a volume that would solicit fawning reviews, win prizes and speak to succeeding generations.

On the other hand, he thought as he watched a fat man in a deck chair page through a John Grisham, writing a blockbusting bestseller might be a better idea.

Perhaps it had not been such a bad thing after all that the promised contract from The Whimsical Press had not come through – not that Percy was of a mind to forgive Lucian Swan just yet. Maybe it was not Lucian's fault that the new owners had pulled the chain on Whimsical Walks but someone had to bear the brunt of Percy's animus. It served the little snot right to be forced to turn his pedantic editorial pencil to the production of porn.

'It's erotica not pornography,' Lucian had said sniffily in the course of the previous week's phone call, 'and you're very welcome to try your hand at it, Percy.'

'What!'

'Well, if not having a Walk to do leaves you a bit short, why not? If you want to make me a proposal I'll give it a sympathetic read, I promise you.'

Percy had not been amused. 'Look, you pretentious turd, the only proposal that springs to mind is that you flush yourself down the crapper along with your filthy books!'

Percy chuckled to himself in recollection. He really shouldn't have been so rude but he'd enjoyed every moment.

'Hey, sport, what's the joke?'

Percy blinked at the blonde girl who had appeared by his side. She wore a white T-shirt with the words 'Cascade Beach Holidays' in red across her chest and carried a clipboard.

'Well, I ... er, it's just a private ...' mumbled Percy. He wasn't used to being accosted by beautiful girls with laughing eyes and flashing teeth.

'Glad to see you're enjoying yourself already,' said the vision in an Antipodean twang, laying a slim bronzed hand on his city-white forearm. 'My name's Carol-Anne, I'm the Entertainments Officer. I'm just putting together the teams for the volleyball competition, so can I add your name?'

'I don't think so. I don't play.'

'Oh come on, it's fun.'

'Sorry.'

Her fingers squeezed his arm and her azure eyes bored into his. 'Please. I only need one more person. We're about to start.'

'Well...' He was wavering. What man wouldn't?

'Great! What's your name?'

'Percy Carmichael.'

'Right, Perce, you're a Plonker.'

'I'm sorry?'

'The teams are Willies, Dickheads, Choppers and Plonkers. The Plonkers are over there.'

She pointed to a collection of bare-chested individuals in a huddle on the beach beside the volleyball net. Percy observed that they were all at least ten years younger than him and that one of them was female. Her chest was bare too. He rose to his feet.

'Wow,' said Carol-Anne. 'How tall are you?'

'Six-five.'

'And you've never played volleyball? Hey, Plonkers!' she shouted at the group on the beach. 'Look what I've found for you.'

The group turned their heads.

'He's a Plonker too,' yelled Carol-Anne.

A cheer went up as Percy loped towards them and a curly-haired man with a barrel chest punched the air. The girl whooped with excitement and her small pink breasts jiggled. Percy found he had an enormous grin plastered to his face. He really was entering into the holiday spirit.

The first game passed in a blur. Percy didn't have a clue and when the ball came to him at the back of the court it skimmed off his palms into the sand. Fortunately his team-mates did not appear to resent his inept play. He noticed that the small girl was almost as hopeless as he was, though the way she threw herself about undoubtedly made her better value for the spectators.

Then he found himself at the front of the court as the players rotated. A bronzed opponent leapt and smacked the ball. Percy stuck up a hand and the ball plopped into the sand on the other side of the net. His first point.

'Great play, Perce,' yelled Curly Head.

The Plonkers served, the Choppers returned and Percy, with his superior reach, swatted it back on the other side.

'Yes!' cried the Plonkers.

'Keep it away from that tall bastard,' muttered a Chopper. But they couldn't and Percy left the court with his victorious team wondering why he had never played the game before. He was obviously a natural.

He let Curly Head – Clive, as he soon discovered – buy him his fifth beer and Jean, the small girl, sat by his side. Her breasts looked even pinker close up. She saw the direction of his gaze.

'I'd better be careful,' she said, 'sunburnt tits are no fun.'

'Don't worry, sweetheart,' said another Plonker – Jimmy – 'we'll oil them for you free of charge. Won't we, Perce?'

Jean made a little moue with her mouth and looked at Percy. 'If we win the final I might let you,' she said to him alone.

So Percy took up position for the deciding game in a haze of squiffy euphoria. He felt suddenly younger, happier, freer. He leapt and swatted, lunged and smashed. He didn't know he had it in him.

It was a tight game, the Dickheads were organised opponents. They served to Percy when he was at the back of the court and he fluffed it; they picked out Jean when she was by the net and she was overwhelmed. But Clive, Jimmy and Garaint from Wales were clever players and the teams were neck and neck as the Plonkers won the serve on match point.

Percy was positioned by the net, straining every sinew as Clive shaped to serve. He'd not felt such a desire to win since junior school, playing football against his elder brother and his friends. A lifetime ago.

Clive served, the Dickheads set and spiked, Garaint kept it alive, Jimmy set it up for Percy. This ball was his, he knew it. It twirled in the air directly above the net and Percy leapt like a vaulting salmon instead of a forty-year-old sedentary male. The biggest Dickhead jumped opposite him to block the ball but it rebounded off Percy's elbow and spun back onto the Dickheads' side.

With elation bubbling in his veins, Percy fell to earth, all the weight of his body slamming the ankle of his left foot against the base of the metal net support.

His shout of agony was lost in the Plonkers' victory roar.

12

'Lucian, dear boy,' said a familiar smoky voice on the other end of the line, 'I'm about to do you the most *enormous* favour.'

'Of course, Marilyn,' said Lucian, trying to keep the weariness out of his voice – and failing. Marilyn Savage, literary agent extraordinaire, never missed a vocal nuance.

'Don't sound so enthusiastic, sweetheart. I'm offering you the hottest book in town.'

'As hot as last time?' *The Dordogne Diaries* by Victoria Venables had left Lucian unmoved. Reminiscences of Sarlat market day and recipes for ratatouille by the literary editor of the *Daily Blizzard* were not Lucian's idea of a bestseller. But then, what did he know? Not much from what Marilyn was saying.

'You missed out there, Lucian. Rodney Branscombe picked it up for fifty thousand and Black Raven start filming next week.'

Lucian sunk deeper into gloom. 'But it was crap, Marilyn. You should be ashamed to take your ten per cent.'

'Fifteen, dear boy. I'm a very special agent.'

'I should say so. So you made seven and a half grand off that old boot's laundry lists. How long did it take you?'

'A morning of phone calls, darling, and—'

'Don't tell me – a lifetime's experience.'

'Precisely, you cheeky boy. You know me so well, don't you?'

That was true enough. He'd first met Marilyn during school holidays when he used to hang around Uncle Basil's house, playing with his cousins. The publisher had specialised in cultivating up-and-coming agents and the gamine Marilyn, with her heart-shaped face and violet eyes, had been a particular favourite. As a pubescent schoolboy Lucian had fallen hard for the tyro agent. And, despite her unpredictable temper and legendary manipulative skills, the torch he carried still burned.

'So what's this new book, Marilyn?'

'Aha. Have I got my little fishy on the line?'

'*Please* don't tease me.'

'But you love it, darling, don't you? It's what makes dealing with you such a pleasure. Unlike some jumped-up little pseuds with MBAs and marketing diplomas and mentioning not the name of Rodney Branscombe.'

'But you sell him all your big books!'

'That's because GrabCo currently have a lot of money. Mind you, the way he's spending it there soon won't be much left. And when that happens he can do his shopping elsewhere.'

'You're being remarkably frank, Marilyn.'

'That's because I know you won't tell. And if you do I'll get my own back and you wouldn't like that.'

That was true. He adored Marilyn but he knew he was dead meat if he crossed her.

'Besides,' she continued, 'frankness is the order of the day as you will see when you read *The Novelist's Wife*. I'm giving you an exclusive look, not just because we're old friends but because it's what you need to get Blue Desire Books off the ground.'

And so it was, he could see that as he pored over the sample pages that night. It wasn't just the nature of the material – the story of an unfulfilled woman wreaking her vengeance in promiscuity on the husband who had robbed her of her dreams. Or even the way it was written – vivid and graphic, with an edge of naïvety which suggested this wasn't a professional writer striving for effect but a woman trying to tell the truth. None of that would have counted for much of course. The book would be dismissed as just another smutty read were it not for the information contained in Marilyn's letter of submission – and the accompanying photograph.

It showed the author on the arm of her husband at a first night or some other ritzy showbiz function. Lucian was pretty certain it was the West End opening of the movie based on Montgomery Hastings' *The Waning Moon*. He didn't have to be a genius to recognise the great author, dapper in his dinner jacket, pressing the hand of the oily Heritage Secretary, Godolphin Sumner. And the woman by his side, slim and dark with high cheekbones and faraway eyes, was the novelist's wife, the author of the lurid sex confession that he held in his hand – the other was absent-mindedly stroking the full-blown erection that had sprung from his loins the moment he had begun to read.

Marilyn's letter made it clear that Karen Hastings wanted to use her real name and trade on the celebrity of her husband. Even if she had looked like the back end of a bus that would be sufficient to cause a scandal. The fact that she was a dark-eyed angel from the valleys, already known to the public as Monty Hastings' refined and respectable consort, was guaranteed to send the newspapers into a feeding frenzy. Caro, for example, would kill for a glance at this material.

There was one obvious catch. Even though it was late, Lucian dialled Marilyn's number. She answered immediately.

'I thought it might be you,' she said.

'I can't publish this, Marilyn!'

'I suppose it's not sexy enough for you.'

'You know it's not that. It's mind-bogglingly filthy!'

'Or is the author not to your taste?'

'The author is elegant and beautiful and a brilliant story-teller.'

'But—?'

'But her husband will sue the shit out of us! It's obvious the novelist in the book is him. She's hardly bothered to change his name – Michaelis Hardy is almost the same as Montgomery Hastings! He cheats on his wife, has orgies with prostitutes, bonks his secretary over her desk every morning and, what's worse, is a lousy writer.'

'Calm down, Lucian. The quality of Monty Hastings' work is surely a matter of opinion.'

'That's not the point. It's the whole picture of the man – the adulterous fraud who'll screw anybody to get what he wants. It's defamatory and he'll sue.'

'No he won't, darling, because he knows he'd lose.'

'You mean it's all true and she can prove it?'

'Got it in one, Lucian. She has sworn affidavits, indiscreet letters and a library of incriminating cassettes. Not to mention naughty videos. As you know, Monty is not one of my favourites, but I almost feel sorry for the little shit.'

'Christ.'

'And as far as indemnity goes, Lucian, don't worry. Karen will sign whatever legal disclaimer your lawyers require. She'll do anything to see this book in print – she'd probably give it to you for nothing. Fortunately I'm here to protect her interests. So go and talk to whoever writes the cheques at your place these days and tell them to get their fountain pen out.'

Lucian put down the last page at midnight. The novel wasn't yet complete but he had read more than enough to know that *The Novelist's Wife* was the most sensational book of the year. Correction – the decade, at least. Provided it wasn't a hoax, of course.

He got up and prowled around his room, his brain gnawing at this sudden possibility. He'd have to meet the author, see the famous incriminating evidence, watch the video ... The thought of the divine Mrs Hastings recording her husband as he ploughed his big-breasted secretary and then masturbating to a series of explosive climaxes with her skirt around her waist on top of a fire escape set

Lucian's cock beating a tattoo against his belly. That had been the last scene, so vividly described, in the manuscript.

So, did that videotape really exist? Was that what he would see – the voluptuous assistant thrusting her muff into the novelist's face, her big satiny buttocks wobbling in his fingers as he sucked her off? And would the angel-faced author sit by his side as he watched her husband betray her in graphic, shaky close-up? And would she then confirm that the lewd spectacle had so excited her that she had plunged her hand between her legs and brought herself off then and there, over and over again?

Lucian's imagination was in lurid overdrive and his loins were in a fever. He could have wept with frustration – not sexual frustration but frustration of purpose. He had – he really had – promised himself that for the present there would be no sex.

He rushed downstairs and knocked on Tania's door. No reply. He pushed it open and cursed at the empty room. Where was she when he needed her? He wasn't sure he wanted the answer to that question.

Returning to his room, Lucian slumped on his bed, his penis an uncomfortable bar across his stomach. It was no use, he was going to have to jerk off. Perhaps he should dig out that photo of Caro? No – that was the one thing he mustn't do. His relationship with Ms Fitzjohn was about to enter a new phase and this time he would be in charge. No back-sliding.

He looked out of the skylight window at the house across the street. Since his first sighting of Nicole Sessions in her bedroom window he had not glimpsed her at all. What with one thing and another – in a word, Tania – he had scarcely looked. A part of him strongly disapproved of this Peeping Tom activity. On the other hand, given what he had seen last time, how could he resist?

His luck was in tonight. A light burned in the bedroom across the street. As before, Nicole sat at her dressing-table brushing her hair. This time her fabulous breasts were encased in a black, push-up brassiere with sculpted cups that squeezed her pretty orbs together to form a deep ravine of cleavage.

Instantly all thoughts of other women, of pert-bottomed Caro, of bronzed and bubbly Tania, of the dark mysterious gaze of Karen Hastings, were driven from Lucian's mind. All he could think of now was the swing and pull of Nicole's slim brown arm as she brushed her hair and the beckoning vee of her golden breast flesh. How he wished he could reach out an invisible hand and slip it beneath the black wisp of material to cup a pouting globe and pull it into view.

It was as if she were listening to his thoughts for, as she continued to work her brush with one hand, she slid the other into the front of her bra and pulled her right breast into the open. It hung there, trembling in the light, and she began to fondle it, running her fingers into the crease beneath and cupping the gourd of flesh, then palpating the areola between her fingers, making the brown nipple jut up like a hat peg.

She put down the brush and brought out the other tit, offering them both up to the mirror before her as she weighed them in her hands. Then she released them and the spheres of flesh settled and separated a fraction on her chest. She wiggled her shoulders and the movement rippled and flowed through her golden bosom, like wind blowing through a ripe cornfield. As she took a nipple between the finger and thumb of each hand and began to pull, Lucian's loins erupted, the spunk shooting unbidden from his tormented tool.

Why, he thought to himself, in the dizzy afterglow of his unexpected orgasm, was Nicole behaving like this? It was hard to believe that this display was for her own benefit. But, of course, it wasn't. For there stood Hugh, his cock in his hand and a shit-eating grin on his face as he appeared from stage left, as it were, and sat on a chair by the foot of the bed. He held his hand out to his wife.

Nicole stood in front of him, holding the hairbrush. He took it from her and she laid her sumptuous body across his lap, her black be-knickered bottom face up. Hugh surveyed it for a moment, running a proprietorial palm across each upthrust cheek. Then he tugged at the waistband and yanked the flimsy material downwards, baring the broad and beautiful ovals of her milky white buttocks. Lucian's cock was now once more straining upwards from his loins.

Hugh hit her first with the bristle side of the brush, a smart swipe onto each fleshy crescent. Then he pressed the brush downwards into her yielding flesh, working it round and across. Her hips twitched under his ministrations and he slapped down smartly with his open palm as if to say, *Be still!*

Methodically he began to spank her with the flat of the hairbrush. *Whack! Smack! Whack!* The night was quiet and, through his open window, Lucian could plainly hear the collision of wood on flesh. And was that a tearful sob, audible between the blows?

Nicole's bum had turned puce now and she couldn't help moving. After each strike she grabbed at her belaboured arse and twitched and writhed. Hugh waited until she was perfectly still again before bringing the brush down once more.

Lucian could hear a woman's voice amidst the erotic sounds. A smack, a cry, a moan and then a shout. The shouts preceded the blows, like commands.

'Nineteen!'

The brush descended, the pink arse danced and Lucian realised that Nicole was calling out the number of her punishment. My God, to think people actually did these things! He'd read about it – in the past few days he'd read rather a lot – but to think he knew people who actually behaved like this!

'Twenty! Aah!'

Hugh threw down the brush and reached behind him. He unscrewed a small jar and dipped in his fingers. Then, very slowly, he began to rub ointment into Nicole's flaming *derrière*. The rounds of flesh squirmed beneath his fingers. Lucian could imagine the cooling balm being smoothed into that abused behind. Could imagine too the pleasure of feeling her silky flesh beneath his fingers. Of soothing the burning skin of her seat, then peeling apart the satiny globes to gaze on the dark and secret valley between – just as Hugh was doing now.

Lucian had a perfect view up Nicole's rear crack. From the black-fringed mouth of her cunt purse up to the pink whorl of her anus, all was revealed. The insides of her thighs were slick with juice and the unfurled outer lips of her pussy glistened. Hugh dipped a finger into the pool within and trailed the evidence of her excitement up the crease of her arse. She wriggled at his touch, bucking her hips in unmistakable need. Lucian held his breath as Hugh pulled her body upwards.

Nicole straddled her husband. Throwing one dancer's leg over his lap, she sat down facing him and, for a moment, her fabulous bust was suspended in his face as she held on to his shoulders and he positioned the big egg of his glans in the junction of her legs. Then she was slithering downwards, the barrel of his tool swallowed in the gullet of her sex as she settled in his arms. Their arms entwined, their mouths locked and her dark curls mingled with his blond locks as their loins enmeshed.

Lucian's stomach churned with lust and envy. Husband and wife had pleasured each other obscenely and now melted into one before him. As he watched, they toppled slowly backwards onto the bed and, a moment later, the light went out. The lewd entertainment had been thrilling and his cock danced between his legs. He suddenly felt an awful emptiness inside. 'Oh Caro,' he muttered out loud.

From below came the sound of a door opening and he shook himself out of his self-pity. What the hell was he doing? Lucian the lovelorn wimp was banished. He was a man with a new resolve, a man with a purpose – and that purpose was Blue Desire Books.

He wondered, as he descended the stairs naked and fully erect, whether it was obligatory for editors of erotica to sample all forms of sexual expression.

And whether Tania liked having her bottom spanked.

13

The unfortunate accident on the volleyball court had not earned Percy any sympathy from his wife. 'You stupid bloody fool,' Felicity had said in the taxi on the bumpy ride to the local doctor. She'd said a lot else besides, most of which was to do with the pathetic nature of middle-aged men playing little boys' games when they were past it. And on the ride back her complaints were redoubled as the implications of the doctor's recommended course of treatment sank in.

'It's all very well for you to sit on your backside and rest for a fortnight but what about me? I'm here for a holiday too, remember? And now I've got to cope with the children single-handed.'

'Don't panic, Flick,' muttered Percy through clenched teeth as the old car rattled down the stony track, sending a lance of white-hot pain up his leg at every jolt. 'They can go to their games and things, can't they?'

'But that's only some of the time, isn't it?' she spat at him. 'You may not have noticed, Percy, but children of five, four and eighteen months need dressing and changing and feeding and putting to bed and sun-creaming and organising and being played with. And you're not going to be much use changing a filthy nappy standing on one leg. How could you *do* this to me?'

'I'll work something out, darling, I promise.'

'You had better, Percy, or I shall personally sprain your other ankle.'

But though Percy's name was now mud in the bosom of his

family, down at the beach bar he had attained hero status. His fellow Plonkers had carried him to a table and plied him with the local gutrot and buckets of sympathy in equal measure. A crowd gathered, which included Carol-Anne. She proposed a solution to his domestic plight.

'I can get you a team of girls to help out,' she said. 'We're all on shift here and there's not much to do when we're off duty except hang around. I bet I could drum up a rota of nannies and waitresses to lend your wife a hand.'

'Fantastic,' said Percy.

'It'll cost you, of course.'

'Of course.'

'I mean, the girls work pretty hard so if you're going to use their free time you've got to stump up.'

'How much?'

'Leave it with me, sport. I'll let you know.'

And she had. The upshot of which now left Percy staring hard at the telephone in the hotel reception on the brink of making one of the most embarrassing calls of his life. Except where his wife was concerned, he was not renowned for resurrecting bridges he had just burned.

'Lucian, it's Percy Carmichael. I'm glad I caught you. How are you, old son?'

Lucian wasn't thrilled to hear Percy's hearty boom. The scars of the pompous fart's abominable rudeness had not yet healed and Lucian would have been quite content to have continued any future intercourse by letter. However, he wasn't surprised. He'd had extensive experience of authors. In many respects they were like donkeys, particularly when confronted by a dangling carrot.

'I'm sorry I got a bit carried away when we last spoke, Lucian. I can assure you there was nothing personal in my remarks. I was just a little disappointed by the new policies of your lords and masters. I realise it's not your fault. You've always treated me with utter professionalism and I regard our relationship as something rare and special in a trade that is becoming increasing tarnished by—'

'What do you want, Percy?'

'Ah ... well, I've been considering the proposal you made me the other day.'

Surprise, surprise. The donkey was after the carrot.

'I don't remember making you a proposal, Percy.'

Let the bastard sweat.

'But, Lucian, you must remember. When you sadly pronounced sentence of death on my *Whimsical Walks in Whelk Country*, you urged me to write for your new list.'

'What list?'

Lucian was enjoying this.

'You know, your ... erotica list.'

'Oh, you mean the *pornography* line.'

'Yes!'

'But that's not your cup of tea, is it, Percy? As you said yourself, I believe. I could hardly expect a writer of your style and sensitivity to lower his standards to such a degree. I deeply regret even mentioning it to you.'

'But you've got to let me do it, Lucian. Please. I beg you.'

There was a pause in the conversation. The note of desperation in Percy's voice was obvious to them both.

'Are you in trouble, Percy?' said Lucian, honour now satisfied.

'Christ, Lucian, you don't know the half of it. I've done my ankle and can't move and Felicity's behaving like a turbo-charged Nazi. I've got to hire half the staff here round the clock to keep her sweet and I can't get a penny back on my insurance – I've gone blind reading the sodding policy.'

'So you need some money and you don't care what kind of book you write.'

'Crudely put—'

'That is how we put it these days at Blue Desire.'

'What's that?'

'The name of our naughty imprint. For which you aspire to write. What's your proposal then?'

'I can hardly tell you over the phone, Lucian. Can't you just trust me? I'll start it here and show you what I've done when I get back. I've got three months before I have to research my history of the Stamp & Mame Corporation and I'll wrap it up by then. I had planned to write *Whelk Country*, as you know, but—'

'OK, Percy, I get the picture.' Lucian was anxious not to open old wounds. 'But you've got to give me some idea what the book's about. Have you got a title?'

'*Distant Equinox*.'

'For God's sake, that won't do.'

'Really? I thought it was rather classy. How about *Reflections on a Sunless Sea*? I've always wanted to write a novel with that title. It's rather poetic, don't you think?'

Lucian sighed. 'Stuff the poetry, Percy, it won't work. We want the grind of nubile flesh, the thrust and pout of busty babes on heat. And the title has got to send the blood rushing to the loins.'

'You mean, like *Oil My Tits*.'

'Blimey, Percy, that's possibly a bit too up-front but, yes, you're on the right lines. Has your hotel got a fax?'

'Somewhere, I suppose.'

'Well, you'd better scribble me out a synopsis tonight, with some sample action if you can manage it, and fax it to me by the time my meeting starts tomorrow morning.'

'Oh, thank you, Lucian, thank you. You've saved my life.'

'Don't get carried away, Percy. Send me a storyline, two pages will do. Just think of pulsing loins and big beautiful breasts.'

Percy looked out of the window at the row of women stripped to their bikini panties on sun-loungers by the hotel pool and smiled.

'Honestly, Lucian,' he said, 'that won't be a problem.'

Percy slaved all night over his outline for *Oil My Tits* – which was only a working title, to be sure, but he wrote it boldly at the top of his pad to keep his literary inclinations from taking over.

It was bloody uncomfortable sitting in the bathroom with his bad leg propped up but he had no option. Felicity's ill-humour had been mellowed to a degree by the presence of Gina and Dyan, two off-duty nannies who had put the kids to bed with cheerful efficiency. All Felicity had had to do was bark orders and tackle the duty-free gin. Now she was fast asleep in the bedroom while Gina listened out for the kids from a makeshift bed on the children's balcony. Which left the bathroom free for the reluctant pornographer.

It wasn't going too badly, Percy thought. He had a plot which had sprung miraculously from his current predicament: Virile mid-thirtyish Max goes on holiday with Arabella, his cold and shrewish wife of seven years. On the first day, Arabella drinks too much at lunch and falls down a flight of stairs, twisting her ankle. With Arabella confined to bed, Max is free to conduct carnal relations with the scores of stunning, scantily clad beauties frolicking on the beach.

Percy enjoyed the idea of turning the tables on reality and having his hero's wife incapacitated. Feeling marginally guilty, he went on to invent a charismatic local doctor who strikes up a rapport with Arabella on his regular visits. Armand, the doctor, is possessed of a freakishly large penis which he uses to comprehensively fuck and bugger the prudish Arabella until she is a slave to brute male passions. In the climax of the story Max, fresh from a three-way orgy with two bikini-clad volleyballing sisters, catches Arabella on her hands and knees sucking Armand's mighty prick, her big nude buttocks thrust invitingly in his direction. Overwhelmed with lust, Max plunges his cock into the proffered arse of his now-shameless wife, symbolically uniting them in a future life of unbridled licence.

'If only,' Percy muttered to himself as he contemplated the finale of his effort. He and Felicity had not had horizontal marital relations since the conception of Crispin, which was well over two years before. He had pinned his hopes for their resumption on this holiday but things had not started off on the right foot. Actually, he thought gloomily as he washed down a paracetamol tablet with a nip of scotch, they'd started on his left. Which was now bust. Hey-ho.

In a haze of pain-wracked nostalgia Percy recalled the image of Felicity's broad and bulging bottom. He'd never been up there, even in their sexiest times. He could imagine the squawks of outrage if he'd tried. Suddenly he laughed out loud as he realised he could fuck the arse off his wife as many times as he wanted in this book. He could write what he liked with her in mind – and any other female he fancied, come to that. That at least would be some satisfaction – to picture Felicity's buttocks spread before him, the dusky dimple of her rosehole yielding at the touch of his knob, parting its velvety folds to suck him in to the hilt!

He chuckled with delight as he crossed out the heading *Oil My Tits*. Inspiration was striking already. Thanks to his wife's arse he had a title: *To the Hilt*.

Percy was out for the count when Felicity found him in the morning, his long frame bent rigid, his swollen ankle propped up on the bidet. A snowstorm of screwed-up paper littered the floor and a half-empty whisky bottle lay on its side.

Percy's snores echoed around the small tiled room, reinforcing the severity of Felicity's hangover and irritating her beyond measure.

'Wake up, you stupid sod,' she muttered and booted him in the thigh. Who said you couldn't kick a man when he was down?

Then she summoned help to scrape her husband off the floor.

14

Brendan O'Reilly was not much of a fellow for books. As a summertime water-ski instructor and a winter whizz on the Alpine pistes, his was an aggressively active lifestyle. And when he was not teaching wobbly-kneed holidaymakers how to stay upright on sea or snow, he had better things to do than read. Brendan O'Bonkers, as his Cascade colleagues often referred to him, was also an expert at serious R&R.

Not that Brendan was stupid. He'd only quit his Physics degree in Dublin out of boredom and the urge to spend time with his estranged father in Australia. In effect the skills he had picked up on the beach in Sydney had opened up a new career for him. Given the state of the leisure industry these days, being a beach bum was a respected vocation.

So woe betide the vacationing desk jockey who thought Brendan would be a pushover in the bar at chess or other intellectual pastimes. One stormy day when the water was too choppy for skiing, he'd run his eye over all the questions in the Trivial Pursuit box and now he was unbeatable. Sometimes it was useful to have a photographic memory.

Brendan was attuned to the needs of the holiday business. Keep the punters happy somehow, was his motto. Which was why he was standing in the office behind the reception desk, coaxing Percy's handwritten memo to Lucian Swan through the fax machine. Naturally he read every word.

His attention had first been drawn to Percy the previous morning.

To be precise, his attention had been drawn to the scowling woman in the next deck chair to Percy. Her displeasure as her husband loped off to the bar was obvious. Brendan usually gave the wife the once-over first, not only because he was a connoisseur of the female form but because, nine times out of ten, she held the key to the couple's holiday happiness. If the wife and mother was having a good time, bet your life the rest of the family were too. And Brendan and his Cascade colleagues had acquired many techniques to keep holiday wives happy.

For a fellow like Brendan who appreciated mature women – grown-up girls with big square hips and bouncing bum cheeks and low-slung, extravagantly curved bosoms that a man could really get to grips with – Percy's wife was a wet dream come true. It was a pity about the pinched mouth and set jaw and emerald eyes clouded with habitual rage. But Brendan wasn't daunted. Tougher cases – and far less attractive ones – had passed through his hands and come out smiling. He looked on a woman like Felicity Carmichael as a challenge.

And so Brendan had been only too delighted to answer the damsel's early-morning distress call and help lift Percy off the bathroom floor. He'd gone further and put an ice pack on Percy's ankle, helped him dress and manoeuvred him downstairs to the restaurant terrace where he now sat, breathing in the fumes of his third black coffee. In the course of this attendance, Brendan had volunteered to send Percy's fax.

It was red-hot stuff, no doubt about that – the outline of a sex novel set in a holiday complex just like Cascade, full of throbbing dicks looking for homes and cock-happy nymphos eager to solve the accommodation problem. It was enough to send a bloke running to the library. He revised his opinion of Percy. He'd already felt sympathetic to the mild-mannered hen-pecked guy, now he resolved to help him all he could. And there were lots of ways he could do that.

* * *

'That's sorted, Perce,' said Brendan as he took the vacant chair next to the invalid and returned his pieces of paper.

Percy blinked at him through his spectacles. 'Are you sure it all went through?'

'No problem. Here's the slip. 'Pages six. Result OK. Failure pages none.'

'Thank God for that,' Percy muttered. 'I'm expecting a reply later today. It's most important.'

'Don't worry – I'll tell the girls on the desk. We'll let you know the moment it comes. I mean, you're not going to run off now, are you?' He laughed and indicated Percy's empty cup to a short busty waitress with a coffee pot.

'Sexy, isn't she?' said Brendan as the girl walked away, her hips swaying under her blue uniform skirt. 'Dynamite body with the temperament of an iceberg – except in the right hands. She'd fit right into your book.'

Percy spluttered into his cup. 'You mean you read my fax? How dare you read my private business documents!'

Brendan was unfazed. 'Keep cool, Perce, anybody would have. You're lucky it was me because I can be of invaluable assistance to you.'

Suspicion gleamed in Percy's eyes. 'What do you mean?'

'This book of yours is going to be set here, right?'

'Well ... somewhere like here, yes. It won't be identifiable.'

'Because you don't want Cascade to sue you?'

'No and I don't want anyone else finding out about it either.' Percy was panicking. His situation was bad enough, it would be intolerable if his fellow holidaymakers discovered what he was up to.

Brendan laid a reassuring hand on his shoulder. 'Relax, my friend. Your secret is safe with me, as they say. Besides, I want to help out.'

'What do you mean?'

'I reckon you need a technical adviser. Someone who knows

what really goes on in a place like this. I could tell you and you could put it in the book. It would make it more authentic – and a hell of a lot hornier than anything you could dream up.'

'If that's true why don't you write your own book?'

Brendan guffawed. 'You must be joking, man. I'm an over-sexed beach bum of twenty-two. When I get to your age I might write about life but right now I prefer living it.'

Percy digested this information. He had already calculated the novel would require upwards of a dozen no-holds-barred passages of uninhibited bonking, preferably with a shifting cast of gorgeous but physically dissimilar types. For a man who had slept with the same woman for over a dozen years and, for the past two, with no sexual contact whatsoever, this was a daunting prospect. He needed help with this book like a blind man needed a guide dog.

But he was still suspicious. 'What do you want in return?'

'I want to be in it.'

'What?'

'I want to be a character in your book, Perce – Big Balls Brendan the superstud of the beach. All you've got to do is tell the truth – well, maybe you could add a couple of inches here and there, know what I mean?'

Perce nodded. He knew all right. He'd give Brendan a two-foot python in his pants if the boy donated enough material to help him dash off *To the Hilt*. The beauty of it was that it didn't matter if Brendan told him a pack of lies – that's all a novel like this was in the first place.

For the first time since he'd smashed his ankle, Percy found himself smiling. He held out his hand. 'It's a deal.'

'You won't regret it,' said Brendan, returning Percy's grip. 'Just wait till I tell you about No Knickers Night.'

'What's that?' Percy was instantly agog, his imagination already working overtime.

'Hey, break it up, fellers.' Carol-Anne, looking spectacular in a skintight electric-blue leotard, appeared out of nowhere. 'Count your fingers, Percy, after shaking hands with this guy.'

'You're looking good today, Carol,' said Brendan. 'The sight of you in Lycra blue could move a man to verse, wouldn't you say so, Perce?'

Percy, trying hard not to look at the girl's breasts exquisitely defined in the straining fabric inches from his nose, grinned stupidly.

'Aren't you required on the beach about now, Brendan?' said Carol-Anne. 'Mr Carmichael and I have to discuss his schedule.'

'Schedule?' said Percy as Brendan jogged off and Carol-Anne took his seat.

'I've worked out a rota with the girls. I've been through most of it with Mrs Carmichael so she has round-the-clock assistance with the children. She says you need nursemaiding too and, as she's going to be busy, I've arranged for people to keep an eye on you.'

'Oh.' Percy hadn't foreseen this. He rather hoped he'd be left alone with his writing pad.

'One of our waitresses, Philippa, is going to take the mornings. She'll put an ice pack on your ankle and fetch and carry for you. Then after lunch, Lucia – she's a local girl who works here in the mornings as a cleaner – will keep you company—'

'Actually, Carol-Anne, I'm not sure all this will be necessary. I mean, I've got a lot of work to do and I was hoping ...'

Percy's words trailed off as he saw the busty blonde waitress who had served him coffee make her way towards them. She had changed into shorts and a blue gingham halter that groaned under the weight of her mesmerising chest.

'Philippa's going to make sure you're comfortable,' said Carol-Anne, 'unless you'd rather be left in peace.'

'Oh no,' said Percy in haste as the luscious waitress stood in front of him. He could make out the individual freckles on her deep cleavage and fine golden hairs glinting on her bronzed bare thighs.

'I've got a first-aid certificate,' said Philippa in the languid tones of the upper-crust Home Counties, 'and I've lots of experience helping chaps with wonky legs. My brothers all play rugger.'

'So you'll be in good hands,' said Carol-Anne.

Percy had no doubt about it.

15

Whack! Felicity hit the tennis ball with all her considerable strength. From the back of the court the ball flew over the net like a bullet and dipped inside the line, leaving Henry, her tennis coach, stranded in mid-court.

'Love thirty,' shouted Felicity with unconcealed satisfaction and marched along the baseline to receive serve. She was enjoying this. Every time she crunched the ball she imagined she was thumping Percy's head. It gave her considerable satisfaction.

Henry was preparing to serve, his jaw set in a determined line. She could see he had not been prepared for her skill or her aggression. He wasn't going to give her an easy ball this time.

He was a tall, lithe youth, agile but not beefy. And he was by no means the best opponent she had ever faced. Though he *was* possibly – a voice in her head suggested – the prettiest.

He served to her backhand, much faster than before, but her old instincts did not let her down. She drilled it across court past his groping racquet. He stood at the net and gave her a rueful grin.

'I thought you said you hadn't played for years.'

'I haven't. I've been breeding – it doesn't give you time for much else. Love forty, I believe.'

She waited for Henry, enjoying the sight of his tight neat rump in his tiny white shorts as he bent over to retrieve the balls. Then she summoned her concentration as she had always done by thinking of something that made her blood boil. That was easy. The picture of Percy reclining on the sun terrace, a beer in his hand and a little blonde trollop fussing around him with her chest half exposed. That *really* fired her up!

Henry served – a kicking, swerving thunderbolt right into her body. She chipped it back and he went for the cross-court line. She reached it somehow, panting hard, and lobbed it over him as he took command of the net. He turned and chased. It was a valiant effort but his return bounced mid-court and she was on it. '*Ugh!*' her grunt rang out as she smashed the ball as hard as she could. It caught Henry, dashing back to cover the net, flush in the solar plexus like a boxer's low blow and doubled him over in windless agony.

She led him to the bench at the side of the court and patted his back as he crouched over, his head between his knees, unable to speak.

'I'm sorry, Henry,' she said without meaning it and thinking that (a) he wasn't much of a tennis coach if he couldn't beat an out-of-practice, out-of-condition mother-of-three and (b) he was a wimp.

But a pretty wimp, said that sly voice in her head again. A handsome, tanned, blue-eyed, youthful wimp whose blond hair was soft and sweet-smelling as she cradled his head on her chest. And whose bare skin was under her fingers, his shirt riding up his back as he sobbed and heaved.

He lifted his head and there was wonder in his azure eyes.

'Christ,' he said at last, 'you're not Martina Navratilova's sister, are you? You're bloody good.'

'I used to be,' said Felicity. 'I was a schoolgirl champion, Junior Wimbledon and all that, but I couldn't give anyone decent a proper game now.'

'Thanks a lot,' said Henry.

'Sorry, I didn't mean—'

'It's OK, Felicity, you've found me out. I'm not the tennis coach. The real one quit last week and I'm standing in till they get a replacement. I thought I was doing pretty well till you came along. You're entering the tennis competition, I take it?'

'I haven't got a partner. My husband's hopeless and anyway he's sprained his ankle.'

Henry sat up straight and rubbed his stomach. 'Don't worry, I'll find you someone. The water-ski instructor is dead keen though he's pretty wild. As he's staff he's only allowed to play to make up the numbers. I guess that's what he'd be doing if he partnered you.'

While he was speaking Henry had stood up, feeling his stomach. Now he pulled up his shirt and tugged his shorts halfway down to examine the damage.

The white skin below his bikini line was a flaming red and the beginnings of a painful bruise could be seen. Felicity gazed at the exposed strip of skin, at the taut and youthful belly and the blond strip of hair running down from his navel in a thickening line, turning a coppery hue as it disappeared from sight into his shorts.

Felicity was hit by a wave of emotion she had thought she would never feel again. A thudding, tummy-turning bolt of lust that she recognised from a distant past and another life. She wanted to bend forward and place her mouth on that exposed skin, to feel the springy curls of Henry's belly hair between her teeth, to plunge her lips down, down into his crotch and root there like a pig after truffles.

And then she realised, from the way he was standing there, gazing at her with those innocent blue eyes, that she could.

'Do you want me to kiss it better?' she asked.

He nodded his head.

If it hadn't been for the blonde girl with the bosom fussing over Percy she probably would have pulled back. But she had seen the way her husband ogled that yawning cleavage, as if he were committing the position of every freckle to memory. Well, two could play at that and, as with most games, she was going to play it better.

She kissed gently round the edge of Henry's bruise, just brushing the skin with her lips. Then she trailed her tongue, snail-like, up to his belly button. He tasted hot and sweaty but not disagreeably so. On the contrary, he was fresh and alive in her mouth, ravishing her senses with the sweet succulence of youth. He was the first young strong male she had embraced in how long – twelve years? Fifteen? Maybe more, way back in her loose-hipped, free-swinging, tennis-playing heyday when she was sought after off the court as well as on it. When the boys at tennis parties had ever-ready, always-reliable, spring-loaded erections in their pants.

Just like Henry.

'Oh yes!' she muttered as her fingers peeled down his shorts to bare a white and throbbing staff, an object of irresistible beauty to her with its curling copper-coloured hairs and the scarlet cap glistening with excitement. She didn't resist.

'Oh yes!' he moaned as she sucked the knob into her mouth, her hot lips sliding down the shaft, swallowing him to the root.

His hands were in the chestnut tangle of her hair and hers were on his bare firm buttocks, her nails cutting cruelly into the taut flesh. Her head bobbed as she gorged on him, the plum of his glans butting the soft skin of her upper palate. He tried to stop her but she was in charge. She ringed his shaft with one hand and pumped him as she conquered him with her mouth. It was all over in under a minute.

'Jesus!' he cried as he emptied himself between her lips, his cock twitching and his legs giving way as she brought him to his knees for the second time in twenty minutes. Not that he was feeling any pain this time.

She sat back on the seat, her mouth overflowing with the salty tang of his juices. She swallowed it slowly, the first draft of young man's spunk she'd tasted in years – probably since those tennis parties. She'd sampled a lot then, she recalled. And after she'd sampled, it was time for her partner to return the favour.

She pulled her tennis skirt to her waist and spread her legs, exposing a bulging vee of white cotton. A line of dark perspiration marked the vertical mouth of her quim. Curling brown hairs peeked out from her panty hem, promising a wild pubic growth that could not be contained.

Henry, still on his haunches before her, stared. She hoped he was man enough to accept the challenge.

She pulled the gusset of her knickers to one side, showing him her tangled bush and the thick wet lips pouting with obvious need. Felicity's was a big hairy cunt – a mature woman's organ that had once gorged on youthful thrills, had given birth three times and had fasted ever since. Now it had a powerful hunger.

Henry shuffled forward and placed his hands on her thighs. He regarded her shyly from under long, girlish eyelashes. He looked about ten years old. But the distended penis that swung up from his loins was not that of a boy. The shaft was long and broad and, praise be, as firm as before she'd taken him between her lips. Her fingers closed round it as his mouth descended on hers and they kissed.

Oh, he tasted good! And he felt good, too, as she hugged him in her arms. A hand delved between her legs to explore the juicy purse of her pussy and, God, that felt fantastic!

Then Henry was all over her, tugging her shirt out of her waist, unclipping her bra and – bliss – crushing her bare breasts to his chest. His fingers were in her crotch, stroking and fondling her labia and rimming her hole and teasing the skin near her aching, needful clit.

She tugged on his cock, muttering, 'Put it in, put it in!' but he wouldn't and just teased and tweaked and pinched her intimate flesh till she was trembling on the brink of that feeling once so familiar and now so foreign to her—

'Oh!' she sighed as his finger circled her clit and 'Ohhh!' as he rubbed the fat head of his penis up and down her gaping crack and 'OHHH!' as he thrust his cock inside her long-neglected cunt, sending her moaning and sobbing over the edge on a wave of ecstasy that drove all the hurt and anger and self-pity from her mind.

It was the best tennis lesson she had ever had.

16

Miranda Lynch dug the point of her pencil into the notepad on her desk, pondering the problem Lucian had set before her. The typescript of *The Novelist's Wife* sat by her elbow, its pages obviously well thumbed.

'It's going to cost a lot, isn't it?' she said. It was the kind of question that did not require an answer, nevertheless Lucian felt duty-bound to fill the silence which followed.

'Marilyn's never been known to undersell a property.'

'I'm aware of that.'

Stab, stab went the point of the pencil, spearing lead-rimmed holes into the paper.

'You know her quite well, don't you?' Miranda said.

'Well, yes. She's an old family friend, I suppose.'

'Right.' The pencil stopped its destructive work as Miranda scribbled something down. She ripped the page out and handed it to Lucian. It said: £25,000.

'That's the most you can offer. It's subject to this legal indemnity she's told you about, sight of the author's documentary archive – and we've got to meet her.'

'OK.'

'If you can pull it off, Lucian, I'll buy *you* lunch at Grimaldi's. Of course, if you don't . . .'

His stomach lurched. 'If I don't?'

'Your P45, remember?'

The swirling grey eyes were on him, full of promised grief. But

the mouth, that pink Cupid's bow, was twitching uncharacteristic-
ally at the ends.

'Just joking,' she said. 'Good luck with your old family
friend.'

Marilyn took the offer as Lucian knew she would – with scorn.

'Twenty thousand pounds! For God's *sake*, Lucian, haven't you
got *any* clout these days? If this were a phone conversation I'd hang
up, that's such a piddling little amount.'

But it wasn't a phone conversation. Lucian had gone round to
Marilyn's mews cottage in Chelsea after work, bearing an
ostentatious bouquet of flowers and a bottle of ten-year-old
MacLavish, her favourite tipple. He'd waited till the flowers were
carelessly flung in a vase and two glasses reverently poured before
he'd made his offer. He'd kept five grand in reserve though it was
little enough room for manoeuvre.

'But, Marilyn, that's about ten times what we'd usually pay
someone to write us an erotic novel. It represents an unparalleled
commitment to a writer in this genre . . .'

'Oh Lucian, *please* don't give me that ghastly publisher-speak.'
She downed her glass of neat malt and reached for the bottle. 'Look,
we both know this book is dynamite —'

'If the legal stuff checks out and if the author is promotable —'

'Are you mad?' Down went another half-inch of liquid nectar
without touching the sides. It occurred to Lucian that he could have
bought five-year-old MacSpit at half the price. 'Karen Hastings is
the most desirable author I have ever represented. In every sense.
Wait till you meet her.'

'I'd love to.'

'You shall, darling boy. The moment she signs a contract with
GrabCo, you can come to dinner and watch Rodney Branscombe
crawl all over her.'

Lucian shot bolt upright. 'Marilyn, you've not shown it to him,
have you? I thought I had an exclusive!'

'And so you have – for the moment. But I'll remind you that the word "exclusive" is close to "elastic" in my dictionary and I'm not sure how much longer I can stretch your first look. Rodney would write me a blank cheque.'

'He's a prick,' muttered Lucian sulkily. 'You said so yourself.'

'True but sometimes a prick is precisely what is required. Have a drop more of this delightful cough mixture.' And she poured him a generous slug without waiting for answer.

'Talking of pricks,' she went on, 'I've always been curious about yours.'

The words came at him through a blur of whisky and self-pity, he was convinced he had lost this battle and in familiar fashion was already savouring his disappointment.

'What did you say, Marilyn?'

'I said I've always been curious about your penis, sweetheart. Ever since you were a schoolboy frolicking in Basil's pool in the summer. Have I never mentioned it to you?'

Lucian swirled the pungent alcohol around his mouth, feeling dull-witted and tongue-tied. 'But, what about it?' he said, wondering what ghastly schoolboy *faux pas* he had committed which she was doubtless about to remind him of to complete his misery.

Marilyn got to her feet, collecting the bottle and her glass. 'I remember that promising bulge in your swimming trunks. I've often wondered just how big it turned out to be in the end.' As she walked to the door she said, 'I'm going to finish getting ready for dinner. Why don't you come and keep me company?'

Marilyn's bedroom was pink and chintzy with Regency-striped wallpaper and a button-backed *chaise-longue* on which she was reclining when Lucian entered the room. She had discarded the silk dressing-gown which she had been wearing and now sat in a tangerine half-slip and matching knickers trimmed with lace.

Lucian hovered in the doorway, bewitched and unnerved. He'd

never seen her like this before. She was an honorary aunt, for Christ's sake! He was embarrassed – but she wasn't.

'Come in, darling,' she said, 'and pass me those stockings on the bed. In fact, why don't you put them on for me? I'm feeling very lazy.'

Lucian obeyed without thinking, slipping to the floor at her feet and fitting her toes into the wispy material. They were the kind of stockings that required no suspender belt. Hold-ups. Caroline had worn them frequently and he was practised at smoothing them up a dainty female limb.

'But what about this book?' he cried. 'You know you don't want Branscombe to have it, Marilyn. Sell it to me, please. It's perfect for Blue Desire. I can go to twenty-five thousand.'

'Ah. *That* might make a difference.'

For a moment Lucian thought she meant the extra money. Then he realised exactly what she did mean. Her small slim leg was extended towards his crotch and her foot was massaging his bulging loins.

'I want to see it, Lucian, don't you understand? Stand up like a good boy and let me look at your cock.'

It was stiff, of course. How could it not be when he had spent the past minute sliding a stocking over the silky sheen of her slender calf and creamy thigh?

'Oh yes,' she whispered as he stood over her, his trousers round his ankles, his thick white wand rearing in her face. 'It's turned out just as I thought. *Big.*'

It certainly was at that moment as she bent forward to scrutinise it more closely, the neck of her slip gaping to reveal the shadowy slopes of her porcelain-pale breasts.

She picked up the remaining stocking. 'I'm going to give you a special treat, darling boy,' she whispered and draped the weightless wisp over his out-thrust limb.

'Oh Marilyn,' he moaned as she wound the material around him, holding an end of the stocking in each hand and pulling it back and forth in a see-sawing motion. The friction was tight on his cock, constraining and exciting him at the same time. The motion pulled on his foreskin, peeling it back off his glans which thrust, rude and red, inches from her lips. She darted out her small pointed tongue and licked it, moving her hands faster.

His cock quivered and strained. He knew it had never been so hard or so huge. This was a dream of his adolescence made flesh – to be masturbated through a silk stocking by the woman who had once starred in those dreams on a nightly basis.

Her thoughts were obviously travelling in the same direction.

'All those years ago,' she said, 'did you ever think of me?'

'Christ, Marilyn, of course I did!'

She chuckled and flick-flicked at his knob with her tongue.

'Did you think of me while you played with yourself?'

'Yes!'

'What did you imagine doing to me?'

'Everything! Especially when I saw you sunbathing topless in Uncle Basil's garden.'

'I remember. I did it on purpose to excite you.'

'Why, Marilyn?'

'It amused me. I liked to imagine you getting worked up with me in mind. If you'd been a little more sophisticated I might have shown you what to do with that whopper in your swimming trunks.'

'Really? God, Marilyn, don't tell me I should have made a pass at you.'

'Well, you should have.'

The see-saw friction on his penis was almost unbearable now and his legs trembled as the sap began to rise from his balls.

'Mind you,' she continued, 'if we'd done it then I doubt if we'd be doing it now. And you wouldn't have a hope in hell of publishing *The Novelist's Wife*. Oh my, Lucian, what a lot of spunk – have you been saving it up? You'll have to buy me a new pair of stockings.'

Dizzy with orgasm, Lucian slumped to his knees. He stared at the wet stocking in her hand and the wicked glitter in her violet eyes.

'You mean you're going to sell me the book?'

'I'm considering your offer seriously,' she said, slipping her knickers down her smooth white thighs and spreading her legs. The mouth of her pussy was a neat hairless slit, the pouting pink lips hungry for attention.

Lucian leaned forward and planted a kiss on the pale dome of her belly. The aroma of her excitement was in his nostrils.

'Mmm, yes,' she sighed and settled down in her seat, her legs opening wider. 'Of course,' she went on as Lucian's mouth began its inevitable journey south, 'I anticipate this being a protracted negotiation. You're going to have to pull out all the stops to convince me, darling boy. Oh that's *good*!'

She seized Lucian by the hair as his lips brushed her labia and pulled his face hard into her crotch. For a second he fought for breath and then plunged his tongue deep into the tunnel of her vagina, pressing his nose against her clit. Her breath hissed through clenched teeth and her hands burrowed under his shirt, the fingernails sinking into his flesh.

As her thighs scissored shut, threatening to cut off his breath completely, he felt the first drop of blood trickle down his back.

'How's it going with Marilyn?' Miranda asked Lucian the next morning.

'I had dinner with her last night,' he said, failing to mention that he'd had breakfast with her as well.

'And?'

'We're in serious discussions. It could take some while.' He stifled a yawn with his hand and winced with pain. The scratches on his back hurt every time he moved.

Miranda fixed him with her most penetrating stare. 'I hope you've got the stamina for it.'

These were Lucian's sentiments precisely.

17

Percy was stuck.

The Whimsical Press had accepted his proposal for *To the Hilt* at once and, as Percy read Lucian's answering fax, a frisson of guilt had stolen through him. The man he had decried so roundly had proved himself to be a real pal. Lucian had even offered to deposit some money in Percy's bank account in his absence to keep the good ship Carmichael afloat. The fellow was more than a pal – he was a saviour.

Which made things worse, some three days later, to be staring at a mere half-a-dozen handwritten pages and knowing that they weren't any good. In the first flush of excitement Percy had thought it would be easy to knock out a few thousand words of erotica a day. After all, he was a professional writer. When he got cracking he could generate a fair pace on topics as diverse as bee-keeping or Alpine gardening or the history of the postage stamp. Once you'd mugged up on a subject, the rest was easy. That was the problem, of course. As far as this subject went, recently he'd not done any mugging up at all.

'Can I get you anything, Mr Carmichael?'

Philippa was looking at him from a reclining chair a couple of yards away in the full glare of the mid-morning sun. Her curvaceous form gleamed with sun cream which had taken fully twelve minutes to apply to every tempting inch of bare skin. Percy knew that because he had timed her. Today she wore a cerise bikini that left even more of her exposed than usual. Percy admired the design of tiny seashells and other marine artefacts that danced along the curve of her bikini top and across the waistband of her minuscule pants. He particularly liked the little seahorse that sat right *there* on the crest of her pubic bulge, its snout poking up and its tail curling down to where the oiled flesh of her upper thighs kissed ...

'Mr Carmichael?'

'Sorry, Philippa – I was miles away. If you're going to the bar you could get me a beer.'

Philippa slid off the sun-bed in one silky movement and bent to slip her espadrilles over her feet. For the umpteenth time in the past few days, Percy found himself staring down the bottomless ravine of her freckled cleavage. How a woman could be so small and yet have so much flesh to put on display was a constant wonder to him.

'Sorry, Mr Carmichael, you'll have to make do with coffee,' she announced as she straightened up. 'I've been talking to your wife and she says that if you drink beer all day with no exercise you'll get fat.'

Her suntanned buttocks, bisected by the cerise thong, winked at him as she walked away. Percy breathed a sigh of frustration as he watched her and surreptitiously eased his smitten penis into a more comfortable position in his shorts. Thrilling though her company was, it was not making his task any easier. She had not yet asked him to show her what he was writing, nevertheless he found her presence inhibiting. Particularly when all he wanted to do was describe blonde pocket Venuses with big freckled breasts and seahorses on their pussies. The alternative was to dismiss her, and the sloe-eyed Lucia of the afternoon shift too. But he couldn't bear to do that – besides he still needed their help.

'That's a terrible heavy sigh for a man surrounded by luscious handmaidens,' said a familiar Irish voice as Brendan took a seat by his side. He wore white shorts and trainers and was mopping his sweat-streaked face. Percy looked enviously at the beaded glass full of amber liquid in his hand.

'I've been playing tennis with your wife,' said Brendan. 'Lord, that's a woman with a powerful backhand.'

'Tell me about it.'

'Thank God I'm on the same side of the net this afternoon. We're playing in the doubles.' He took a deep draught and smiled in contentment. 'How's the book going?'

Percy pushed his notepad across the table without comment. It would be interesting to see Brendan's reaction. He, after all, was the target audience.

Brendan eyed the top page and his face fell. He took another gulp of beer and his brow furrowed in concentration.

'What does "callypygian" mean, Percy?'

'Having beautifully shaped buttocks.'

'And "cyprian sceptre"?'

'That's a penis.'

'So what this bit means is the sight of her pretty arse made his cock go stiff?'

'Yes.'

'Then, for God's sake, man, why don't you say so? Do you expect people to read your book with a dictionary in the other hand? How the hell are they going to jerk off?'

Percy looked pained. 'Well, I did expect some kind of intellectual response as well as the purely visceral.'

Brendan snorted. 'Don't kid yourself, Percy. Guys read these books to get turned on and then they have one off the wrist. Or else their wives get lucky. It's a feel-good thing, not a degree course in etymology.'

Percy smiled. '*Touché*, Brendan. I bow to your superior knowledge of the genre.'

'You bet it's superior. Anyhow, I'm going to be in your book, right? And I want a cock not a cyprian sceptre.'

'Not even a bloody enormous cyprian sceptre? OK, I admit it's not right yet.'

Brendan grinned. 'What's the problem, Perce? Don't tell

me your nurses are not inspiring you.'

'To be honest, they don't help. I'm so busy ogling them I can't work. And then I'm embarrassed to write what I really want to in case they read it.'

'Embarrassed?' Brendan looked nonplussed, the concept was alien to his nature. He thought for a moment.

Below them, Philippa could be seen emerging from the beach bar carrying two cups of coffee. Brendan spoke quickly.

'I can assure you Philippa won't be bothered by anything you write. Just don't attempt to lay a hand on her.'

'I'd never dream of doing such a thing—'

'Of course you would, Percy, any horny guy would. Just don't do it. Dream all you like then write it down. If she reads it I guarantee she'll be flattered. I mean, is that girl an exhibitionist or what?'

Both of them paused to watch Philippa climb the steps to the terrace. She moved gracefully. There were no ripples in the coffee she carried but at each step the upper slopes of her exposed breasts quivered deliciously. As she undulated towards them and the little seahorse in her crotch thrust out its snout in Percy's direction, he realised she loved showing off her body.

'The little pricktease,' he muttered, suddenly aware that – on paper at least – he could do just what he liked to her.

'Got any money on you?' asked Brendan.

'Forty or fifty thousand lira.'

'Great. When Lucia asks you for it this afternoon, just hand it over.'

'Why?'

But Brendan was gone and Philippa was placing the coffee on the table by his side. The seahorse was inches from his face and he studied it closely, turning over in his mind the words to describe that bikini – and the scene which would follow as his hero, Max, sank his teeth into the scrap of cerise and tore it off an imaginary blonde's pretty arse.

By the time Lucia arrived that afternoon, Percy was riding a streak of inspiration. Max had seduced a big-chested blonde with freckles, Simone, in a changing cabin at the back of the crowded riviera beach, ripping her bikini off and sitting her on his rearing cock as he leaned against the wooden door for support.

Percy had imagined what it would be like to circle Philippa's small waist with his big hands and then described Max plunging such a woman up and down on his penis, her swollen breasts rubbing against his chest and her hot little mouth on his as they tried to keep the lid on their moans of lust. But that had proved impossible for Max and Simone and as she came for the third or fourth time, shrieking out in ecstasy, someone yanked open the cabin door and the pair of them tumbled nude into a crowd of onlookers.

Percy barely looked up as Felicity came by, her hair sandy and wet and her face brown from the wind after her sailing lesson.

'I say, well done, Percy,' she said as she took in his industry. 'You might as well crack on with it. The girls can supervise the kids at lunch. I'll get one of them to bring you a sandwich.'

'And a beer,' said Percy hopefully.

'Righto,' she said and strode off. It was the first pleasant interchange he'd had with his wife for days.

He turned back to the page before him and decided to have Max straddle Simone's chest and place his straining penis between her heaving freckled melons.

He was barely conscious of the moment when Lucia took her seat beside him but when he looked up he found the Italian's dark and soulful eyes fixed upon him.

' 'Ello, Signor Percy. You work 'ard.' She smiled, revealing her brilliant white teeth. She too was a small girl but there the resemblance to Philippa ended. She was olive-skinned and slender, with a straight nose and lustrous black hair that fell to her shoulders. She wore a collection of bracelets on her wrists that rattled as she moved and long dangling silver earrings that tinkled when she turned her head. Her tiny feet were in white leather sandals with heels that rapped loudly on the flags of the terrace and when she spoke in Italian the sound was like a volley of machine-gun fire. All in all, her presence could not be overlooked and, so far, this constant noise had been distracting to the writer.

His cock had also found her distracting. Though she wore many more clothes than Philippa, her body, in its own way, had as powerful an effect. The eyes and the lips spoke of untold exotic pleasures for a lover. The little hands changed the dressing on his ankle with a lingering sensuality – as if they were reluctant to leave his flesh. She would often lay a small cool palm on his brow and gaze at him with tender concern, as if she were checking the temperature of an ailing infant. But her touch was more than motherly.

Her garments concealed her body like veils around an exotic dancer. She wore layers of clothing, open shirts over tiny vests, gauzy hanging scarves, thin wispy things that somehow placed emphasis on the unfettered curves of flesh beneath. Percy had often fancied he could see the shadows of her nipples through the flowing material. She wore no bra, he was certain of that from the way her flesh shifted, and her last layer always seemed to be white and thin, revealing the dark smudges beneath.

Now she laid a hand on his bare knee, the fingers just touching the flesh on the inside of his thigh. It was a typically intimate gesture.

'You 'ave money?' she said.

Percy remembered what Brendan had said. He put his hand in his pocket and pulled out a small bundle of blue notes. She took them from him and counted them. Then they disappeared into her clothing, conjured away by those magic fingers.

'Come,' she said, taking hold of his arm with one hand and picking up his stick with the other. 'We walk.'

Percy wanted to protest. It was still difficult moving around and he saved his energies for hobbling to the loo and getting up to his room. But Lucia was tugging him to his feet and, remarkably for such a small woman, bearing his weight as she urged him forward.

They didn't go far, just along the walkway and behind a wicker screen which took them down the side of the hotel building. Chairs and tables were piled up here – it seemed this part of the terrace was not in use. Lucia pulled a sun-lounger with an adjustable back from behind a stack of chairs and tugged it into the open. She indicated that Percy was to lie back on it. He did so, gratefully taking the weight off his injured foot while she fussed around him. Then she perched on the side of the recliner, her hip pressing companionably into his.

'Is OK?' she asked.

He looked over her shoulder. To the left were the gorse and scrub-packed slopes of the nearby hills, to the right was the bay where a vermilion sea twinkled beneath a cloudless sky.

'Is very OK,' he said.

'*Bene*,' she said and kissed him.

It was an exotic foreign kiss. It tasted of espresso and tobacco and hinted at devilish sensual pleasures he had never before tasted. He wrapped his arms around her and pulled her to his chest.

'Ooh, Signor Percy,' she whispered in his ear and bit the lobe.

'Ow!' he cried. It was like being stung by a wasp. She laughed, a low husky chuckle, and pulled away from him.

To his astonishment he found himself staring at her naked breasts. Somehow she had rearranged her clothing to unveil high shallow bowls of flesh which curved upwards to coal-black points. She took his hand and led it to her bosom, her bottomless brown eyes twinkling with mischief.

His hand shook as he felt her. The small rounds seemed to swell and leap at his touch, the nipples long, ridged and hard against his palm.

'*Bella, bella*,' he muttered, cursing his ignorance of Italian. 'You are beautiful, exquisite —'

'Ssh,' she said and offered her teats to his lips, holding back her shirt so he could explore her thoroughly with hands and lips. As he did so, a little bit of his brain said, *Make notes in your head! You can use this in your book!*

He was so engrossed with her tits he was not aware she had unfastened his shorts until he felt her hand on his cock.

'Oho!' she cried with a chuckle. From her broad smile it was apparent she liked what she had found.

'*Grande, molto grande!*' she cried and slid her little fingers into his underpants to fish out his balls.

'Oh Lucia,' groaned Percy, all thoughts of note-taking completely banished. It had been many years since any woman, let alone a sloe-eyed Italian beauty, had taken the tiniest interest in his sexual equipment.

His genitals did look enormous in her small hands, the tool stretching fat and stiff up over his belly, the sack of his testicles overflowing one hand, the shiny scarlet glans rearing from between the fingers of the other. She squeezed his shaft and his whole body twitched. He was wound up so tight he might explode at any second. They both knew it.

She teased him. She fluttered her fingers up and down his straining weapon, then circled it with both hands, pulling back the foreskin till the knob stuck up like a purple lollipop. Then she dipped her shoulders and touched the black spike of each nipple in turn onto the gleaming head.

Percy's mind was in a mist as she played with him like this, wantonly, obscenely. God, it was fantastic!

She pressed his tool to her lips and, looking up at him and laughing, flicked her tongue out, the tiny tip seeking the eye of his glans.

'Good Lord!' he cried, then, 'My God!' and 'Oh Christ, Lucia!' as half his big tool disappeared between her lips, distorting her pretty face, and her jaw worked and the earrings tinkled and her fingers jacked his shaft up and down in a rattle of bracelets and then

116

he convulsed, shooting every drop of his long-stored-up and disregarded jism down her adorable throat.

She kept his cock in her mouth as he slowly became soft while he stroked her lustrous midnight-black hair and thought that that was the best fifty thousand lira he had ever spent.

18

Lucian had thought hard about his first editorial session with Caroline. It was important to establish a new order in their relationship – this time round he was determined to hold the whip hand. Maybe literally.

'Lucian, darling,' cried Caroline as he opened the front door, bussing him on both cheeks in a cloud of *Intime*.

'You're five minutes late,' he said. 'This is meant to be a professional arrangement, Caroline, I trust you're going to take it seriously.'

She raised a pencil-thin eyebrow and preceded him up the staircase without comment, her provocative bottom swaying beneath his nose as they ascended.

'I hope your Australian tart is not lurking around somewhere,' she said loudly as she entered the flat. 'If she is, I'm not staying. You can buy me dinner at that Italian place on the corner.'

'As it happens, Caroline, Ms Pilgrim is not at home this evening. And, as a fellow author on the Blue Desire list, I suggest you treat her with the respect she deserves.'

'Are you all right, Lucian?' Caroline's milky-blue eyes registered – possibly – concern. 'You're sounding just a teensy bit uptight.' She placed a small hand on his shoulder, warming his skin through the cotton of his shirt. 'I can understand you being a bit nervous, darling, but don't worry. This is just a working relationship. I promise I won't muck you about.'

Lucian said nothing, pushing open the door to the living room and ushering her ahead of him.

Caroline dropped her briefcase on the sofa and was in the act of removing her jacket when she froze.

'What's *that*?' She was staring at the coffee table on which stood a bottle of wine, two glasses, a document bearing the letter head of The Whimsical Press, an artist's sketchpad and a large pink object.

'A rather good Chablis and a signed copy of your contract,' said Lucian. 'And some props.'

'*Props*!' she spat the word out with scorn. 'That's a dildo!'

Lucian opened the wine.

Her eyes were fierce narrow slits as she bristled with outrage. 'How simply revolting! I suppose it belongs to that Pilgrim woman.'

'As a matter of fact, I made an embarrassing foray into Soho and bought it especially for our session this evening.'

'What! You mean it's something to do with me?'

'Of course. You've got one in your book, don't you remember? Obviously you are familiar with how they work.'

'I've had enough.' She grabbed her briefcase. 'You can speak to me about the book over the phone, Lucian. I'm not putting up with your smutty little games.'

'Aren't you forgetting something?' Lucian took a slip of paper from his shirt pocket and unfolded it.

'My cheque,' she said and held out her hand. 'Give it to me, Lucian.'

He grinned and replaced the paper in his pocket. 'Not until you comply with the terms of our agreement.'

'What do you mean?'

'It says in the contract that we will pay you in instalments provided you follow the firm's editorial guidance. That means, darling Caro, that you do what I say. Walk out now and I tear up this cheque. Our deal's off.'

Caroline stared at him, gimlet-eyed. But beneath the hostility

Lucian could detect something else – uncertainty maybe. She was used to walking all over Lucian and this was a new experience for her.

She put down the briefcase. 'What do you want me to do?'

Lucian smiled and said, 'Take off your clothes, Contessa Strepponi.'

'What!'

'I can tell from the sneer on your beautiful face that you fear contamination from the unpretentious nature of my humble home. Take off your expensive designer gown so it will not spoil.'

She stood completely still, her face blank, as if in shock.

'I wrote that,' she said.

'You certainly did. Let's see if you really meant it. Remove your gown.'

'But...' She made a rather forlorn gesture with one hand. 'I'm not wearing a gown. Is this really necessary, Lucian? I'll feel silly.'

'Remove it at once, Marietta, or I shall rip it from your exquisitely beautiful back.'

As if in a trance her hand went to her bodice and she pushed the first button into the eye of the buttonhole. Then she slowly unfastened the front of her blouse. 'I'll never forgive you for this, Lucian,' she said but her voice was small and lacked conviction.

'My name is Bruno, Marietta. I am an artist and you are my model – remember?' And he took the blouse from her and tossed it onto a chair as she stepped out of her skirt.

With trembling hands she peeled her tights down her rounded thighs to stand before him wearing only a pink lacework brassiere and matching knickers embroidered with little roses. Lucian's cock twitched in his pants. It was as if he had never seen Caroline in underwear before. It was incredibly exciting.

'And the rest,' he commanded.

'No,' she cried, holding an arm over her chest and a hand over her crotch to shield her pubic bulge, just as she had described in her book. There was no doubt now that she was going to play along.

'How else am I going to paint you if not naked?' he roared on cue and watched in triumph as she unhooked her bra and dropped it on the sofa. Then she slipped her hands into her panties and pulled them down her legs, her pear-shaped breasts dangling as she bent forward. Lucian fought the urge to reach out and cup them in his hands. That would break the spell, he was sure.

He savoured the sight of her nudity. Had those breasts grown a little fuller since he had last smothered them in adoring kisses? He could not remember her nipples being so long and swollen, nor her areolae so pink, nor her belly so prettily curved.

'Turn round,' he barked, aware he was departing from the script but eager to see her bottom. She turned without a murmur.

It was still the arse of his dreams, two full teardrops of flesh flowing outwards from her narrow waist like twin petals on a perfect tulip, the skin smooth and flawless, except when – *smack! smack!* – a firm hand was laid across her buttocks, setting the pert rounds in pink and quivering motion.

'Ow!' cried Caroline and Lucian thought his impulsive gesture had broken the spell. This was not part of her scenario. Maybe he had overstepped the mark.

And then she said, in a small wimpering voice, 'Please, Bruno, not again!' and he laughed out loud. 'Bruno' indeed! His victory was complete. All he had to do now was make the most of it.

'Sit on the sofa,' he ordered, 'and spread those pretty legs.'

She did as she was told, opening her thighs in an inviting vee.

'Touch yourself,' he commanded and she didn't even bother to protest but ran her hands over her body. Her left hand tweaked her nipples, moving back and forth, until the ridged pegs of flesh stood up like scarlet thumbs. Her right hand roved across her belly and down her thighs, weaving round and round in a circular pattern, closing in on the bull's-eye of her sex.

Lucian was sitting opposite her, drinking in the sight of a woman on erotic autopilot. Though he had picked up the pad and pencil it seemed an unnecessary piece of play-acting – Caroline had no need of external aids to her performance.

The hair between Caroline's legs was a vertical blonde strip that concealed nothing. As she lolled back on the cushions her pubis was thrust into exaggerated prominence, revealing every sugar-pink fold of her delicious crack, from the shy hood of her clitoris down to the pouting divide of her bulging rear cheeks.

Her fingers had reached the in-rolled lips of her exposed pussy and they fluttered up and down the inviting slit, hardly brushing the flesh. Then, as if she had teased herself enough and could resist no longer, she pressed two fingers into the light fuzz at the top of her split. She worked them down and round, building a steady rhythm, bearing down on the flesh around her clit.

Lucian was fascinated. He had once asked Caroline to masturbate for him and her response had been withering. She had claimed to be revolted by the notion and said that self-gratification was utterly foreign to her nature. Lucian had been sufficiently cowed to believe her but now, as he watched the familiarity with which she handled herself, he recognised it for the hypocrisy it was. She was so bloody good at it she was coming already.

'Oh crumbs,' she moaned, her fingers plucking at her nipples, her head bowed as she watched her other hand busy in her wide-open crotch. 'Oh gosh, oh crikey, oh . . .'

Lucian had always found it endearing that, in expressing erotic pleasure, Caroline's vocabulary reverted to the sixth form. He knew for sure that she was really worked up.

She pumped her hips, lifting her loins off the sofa, both hands busy between her legs. 'Oh my, oh my!' she muttered, pushing two fingers deep inside the pink velvet crease of her quim. Then her eyes locked on Lucian's.

'Give it to me,' she said.

He grinned. He knew just what she wanted.

'Ask me nicely,' he replied. That's what Bruno said to Marietta at this point.

'Give me the dildo – *please*!'

It was a monster, twelve inches long, the biggest they'd had in the shop. Caroline took it all, inch by inch, carefully easing it up her tight but insatiable pussy. And when it was deep inside, she gave him quite a show, tweaking her clit till it stood up blood red, stuffing the big machine deep into her vagina and corkscrewing a finger into her anus as she pushed herself over the edge. By the time she had finished she had shagged herself to delirium and back – much like her creation, Marietta Strepponi.

Finally she flung the phallus across the room and lay panting on the sofa. Only her ragged breathing broke the silence.

'Fuck me now please, Lucian,' she said at last.

'No, Caroline.'

'For God's sake, I need a real cock in me. *Please*.'

'Sorry. That's not how you wrote it. Bruno doesn't fuck Marietta in that scene.'

She gave a cry somewhere between a curse and a sob and, grabbing her clothes, rushed from the room. Lucian heard the sound of running water from the bathroom and two minutes later she reappeared. She looked as composed as she had when she arrived but her mouth was set in a thin line. She picked up her briefcase.

'Have you got any more copy for me?' he asked.

'I did have,' she snarled, snatching the cheque that Lucian held out to her, 'but in the light of this . . . meeting, I'm going to revise it.'

'Really?'

'Yes!' she hissed. 'Though I hate to say it, you sly manipulative bastard, you've given me some bloody good ideas.'

'See you next week then,' said Lucian as the front door crashed behind her.

He quickly dialled Marilyn Savage's number and sighed with relief when she answered on the second ring. Negotiations for *The Novelist's Wife* were still ongoing. It would be appropriate to donate the crippling hard-on in his trousers to the cause.

19

Her current situation was a puzzle to Felicity. She couldn't explain it to herself. How could she, a respectable wife and mother, secretary of the Spawnshire Infants Trust, relief counsellor for Parents Under Stress and treasurer of the St Marchmont's Operatic Society, be doing *this*?

Because she was on holiday.

Because the kids were out of the way and her husband was conveniently laid up.

Because, at bottom, she was a shameless slut.

And because – oh yes – because it felt *good*!

Of course the Irishman with his tongue in her vagina was also to blame. Admittedly she'd had Henry the tennis coach before allowing Brendan any liberties but it had been different with Henry. He'd been in awe of her and she'd bestowed on him the gift of her body as if he were yet another of her Good Works. That was not the case with Brendan. With his tousle-haired charm and what-the-hell attitude he could probably have had taken his pick from the week's entire roster of female guests. And when he'd kissed her after their first-round tennis victory, his toffee-brown eyes twinkling into hers, his fingers slyly squeezing the flesh of her hip, the boot of generosity had been on the other foot.

And now she was in bed with both Brendan and Henry, their impatient hands sharing her bountiful body, their mouths gorging on her most sensitive openings, their firm young cocks pressing against her flesh. God, she was loving every minute of it.

In a way it was a relief that things had gone this far. After the first encounter with Henry she had suffered pangs of conscience. These had been counterbalanced not only by the little hussies flitting around Percy but the sudden remembrance of how important good sex was. In the hurly-burly of child-rearing and wage-earning, Felicity and Percy had allowed that side of their lives to fade and die. In any case, it was difficult to feel romantic about a middle-aged man whose nightly presence in your bed was merely a snoring, farting impediment to a deserved night's sleep. To be frank, Felicity had come to the conclusion she could live without sex.

But the feel of Henry's beautiful cock inside her had changed all that. Suddenly it had become desperately important to her happiness that she had sex again. And, even if she could only enjoy it for the length of this holiday, she was going to pander to her long-neglected sexuality. For the rest of the fortnight she was determined to get laid – lots.

So when Brendan had given her a smacker on the lips on the tennis court, she'd slipped her tongue into his mouth in a flash. They'd rushed straight back to her room in the knowledge that Percy wouldn't be disturbing them and had spent a torrid hour testing the bed springs.

Today, prudence prevailing, Felicity had gone ahead to the room on her own, and Brendan had joined her a few minutes later under the shower. Later, in bed and on the verge of her second orgasm of the afternoon, Felicity had thought she'd heard the door open. And when she opened her eyes, her pleasure temporarily sated, she'd seen Henry standing by the bed, his tall bronzed body stark-naked, his long white penis jutting from the pale triangle of his loins.

There were many things she could have said, 'Get out' being the most obvious. But for these few days Felicity Carmichael was functioning by different rules. She'd already crossed her Rubicon and now all she could see ahead of her was a unique opportunity for erotic indulgence. So what she actually said as she opened her arms to the new arrival was, 'You planned this, didn't you? You naughty boys.'

By now they'd both had her and she'd come three or four times herself so all immediate desires had been assuaged. She sprawled on her back, big breasts lolling and thighs spread, basking in the admiration of the men on either side of her.

Henry was stroking a large creamy breast, rubbing the engorged nipple with his thumb until it stood up like a brazil nut. His eyes were on Brendan who raised the knee nearest him, exposing Felicity's groin. He slipped his fingers into the damp bush of hair and gently traced the roll of her labia. Her belly quivered at his touch. The two boys had worked her up to a plateau of sensual response and she was aching to go higher. What would they want of her next? she wondered. The anticipation was thrilling.

Henry's hand joined Brendan's between her legs, pulling her legs open further then resting on the plump and silky flesh of her inner thigh, the tip of his thumb just a whisper from her yearning clit.

'Let's do something together,' she heard herself murmur and her hands closed on their cocks, both satisfyingly stiff and eager.

'What did you have in mind?' said Brendan, pushing a finger inside her. It made a rude sticky sound as he lazily moved it in and out.

'I don't know. I've never ... there must be something.'

'If there's anything in particular you'd like, just tell us. Henry and I aim to please, don't we?'

'You bet,' said Henry and his thumb pressed into her for an instant sending a current of lust flickering through her veins.

'Oh God,' she groaned. 'I can't ... I don't ... please, just take me. Both of you. Now, *please*.'

Brendan laughed, a wicked sound that fuelled Felicity's excitement, and removed his fingers from her pussy. 'Come here, my darling,' he whispered and pulled her on her side into his arms.

It was intoxicating to be embraced by him, his long muscular body holding her tight, the barrel of his cock pressing into the groove of her pubis. As they kissed she was aware that Henry had left the bed and she heard his bare feet on the tiled floor.

Brendan put his hand on her leg, pulling her thigh over his hip, nudging the end of his tool into her impatient crack.

'Well now, look at that,' he said and she did so, gazing past the foot of the bed at the dressing-table. Felicity could see now what Henry had been up to. He had adjusted the mirror so it reflected the activities on the bed.

Felicity gasped at the sight. Viewed from this angle she could see every detail of her exposed crotch – the curves of her legs and thighs, the tangled bush of belly hair, the wide-open cleft of her pussy and the jut of her swollen buttocks.

'My God, I look vast!' she cried.

'And beautiful,' murmured Brendan. 'You're a Venus of perfect proportions – isn't she, Henry?'

'Oh yes,' he agreed, cuddling up behind her.

'There's certainly enough of me to go round,' she said and giggled. The sight in the mirror was compelling, obscene but incredibly arousing. She watched herself trace a finger the length of Brendan's fat pink sausage of a cock. It too looked huge from this angle. She wondered what it would look like sliding into her pussy and shivered with excitement, for she was about to find out.

Brendan spread juice from her quim onto the head of his tool and lodged it in her slit. He deliberately held it there for a moment, so they could all savour the sight of the purple glans nuzzling between her long pink labia. Then he pushed and the end disappeared inside her.

'Ooh,' moaned Felicity, thrilled by the sight and sensation of being filled. Her vagina was like a mouth, stretching wide to swallow the thick invader. By reflex she bore down and saw her cunt, like some exotic sea anemone, swallow his organ to the root.

'My God,' muttered Henry, his voice thick.

Brendan chuckled and pulled Felicity closer to him, stretching her buttocks wide so the furrow between gaped open, from the brown whorl of her anus to the distended lips of her sex. As the thick shaft of his cock shunted gently in and out of her in small, titillating movements, Brendan's hands roved the satiny expanse of her splayed buttocks.

'Did you ever see such an inviting target?' he said to Henry.

The blond boy simply grunted and unscrewed a bottle of body lotion he must have taken from the dressing-table.

Even watching in the mirror as Brendan palmed her arse cheeks and Henry coated his tool with white cream, it did not dawn on Felicity what they were planning to do to her. Only when Brendan touched the dimple of her bumhole with a blob of ointment did the realisation hit her. She was not only to be fucked but buggered at the same time.

Buggery. It was a word that thrilled and revolted in the same breath. Felicity had done it in her youth to please a particular boyfriend. He'd got her to like it and when they'd split up she'd rather missed it. No one had done it to her since then and her husband had never even suggested it. Her partiality was a forbidden secret that lay long buried. And now Henry was going to do it to her in these outrageous circumstances. She was on the brink of orgasm at the thought.

Henry misunderstood the shiver that vibrated through her agitated flesh.

'I'll stop if it hurts,' he said as he pressed the head of his penis to the opening that Brendan was massaging so skilfully. 'I don't want to cause you any pain.'

But the pain of his entry was not something that worried Felicity. She had a high tolerance to physical discomfort and the wimpish behaviour of others was top of her list of irritations. More to the point, she had endured childbirth three times without pain relief of any sort. Beside that, the intrusion of Henry's long thin penis into her rectum was not significant.

And when it was in – lodged deep within her bowels, pulsating in her guts with Brendan's cock buried in her from the front, their young strong bodies enfolding her in a carnal embrace that made her dizzy – oh how glorious that was! Their hands were all over her, stroking and tweaking and hefting and squeezing until her senses were overloaded. She came almost immediately as Brendan touched her clit and then again and again, every inch of her flesh seeming a separate erogenous zone, in a string of climaxes like fireworks shooting off into the night.

But it wasn't night-time it was a blazing Italian afternoon with a sea breeze ruffling the thin white curtain in front of the balcony shutters. The three of them stopped for a rest, glued together by sweat and the juices of sex, and she watched that thin curtain blow back and forth. Outside there were voices of distant merriment by the hotel pool and, closer, the rumble of male conversation a few balconies along. What would these people think if that curtain should fall and they could see her now? Felicity looked in the mirror at their lewdly sandwiched bodies and realised that she couldn't care less.

Her lovers saw the direction of her gaze and lifted her upper leg high in the air to display the three way conjunction more fully. The two cocks were buried in her, fore and aft, like smoking guns. She longed for them to shoot inside her.

'Don't stop now,' she said, her voice urgent with desire, 'fuck me some more.'

So they did. Back and forth in a rhythm, their organs like pistons, driving to the hilt in turn, shunting her quivering, spasming flesh between them until they lost all control. The three of them tumbled over the edge together, locked in one rushing climax that reverberated between their bodies until long after their limbs had ceased to twitch.

They lay as if dead.

At length she said, 'You sods, you've done this before, haven't you?'

Brendan kissed her. 'Believe me, my darling, I've never done anything quite like that.'

Henry just sighed with contentment and pressed his wilting penis into the sticky pool of spunk between her big round buttocks.

20

Though it was on the mend, Percy's ankle still looked ghastly, blue and mottled and fat, like an aubergine with toes. But it didn't hurt like before. The lancing pain up his leg had faded and he could walk without support if he had to. The point was that he didn't have to. Both Philippa and Lucia were practised at manoeuvring his long frame about the terrace and up and down stairs. When they weren't around he hobbled ostentatiously, stick in hand. Only Brendan knew of the improvement in Percy's condition and he was sworn to secrecy. Things were fine just the way they were.

In fact this morning, a week after Percy's doomed heroics on the volleyball court, things were finer than ever. The children had gone rushing off to their activities with squeaks of joy and Felicity had shown him, albeit briefly, the kind of doting consideration she reserved for charitable causes.

'Percy, my darling, just look at your poor foot! You must still be in agony.'

'It's not as bad as it was, Flick. I'm only sorry I'm not able to keep you company. Give you a knock-up on the tennis court and all that.'

'Oh don't worry. There's plenty here who'll give me a knock-up if I ask them. I'm not shy you know!'

Felicity had always had a fine figure, he reflected as he watched her walk down to the beach, her big bottom swinging beneath a flowered cotton wrap tied sarong-style about her hips. He was looking forward to the scenes in *To the Hilt* when Max would get to grips with an arse like that.

In this glow of conjugal satisfaction, Percy had savoured the sight of Philippa's sun-cream routine. It took fully fifteen minutes this morning, the extra three being attributable to the doffing of her top and subsequent oiling of her awe-inspiring mammaries. Percy made no attempt to hide his interest in proceedings. He eyed every daub of cream and quiver of flesh with undisguised admiration. Philippa had been working up to this moment of revelation and to deny her his appreciation would have been churlish – not to say an act of complete hypocrisy.

When she had finished and her oiled breasts were pointing at him in a manner that defied gravity, she said, 'Well, if you're going to write about them, you might as well get the details right.'

'I'm deeply grateful,' he said. 'You're not only beautiful, Philippa, but generous with your beauty.'

'Creep,' she muttered and lowered her eyes to her book. All the same, she couldn't hide a blush.

Percy reflected that a blush would hardly cover her confusion were she to know that this was not the first time he had scrutinised her tits in their entirety, not to mention the rest of her.

'Can you walk yet, Perce?' Brendan had said to him the previous day, just after lunch. 'If you can manage it there's something you should see. Be great for the book.'

So Percy had followed Brendan into the stunted growth of trees at the back of the beach, making the happy discovery that his ankle was fast regaining its strength. They had followed a sandy path for a few hundred yards and then scrambled up a dune topped with scrub and gorse. Ahead of them was the sea and below them a clearing, hidden from the beach. Brendan had pointed downwards with a finger and winked. Percy understood he was to keep quiet. In any case the sight before them required no commentary.

Two girls lay on a rug, both nude. One was Philippa, the other a dark-haired child-minder who occasionally looked after Percy's kids. Her name was Gina.

Their bodies baked in the heat of the sun but sunbathing was not the name of their game. They were kissing fiercely, their arms wrapped around each other as they lay on their sides, their loins mashing and bumping together.

Percy was rigid with shock and desire. He had never seen women making love before – he'd never seen anybody making love before. It was incredible.

Philippa pushed the other girl onto her back and slid a hand up her bronzed thigh into the black thatch of her crotch.

'Ooh yes!' hissed Gina as Philippa opened her up like an oyster and slipped a finger inside.

'Good grief!' thought Percy and adjusted the erection in his shorts.

'Don't get any ideas about lending a hand,' muttered Brendan in his ear. 'Lay a finger on either and they'll blow a fuse.'

It looked to Percy like they might be blowing fuses without help from him or any other lustful male. They had tongues in each other's mouths and fingers in each other's pussies and Gina was already whimpering and squealing out loud.

'All the guys sounded them out at the beginning of the season and got the big frost,' continued Brendan. 'Then the next thing we know is they're dancing the slow ones together on Romeo and Juliet Night.'

'Which one's Romeo?' whispered Percy but he'd already made up his mind. Philippa was definitely in charge. She'd brought Gina off with her hand and now knelt between the girl's thighs, her big breasts hanging down. She bent Gina's legs back over her body, pushing the girl's knees into her chest and spreading wide her arse and pussy crack.

Percy gulped as he feasted his eyes on Gina's exposed crotch. Her nest of hair had parted to reveal a pretty coral-pink mouth which seemed to plead for attention. Philippa teased her. She blew a hot whisper of lust over those pouting lips and then, to Percy's amazement, dipped her shoulders and nuzzled the open crack with the end of one dangling breast. She did it again with the other. Then back and forth in a swaying, rippling blur of flesh until, with a moan, she crushed her bountiful chest between the girl's wide-spread legs.

'That woman can do anything with those tits,' muttered Brendan. 'Shell peanuts and open a bottle of beer, I bet. It's a mortal shame that's the only way she'll ever give a fellow satisfaction.'

Percy chuckled at the memory now as he shamelessly ogled Philippa's bared bazookas.

'I hope you're not laughing at me,' she said, staring at him over the top of her sunglasses.

'Good God, no,' said Percy. 'It's, er, to do with my work.'

'Your porno book, you mean. Tell me, what's my character doing now? Gangbanging a busload of yobs with tattoos on their willies?'

'Hardly.' Percy was mildly affronted. 'Simone's got far too much class to go in for that.'

'You could have fooled me,' said Philippa and grinned, her breasts shifting delightfully on her chest.

Percy laid his writing pad on his lap to cover his erection. These little chats with Philippa, a recent development, were a highlight of the morning.

'Actually,' he said, chancing his arm, 'Simone is about to meet someone very interesting. A female language professor in the throes of a broken marriage who has decided to give up men.'

Philippa's grin broadened, her tits swayed, Percy's cock twitched. 'Simone's gay?'

'Simone slept with girls at school. As for the professor, the aesthetic possibilities of woman-to-woman love have always appealed to her. Now she wants to try the real thing. What do you think?'

Philippa considered the matter, she didn't seem fazed by the turn the conversation had taken. 'What's the professor's name?'

'Lauren.'

'I knew a Lauren once. She was pencil-slim with wonderful hair that hung down her back like a curtain of gold.'

'My Lauren has golden hair too.'

Philippa's grin softened to a wistful smile. 'She had a little pointed chin and big brown eyes. No tits to speak of. We were quite the opposite shape. We used to think it was funny.'

Philippa's hand had fallen, perhaps unconsciously, to her breast and her fingers toyed with a rigid rosy nipple. 'Who makes the first move?' she asked.

'It has to be Simone. She finds Lauren in tears in the hotel bar – she's being pestered by some men – and Simone suggests a walk on the beach. It's sunset and very beautiful. Lauren pours out her unhappiness. Simone tells her to be brave and take a chance on a new life. Then she says Lauren needs to perform a symbolic act to signify a break with the past.'

'So she takes her to bed?' Philippa raised an eyebrow and the finger on her breast stopped circling the areola.

'Not yet,' said Percy hastily. 'Simone persuades her to strip off all her clothes and they bathe nude in the warm sea as the sun kisses the horizon. Afterwards they run back to the hotel and share a bottle of cognac in Simone's room.'

'And then they fuck?' Philippa's fingers were busy again and Percy was amazed to see that her other hand was openly stroking the bulge of her pussy through her bikini panties. 'Tell me what they do, Percy.'

'Well ... they're shivering after being in the sea so they get into bed and hug. Of course, they're naked and they giggle as their breasts and bellies touch. Then Simone kisses Lauren. It's the crucial moment. Will she run screaming from the room?'

'I bet she doesn't,' said Philippa, her index finger sliding up and down the groove of her sex through her bikini. Percy could see the pale blue material turning to navy with her dampness.

'She responds to Simone's kiss with passion. It's like turning on a switch. She clutches Simone's breasts and rubs her pussy against her thigh. She's wet and open and willing, Simone's to do with as she wishes.'

'Mmm, sounds great,' muttered Philippa, pulling the gusset of her pants to one side and slipping a finger inside. 'Go on, don't stop. Does Simone eat her out?'

'They swivel round and sixty-nine. Lauren's clumsy at it but she buries her face between Simone's legs and tastes the honey of her juices.'

'Tell me about Lauren's sex, Percy.'

'It's a secret nook that leads to an untapped well of sensuality—'

'With glossy honey-brown hairs that part under your tongue,' interrupted Philippa, her eyes closed and her face held up to the sun. 'And when you kiss her pussy you must treat it like a mouth, trace her lips with your tongue, nibble and suck and then plunge in deep. Lick the length of her crack, tickle her bumhole with your finger, blow on her clit but don't touch it. Then she'll be squirming and squealing and pushing her fanny into your face and begging for it.'

Philippa was staring straight at Percy now. Both hands were in her crotch, one pulling wide the panty gusset, the other masturbating the pink and golden flesh beneath. Percy could plainly see that four fingers were buried inside her vagina and her thumb was rubbing the flesh around her clit.

'And then,' she continued, her voice tight and her breath short, 'when you've teased her enough, you let her have it.'

Suddenly, before Percy's incredulous gaze, Philippa began to bounce up and down on the hand jammed deep inside herself, her thumb squeezing tight and the nail white with pressure, her face rigid with effort and those fabulous big breasts dancing and juddering.

Her orgasm seemed to go on forever and Percy drank in every detail of her pleasure. At last she slumped back in her seat and her swaying, tantalising flesh became still. She smiled at him, her sticky thighs spread and her fingers still embedded deep within her vagina.

'I hope you had a good look, Percy,' she said. 'I've always wanted to inspire a great writer.'

21

By the time Lucian arrived home, Caroline was waiting for him in the living room. Tania, who sat opposite, must have let her in. The tension between the two women was obvious but, at least – Lucian thought – they weren't scratching each other's eyes out.

'Goodbye, Caroline,' said Tania with excessive politeness. 'I hope your meeting is ... constructive.' She left the room and, a moment later, Lucian heard the front door open and close.

Caroline made no acknowledgement of her exit or his entrance but her eyes were glued to the long thin parcel Lucian held in his hand. She stood as he laid it on the table.

'Unbutton your coat, Contessa,' said Lucian, plunging at once into the required scenario. Caroline lifted her hand to her throat and began to unfasten her long mackintosh.

It was a bizarre garment to be wearing on this warm summer evening but Lucian could guess why she wore it – and what he would see when she removed it.

He poured himself a drink and savoured the sight of her trembling fingers picking at the fastenings, holding the coat closed until she had undone it all the way down.

He had spent a hard week – the Lynch woman had doubled his workload and his body ached and smarted in many tender places from his protracted negotiations with Marilyn Savage. For two pins he'd have cancelled this encounter with Caroline and tumbled into bed – alone. But Caro had sent him the latest instalment from her book. He'd read it that morning and he knew what was required of him. He was rigid with excitement already.

'There you are, you swine,' muttered Caroline, shrugging the coat from her shoulders. Beneath it she was all but naked. She wore just a thin white camisole that reached to her waist with matching stockings and suspenders. The points of her nipples and the circles of her areolae were plainly visible through the flimsy top. The pale dome of her belly and the strip of honey-coloured curls at the junction of her thighs were framed by the suspender straps. To Lucian's eye she had never looked more ravishing.

'I hope you're satisfied,' she said bitterly.

'Not yet,' replied Lucian, 'but I intend to be. Tell me, Marietta, did you enjoy walking the city streets knowing that only your coat concealed your most intimate secrets?'

'I was humiliated and ashamed.'

'Excellent. What else did you feel?'

'I don't know what you mean.'

'Admit it, Contessa, you were excited. The thought of all those coarse peasants so tantalisingly close to looking at your pretty cunt turned you on. Didn't it?'

'No. I swear it.'

'Let's see, shall we?'

'No, Bruno, no – don't touch me!' she cried as Lucian slipped to his knees in front of her. But her feet moved apart of their own accord to allow his hand to slide between her thighs. The musk of her arousal was thick in the air, her bush inches from his face as he slipped a finger between her labia. Her pelvis jerked at his touch and the mouth of her pussy sucked him in eagerly. He wanted to plunge forward and kiss those pink and gleaming lips but he restrained himself. It wasn't in the script – yet.

'Aha,' cried Lucian, rising to his feet and holding a glistening finger in front of her. 'You are wet with need, Contessa. Your aristocratic cunt is dripping with desire for an artisan's cock. You must be punished.'

'No!' wailed Caroline.

'Unwrap the instrument of your pleasure,' he ordered and pointed to the thin parcel on the table.

Caroline continued to protest but her fingers ripped open the paper with an eagerness she could not conceal. In the shop, the cane had looked innocuous and silly. In Caroline's trembling hands, next to her exposed flesh, it looked vicious.

Lucian pulled a straight-backed chair into the centre of the room. 'Bend over the back,' he commanded. 'Present those delectable buttocks for chastisement.'

'You wouldn't dare,' cried Caroline in defiance. 'If you mark my flesh my husband will have you killed.'

'I think not, Marietta. Haven't you realised that this is all the Count's idea?'

'No!' wailed Caroline. 'It can't be!'

'Oh yes, my little one. And I have precise instructions how I am to decorate your arse.'

'God have mercy,' cried Caroline and threw herself over the back of the chair.

It was a corny scenario, Lucian considered, though he had rather enjoyed hamming his way through his lines. And Caroline had acted her part as if she were auditioning for the RSC. One thing was certain about her book, if it had the same effect on future readers as it did on his cock all parties would be well satisfied.

The back of the chair was not high and Caroline was able to bend over it from the waist, thrusting the creamy ovals of her incredible buttocks high in the air. Though Lucian had never felt a desire to cane a woman before, he had to admit the peachy moons formed a tempting target. He made an experimental swish through the air with the cane and the thing seemed to leap in his hands with a life of its own. Lucian felt a pang of alarm. Christ, he didn't want to really hurt her.

'Don't leave me like this,' she cried. 'Get on with it if you must.'

He brought the cane down on her right cheek, trying to inflict the minimum amount of pain. The flesh wobbled as it absorbed the blow but retained its flawless pallor.

Caroline jerked her head around and glared at him. 'Do it properly, Lucian,' she hissed and for a moment they were no longer acting out her drama.

In a flash, other memories of their time together crowded into his head. The sneer in her voice, the contempt in her eyes, another man's cock in her mouth . . .

Smack! The sound was like a pistol shot as the cane cracked onto the meat of her arse. Then *smack* again, this time onto the left cheek in a backhand swipe that left a long pink stripe emblazoned on her flesh.

'*Oh!*' squealed Caroline and her buttocks quivered with the force of the assault.

Lucian waited for her to compose herself. She had a weal on each side now and, according to Caroline's own instructions, she was to have a couple more. He conjured up the picture of that Polaroid again and let her have it.

'No, please!' she moaned. 'Don't do it, Bruno. Don't – *aah!*'

But Lucian took no notice. This is what she wanted – what she had explicitly asked for. And what she was going to get.

When he had finished he flung the cane to the other side of the room. It had done its job. Caroline's twitching, clenching arse was symmetrically striped with cuts that would surely take many days to fade. Who else would see them? he wondered with a pang of jealousy.

But now was no time for wimpish thoughts. Caroline cum Marietta was still doubled over the chair, her body shuddering as she sobbed out her pain – real or assumed, he could not tell. Her pink and blazing bottom beckoned like a beacon, her stockinged legs open in a vee, the pouting purse of her pussy winking wetly at him. He quickly pulled off his clothes.

Her cunt was dripping like a tap, her sex juices running down her thighs to her stocking-tops. He had never seen her so turned on and, as he sank his tongue deep into her honeyed circlet, he felt her shaking with desire. He gorged on her wet sex like a starving man, holding her cheeks apart with his hands, squeezing and fondling her tender buttocks as he licked her from arsehole to clit and back again while she squirmed in excitement upon his face.

He stood and sank his cock in her to the depths, the first time he'd fucked her for weeks. It was if he were inside a different woman – as if this were a new cunt around his cock and each movement of her body a revelation. In a way, of course, this was true. He was not Lucian worshipping Caroline, he was Bruno fucking Countess Marietta.

And Bruno's lust was insatiable. He thrust on and on, bulling his cock into the heart of her until she screamed out in orgasm. Then he slowed, stroking her abused flesh, pushing the camisole down her back to caress the fair skin, reaching below her to fondle the swollen pear-shaped breasts and all the time shunting his big organ in and out of her sex.

Lucian realised he could do anything he wanted to her now. She had come a lot and he had held back. After his debilitating week he reckoned he had one big climax left in him and he wanted it to be special. And what could be more special than finishing between the twin globes of flesh that he so adored and which now burned with the marks he had inflicted? There would never be a better time to fuck her arse.

Lucian pulled his tool from Caroline's pussy and moved it up the few centimetres to the dimple of her anus. It wasn't in the script she had ordained but she was so on heat he knew she wouldn't object.

If Caroline was surprised she didn't show it. She merely pressed her bottom back against him as he pushed. For a few seconds her flesh resisted, then came a moan from her, a grunt from him and – oh bliss! – his glans was suddenly corked within her anal ring and his entire cock was being devoured in the heat of her most private orifice. He drove in and she thrust back. He had his hand in her crotch, playing with the wet folds of her pussy lips, pressing his fingers against the hard nub of her clit, urging her towards a climax to match the one now building in his loins like an unstoppable wave.

The chair tipped over as they came and for a moment they lay glued together in a sated, shuddering heap. Lucian's face was buried in her hair, the smell of her in his nostrils, his heart hammering and yearning for her. 'God, Caro,' he muttered into her neck, overwhelmed by the moment and on the brink of saying things he knew he shouldn't. Like, *don't leave me, my darling, I beg you. Come back to my bed*.

But she was pushing him off and reaching for her coat, her face a mask of disgust.

'You buggered me, you bastard,' she hissed. 'That's not in my book.'

'Well, perhaps it should be.'

'Did you have to make such a meal of it? God, I hate you.'

'Don't look on it as buggery, Caro. Consider it an editorial suggestion.'

But Caroline wasn't listening, she had done up her last button and stalked from the room.

Lucian called after her, his voice as stern as he could make it, 'Same time next week, Marietta. And don't be late.'

The front door closed with such violence the whole house shook.

To think he'd almost told her he still loved her. The new Lucian had had a lucky escape.

22

Percy was feeling no pain. Thumping rock from the sound system merged with drunken laughter and wrapped him in a cocoon of noise. He swallowed a mouthful of brandy and grinned stupidly at the bronzed and beaming revellers who surrounded him. The children were all in bed, dinner had been consumed and the booze was flowing. It was the last night of the holiday and all those crammed into the beach bar were determined to make the most of it.

Percy was pleased to see that even Felicity was entering into the spirit of the occasion. He watched her as she laughed at something Brendan said, her head thrown back and her hair hanging loose in a chestnut cloud over her bronzed shoulders. He knew that his were not the only admiring eyes on the gleaming cleavage revealed in her black figure-hugging cocktail dress.

Brendan leaned across to him and whispered in his ear. 'I hope you're making mental notes.'

'What do you mean?'

'Remember I told you about No Knickers Night?'

'Yes?'

'Well, this is it. Look up there.'

Percy looked. On the rail above the bar hung flags and straw-covered Chianti bottles and bunches of plastic grapes. And also, as he could now plainly see, half-a-dozen scraps of lace and cotton that he immediately recognised as women's undergarments.

Brendan explained further. 'John and Ginger behind the bar put

145

the word out. They'll let any woman drink for free if she'll take her knickers off and hang them up.'

'Good God.' Percy peered closely at the girls around him and then up at the flimsy trophies on display. The thought that there were half-a-dozen knickerless women so close to him had his imagination working overtime.

'Sometimes it's the most unlikely types who end up bare-arsed,' continued Brendan. 'You wouldn't think it of Mrs Wootton-Smythe, would you?'

Amanda Wootton-Smythe was an elegant blonde who had made herself universally unpopular throughout the holiday fortnight. Her husband was taciturn, her children were brats and she herself was civil to no one. She and Felicity had had a stand-up row following a queue-jumping incident at children's tea-time.

Now Amanda was perched on a bar stool talking to curly-headed Clive, the volleyball Plonker. She wore an emerald-green wrap round skirt which, to Percy's eye, revealed only long lean leg and thigh right up as far as he could see. As he watched, the barman placed a tall frosted glass in front of her filled with foaming lemon liquid and topped with a paper parasol.

'She's drinking Ginger's specials,' muttered Brendan. 'I guarantee you'll get an eyeful if you stay just where you are.'

'Bloody hell,' muttered Percy, his eyes on stalks as he willed the green flap of her skirt to gape a little further between her thighs.

'It's not just her either, Percy. I reckon little Jean and Dyan and Garaint's wife have all opted for the free bar. You don't know where to look now, do you?'

That was true. Percy's eyes were darting madly about, seeking out the women Brendan had named. Jean and Dyan were dancing on the dais behind the speakers on the other side of the bar. From the roars and whoops coming from the knot of lads standing below them he could guess that what Brendan had told him was correct.

'You want to make the most of this, you know, Percy. For the book and all that. Would it help if I got your wife out of the way?'

Percy gazed at Brendan with pure gratitude. For such a young man he did seem to have a mature understanding of Percy's requirements. Peeking up women's skirts with Felicity sitting next to him was not the most sensible course of conduct.

'Look,' continued Brendan, 'I think I can persuade her to play boules with me. I've told her I'm better at that than tennis and she says can still beat me.'

'Sounds like Felicity. Do you think she'll go for it?'

But Brendan was already whispering in Felicity's ear. She gave him a look Percy couldn't fathom and then placed her hand on Percy's shoulder.

'Darling, I'm tired,' she said. 'If it's all right with you I'll give this silly boy a game of boules and go straight to bed.'

'Of course, Flick.'

'There's no need for you to come though. Stay up as long as you like and enjoy yourself.'

Then she pecked his cheek and disappeared up the steps to the hotel with Brendan at her side. Percy smiled with satisfaction. This holiday had really done her good, there was no doubt about that.

He turned his attention to Amanda Wootton-Smythe's incredible legs.

The boules pitch was in darkness – which suited Brendan and Felicity just fine. They didn't need illumination for the game they were going to play.

'I must be mad,' said Felicity as he slipped the strap of her dress from her shoulder, baring the bountiful curves of her left breast.

'You're not mad, you're beautiful,' he said and exposed her right breast to the moonlight.

'Mad for your big Irish cock, at any rate,' she muttered, dragging his jeans down his hips.

His mouth was on her nipples, teasing them to hardness, his spittle glistening on the saucers of her areolae. His hands were under her skirt, gripping the solid globes of her buttocks, wriggling a finger into the moist crease between.

'Oh God, Brendan, I'm going to miss this,' she muttered, pulling his penis into the open and tugging it towards her crotch.

'Steady on, woman, let's get comfortable. We've got plenty of time.'

'But I need it now, Brendan! This is my last night and I want to you to fuck me and fuck me and—'

He shut her up by covering her mouth with his and pulling her down on top of him into the dusty grass by the boules pitch. Her skirt was round her waist and her legs were spread. And as Brendan thrust his tool into the wet and welcoming crevice between her thighs he met with no impediment. Such was Felicity's intention to make the most of her last night, she too could have drunk at the bar for free.

23

The half-hour following Felicity's departure was one of the most extraordinary Percy had ever spent. Wedged in his seat, he watched the comings and goings around him with mounting disbelief. Suntanned and sozzled, aware that the sands of holiday time were fast trickling out, everyone it seemed was prepared to let their hair down.

The mysteries of Amanda Wootton-Smythe's wrapround skirt had long been revealed to Percy – and to anyone else who cared to look. The sourpuss expression had slipped from her face to be replaced by a loose-lipped grin and beside her on the bar were five discarded paper parasols. She sat on the bar stool with one leg on the floor, the other resting on the stool rail, her thighs bare and wide. Clive stood in front of her, making jokes and laughing as if he were unaware that his companion was all but naked from the waist down. But his right side was turned to Percy and his left hand could not be seen. Percy had his suspicions just where it was hiding.

Couples were now slow-dancing between the tables and Percy had located two more knickerless women: Garaint's wife had her bottom on view as the Welshman waltzed her around the chairs and Dyan had fallen asleep at the opposite table with her frock hiked to her waist.

'Hiya, Percy,' said a familiar voice in his ear. He tore his gaze from Dyan's overflowing buttocks to see Carol-Anne, the Entertainments Officer, taking a seat by his side. Her pretty face was creased by a frown.

'God, am I pleased to see someone who's not behaving like this is a remake of *Caligula*. I swear it's the worst part of my job – having to put up with this kind of obscene conduct on the last night. Honestly, I don't know what gets into people. I can only apologise, Percy.'

'There's no need, Carol-Anne. You must allow the holidaying work-slave a little licence at the end of his sojourn in the sun.'

'Gee, that sounds profound. You're a wise man, Mr Carmichael.'

Percy blushed. Flattery from a woman as young and scrumptious as the blonde Australian was as potent as the cognac burning in his belly.

'Say, Percy, would you do me a favour and get me a drink? I mean, if your foot's up to it.'

'Of course. I'm supposed to exercise it these days anyway.'

Percy hauled himself to his feet, cursing the giant erection that stretched his trousers to bursting. He turned his back to Carol-Anne quickly, hoping she wouldn't notice.

'So she sent you this time, did she?' said Ginger as he poured Percy's order.

'What do you mean?'

'Just a little joke between Carol-Anne and us guys behind the bar. She's on our case all week so we say we'll *only* serve her on party night if she gets her kit off. We'll get her before the season's over, no sweat.'

Ginger finished swizzling a long green drink and decorated it with a cherry on a stick. 'There you go, mate, and good luck. They say she's got great acceleration if you can just get her engine started.'

But Percy was scarcely listening, he wanted to satisfy his curiosity on another point. His position at the bar was just behind Amanda's chair and if he leaned forward and to one side – Good God! It was as he had suspected but the blatant rudeness of the sight still took him by surprise. In the spread vee of Amanda's thighs he could see Clive's hand stimulating her cunt. With two fingers embedded deep between the sticky labia, Clive's wrist was moving, slowly in, slowly out, as he gently masturbated her. From the murmur of sound from her lips it seemed he was playing her like a fish. Percy strained to hear.

'Promise me you'll fuck me soon, Clive darling, oh that's so marvellous in my pussy, one more drink and fuck me with your lovely lovely cock ...'

Percy turned back to the table with his erection intact. There was nothing he could do about it. As he took his seat, his loins poised momentarily next to Carol-Anne's face, he thought his distraught penis might burst from his trousers and poke her in the eye. He sank into his seat with relief.

'Thanks a bunch, Percy.'

'My pleasure. Thank *you* for helping me out this past couple of weeks. Your girls were brilliant after I smashed my ankle.'

'We aim to please. I'm just thrilled we had a real writer staying here. Now tell me, exactly what is it you're working on?'

There was a moan from Amanda's direction, followed by another and another. The kind of moan that, in certain women, heralds the approach of a noisy orgasm.

Percy tried to ignore the distraction. Carol-Anne's earnest face, the eyes big with interest, demanded a response.

'It's a, er, study in human relations—'

'Oh. Oh! OH!'

'An exploration of how men and women interact in their leisure time—'

'Oh God, oh God, oh GOD!'

Carol-Anne's brow puckered in puzzlement. Percy fought to keep his eyes on her face. Over her shoulder, on the dance floor, he saw Jean on her knees with her boyfriend's cock in her mouth. By the bar Amanda was now shouting out an unstoppable flow of obscenities.

'Is it a sociological book then?' asked Carol-Anne. Only the speed with which she had disposed of her green drink betrayed any awareness of the mayhem developing around her.

'Cock! I want cock! Give me COCK!' yelled Amanda.

At the next table Dyan was now snoozing on Garaint's lap while he fingered the pale white globes of her big bottom. Garaint's wife was straddling Pete from Preston, one hand holding her skirt high, the other directing a thick red penis into the black fur of her nook.

'Well, yes, er, I suppose it is,' mumbled Percy. 'I mean it does have sociological relevance though it is not meant to be academic in any sense . . .'

'It sounds great,' said Carol-Anne with a brilliant smile, her little white teeth gleaming in the dim light. 'That's just the kind of thing we need in the Cascade Hotel library.'

'There's no doubt about that,' said Percy.

Clive was now giving Amanda the relief she had been screaming for, skewering his tool into her as she braced herself on top of the stool – a remarkable feat of sexual coordination that had no effect in lowering the volume control. On the dance floor, Jean was getting it at both ends from her admirers, who were queuing up. Percy noted that her desire to acquire an all-over suntan had paid off.

Carol-Anne took a despairing suck at her straw though her glass was plainly empty.

'Allow me,' said Percy but she pushed him back into his seat.

'No,' she said, standing up. 'It's my round and I can't keep putting it off. Here, give me a hand.'

To Percy's complete amazement, she began to wriggle her tight leather mini-skirt up over her hips. Beneath, powder blue panties clung to her delectable loins like a second skin.

'Do you mind taking my knickers down?'

Percy was dumbfounded.

'Come on, Perce. I'm parched and this is the only way those bastards will serve me.'

Despite other distractions, John and Ginger were staring at her from behind the bar.

'But I'll go, Carol-Anne. Please sit down—'

'What's the matter? Don't you want to look at my puss? Help me, Perce. Pull 'em down.'

So he did, holding the wisp of material reverently as he lowered it over her firm boyish buttocks and down her slim finely toned thighs. And as he removed the garment, his face was an inch or two from the smoothest, prettiest, nudest pussy slit he had ever seen.

She placed a hand on his shoulder and raised her leg to slip the knickers off her feet. As she did so the hairless pink cleft stretched and pouted before him as if begging for a kiss. Then her skirt was back in place and she was marching to the bar where Ginger and John were leaping and high-fiving with glee.

Percy now no longer had eyes for the erotic exhibition taking place around him. A half-naked conga line had formed, snaking round the tables and then out onto the beach.

Only those too drunk or too engrossed were left as Carol-Anne returned. She carried a tray which bore a jug of her preferred green cocktail, a bottle of cognac and two glasses.

'At least they reckoned my tush was worth something,' she said. 'Come on, Percy, let's get out of here,' and she marched straight past him towards the stairs leading up to the hotel.

Percy followed her without a backward glance as she crossed the hotel reception and strode up the main staircase to a room on the first floor. He held the tray while she unlocked the door.

She led him straight out onto the balcony and breathed a sigh. 'Thank God we're out of that. Some nights things just get out of hand, don't you think?'

The view from the balcony was sensational. The velvet sky above the bay lit by the pinpoints of tiny stars; the half-glimpsed shadow of the mountains inland; the lights of small bobbing boats out at sea. And the beach laid out just below them – a group of shadowy figures splashing in the lapping surf and the floodlit volleyball court alive with leaping, wobbling, nude men and women.

'Good God,' muttered Percy.

'I know,' said Carol-Anne, adding as if it were the ultimate sacrilege, 'there were even people fucking on the boules pitch.'

'No!' said Percy, trying hard to stifle a giggle.

'Yeah, I know. What people don't realise is that I've got to organise a competition on that pitch next week. I don't need it all messed up. Now, wait here. I'll be right back.'

'Er, um, yes,' said Percy, dumbfounded by the turn of events.

She returned a moment later holding a pair of binoculars, a pencil and a clipboard. She had also removed her skirt and stood before him in just a pink halter top and a pair of trainers. She made no reference to her state of semi-nudity.

'Right, you guys,' she muttered as she leant on the balcony rail and trained her binoculars on the beach, 'I'm going to make a report.'

Percy marvelled at her glorious body, so different from the ripe maturity of Felicity, the bounty of Philippa, the olive-skinned beauty of Lucia. How wonderful women were in their variety!

'OK, that's Kiwi Jim with a girl in the canoe. That's major misuse of equipment. And they're not wearing buoyancy aids on the water so that's a breach of safety regulations—'

Carol-Anne had the lean, toned figure of a fitness follower. Her thighs were long and strong and there were muscles in her slender arms. And those buttocks, jutting back at Percy as she pressed forward against the balcony railing, were firm and gently curving without an ounce of surplus flesh. Why, he'd wager they wouldn't wobble an inch if he slapped their cheeky crescents—

'—oho, Ginger! Gotcha! What are you doing with her? You're on duty behind the bar till two. You'll get your pay docked for this!'

—but what he really wanted to do, what he was *going* to do was to explore that little pocket of pink flesh peeping at him beneath the rounds of her buttocks at the junction of her thighs. Mmm, yes, that delectable vaginal opening so memorably glimpsed already.

Suppose he slid to his knees behind her and pressed his lips to her pussy just like this—

'—God, look at that, those two guys doing it to her on the volleyball court. That's disgusting! She's shaking her butt faster than she ever did in my aerobics class—'

Percy had his tongue deep inside her now, kissing her pouting recess with all the pent-up frustration of the past few hours. And her cunt kissed him back, it seemed, the lips swelling and fluttering, the juice of her excitement bubbling from within her. And all the time her other mouth maintained its stream of recorded misdemeanours. Percy smiled to himself as he pulled his prick from his trousers. *Let's see if she can talk through* this, he thought.

'Jesus, that's terrible! They're doing it in a chain right on the court! I'm going to fax London tomorrow about this— OH!'

Silence followed and it was blissful. A silence which was broken only by the sounds of their bodies pressing wetly against each other. His hands were on her breasts, his mouth on her neck, his penis buried deep within her. His loins buffeted her small pliant arse as he gave her what she really craved and she never said another word until after she came.

'Mmm,' she whispered later as they lay on the sun-bed beneath the stars, 'when I first saw you I never thought you'd be so sexy.'

Most of their clothing had disappeared and the balmy night was gentle on their bare skin. Percy stroked her full soft breasts and said, 'To be honest, I thought I'd said goodbye to sex for ever.'

'That just shows how wrong you can be,' she replied and, with a wriggle of her hips, she sheathed his distended penis in the hairless mouth of her vagina.

'Yes,' he muttered, pumping into her honeyed sweetness. 'Doesn't it just.'

24

In the end, Lucian's capture of *The Novelist's Wife* was rather an anticlimax, which was more than could be said for the protracted period of negotiation that preceded it. During the course of ten days Lucian had climaxed with Marilyn Savage in an outlandish selection of positions and situations and she had out-climaxed him three-fold.

On the tenth morning he woke in her bed after two hours of fitful sleep and dragged his bruised and battered body into a sitting position. Marilyn had humiliated him the previous night at dinner before two of her female friends and the memory burned hot and shameful.

After the coffee she'd ordered him beneath the table and commanded him to suck her off. Then she'd insisted he bestowed the favour on her two companions, a literary journalist and a yachtswoman who was writing her memoirs. They'd sniggered and giggled and criticised his technique as he'd pleasured them and his only satisfaction had been in making the yachtswoman come so volcanically that she'd knocked over a bottle of brandy. And all the while he'd been down there in the musky dark, tonguing their insatiable vaginas, listening to their vile remarks, he'd been spurred on by one thought: he had to sign *The Novelist's Wife*. Unless he performed every bizarre act she ordained, he knew Marilyn would sell it to Rodney Branscombe. She'd made no bones about it.

And now, as he lay shattered in Marilyn's bed, scarcely

recovered from the orgy which had followed his under-the-table demonstration, he remembered something. Something so blindingly obvious that even the most junior editorial assistant would have been aware of it. He was furious.

'Marilyn!' he roared. 'Get in here!'

The bathroom door opened and Marilyn emerged, her hair wet, a towel wrapped around her sumptuous body and a familiar mocking grin on her face.

'You are the biggest bitch in the business,' he cried and jumped from the bed to grab her.

'That's my reputation,' she said as he yanked the towel from her damp body and pulled her face-down over his lap. 'Lucian – please!'

The first few slaps were delivered with anger, setting the smooth white cheeks of her bottom in motion, swiftly turning them to puce then scarlet.

'Ow! Lucian! Stop it!'

'You've tricked me, haven't you?' He slapped her some more.

'I don't know what you mean. You didn't have to get under the table, you could have said no. Ouch! Now stop it.'

He held her down firmly with his weight on the centre of her back. He watched her livid arse wriggling across his lap.

'If I'd refused you'd have rejected my offer for the Hastings book, wouldn't you?'

'Well, there are other editors who are more cooperative than you are turning out to be.'

'Who?' He slapped her again and this time left his hand on the burning flesh. She pushed her bottom against it.

She chuckled. 'I thought you didn't like me to mention his name in your presence.'

'Say it now.'

She was looking up at him over her shoulder, her eyes twinkling with merriment. Evidently this was not that painful an experience.

'Rodney Branscombe.'

'You're a liar.'

'Lucian, please. That's a most unprofessional remark.'

'But, Marilyn, you know very well that the last book in the world Branscombe could publish would be *The Novelist's Wife*.'

'Oh really.' He no longer held her down now and she raised her head to look at him. Her loins were grinding into his wantonly as she said, 'Why is that?'

'Because GrabCo have just spent a million on Monty Hastings' new contract. They can't publish his wife's book, he'd go ballistic.'

Her smile of triumph was unconcealed.

'And you've been stringing me along,' cried Lucian, 'dangling Rodney bloody Branscombe over me, turning me into your personal sex-slave, when all the time you know there's no point in even talking to him about it.'

'Poor Lucian,' said Marilyn and put her hand between his legs. His erection was enormous. 'I imagine it must have been terrible for you, spending night after night in this bed with me.'

'No, of course not, Marilyn. You're fabulous but—'

'But?'

She was sitting up now and stroking his cock gently, fluttering her fingers along the top of the shaft just the way he liked it.

'I feel I've been used. Taken for an idiot.'

'I see.' She slipped onto her knees between his legs and considered the big swollen organ in her hand. 'I didn't plan it, Lucian, but it's not my job to point out the obvious, now is it?'

She dipped her head and took one testicle into her mouth. In the full-length mirror behind her Lucian could see the violin curve of her waist and hips and the flaming moons of her abused buttocks. She took the other ball between her lips and a frisson of delight ran through him.

After a moment she raised her head. 'I do feel a teensy bit guilty about making you do some things. But I never thought you'd do everything I asked.'

She pumped his cock with one hand and flicked her tongue across his scarlet glans. 'Like when I made you spunk off at that Pirandello play.' She laughed and her small breasts quivered, the nipples dark and swollen.

'I thought I was going to get arrested.'

'It was such a bloody boring play, darling, everyone in our row was glad of the entertainment.'

Her hand had found a steady rhythm and his knob was turning purple. She fondled his balls as she wanked him. 'Anyway, don't tell me you didn't enjoy last night. Three women to keep you happy must be every man's dream.'

'Please, Marilyn, I'm shattered.'

'You don't look it from this angle.'

That was true. His distended penis loomed over her small, heart-shaped face.

'I admit,' she continued, 'that I probably owe you a favour or two in return. Suppose in future I give you a blow-job every time you buy one of my books?'

'But, Marilyn, you never *sell* me any of your books – oh!'

She had slipped her pink lips over the end of his swollen tool and he watched in wonder as his entire length disappeared into her face. She came up for air and then swallowed him again. And again. Then her hand was jerking on his shaft and her tongue was rimming his glans. In the mirror her pretty buttocks quivered and, as she shifted her stance and he glimpsed movement between her legs, he realised she was diddling herself with her other hand.

It couldn't last long like that. Not with her gumming his tool and wanking his shaft and the sight of her playing with her pussy in the mirror.

'Christ, Marilyn!' he cried as he erupted down her throat. And she lifted her face from his cock and swallowed as she orgasmed on her fingers.

'Well,' she said eventually, 'how did you like your first pay-off?'

'You mean . . . ?' As ever, it took a while for the penny to drop.
'Congratulations. You've now bought *The Novelist's Wife*.'
On second thoughts, it wasn't an anticlimax at all.

Three

NAKED IN THE ROSES

25

Staying at a hotel just ten miles from her own home seemed an extravagance to the teacher's daughter from a terraced cottage in the Rhondda. But Karen Hastings had come a long way since she was plain and spotty Karen Jenkins, the school swot of Llangavenny Grammar. Now she was married to a leading literary lion and soon to be a published novelist in her own right.

Though she was the beneficiary of a generous monthly allowance from her husband, it gave her a particular thrill not to be spending Monty's money on her stay at Swivenham Hall. Thanks to Marilyn Savage she had received a cheque from Blue Desire Books which she had just deposited in a new and separate bank account. This was her own, hard-earned cash and she was going to blow it just how she fancied. And she fancied spending some of it on her friend Adele, from the bookshop in Long Swivenham, and Adele's fiancé, Will. If all went as planned, she could always claim it as a tax-deductible expense.

Apart from anything else, Swivenham Hall was delightful. An Elizabethan manor-house with its Tudor exterior lovingly preserved, it overlooked topiary gardens, tumbling terraces and a vast ornamental pond. A short walk from the rear of the house led to the main attraction for one of the party of three enjoying the brilliant summer day – the golf course. Will was an enthusiastic golfer with insufficient funds to pursue the game as he would wish. Today, as Karen's guest, he was able to enjoy the rolling fairways, polished greens and devilish long rough of the most challenging course in the district. He was half in love with Karen already.

Adele jabbed Karen in the ribs as she studied Will standing over the ball on the seventh tee. He was a big man, broad of beam and shoulder with a shock of fine sandy-blond hair and melting spaniel-brown eyes.

'Take your lecherous eyes off my feller,' she hissed.

'He's worth looking at,' said Karen, wondering what it was like for Adele to have that big muscular body pressing down on her of a night.

Crack! Will smote the ball into the distance and followed its flight, a smile of satisfaction on his face.

'How's that, girls,' he cried in delight; 'girls' emerged from his lips as 'gurrls' – he was from Edinburgh. Then he picked up his bag and strode off, full of bristling purpose. His companions sauntered along behind him. Playing golf was not on their agenda.

Adele linked arms with Karen. 'You *will* come to the wedding, won't you? It's a pity you can't be my maid of honour.'

Karen chuckled. 'You'll have to get one of your other girlfriends for that.'

Adele sighed. 'Now I've met you I haven't got any other girlfriends.'

'I'm pleased to hear it. For Will's sake. You've got to be straight with him.'

'But what about us? I can't imagine giving you up.'

'Don't go all moony on me, Adele.'

'Well, do you want to stop seeing me?'

The truth was that Karen didn't. Since she and Monty had ceased communicating, and despite her many other dalliances, Adele was the closest friend she now had. Perhaps her only one, she thought with a stab of self-pity.

'No,' she replied, 'but the sex is only part of it. We can be friends without it once you're married.'

'So we should make the most of it before then?'

'That's not exactly what I said, Adele.'

'But I know how you think, you randy cow. I bet right now you'd rather be in bed with me.'

Karen grinned. 'How about those woods over there? No one would see us.'

'Sure, but what about Will?'

'Right, you demon Scotsman, show me how you whack the ball.'

Will regarded Karen with amusement – tinged with desire, of course. Her salmon-pink shorts revealed more of her rounded brown thighs than was customary on the golf course. She had seized the club from his hand as he evaluated his shot off the next tee.

'It will be my pleasure,' he announced and led Karen with much patronising ceremony to the ladies' tee. There followed a deal of banter between the two, both verbal and physical, as the tall Scot crouched over her from behind, demonstrating how to swing the club. Karen simpered, leaning back into the bear-hug embrace of his burly arms. She winked at Adele and shamelessly ground her buttocks back into his crotch.

Will leapt away from her as if stung, his cheeks flushing beet-red.

Karen swung the club. *Ping!* The ball flew like an arrow up into the sky and then plunged into the woods to the left of the fairway. From 150 yards away they could hear the sound of it clattering through the branches.

'Ooh! That was fun,' cried Karen. 'Can I have another go?'

Will stared in the direction the ball had flown, somewhat bemused.

'That was actually quite a good shot,' he said. 'It's a pity you hooked it a wee bit.'

Karen resumed her stance, Will produced another ball and Karen deposited it in almost exactly the same spot.

'Oh dear,' she said. 'Let me try again. I promise I'll get it straight this time.'

But she didn't. The hit was clean and the ball soared high into the blue only to land even further into the stand of trees.

'I'm awfully sorry, Will,' Karen said even as he was rummaging in his bag to find another ball. 'I'm obviously programmed to hit it off line.'

'I don't understand it,' he replied. 'You've got a great swing and you smack it clean as a whistle. You ought to have proper coaching.'

'Well, maybe you can give me some. But not today. I'll go and hunt for your balls.'

'We'll all go,' he said. 'It won't take long.'

'Don't be bloody daft,' said Adele, catching on. 'It could take ages. Why don't you finish your round? We'll follow you.'

In the woods they didn't waste any time on golf balls. Adele pushed Karen onto a bank of grass and plunged her tongue down her throat as she manipulated the fastening of her shorts.

'I swear you're the most impatient lover I've ever had,' said Karen.

'I can't help it,' whispered Adele, slipping Karen's panties off her feet and spreading her thighs to gaze with longing on the strip of coal-black curls and the glistening labia beneath. She dipped her head and slithered her tongue into the pouting pink groove, separating the soft petals and licking the juices which welled up from within.

Karen hadn't realised she was so turned on. She never thought about women in the abstract, never eyed them in the street or lusted after them on screen. But Adele had an effect on her, there was no doubt about that. In the weeks since their first tryst they had met regularly. At first there had been the pretence that their get-togethers were out of simple friendship – and they did spend time exchanging confidences and gossiping. But the talk was sandwiched between bouts of lovemaking that were as intense in their way as any Karen had ever had.

By now Adele had one arm wrapped around Karen's waist, the fingers of her other hand buried to the knuckle in her lover's wet cunt. Seized by a spasm of desire, Karen pressed Adele's face into her crotch with both hands and rubbed her clit along the bridge of the girl's nose. It was glorious. Karen used her girlfriend's face and hand shamelessly, rubbing herself to orgasm in the knowledge that her taking was giving them both intense pleasure.

Karen came with a long-drawn-out hiss of breath as her body convulsed and her limbs quivered. When she relaxed her grip on Adele's hair, the girl remained where she was, inhaling the musk of Karen's spent excitement and planting little kisses on the soft skin of her thighs.

Eventually Adele said, 'What are we going to do about Will?'

'Show him the time of his life. Unless you've changed your mind.'

'No, I haven't. But I'm worried. Suppose it all goes wrong?'

Karen pulled Adele up from her squatting position and hugged her.

'Then he'll blame me and you'll be in the clear. It's worth the risk. If you're going to live with this guy for the rest of your life he's got to know what you're really like.'

Adele was not mollified. 'It's just that he's so straight down the line. Did you see how he jumped when you pushed your bum into him?'

'That's guilt. He doesn't know how to handle the fact that he wants to fuck me. Just like you.'

Adele buried her face in Karen's hair and moaned as the older woman slipped her hand up under her dress and began to explore her treasures.

'My, Adele, your knickers are flooded. Stand up and let me take them off.'

The girl did as she was told, holding her skirt to her waist as

Karen pulled the sopping garment down her long thighs. She made Adele wait like that, the sun slanting through the trees onto her pale loins and the wispy brown curls on her prominent pussy mound. Her bush was beaded with sex dew and moisture glistened in rolling droplets on her thighs. Karen licked along one leg, travelling up from the knee to capture the little tears of arousal on her tongue.

'Oh, Karen,' sighed the girl as Karen's mouth approached the apex of its journey and then moved to the other thigh to begin all over again. 'You make me feel so sexy. I can't get enough of you. I could come just like this.'

'Why don't you then?' said Karen and closed her lips over the girl's open-mouthed vagina.

The birds in the trees took wing as Adele's shout of release rang through the wood. As ever, it seemed, Karen did not have to do much. The intensity of the girl's own desire was such that the first touch of Karen's mouth on her overheated sex took her tumbling over the cliff of ecstasy.

As Adele came, her knees buckled and she clung to Karen for support. The pair of them toppled off the bank and rolled down the slope into a heap of dry bracken.

'Ouch,' muttered Karen, coming to rest on something hard in the small of her back. She pulled the object from beneath her.

'What's that?' said Adele and smiled when she saw the small white article in Karen's hand.

'At least that's one of Will's balls we've found,' said Karen 'and we know where to look for the other two, don't we, Adele?'

26

'So why are we here, Lucian? Aren't you going to treat me to one of your swanky publisher's lunches?'

'Not today, Tania. This, I promise you, will be far more memorable. Have a sandwich.'

'OK then.' She leant companionably against him on the bench and looked around the small park. 'I suppose this *is* prettier than some smoky old restaurant.'

Lucian squeezed Tania's hand. She was the most even-tempered woman he'd ever had; sulks and wild mood swings were not part of her nature. Perhaps he should confine himself to Antipodean women in future – cheerful can-do girls like Tania who shrugged off disappointment and got on with life. Then he could forswear the neurotic English beauties who gave him overdrafts and heartache in equal measure. Like Caroline. Who was the reason the pair of them were sitting on a park bench, sharing a tuna-and-cucumber-on-brown when they could be savouring *langoustines à la Luigi* at Grimaldi's.

'Did you bring your camera?' he asked.

'It's in my sack. I thought it was a pretty funny thing to be asked to bring to lunch.'

Lucian wiped crumbs from his mouth and swigged from a can of Coke. He passed it to Tania.

'This is a working lunch. We're going to try and shoot a cover photo for Caroline's book.'

Tania's face registered surprise but she said nothing as Lucian continued. 'It's Caro's idea and Miranda Lynch thinks it might work. It'll be a good publicity shot anyway.'

'Why involve me?'

'Because somehow Caro knows you're a photographer.'

'I told her about it that night you were late. But I thought she hated my guts.'

'She hates mine too. But that's what her book's about. The more she hates, the more she gets turned on. Come on, we're meeting her over there in the rose garden.'

'Why?'

'Because that's where you're going to take her photo.'

'Strewth.' Tania stood and hoisted her rucksack onto one shoulder. 'I still don't understand, Lucian.'

'You will when I tell you her book is called *Naked in the Roses*.'

A Central London park at lunchtime on a sunny day is not the most discreet spot for a nude photo session. Even though the entrance to the rose garden was tucked away on the far side of the pond, there were many who had made their way there to enjoy its relative seclusion.

'Is she really going to flash her butt here?' said Tania.

'*She's* not,' said Lucian, 'but Contessa Marietta Strepponi is. She's the central character in Caroline's book.'

'Oh right.' She flashed him a knowing grin. 'And every week you and the Contessa act out her new scenes.'

'Er, yes. I'm her brutish tormentor, Bruno.'

'And what about me?'

'You feature in the new stuff she sent me. I should have warned you, I know.'

'Don't apologise till you get the bill for the photographs. Just tell me how I fit into Miss Weirdo's book.'

'Bruno takes her to a public garden and makes her walk naked through a bed of roses. A blonde female photographer records the event.'

'And that's me?'

'Actually she's referred to as Bruno's Australian bed-slut. He uses her to humiliate Marietta.'

'Really? Does Caroline like girls then?'

'Tania, I haven't got a clue what Caroline likes any more. Marietta, on the other hand, is game for almost anything. Here she comes now.'

Through the wrought-iron gates of the park walked a slim blonde figure in a white shift that fell to mid-thigh. Caroline. Behind her in the summer breeze trailed a green scarf as light as air and on her feet were open-toed sandals. Apart from that, as was evident from the sway of her breasts and the dark shadowing at her crotch, she wore nothing. She made no signal to Lucian and Tania but drifted towards them past a group of open-mouthed office-workers picnicking on the grass.

'You're late, Marietta,' snapped Lucian as Caroline came up to them. 'Apologise to Tania.'

Her milky blue eyes flashed with anger. 'What's one of your whores doing here?'

'She's here because it amuses me,' said Lucian, 'and to take photographs of your pretty pink arse. Now say you're sorry.'

Caroline glared at Tania. 'I'm sorry I'm late,' she said icily and turned to Lucian. 'Satisfied? Now let's get on with it.'

She wheeled around and marched off, the cheeks of her bottom quivering beneath the thin slip. Lucian knew that her script called for those self-same shuddering globes to be well attended to before the afternoon was over and his cock was already salivating in his pants at the thought. He noted with satisfaction that Tania had her camera at the ready and was following close behind Caroline's thinly clad form.

The garden was artful rather than formal. The roses themselves, of many varieties and hues, were arranged in banks of colour blending into the surrounding shrubs and a small copse of trees. As Caroline walked towards a bed of old-fashioned scarlet tea-roses, she slipped the straps of her dress from her shoulders and stepped out of it, leaving it behind her on the grass. Tania's camera began to click as the nude woman stepped into the flowers.

Lucian glanced over his shoulder. They had turned behind some large bushes which now concealed their activities from the picknickers. He had no doubt, however, that they would soon be an object of curiosity.

'Ah!' Caroline's cry was of pain as she moved her body through the roses' thorny embrace. Tania's camera was clicking fast, capturing the white flesh against the rich ruby of the petals. In the heart of the undergrowth the bushes grew wild and tall, framing Caroline's face, her blonde hair tousled, her eyes wide and unseeing. Rose blooms were crushed against the swollen orbs of her breasts and small flower-buds pressed against the lily-white bowl of her belly.

'Great,' cried Tania in enthusiasm, evidently excited by what she could see through her lens.

'Tell her what to do,' muttered Lucian. 'Bully her around, that's what she likes.'

Tania lifted her face from the camera and gave him a quizzical look. Nevertheless, she began to bark out orders that Caroline instantly obeyed.

'Hey – squeeze your tits. That's right. And play with your nipples, make them stick up. Quick! Now, with your other hand, open your legs. Show me what you've got, slut!'

Lucian was amazed to see his cool and contemptuous former fiancée splay her thighs wide and plunge two fingers deep into the well of her vagina, openly masturbating for the camera. Her cheeks were pink and a pre-orgasmic blush suffused her naked throat and bosom. Crushed rose petals stained her fair skin and blood wept from the thorn pricks that punctured her flesh.

'Bloody hell!' whispered a hoarse voice from behind Lucian. It was a be-suited office-worker, another in tie and shirtsleeves by his side. 'What the fuck is she playing at?'

Lucian had prepared an explanation for this eventuality, namely that they were taking photographs for a book cover and the proceedings were entirely legitimate but private so bog off please – to be delivered in a suitably snotty voice of authority. So he couldn't account for what he actually said.

'She's escaped from the Hospital for Nymphomaniacs up the road.'

'Who are you then? A doctor?'

'That's right. Now leave us alone, please. This is a delicate matter.'

'Why's that bird taking photos? You sure you're not from some mucky magazine?'

Lucian snorted in exasperation. 'Look, this patient is sexually disturbed and it is important we have visual record of how her condition manifests itself. Will you please go away.'

'No fear,' said the other man, 'I've never seen a dolly wank herself off in a flowerbed before. You'd pay a fortune to see this in Soho.'

'How long's the show going on for?' said the first man. 'Have I got time to nip back and fetch everyone else?'

'Oh, oh sweet Jesus!' Caroline was moaning, her fingers working rhythmically between her legs.

'For God's sake, doctor,' said Tania, 'this patient needs proper relief. Since these men are here, perhaps they'd like to help out.'

You dirty little minx, thought Lucian, excited by the prospect. Caroline had shivered through one orgasm already and was obviously primed for more. He had no doubt she'd do anything he said.

The two men were devouring the nude woman with their eyes. Lucian said in confidential tones, 'Look, there's no time to waste. She needs satisfying right now or she'll lose her grip on her sanity. If you'd care to slip out of your clothes ...'

Maybe it was the unreal situation or the thought of all those thorns but they hesitated. Lucian said, 'She was in the Cocksuckers' Ward. Consider it like giving blood.'

That did it. In a flash they were on her, trampling on the roses as they pulled at their clothes.

'You brutes,' cried Caroline even as she flung her arms around the first man's neck and his large square hands closed on her breasts.

'You must satisfy them, Marietta,' called Lucian. 'Drain them dry of their desires or it will be the worse for you.'

But Lucian's threats were unnecessary. Caroline or Marietta or whoever she was at that moment, had every intention of fully gratifying her new admirers. She was on her hands and knees between them and their cocks were in the open air. In a flash, one tool was spearing down her throat, the other plugging the back-thrust vestibule of her hungry vagina.

'Good God,' muttered Tania, leaning against Lucian and rubbing her bottom into his bursting crotch, 'I've never seen anything like this before. A pity I've used up all my film.'

The man behind Caroline was shafting her steadily, trying hard to make it last. His thick red cock was visible on the out-stroke, glistening with sex juice, and his testicles swung with each thrust. His hands were on the cheeks of Caroline's bottom, holding the plump moons apart so he could study the deep groove of her arse crack and the sight of his member ploughing her furrow.

At her other end, office-worker number two was already approaching his short strokes – except that it was Caroline who was doing the stroking. One arm was fastened around his waist for support and her free hand was wrapped around the base of his penis, pulling the skin back and forth as she jacked him towards his crisis. Her head dipped and bobbed while she guzzled his long blue-veined cock. As she sucked and wanked, her hanging breasts swung neglected beneath her. Lucian fought the urge to step forward and join in.

'I told you this would be memorable,' he whispered into Tania's ear.

'You did,' she replied. 'And it's going to be truly unforgettable in a moment. There's a park-keeper and a policeman heading this way.'

27

It was too late for lunch by the time the golfing party had finished their business on the course. At Karen's suggestion they returned to her room and ordered sandwiches.

'We'll make up for it at dinner,' she said as a room-service waiter arranged plates. 'And don't tell me you can't stay. It's my treat and I insist.'

So that settled that. Will beamed at her in gratitude as she produced a beer for him from the mini-bar. He reached for another rare-beef sandwich.

Adele was unbuttoning her dress. 'Do you mind if I have a shower, Karen? I feel all icky after scrambling through the undergrowth.'

Which left Karen and Will. Karen poured him another beer and sat opposite him. They didn't speak. Will ate like a starving man and Karen swung her bare brown legs directly in his line of sight. Will stopped munching and sipped his beer. Karen sighed contentedly. There was complete silence apart from the sound of hissing water.

'Will!' Adele was calling from the bathroom.

He raised his eyes from Karen's thighs with a guilty start.

'Come and scrub my back!' Adele shouted.

'Er...' he muttered, rising to his feet.

'Go ahead. She needs you,' said Karen.

She gave them five minutes. She and Adele had decided that would be time enough.

The happy couple were both naked in the shower stall when she burst into the room.

'Don't mind me,' Karen said, pulling down her shorts and sitting on the toilet seat. She peed noisily. 'Sorry but I couldn't wait.'

Will was staring at her open-mouthed over his shoulder. Karen enjoyed the sight of his big naked body: the thick columns of his legs, the white apple-cheeks of his bum and the broad brown slab of his back glistening beneath the rain of spray. Adele's body was obscured by his bulk but her face peeped around his body, a secret grin upon her face.

Karen stood up and patted her bush dry with a leaf of loo paper. She made no attempt to hide her dark-curled pussy mound. She turned to flush the toilet, showing him her bare buttocks.

Will's face was fixed in horror.

'What's up?' said Karen pulling her T-shirt over her head and reaching behind her to unfasten her bra. 'Never seen a woman have a pee before? That'll change after you're married, won't it, Adele? Come on, make room.'

It was a squash for the three of them in the small cubicle. There was no way for Will to avoid touching Karen's flesh even had he wanted to. And she knew how much he didn't want to. The evidence was there in Adele's hands, a vast club of a cock distended to its limit. It emerged from a cloud of soap bubbles, the foreskin peeled right back, the glans maroon with pent-up desire as Adele stroked and tickled the fat shaft.

'May I?' said Karen and took charge of the big tool. She slipped to her knees in the swirling suds and looked the monster straight in the eye.

'My God, Will, you've got a nine-iron here!'

When she stretched her jaw wide to take it between her soft full lips, he lost control.

'You witch!' he cried, grabbing her hair and forcing his rigid flesh deep into her mouth. 'You luscious, sexy, teasing whore. God, I want to fuck and fuck and—'

Fortunately for Karen that was all it took for him to explode in her mouth, flooding her with an un-dammed river of Scottish spunk. She clung dizzily to his tree-trunk thighs on this thirty-second journey to ecstasy and swallowed all he gave her.

When she took her mouth from his shrinking cock she found herself staring directly at the pouting pussy lips of Adele. Karen transferred her lingual attentions. This weekend was their treat, after all.

As Karen explored the familiar but no-less delicious folds of Adele's cunt, from above she heard the sounds of weeping interrupted by soothing murmurs and sudden intakes of breath. Husband- and wife-to-be were working things out.

'Adele, I'm sorry. I'm a brute, I know. I couldn't help it—'

'It's all right, Will. I still love you.'

'But I shouldn't have. I've been unfaithful to you.'

'Don't be silly. By my presence I gave you permission, it doesn't count – oh!'

'Adele, are you all right? What's the matter?'

'It's nothing. It's what Karen's doing to my clit. Will, just kiss me while I come!'

While her young guests took their time drying themselves, Karen pulled the covers off the big bed and hung the Do Not Disturb sign on the door. The others might be feeling sated and indolent, but she had a fire in her belly which would take a deal of putting out.

Will did not protest when Karen wound her arms around him and pressed the hard nubs of her erect nipples into his chest.

'Tell him it's OK to kiss me, Adele.'

'It's OK, Will.'

And so he did. His chest was almost hairless and banded with muscle. There was no flab anywhere on his body – Karen looked.

His club was stiff between his legs again and his fingers were no longer wary of exploring her taut and sumptuous flesh. They fondled each other with relish while Adele looked on, fingers idly paddling between her legs. There was no rush now. It was obvious even to Will how they would fill the time until dinner – though how it had all come about was a mystery he would ponder for a long time.

'Adele,' said Karen, tumbling Will backwards onto the bed, 'tell him it's OK to fuck me stupid.'

Adele dived onto the white sheet beside them. 'Actually, it's not,' she said, 'unless he does it to me at the same time.'

Will looked perplexed as the women arranged their supple limbs on his supine body. But as Karen straddled his hips to bury his straining cock in her hot nook and Adele's bottom descended on his face to offer her smiling cunt to his lips and tongue, he soon caught on. He had never played this game before but if he practised he was sure he could soon get his handicap down.

Later, when the women had drained him dry, Will was introduced to other delights that he had only dreamed of. As he watched Adele and Karen embrace upon the bed, their summer-brown beauty brilliant against the white sheet, their mouths and fingers and limbs skilful in the ways of pleasure, it never occurred to him that they weren't performing just for his benefit. Which, in a way, they were – though, with her head buried between the long lean thighs of her female lover, Karen had trouble remembering Will was even in the room.

She remembered well enough half an hour before dinner, when his revived erection pressed between her buttocks and thrust into the moist pocket of her vagina while she was sucking Adele's pussy to orgasm for the umpteenth time. Then, with Will's massive engine shunting steadily in and out of her cunt and her tongue buried to the root in his fiancée's most intimate orifice, she reflected with sorrow that she had now finished her research for *The Novelist's Wife*. It had turned out to be a true labour of love.

28

As gently as he could, Lucian caught the tiny splinter of wood between the jaws of the tweezers and eased the thorn from the lightly tanned flesh above Caroline's left shoulder blade. A crimson bead oozed from the wound and he dabbed it with a tissue soaked in iodine. The girl flinched and moaned, pressing her face further into the pillows of Lucian's bed. A few feet away, Tania carried out the same operation on a puncture just behind the journalist's knee. The air was thick with the smell of antiseptic and Caroline's nude body was studded with scratches and weals and pinpricks of blood. It was an extraordinary scene.

But not as extraordinary, thought Lucian, as the one they had left behind in the park. Two men on their knees in the flowerbed, their trousers round their ankles and their cocks on display, one hosing the empty air with gouts of semen even as Caroline was plucked from his grasp by Lucian. Behind them the park-keeper was yelling in indignant tones about the state of his roses and the policeman had broken into a trot. As Lucian bundled a naked Caroline ahead of him and shouted to Tania to follow, he saw the remaining picnickers emerge from behind the bushes hard on the heels of the park-keeper.

Caroline's unknown lovers were too bewildered by the turn of events to even cover themselves up. Office-worker number one, whose enjoyment of Caroline's succulent pussy had been so unhappily interrupted, still sported an angry hard-on which was an object of discussion to the gathering crowd. 'Christ, they're a pair of gay boys on the job,' said one voice even as the officer began to intone the caution.

Lucian glimpsed these proceedings through the branches as he led Caroline and Tania along a small footpath which ran between the garden and the back wall. He knew the park well from a period some three years back when Uncle Basil used to bring Aunt Sophie's miniature poodle to the office. Lucian was usually deputed to take Tristram on his constitutional and the little fellow loved to take a dump along this obscure pathway.

'Put your dress on, for Christ's sake,' he muttered to Caroline as they reached the abandoned gardener's hut. This was the tricky bit. The wall was lower here and Lucian manoeuvred an old petrol drum up to it and placed a plank across the top. It held as he climbed up and looked over into a quiet residential street. On the corner fifty yards away was a stream of traffic. Even as he looked he saw two taxis speed by.

With Tania's help he got Caroline over the wall somehow. In fact it was easier than he might have expected. If she had been her normal self she would have whinged and bitched a blue fit. But it was as if she were in a trance and she followed Lucian's instructions without a murmur.

Lucian sat in the jump-seat in the taxi, facing the two women. Caroline lolled like a doll, her eyes closed and her dress riding high over her spread thighs; the white cotton was spotted with grime and grass stains and blood. Tania had her fist jammed down her throat trying to stifle her hysteria, tears of merriment rolling from her sparkling eyes. Her dress, too, was hiked high and her panties were on view. It occurred to Lucian that, despite the nerve-jangling, heart-stopping stress of their escape, he had had an erection the whole time.

He made the taxi drop them by a parade of shops two streets away from his flat. The weasel-faced driver had thrown them far too many curious glances for his liking.

'What's up with them two?' he'd said as Lucian pulled out his wallet.

'We've just been celebrating a birthday,' Lucian said. 'They're a bit tiddly. Here, have a drink on us later,' and he pressed a fiver into the bony hand.

'Ta very much, guv,' said the cabbie, suspicion instantly replaced by bonhomie. ''Ere,' he added, 'when you're shaggin' 'em, give 'em one for me.'

Now, with an assortment of first-aid equipment, Lucian and Tania were ministering to Caroline's wounds. She lay unprotesting as they nursed her abused body. In fact she'd not said a word since her exclamations in the rosebed in the park. So Lucian was taken by surprise when, as he cleaned a nasty slash on her upper arm, he heard her murmur, 'Oh, that's nice.'

Caroline's face was hidden from him, buried in the pillow, but the sound was unmistakable. 'Yes, please. More. Oh, that's heaven.'

He looked at Tania who was on her knees by the side of the bed, attending to Caroline's legs. And, he could now see, other tender portions of her rear anatomy. Caro's milky-white arse cheeks were tilted up off the bed, her thighs spread sufficiently to give Tania access to the rear-facing split of her pussy. Lucian leaned over to see Tania's forefinger disappearing between the slick swollen lips of Caroline's vagina.

'What do you think you're doing?' he hissed.

'Giving her a thrill. She loves it. Look.' And Tania inserted another finger, then another. 'She's so turned-on you could put your whole arm in there, I bet.'

Lucian was unaccountably miffed. 'We're supposed to be patching her up, not touching her up.'

'Ohh!' groaned Caroline. 'Don't stop.'

'You see?' said Tania. 'Why don't you get the splinters out of her arse? I'll try and keep her mind off what you're doing.'

Lucian couldn't think of any reason why not. The only problem was that, as Tania soothed the inflamed membranes of Caroline's swollen genitals, the success of her efforts reverberated through the girl's buttocks making them twitch and clench. Delightful though this was to the eye, removing thorns from the quivering bum flesh was a trifle difficult. Lucian pinched together a fold of creamy buttock and applied his tweezers.

'Aah!' squealed Caroline, grinding her pelvis against Tania's hand at the same time as Lucian probed.

'You hurt her,' said Tania.

'That was a cry of pleasure,' said Lucian and held up a sliver of thorn in triumph.

Caroline's arse spasmed, bouncing up and down in a flurry of agitation, the pink-and-cream cheeks a riot of motion.

'See,' said Lucian, waiting till the crisis had passed before seizing a pinch of flesh and re-applying his pincers. The movement spread wide the girl's arse furrow, revealing the puckered dimple of her anus and the pale-furred purse of her pussy still distended by Tania's probing fingers.

'Don't you want to fuck her?' said Tania.

Lucian did not reply. The wanting-to-fuck-her feeling went without saying.

'Do her now,' said Tania. 'I want to watch. Do her here.' And she dipped her head, extending a long pink tongue to circle the pretty fissure of Caro's bumhole. The supine girl moaned at the lascivious touch and butted her spread buttocks back into Tania's face.

The Australian lifted her head, her eyes shiny. 'See, she wants it.'

Lucian threw his clothes off in seconds.

It wasn't easy to position himself because Tania had the urge to keep her fingers in Caro's cunt. They compromised by letting Lucian arrange himself on Caroline first. Tania fetched some cream and worked it into Caro's bum. She did it very thoroughly, pushing big dollops right inside. Finally she sucked Lucian's bursting tool into her mouth, wetting it thoroughly with her spittle.

'Go on,' she urged. 'Put it up her now. She's dying for it.'

The truth was, they all were. Lucian gritted his teeth as he pushed his purple glans against the glistening star of the girl's fundament. It resisted. Tania took charge and pressed the knob in. The slippery flesh yielded, the tiny circlet stretching to engulf the rounded end, then closing over the shaft as Lucian slid smoothly, sweetly home, deep into the intimate crevice of her arse.

'Ooh!' squealed Caroline and pressed her buttocks hard against his belly, trying it seemed to get even more cock inside her. Lucian lifted her by the hips and Tania slipped a pillow beneath her belly, then the pair slumped back upon the bed, squirming and pumping.

'Wait! Wait!' cried Tania as she knelt behind them and pushed her hand beneath Lucian's leaping balls to fondle Caroline's neglected vagina. The three of them were connected, plugged into a hot sexual current that raced through their veins like electricity.

Lucian knew he couldn't last long. All that had happened in the last few hours was enough in itself to send him over the edge, not to mention the release of tension after the escape from the park. And now to have his cock buried in the most delicious arse of his sexual acquaintance, with another girl's hand foraging in the pocket of his lover's vagina – he could feel Tania's fingers stroking his cock through the thin membranes of sex tissue – was incredible. Caroline was writhing and panting beneath him in a crescendo of movement and he could hear Tania's heavy breathing behind him as she urged them on with a string of obscenities. He had no doubt she had her other hand between her own legs.

They all came together.

Then they collapsed and went to sleep.

When the phone rang only Lucian stirred.

'Miranda wants to know what you're up to,' said his assistant.

'Tell her I'm working at home,' he replied and hugged the two authors closer to him on the bed.

29

When Lucian woke up he was alone. He stretched languorously across the bed and the late afternoon sun fell on his face. He felt as if he had taken some weird hallucinogen for his mind was a whirl of indistinct erotic images – blood-beaded white flesh and soft-furred cunt-clefts and heavy, hanging breasts. He sat up and peered around him, the events of the day slowly assembling themselves in his memory. The disarray of his room and the smell of antiseptic confirmed that it had all been more than a sex-mad dream.

He padded down to the kitchen, suddenly ravenous. There wasn't much in the fridge but enough to satisfy him, thank God. He washed down cheese, salami and an apple with a glass of iced water. It tasted like the best food he had ever eaten.

On the table was a note from Tania: 'Gone to Paul's to develop the film. See ya when I see ya. Big kisses. T.'

The thought of the pictures of Caro in the roses sent a twitch of excitement the length of his cock, which was now inching, turgid and expectant, along his thigh. With his belly full and his brain awake and buzzing, he realised he had hardly begun to exhaust the possibilities of being in bed with two women. They had been hot and eager, as horny as him, and now they had gone. He had little expectation of seeing Tania again that day. Paul was another roving Australian who had access to a photo lab somewhere in town. Lucian had no doubt that Tania's relationship with him involved exposing more than rolls of film.

He returned to his bedroom and began to clean up. He pulled the sheet off the bed, stained with dots and smears of blood and other telltale soggy patches. He collected all the wads of tissue and discarded dressings. He threw open the windows, including the skylight above his bed. As he did so, naturally he looked across the street.

Nicole was there. His heart thudded and he froze, his fingers pressing white-tipped to the window sill. She was, as ever, heart-stoppingly beautiful.

She wore her tennis outfit – white T-shirt, white pleated skirt, white socks, white plimsolls – the classic ensemble from the days of amateur Wimbledon. On her it looked classically cock-stiffening. Lucian was very stiff indeed.

Nicole was talking to someone out of sight. No doubt Hugh was also relishing the sight of her pirouetting up and down, the skirt whisking across her delectable thighs, her full bosom straining the cotton of her shirt. For a married woman, Nicole certainly gave good value. Parading around her bedroom, everything she did was calculated to set her man on fire.

Now she reached under her skirt and wriggled. It could only mean – yes! Her panties were skittering down her long brown legs. She bent to pick them up, offering Lucian the tiniest glimpse of pale buttock, before throwing them to Hugh who was still hidden from his sight.

She performed a few stretching exercises, arms reaching to the sky, then to one side, then the other, the hem of her skirt lifting each time to just below her crotch. She turned to face the window and bent down to touch her toes. Lucian imagined the view Hugh was getting. He groaned.

Then she took her top off to reveal a white sports bra with crossover straps. For a woman with her superstructure, Nicole needed some serious support on court. The bra did not remain long. Lucian was almost drooling as he watched her fingers reach between her shoulder blades and unclasp the garment. Though he could not see, he could imagine the shift of flesh outward and downward as her magnificent chest globes were freed from constraint. His fingers itched to caress her.

The exercises resumed. There was more arm-waving and this time Lucian could glimpse the golden shimmer of tit as she twisted her torso. He clasped his jumping cock firmly in his fist, determined not to give himself relief just yet. But Nicole's exhibition was becoming more than he could bear.

And more than her other watcher could bear too, it seemed. A figure suddenly stepped into Lucian's view, smiling and closing fast on Nicole's irresistible body. Lucian was flabbergasted. The man with his arms around her, pressing those big breasts to his chest and subjecting her to a soul-searching kiss, was not her husband. What's more, his naked torso was the colour of bitter chocolate and Lucian recognised him. His name was Freddy Cameron, an investment banker with a Rolls that took up two places in the tennis-club car park. He was also the owner of the biggest cock Lucian had ever seen.

The kiss continued across the street as Lucian tried to come to terms with the emotions that were now storming through him. The first he recognised as simple jealousy – if jealousy could ever be simple. Though he had wanted Nicole ever since he had set eyes on her, and his desire had increased tenfold through witnessing her antics with her husband, he had never felt jealous of Hugh. In fact, he took his hat off to him. For a fellow to have such a hot and eager wife after five years of marriage roused in Lucian only admiration.

But for that wife to cavort and display herself for another man – that changed things. If Nicole was going to play away there was an enthusiastic partner for mixed doubles just across the street. Now Lucian really *was* jealous.

Then there was the question of Hugh himself. The poor sod was probably on a business trip, stuck in a hotel off a motorway somewhere thinking his ever-faithful other half was pining for his presence. So was he, Lucian, now duty-bound to inform his tennis partner that Nicole was playing singles? No was the answer to that. Quite apart from anything else, how could he put it? 'Look, Hugh, I just happened to be watching your wife undress the other night when I noticed there was some other chap giving her a hand...' Which was true, Freddy now had her little skirt off and his strong black fingers were kneading the white cheeks of her bottom like dough.

Which brought Lucian to the question of Freddy himself. He liked him, everybody did. Freddy was an affable guy with a charming manner and an open wallet come drinks time. His family had fled from Timbanda after most of them had perished at the hands of the dictator before last. Freddy had duelling scars on his cheeks and a missing finger on his left hand. 'You wait till I write my book,' he often said to Lucian. 'It will make your hair stand on end to learn how I lost my family and my finger.' But as for things standing on end, what really interested Lucian about Freddy was his cock.

He guessed Nicole would shortly be finding it pretty interesting too for she was on her knees in front of Freddy, pulling his shorts down his coal-black thighs.

When Lucian had first met Freddy, in the changing room at the club, the African was naked. He had stood in the shower, facing the room, conducting a loud conversation about the legs of Steffi Graf. He was not a big man, five-seven tall at most with a slim build – but his penis looked as if it belonged on a giant. It hung between his thighs like a black banana, as thick at the root as at the tip, there being no discernible bulge to the glans beneath the hooded foreskin. Unlike any other willy of Lucian's acquaintance, hanging there limp and detumescent it was a thing of power and beauty. He'd not been able take his eyes off it.

He'd seen it many times since for Freddy was proud of his symbol of masculinity. He spent a lot of time in the changing room, most of it with his prick on display. When Freddy undressed, the first items of clothing to come off were his trousers and underpants, and they were the last to go back on again. Freddy had the biggest dick in the club and, though his tennis was lousy, everyone knew he was the real cock of the walk.

And now Lucian would be able to satisfy his curiosity on one important matter – just how big did Freddy's dick get?

Nicole had uncovered it and, though Lucian could not see her face, her posture revealed the awe she felt. She fell back on her haunches, the delectable globes of her arse resting on her feet, to consider the discovery she had made between Freddy's open thighs. And now Lucian could see the dark glistening cock that was of such abiding interest to all. To his surprise it looked exactly the same as it always did, like a length of heavy rubber hose looping from the springy black curls at the base of Freddy's belly. This was curious. Any other male, he was sure, would have an upright member quivering like a tuning fork at the prospect of playing a symphony on Nicole's pneumatic flesh.

She reached out a hand and nervously began to stroke the sleeping prick, as if she were petting a snake. Freddy smiled encouragement at her, his eyes flashing. Gradually she became bolder, enfolding her fingers round the dangling pipe. It seemed to Lucian that she could not grip him all the way round. Then she lifted the head of the snake and her mop of black curls dipped. Lucian could not see her exploring Freddy's penis with her lips but he could imagine it only too vividly. Similarly he could not tell exactly what she was up to with her hands but he could guess. When at length she leaned back to admire her handiwork, Lucian saw that it had been effective.

At last Freddy's great cock was waking from its slumber. Nicole had let go of him and was now watching, doubtless in wonder and trepidation, as the beast began to stir. The mighty tool erected in stages, jerking up to the vertical in a miracle of genital engineering. It stretched up to Freddy's navel and beyond, dwarfing its diminutive owner. The gleaming tower of power thrilled and frightened Lucian from his vantage point across the street. God alone knew what it was doing to the naked and expectant Nicole who was squatting just inches below it.

Freddy said something to her and she got up and rummaged in her dressing-table drawer. Lucian recognised the pot that she retrieved – it was the one Hugh had used to rub cream into her bottom the night he had spanked her. Now Nicole stood with one foot up on the bed beside Freddy and began to anoint her vagina. She took her time smoothing lots of cream deep into her crevice. Lucian didn't blame her. The black monster between Freddy's thighs looked like an upright battering-ram.

There was further conversation between the two. Freddy's fingers were in Nicole's crotch, double-checking her lubrication work possibly, while she placed both hands on his weapon, pulling back the thick hood to reveal a bulging purple knob.

Preliminary negotiations over, Freddy lay back along the bed and Nicole climbed over him. She balanced on top of his cock for an age, it seemed, before she had the courage to bear down, thrusting the thick bulk up into her well-oiled entrance. Lucian watched the impaling from the rear – the globes of her milky buttocks jutting and pouting, the veined black column spearing up between her slim thighs, the dark-fringed orifice of her open-mouthed vagina swallowing and swallowing, inch by inch . . .

'Good God,' muttered Lucian to himself. Nicole had taken all of the giant member inside herself and now swayed on top of Freddy's prone body, plugged to the hilt. For a moment she was still, then she tried a little jerk, then another, raising herself up and down on the black pole in her belly. Then she began in earnest, lifting and sitting, her buttocks flexing, her pelvis grinding. Freddy's hands cupped her arse rounds and he helped the up-and-down motion. Lucian could see him palpating her cheeks and running his fingers into her crack, the stub of a finger on his left hand clear in the bright evening light.

They couldn't hold the position for long, Lucian reckoned – not without Nicole suffering damage. But first they changed up a gear and suddenly their bodies were clutching and lifting and heaving together in a blur until, with a shriek that was audible from across the street, Nicole announced her climax.

With two strokes Lucian erupted his frustration and lust and jealousy into his fist. He rested his forehead against the window ledge, panting hard, his eyes closed.

When he opened them he saw that Nicole was sitting on the bed with a daft grin on her face. Freddy was looking out of the window, idly scratching his big hanging testicles. His penis was as spectacular as before, wet and fully extended. When he turned towards the bed, his cock moved fractionally later than the rest of him, swinging in front of him like a great boom.

The grin on Nicole's face disappeared and another expression took its place – dreamy, lustful, compliant. Slowly, as if in a daze, her hand reached for the big glistening penis and she opened her mouth as wide as she could.

30

When Monty Hastings announced to his wife that he was off to Venice to attend a writers' conference, Karen did not turn a hair. The fact that Monty would be café-hopping in St Mark's Square, downing Bellinis in Harry's Bar and sleeping at night in a refurbished palazzo with the lapping of the Grand Canal for a lullaby was of no concern to her. It was well known that writers' workshops were all hard graft. She suggested that he took his industrious researcher, Harriet Pugh, with him to ease the burden.

With those two out of the house, Karen turned her attention to the affairs of Blue Desire Books. Lucian had been nagging her – in the nicest possible way – to allow a visit from a photographer. It was all to do with 'packaging' and 'launching the imprint' and 'creating an image'. Karen was no fool, she knew he wanted a sexy photo of her to bung on *The Novelist's Wife* so whatever he wanted to call it was fine by her.

The photographer was an intimidating smoothy with a shock of dark bushy hair and a practised smile. 'Darling, you're ravishing!' he cried as Karen opened the door. 'I'm going to *adore* shooting you.' Karen had been relieved to see Lucian standing behind him. They'd only met once before but they'd talked so much on the phone since then she felt he was an ally.

'I'm Cliff's assistant for the day,' said Lucian as he carried some lights from the photographer's Range Rover.

'And I'm Karen's,' said Adele, pitching in and picking up a tripod. 'She's asked me along for immoral support.

'And, God, are you going to need it,' she added in a whisper to Karen as the two men hustled around with equipment.

'What do you mean?'

'I hate to think what you'd get up to with these two left on your own. They're really dishy.'

'Do you think so? That photographer guy is too full of himself.'

'Of course, he's Clifford Rush, he's *famous*. We've got big arty books by him in the shop. He takes really sexy photos.'

'Oh.'

'And your Lucian's got a lovely grin. I bet you really enjoy working with him.'

'He's OK but ours is a professional relationship, Adele. Hey, leave my skirt alone. What the hell do you think you're doing?'

'Just checking.'

'Adele, please! They'll be back any moment! Take your hands off me!'

'OK but tell me that this isn't pussy juice on my fingers? You're turned on already, you sexy bitch, and don't deny it.'

Karen didn't try.

Turned on or not, the morning session did not go well. There was a lot of hanging around while Cliff fiddled with equipment and made calls on his mobile phone. Then he took some staid shots of Karen posing in Monty's study which she didn't feel comfortable about at all.

Over lunch in the kitchen Lucian produced the cover design for one of the other Blue Desire launch titles.

'Talk about literal,' sniffed the photographer as he peered at the shot of a nude blonde posing in a rosebed beneath scrolling blue typography that read *Naked in the Roses*.

The women were more impressed.

'God, look at the expression on her face,' muttered Karen.

'I bet she's having an orgasm,' said Adele.

'You can't actually see anything.'

'But it's dead sexy.'

Cliff Rush cut in. 'I suppose it's not too bad but it's *nothing* to what I can do with you, sweetheart.' And he seized Karen by the hand and dragged her towards the door.

Lucian half rose but the photographer stopped him from following. 'Leave us alone, dear heart. This is the moment I earn the pittance your firm is paying me.' And he whisked Karen off upstairs.

Lucian watched him go and shrugged. Adele took a bottle of wine from the fridge and refilled their glasses. She looked again at the shot of the blonde in the roses.

'What *is* she doing exactly?'

He told her. It was a good story and she took in every word.

'So I was right, she *is* having an orgasm.'

'Yes.'

'And that's the kind of thing you want from Karen?'

He looked embarrassed. 'I don't know. I mean, is she game?'

Adele just laughed. This sweet boy obviously didn't know Karen at *all*.

Clifford had set up in Karen's bedroom. As they entered the room he spun her around and pressed her up against the wall.

'This is it, darling,' he said, his hands squeezing her arms, his blue eyes gazing into hers. 'I want you to trust me completely. Give me your mind and your body for the next hour and I'll make you look like the sexiest woman who ever lived.'

Karen giggled but the mad-eyed photographer shut her up. 'Look, I'm told you've written a novel so hot that readers will spontaneously combust with desire. I want you to give me some of that. I want lust in my pictures. I want wild wanton sex. Can you do it?'

Karen nodded. 'I-I'll try—'

'NO!' Cliff roared and thrust his pelvis against hers. The hard bundle in his crotch ground against her mound, taking her breath away. 'I don't want you to try – I want you to *give*!' And he kissed her. She squirmed and wriggled. *How dare he*? She pulled her mouth away.

'Get off me!' she hissed.

'Great,' he said, suddenly releasing her. 'That's it! Give me some of that.'

'But I'm angry not turned on, you idiot.'

He grinned and she felt a sudden stab of sympathy for him. 'Who cares? You *look* damn sexy. I think we're going to have some fun.'

Karen wasn't sure about that but she wasn't sure about much at present. He was crazy and unpredictable and, she couldn't deny it, highly desirable. The skin across his firm jaw was smooth and his bottomless blue eyes were laughing as he took in her confusion. He pulled off his shirt to reveal a tanned and muscular chest.

'I always strip off when I'm working,' he explained, reaching for his camera. 'It's hot under these lights.'

That was true. Suddenly Karen felt oppressively warm. There was sweat under her arms and her breasts. It called to mind the heat of her locked room as she worked at her book. Then she knew what was expected of her.

'Yes!' cried Cliff as Karen's fingers found the buttons of her summer blouse. 'Oh yes, my darling, take it slowly and give me everything you've got.'

It was a frustrating afternoon for Lucian. He and Adele repaired to the parlour across the hall from Karen's bedroom to be on hand in case they were needed. So far they had not been and Lucian's attempt to sneak a look inside had been met with an emphatic instruction to 'Fuck off, darling, there's a love.'

'Genius at work, obviously,' Lucian said and Adele smiled without conviction, sipping nervously at her wine.

They conversed feebly about books and publishing and poor trade in the bookshops until they dried up completely, both of them mesmerised by the sounds filtering through the closed bedroom door.

Most of the noise came from the photographer: excited yelps of glee and shouts of 'Yes, that's it!' and 'God, you're gorgeous' and 'Oh darling, that's *fabulous*'. Then there were fewer discernible words and more frequent grunts and groans and squeals of vocalised excitement. And among the masculine effusions, feminine notes were heard as well: low moans and throaty cries and higher, long-drawn-out ululations that spoke directly to the throbbing prick in Lucian's pants.

Adele seemed deeply affected. As the sounds of Karen's excitement mounted, the girl's hazel eyes grew round and the breath was expelled in short gasps from her thin, curving lips. A pulse beat in her throat and her hands gripped her glass so hard Lucian feared it might shatter.

'Oh God, I can't stand it,' she cried suddenly. 'I'm going to stop him.'

Lucian caught her before she reached the door.

'No, Adele. Let him do his job. These photos are important.'

'But,' she moaned, her slender frame squirming against him, 'you don't understand. I want to be with her. She needs me.'

Adele was almost as tall as Lucian and her big eyes looked directly into his. The points of her nipples were hard against his chest through their thin clothing and his erect cock butted against her soft belly.

'You men are so vile sometimes,' she said. 'You stick together. I bet he's raping her in there and you're just an accomplice.'

A cry of excitement rang out from the bedroom. 'Yes, Cliff, yes!'

'You see, she's fine,' said Lucian, aware that their pubic mounds were rubbing together, the barrel of his cock seeming to fit directly into the groove of her hillock.

'I bet he's got it in her,' Adele spat. 'His big fat ugly penis. He had an erection when he dragged her upstairs. And you've had one all afternoon, you filthy sod.'

'I'm sorry,' spluttered Lucian and tried to lever her belly off his.

'You see? You're sticking your thick thing into my tummy, you pig. I suppose you want to do me like he's doing her.'

'No!' he cried and attempted to disengage their bodies but somehow their loins were glued together. She was squirming open-thighed on him now and her face was flushed with anger or distress or – 'Oooooh!' she wailed – orgasm.

Lucian caught her reed-slim frame before she fell to the floor and laid her on the small sofa in the bay of the window. Her skirt seemed to have become caught high up on her long thighs and he found himself staring at her skimpily-knickered pubis. Brown curls poked from beneath the pink cotton and a dark wet line denoted the vertical spread of the folds beneath.

Adele lay limp and unseeing, making no attempt to cover herself. Lucian drew the obvious conclusion as to his expected course of conduct.

'Oh God,' she wailed as he pulled the damp gusset free of her tangled bush and she lifted her hips to allow him to bare her completely. Her pussy smelt musky and sweet and her lips were long and curling. He teased them apart gently with a finger, right up to the hood of skin which peeled back at his touch to reveal the tiny stalk of her clit. He blew a gentle breath across the plain of her belly and her pelvis convulsed. This was a woman burning up with hunger for sex.

'Kiss me, Karen,' she moaned. 'Kiss my cunt, you lovely darling. Please.'

Lucian gazed at the moist and perfumed folds of this delirious woman's sex and contemplated the morality of bestowing cunnilingus under the guise of mistaken identity.

'Please, Karen, *please*!'

The pale thighs opened still further. The pretty pink lips wept with desire. Lucian had no wish to deceive but he could recognise an overriding need when he saw it. He bent his head to administer the kiss of life.

In the bedroom, Karen was oblivious to everything but the scratch of paper on her skin, the satisfaction of completing another vengeful swipe against Monty – and the enjoyment of a thick penis in her yearning cunt.

She was on her knees on the bed, her nude buttocks thrust high and spread wide to take the force of the photographer's buffeting from behind, his stiff pole gliding and swooping the length of her moist passage in a steady rhythm. Beneath her lay the crumpled remnants of a few hundred pages of A4 paper.

It had been Clifford's idea for her to recline naked on a pile of typewritten pages but it had been Karen's inspiration to use the typescript of Monty's last novel for the purpose. To lie on a bed of her husband's overblown prose, displaying every inch of her flesh for a celebrated exploiter of the female form, that had given Karen real pleasure. Had turned her into a shameless wanton for Clifford's camera. Had spurred her on to stroke her breasts and pinch her nipples and tweak her clitoris to orgasm, time and time again. Until at last Cliff had called a halt and fallen on her himself, giving her the benefit of the very special telephoto lens he carried between his legs.

'Fuck me, fuck me, Cliff,' she cried. 'Do me with your big prick until I come again.'

The great photographer smiled as he went about his work and the pair of them tumbled on Monty's bed of prose until every page was creased and torn and stained with the juices of their coupling.

Karen shuddered to her final orgasm and shivered with pleasure as a lake of semen pooled on the paper spread beneath her loins. At last she had fallen in love with the literary life.

31

Miranda Lynch was as good as her word. As promised, she took Lucian to lunch to celebrate his acquisition of Karen's book. But if he expected her no-nonsense façade to crack during a long and languorous prandial experience he was disappointed. His enjoyment of wind-dried guinea fowl on a bed of *focaccia*, stuffed with cranberries (a Grimaldi special) was severely curtailed by a review of Blue Desire's progress.

'We're scheduled almost to the end of next year,' he was able to report, a feat which entitled him in his opinion to a bottle of the second-best claret. To her credit, Miranda had allowed him to order it without objection even though she – wouldn't you know it – barely touched her own glass. The result was that he was a bit squiffy by the time he laid down his knife and fork. Under the scrutiny of the toughest woman in publishing this was doubtless an error of judgement. For the moment, however, judgement was not at his command.

'You know, Miranda, my Uncle Basil is a great admirer of yours.'

Was that a glimpse of a smile on her perfect pink lips?

'I was at his house last night,' continued Lucian, 'and he was talking about you.'

'Really?'

'Yes. He said he only accepted such a piddling pay-off from the firm because you were so scrumptious. All the time you were negotiating he couldn't take his eyes off your legs.'

This time she did smile, there was a small twitch of the mouth. Or was that a snarl?

Lucian blundered on. 'He also said he couldn't get over the discrepancy between your image and your behaviour.'

She nodded. 'Discrepancy,' she repeated in an encouraging tone.

'Yes. The way you look like a brain-dead Barbie doll and behave like a corporate stormtrooper.'

'Oh?' The lips might be smiling but clouds were gathering in those swirling grey eyes.

'That's just his way of saying how impressed he is by you. You know Uncle Basil.'

'I do indeed. I'll call him when we get back and invite him to lunch.'

The clouds had dispersed, Lucian was relieved to see. He spoke with more confidence as he examined the dregs in the wine bottle. 'He says he's not lunching at present. He's trying to catch up with all the Baxendale stuff. I mean, buggering off on that cruise with Aunt Sophie for the summer put his schedule up the ... oh dear, I've just made a boo-boo.'

'You have?'

'No one's meant to know he's one of the Baxendale judges. I only found out because I went into his study. He swore me to secrecy. You won't tell anyone, will you? Please?'

To his surprise he felt her hand on his, stilling his agitation. It was warm and her voice was soft. 'Calm down, Lucian. These things always get out. It's impossible to keep them secret.'

Lucian knew this was true but he didn't feel any better. One of the many peculiarities of the Baxendale Prize was that the identity of the judges was not to be revealed before the prize-giving dinner – on pain of the prize being rendered void for that year. This particular stipulation in Gwendoline Baxendale, the benefactor's, will had been designed to avoid the public dog-fight between judges that annually affected the other literary prizes. It was an idiotic condition which had nullified the competition for the past two years running.

The hand squeezed his. 'Don't worry, Lucian, I shan't blow Basil's cover.'

'Thanks, Miranda. I've put my foot in it, haven't I?'

'Actually, Lucian, you have been most interesting, so cheer up.' She glanced over his shoulder. 'I understand you're rather partial to dessert wine. Why don't we invite these two ladies to share a bottle?'

Lucian looked up to see the familiar figure of Marilyn Savage approaching, a buxom brunette in a grey-patterned power-jacket in tow. He hastily stumbled to his feet.

Marilyn greeted Miranda like a long-lost sister, which puzzled Lucian since he'd gathered the impression a certain *froideur* existed between the two of them. She introduced her companion as Cherry Shaftoe, a big wheel on *The Sunday Badger*. It transpired that the two of them had been lunching in the adjoining room. What a coincidence!

'So you're the one who bought Karen Hastings' book,' purred Cherry as she sat down next to Lucian.

'I've been telling Cherry a little bit about it,' said Marilyn. 'It would be just perfect for the cover feature in the *Badger* colour sup.'

'Absolutely,' burbled Lucian, swigging from a glass of golden liquid that had appeared by magic at his elbow.

Cherry swigged too, her full red lips kissing the glass in an intriguing manner. For a woman in her middle years, she had a decidedly mischievous look about her. Her wide, burnt-sugar eyes twinkled at him in a conspiratorial fashion. It struck Lucian that she was as tipsy as he was.

'I'll certainly be giving it serious consideration,' she was saying. 'But all you publishers are after our cover slots. The competition is *stiff*.' And she shot Lucian a look brimming with significance.

'Marilyn's been telling me what a persuasive negotiator you are,' she continued, turning to him so that he couldn't help but be impressed by the undulating vista of the silk-clad hills beneath her jacket.

'Er, well . . . Miranda would have fired me if I hadn't bought it,' he said with an unconvincing grin. Nobody laughed.

Cherry placed a hand on his forearm and squeezed hard. 'So you went flat out to get it. I admire a man who'll give his all for what he wants.'

'I'm sure Lucian really wants Karen in the *Badger*,' said Marilyn.

'Oh *good*,' breathed Cherry, leaning back in her chair and gazing at him hungrily. It struck Lucian that he'd be really worried if he didn't know that she had already eaten. On the other hand, she looked like a woman who could easily accommodate two puddings.

'I was telling Cherry about your table-top technique, Lucian,' said Marilyn.

'Table-top technique?' He was nonplussed.

'Or should I say, *under* the table top,' continued Marilyn. 'You remember that, Lucian. My yachtswoman friend was particularly impressed.'

Lucian choked on his wine. A memory of sore knees, soft white thighs and shrieks of orgasmic hysteria flashed into his mind – the night he had sucked off Marilyn and her pals beneath the dinner table. *Oh my God! She wants a repeat performance!*

'Marilyn, I . . .' His mouth was opening and closing like a landed fish. He looked to Miranda for help. She said nothing. It would have been as profitable to appeal to his wineglass or the tablecloth. With a pounding heart, he drained the former and lifted the latter.

There was an eerie half-light beneath the table. They were sitting at the rear of the restaurant, a position sheltered from prying eyes but a little short of natural light. And here, under the canopy of table and cloth, the three pairs of female legs glowed in the gloom like objects in a dream.

Marilyn's he knew well. Slim, delicate, waxed to a satin smoothness, her bare brown limbs were nonchalantly crossed, one shoe dangling from a painted toe, rocking from side to side in a rhythm that betrayed her emotion. Lucian could well imagine the river of excitement wetting her tiny lace panties.

Miranda, on the other hand, was an enigma to him. That her incorruptible beauty could countenance such shameless acts as were about to be committed was a shock. Perhaps she didn't realise what he was about to do? But that could hardly be the case – she must have set the whole thing up. Her grey eyes had held a gleam of curiosity as he sank beneath the table, the kind of bloodless curiosity exhibited by scientific researchers and members of the judiciary. Lucian had no doubt that, on this performance as on any other, Miranda was sitting in judgement.

Her legs were long and slender, encased in some kind of opaque shiny material that doubtless protected her entire lower anatomy from contamination by dirt, wind and human contact. Not that Lucian could see further than the hem of her oyster-pale skirt which finished primly just above the knees. Inevitably, in Miranda, those bony promontories were neat, exquisitely turned and clamped tightly together.

Not so the knees of the VIP journalist. Her legs were spread in a welcoming vee, her scarlet skirt riding half-mast across nude dimpled thighs. The invitation was blatant. Naturally, Lucian accepted it and began to explore beneath that scarlet pelmet.

There was a loud intake of breath from above the table, followed by a throaty gurgle as Lucian brushed his lips across the skin of Cherry's left thigh. His fingers delved upwards, stroking, probing, seeking out her special places with his fingertips. He wanted to tease her, to set her wriggling and writhing and begging him to do obscene things to her. But the moment he was lodged between her spread limbs, his hands on the butter-soft skin and her musky perfume in his nostrils, he was seized by passion.

He bared her pussy with a rip of her knickers. She squealed but he knew she loved it from the way her big bottom lifted from the seat and her exposed pubis was thrust into his face. There was barely a fringe of hair on her belly. She was all slippery sweetness and smooth smooth flesh. As he pressed his lips to her vagina and roved her perfumed folds with his tongue, he slipped his hands beneath the cheeks of her bottom and spread them apart.

Above him he heard voices.

'I give you my word Karen Hastings won't talk to anybody else before publication.' That was Miranda.

'You can stay with her for a couple of days. She's quite adorable.' Marilyn.

'Ooh, that's nice.' Cherry.

'We've had six-figure offers from the *Dog* and the *Bunny* though I'd rather run with a quality paper.' Miranda.

'You see, darling, we can't let it go for peanuts. You'll have to go some way to matching the money.' Marilyn.

'Six figures for a smutty novelist!' protested Cherry. 'I don't see how we could – oh God! Mmm, oh that's fantastic! You're right, Marilyn, the boy's a *musician* on the clitoris.'

Lucian ceased titillating that sensitive little promontory and blew a gentle breath across the tender folds of her nether lips. Now was not the time to ease her agitation. It was a crucial stage of the negotiation.

'Suppose,' said Miranda, 'you ran the profile of Karen for the colour sup and then serialised the book in the news section around publication.'

'You'd sell a hell of a lot of papers,' Marilyn chipped in.

'Oh my God, that's *good*!' moaned Cherry as Lucian curled his fingers into her bum crack and began a sly manipulation of her rosehole. Her abundant flesh leapt and quivered in his hands.

'We've got some sensational photos of Karen you could use,' said Miranda.

'Clifford Rush took them, darling, so you can imagine how wicked they are.' Marilyn.

Cherry's fingers were in Lucian's hair, tugging his face into her agitated crotch. 'Please, please!' she moaned.

'So, two hundred grand would be cheap at the price when you think about it.'

'What do you say, Cherry?'

'Yes, for God's sake, yes! Only just let me—'

Lucian plunged his tongue inside her, pressing the bridge of his nose the length of her split and sliding his forefinger deep into the slippery fissure of her anus.

'AAH!' shrieked Cherry and her thighs closed on Lucian's ears shutting off all sound.

When she finally relaxed her grip, Lucian heard Marilyn's voice saying, 'How about some champagne to celebrate our agreement? What do you say, Cherry?'

'I say that sounds a wonderful idea but I'm not drinking it with you two tricky bitches.'

'Really?' The satisfaction in Miranda's voice was palpable.

'No. I'm drinking it with your lapdog of an editor. I'm taking him to that hotel over the road right now. Any objections?'

'None at all,' said Miranda. 'You can keep him till next Monday. Just let me have him back in one piece.'

Beneath the table Lucian rested his head on the soft cushion of Cherry's thigh and allowed her hand to slip inside his shirt. She abraded her thumb across his nipple and a shiver ran through his drunk, disbelieving and desperately horny body. He placed a gentle kiss on her warm skin.

'Move it, you little tart,' said Marilyn as she prodded him with her shoe. 'On your feet and give the lady her money's worth.'

Four

THE BOTTOM LINE

32

'Nooo!' wailed Crispin Carmichael, his little face as red as a ripe tomato.

'Yes, Crispin, yes!' yelled an infuriated Felicity, struggling to keep a hold on her squirming two-year-old as he flailed against her knees. They were standing on the front-garden path of the Carmichaels' house having their daily battle about Crispin's new coat.

'No coat, mummy,' cried Crispin, breaking free and running headlong down the path, the despised garment trailing from one arm. As the pristine blue denim splashed through a large puddle, Felicity lunged for it and fell face down into the muddy water.

'*Shit!*' she screamed and then, 'Crispin, *come back!*' But her son was gone, out of the gate onto the pavement. '*Crispin!*' she yelled again in despair as she realised her back was spasming in pain and her legs would not push her to her feet fast enough to catch him.

The low winter sun shining in her eyes was suddenly blotted out by a looming shadow.

'It's OK, Felicity, I've got him,' said a voice she could not place and she made out the familiar shape of Crispin nestling in a tall man's arms.

'Thank you,' she said, sitting up slowly, her heart pounding and a knotted ball of pain lodged in the small of her back. 'Do I know you?'

The man chuckled as he held out his free hand to help her climb to her feet. 'Well, *you* don't do much for a fellow's self-esteem,' he said in a soft Irish brogue that formed itself into a name in her head at the very instant Crispin said –

'Brendan!'

Inside the house, Felicity sat gingerly at the kitchen table, a cushion at her back, while Brendan unearthed tea things, Crispin sitting cheerfully on his shoulders. As the kettle boiled, he whisked dirty dishes from the table and stacked them in the dishwasher.

'Things are a bit of a mess,' she said. 'The au pair left last week and I'm trying to do a million things at once.'

'Just you sit there,' said Brendan, setting a steaming mug in front of her. 'I'll clean up, it's no problem.'

And he did, clearing the work surfaces, stowing food back in the fridge and picking squashed banana out of the rug. To Felicity's amazement, Crispin helped him pick up bits of Lego and collect all the squidgy balls of Play-Doh that had rolled under the table.

Felicity swallowed three aspirins and tried to stand up. 'Christ,' she muttered between clenched teeth as the pain seized her. 'I really am in trouble. Crispin's due at a birthday party in an hour, I've got to pick up the other two from school, I swore I'd drop off the accounts to the Operatic Society and I doubt if I can even *drive*. And, *oh shit*, the fucking Presleys are coming to dinner!'

'Sit down, Felicity, and relax,' said Brendan. 'As a matter of fact, your luck is in.'

'What do you mean?'

'I mean that, after Cascade Holidays, I'm an expert in a crisis.'

Felicity lay on her stomach on the bed with her blouse off and her bra undone. Her immediate concerns had been dealt with: another toddler's mum had taken Crispin to his party, her elder children were being collected from school by a classmate's nanny and Brendan was shortly to drive to the High Street and deliver the promised accounts. On the way back he would shop for dinner and a friend of his had been summoned from London to cook it. But first he was going to attend to Felicity's back.

'You'd be surprised,' he said as he began to manipulate the flesh along her vertebrae, 'just how many people do their back on holiday. Every week you can bet somebody buggers themselves having a go at an unfamiliar sport. I got quite good at patching people up. Oho, you've seized up here, haven't you?'

'Yes!' she squealed as his fingers dug into her.

His hands were at the base of her spine pushing at the waistband of her clothes.

'I'll have to get under here,' he said, unzipping her skirt.

'Just don't get any ideas,' Felicity said as he tugged the garment down and then peeled back her tights.

'I'm sure I don't know what you mean, Mrs Carmichael,' he said, getting to work with his big strong hands.

'It's not that I don't appreciate your help, Brendan, and I admit that we did, um, enjoy one another's company on holiday. But that was then and this is different so don't, *don't* try anything on. Is that clear?'

You bloody hypocrite, Felicity said to herself as Brendan began to work on her aching spine. *An hour after he turns up he's got you half naked on the bed. Think what you must look like with your arse sticking up and your tits bulging out under your arms. You're dying for it.*

No, I'm not. I can live without sex. It's not important to me.

You didn't think that on holiday, did you? You couldn't get enough of him then, could you? And his friend.

That's what holidays are for. This is real life. I've got the kids and Percy to cope with and lots of work to do and somehow I've got to find another au pair who has more brains than that miserable Swede and actually likes children. The last thing I need is sex.

Is it? Really? You've missed it, haven't you? Missed his big cock up you. Missed his tongue in your mouth and his mouth on your breasts. And his magic hands on your body. Like they are now.

But this is different.

Is it? He's making your pain go away and your nerves jangle and your skin glow and now you want—

No.

—fucking. Don't you?

No!

Yes, you do. Admit it.

No, no, no! Oh God, yes. Of course I do.

You horny cow.

Yes. Yes, I am.

'There, how's that?'

Brendan had worked all the way up Felicity's spine, cajoling her stiff tendons and freeing up the joints. He had finished off by folding her in a body-crunching embrace until, with an unexpected twist of his arms, her last vertebra had clicked loose.

Now she felt as if she were floating in the air, her mind and body freed of their habitual tension. Even the dialogue playing in her head had ceased. She didn't care that she lay on her side, her breasts lolling and her bottom almost completely exposed. She didn't care about her domestic anguish. She didn't care how or why this marvellous Irish boy had appeared again in her life like a saviour.

But she did care, fiercely, that he shouldn't leave her alone just now. That he should see to her every need. That his thrilling fingers should remain on her tingling skin to rove at will, to cup and squeeze her big dangling breasts, to lay bare her thrusting buttocks and plunge into the wet warm cavern between.

He did not let her down.

When he was finished and her every atom was singing with contentment, he pulled the bedspread over her flushed body and, for the first time in months, she slept without a care in the world.

33

Percy plodded the half-mile from St Marchmont's station to his home with a heavy heart. Since the birth of Crispin he had worked in the spare office of a designer friend near St Pancras. The rent was negligible, the train journey short and he had been able to avoid the daily dramas of domestic strife that ate into his time when he used the study at home. At the end of the day, however, he returned to the bosom of his family with little expectation of domestic harmony. Felicity resented his absence, though she was never overjoyed by his presence, and since their blissful summer holiday things had got worse.

Tonight, Percy knew, there would be trouble. After a frustrating day grinding out his company history of Stamp & Mame, he'd gone for a drink. Only after it was too late to make the seven-fifteen train had he remembered that two of Flick's operatic friends were coming to dinner.

He put the key in the lock with dread and stepped into the house. Since Ingrid had walked out the week before the place had been littered with dressing-up clothes, junk models with flaking paint and up-ended boxes of jigsaws. So he gazed in surprise at the tidy hallway and the fresh flowers on the table. Of jigsaw pieces and stray toys there was no sign. And someone had replaced the blown bulb in the alcove lamp.

From the front room came the sound of a string quartet and in the air was the faint aroma of food being prepared – herbs and wine and roasting meat. He remembered he hadn't eaten all day.

A smiling woman in a scarlet sheaf dress cut low on the bust and tight on the hip emerged from the front room and kissed him. Her thick chestnut hair was loose over her creamy shoulders and she was warm and scented in his arms. For a split second he did not recognise his wife.

'Flick, I'm sorry. I got held up and missed the train. Tonight of all nights – I'm mortified. What can I do?'

'Calm down, Percy. There's no rush.'

'But don't you need me to clear up or make gravy or read to the kids or—?'

'Ssh, darling. Everything's under control. You go and freshen up. The Presleys won't be here for a few minutes.'

Percy climbed the stairs in a daze. What the hell had happened? Whatever it was, he was all in favour.

As he was about to step into the bedroom, he looked up the next flight of stairs and froze in disbelief. A young woman in a tight pink top and a black mini-skirt was standing outside Crispin's room, her ear pressed to the door. From this angle Percy had an unrestricted view up her bronzed and deliciously toned thighs. Percy remembered those thighs well – and what lay between them. He'd thought about this gorgeous blonde vision almost every night since he had returned from Italy but had never dreamed he would ever see her or her legs again. Or the wide pretty face that now turned to him, a finger pressed to her lips.

'He's just dropped off,' said Carol-Anne as she descended the stairs, her big blue eyes smiling.

He ushered her into the bedroom, his arm looping round her waist without conscious intent.

'Hiya, Perce,' she said and lifted her face to be kissed. Her tongue was in his mouth before he knew it.

'Good God,' he said as their mouths drew apart. 'What are you doing here?'

'Aren't you pleased to see me?'

'Pleased? I'm ecstatic.'

'Yeah, I can feel it,' she said, palming his stiffening cock through his trousers. 'Take it out and show me.'

'What?'

'Come on, Perce, don't play hard to get. Your guests aren't due for five minutes. Time for you to slip me a length.'

It was an utterly mad situation, Percy knew that. His brain was bursting with all sorts of questions that his sane, boring, workaday self needed an answer to. Like: is this glorious girl real? What's she doing here? Is she actually pulling her skirt up so I can fuck her? And: how long will I have left to live when Felicity walks in and catches me?

The Australian appeared to read his mind. 'It's OK, Perce. The kids are asleep and Brendan's in the kitchen with your wife. They'll be fixing up the hors d'oeuvres. Seize the moment, sport, and fuck my pussy. Or have you gone off me?'

He threw her backwards onto the bed and dived on top of her. Somehow her hand was in his fly and her tiny skirt was round her waist baring the long slim limbs he dreamed of nightly. His cock was hard and thick in her small hand and she was pressing the gleaming red head into the soft cleft at the base of her belly, tugging at him urgently as if she too could hardly believe her luck.

In a flash he was inside her and pumping, her supple body cleaving to him, her mouth on his and her fingers beneath his shirt. There was no time to savour the reunion, just time to grab and squeeze and fondle and thrust-thrust-thrust, his swollen length plundering her soft hairless nook in greedy juddering jolts as he lost all sense of time and place and, all too soon, erupted inside her.

For a moment they lay panting in a sticky heap on the ruined bed. It occurred to Percy it must have been all of ten minutes since he had walked into the house.

Downstairs the doorbell rang.

Later, when the asparagus and the roast lamb and the *tarte Tatin* had been washed down by Chablis and Fleurie and Armagnac, when the Bendicks mints had been scoffed and the coffee cups cleared and the dishwasher sent on its second merry cycle, when the Presleys had lurched cheerfully into the night, replete and impressed, Felicity and Percy lay side by side in bed and talked.

'It was a miracle,' said Felicity.

'Amen to that,' said Percy, 'but I still don't understand why they're here.

'Brendan was looking for you, he said. Something to do with that book you were writing on holiday.'

'Oh?' Percy tried to sound disinterested. 'That book' was a potentially dangerous subject – Felicity did not approve. But for once she was not interested in picking a fight.

'He just took over. Fixed my back, organised the children and rang up Carol-Anne to help out.'

'That was the best dinner party we've ever had.'

'And the children went to bed on time and the house was cleaned up.'

'Perhaps they should move in permanently.'

'You know, Percy, I was thinking that. But could we afford them?'

'If they took the load off you, you could earn some money to pay them. But frankly, Flick, they're worth their weight in gold. I've not seen you looking so happy since that holiday. Or looking so good either. You were lovely tonight.'

'You old shmoozer, Percy,' she said but she rubbed her cheek against his on the pillow. Then she sighed. 'They'll never go for it, though,' she said.

'Why not?'

'I don't think they get on that well. Brendan said they were just sharing a flat because they knew each other from Cascade. They wouldn't want to live in that little room upstairs.'

'How are they managing tonight then?'

'She's got a sleeping bag so I guess one of them is dossing down on the floor.'

'Oh,' said Percy, relieved by this information even though it spelt the end of his hopes for installing the pair on a long-term basis. He yawned and muttered, 'Goodnight, darling.'

'Goodnight,' she replied and wormed her hand into his. He squeezed it companionably.

Percy's last thought before he drifted into sleep was that he could still smell fucking in the air. Next to him, a smiling Felicity was thinking the same thing.

On the floor above, in the attic bedroom, two naked bodies were wedged together in the small bed, gently savouring the proximity of their most intimate flesh.

'You're a horny sod, Brendan O'Reilly,' said Carol-Anne, clasping his outsize erection in both hands. 'I bet you really enjoyed putting this wicked thing in her again.'

'Of course, I did. She's a glorious woman.'

'She's twice my size.'

'And twice as sexy. Ow! That was a joke. Now, are you going to put my cock somewhere safe or are you planning to pull it off?'

'I thought I might milk you all night, so you've nothing left to give our hostess in the morning.'

He chuckled and rolled her onto her back, his strong hands spreading her legs. 'If it's an all-night shag with me you're after then I guarantee you'll not be able to face Percy either.'

She tilted her pelvis to ease the passage of his big knob into her vagina and moaned in contentment as it slid all the way home. She wrapped her arms round his broad back and yielded to the spiral of lust that flickered upwards from her quivering belly. 'Do me quick then, Brendan. In this house I think we're both going to need our beauty sleep.'

He clasped her buttocks and began to thrust.

34

Publishing parties were not Miranda Lynch's favourite events. She didn't drink much and hated cigarette smoke and couldn't stand the shifting crush of half-sozzled nonentities. But, as an industry mover-and-shaker, she was obliged to play the game and now she had it down to a fine art. Stick to one glass of wine, only talk to important guests and leave within an hour of arrival – those were her rules.

Tonight she was cutting it fine. She had five minutes to go and she'd failed to stop a waiter topping up her glass. Her attention had been on a group of pinstriped men in the far corner, wreathed in cigar smoke. Dinosaurs, all of them, in her view – old-style publishers who treated the business like a horse race: back enough runners and you're bound to have a winner. Miranda despised that philosophy. To her, book publishing was a modern industry in which planning and method could eliminate risk, not a seat-of-the-pants skylark for indulgent amateurs like these chortling inebriates.

She approached the group, ignoring other invitations to chit-chat. She knew most of these men, she had even been employed by one or two in the distant past. Back then, of course, they had considered her perfect employee fodder – an eager workhorse with great legs. Too late they had discovered she had brains as well as a body. Now they feared her, though their admiration of her physical allure was undimmed. They knew she was the future of the industry and they were heading out to grass. And some of them were meant to be grazing full-time. Like her quarry, Basil Swan.

'Miranda, sweetheart, how wonderful to see you. You're looking as sexy as ever.'

'You, too, Basil darling,' replied Miranda giving him the benefit of her best teeth-and-eyes smile as she kissed both his smoothly shaved cheeks. Miranda knew how to go through the motions when she had to.

She took his arm and neatly cut him out from the herd. 'You've been avoiding me, Basil.'

'Never!' His bushy eyebrows shot upwards and his murky eyes bulged with sincerity. 'Miranda, you are the *last* person I would wish to avoid, I swear.'

'But I've been calling you for months.' Miranda couldn't keep the pique from her voice, the matter irritated her too much.

'Well, I have been frightfully busy recently. Been living like a hermit. This is my first party for yonks.' He grabbed a glass of wine from a passing waiter and downed half of it.

'We need to talk, Basil. I have a proposition for you.'

'How exciting. Why don't you ring my assistant and we'll fix something up.' His eyes were already gazing over Miranda's shoulder, looking for an avenue of escape.

'I have called your assistant dozens of times, Basil, and frankly she is downright rude.'

'Really? Lorna? I'm most surprised. I'll get her over.'

He raised his hand to wave to a tall girl with a mop of henna-ed hair who was giggling amongst a group of low-grade editorial pond life. Miranda's surprise was momentary. She had wondered why the voice on Basil's phone was familiar.

'I didn't know Lorna Prentice was working for you.'

'Oh yes, marvellous girl. I took her on at Whimsical, you know, so I was only too keen to give her a berth when you kicked her out. Big mistake, if you ask me. That girl's going far.'

'Not if she can't pass on a simple message.'

'Ah, well, I will have words with her—'

'Don't bother, Basil. Just tell me when we can meet. How about now? I'll buy you dinner.'

'Sorry, Miranda, I'm booked.'

'Tomorrow morning then. I'll come to your house at eleven.'

'I say, Miranda, you are persistent. You make a fellow seem truly desired.'

She stepped closer to him so he was backed into the corner. 'You *are* desired, Basil,' she replied and enjoyed the starburst of surprise in his big watery eyes as she palmed his crotch.

'Miranda! Good God!'

'There's only two ways to get your attention, Basil. And this is one of them.' She fondled the expanding bulge in his trousers.

'And what's the other?'

'A deal, of course. The deal we're going to talk about at eleven tomorrow morning.'

'Basil!' A woman's voice intruded from behind Miranda. 'Let's go. I booked the table for half an hour ago.'

Miranda turned to look into the face of Lorna Prentice. 'Hello, Lorna,' she said, her voice warm.

'Hello, Miranda.' Lorna didn't sound quite so enthusiastic.

'You'll be delighted to hear I've finally managed to pin Basil down to a meeting. Thanks so much for all your assistance. I'll leave him in your hands now.' And she stepped back so Lorna could appreciate the sight of Basil standing with embarrassment on his face and an enormous hard-on straining at his trousers.

'You told me you hated her,' snarled Lorna. 'You said she was poison – the biggest bitch in the entire book business. You're a two-faced bastard, Basil Swan.'

'Calm down, Lorna. There's no need to blow this out of proportion.'

'Your bloody cock was out of proportion, Basil. That's the point. How could you?' And she burst into tears.

They were sitting in Basil's BMW, supposedly en route to Chez

Adolfo after the party. But they hadn't moved an inch before Laura's outburst began.

Basil let her snivel into his shoulder and hugged her tight. 'Look, my darling, I've been doing my best to avoid her, as you know. But I couldn't duck her tonight.'

'But why did you have an erection? You fancy her, don't you? I bet you had an affair and now she wants you back and you're going to chuck me and I'll have to find another job —'

Basil shut her up in the time-honoured fashion. As they kissed, the tension began to ebb from the slim body in his arms. He stroked her hair and slipped a hand inside her coat to find the gentle curve of her small breast. He took his mouth from hers and gently licked the tears from her cheeks.

'You silly, lovely, adorable girl. Believe me, I've never had an affair with that witch and I swear I'll never let you go. You can work for me for as long as you like, I promise. I think I'm the luckiest, happiest old publishing fart there's ever been to have such a passionate and sexy girl prepared to let me make love to her like this – and this – and this . . .'

Basil had had a long experience of women and knew just when to let them shout and scream, when to fold their trembling bodies in his arms and when to take their clothes off. He was very good at all these things and within seconds, it seemed, Lorna's supple coltish body was bared beneath the warmth of her winter coat. Fortunately Basil had also had the presence of mind to put the heating on.

He slipped to the floor between her legs, wedging his bulk with surprising agility into the space in front of the passenger seat. For the millionth time in recent months he congratulated himself on having taken his health in hand last summer.

Beneath her coat Laura's breasts were naked, the nipples dark and wet with his saliva. Her frock had been raised to her waist and he lifted her apple-cheeked bottom to slip her panties down her slender legs. The black muff of her curls was soft on his cheeks as he bent to kiss the pouting mouth of her pussy, slicking the length of her cleft with his tongue.

He leaned back and released his cock. It looked huge in the small space, broad and veined and thick as a club. Basil felt a surge of masculine pride as he pulled it into the open, easing his full balls out of his trousers as well. A memory of what used to happen in situations like this flashed into his head. He banished it swiftly, negative sex images and thrusting erections were not compatible in his experience. He focused on the succulent and gleaming split of flesh spread before him and prepared to take his pleasure.

She stopped him.

'Basil, I . . .'

Her large green eyes implored. There was still doubt in her mind. An unanswered question that Basil knew he'd have to address in the end. Fortunately, he'd now thought of how to do it.

'You want to know why I had a hard-on, don't you?'

'Yes!'

'While I was talking to Miranda I remembered what you'd told me about your last day at Whimsical.' He lifted her thighs, folding her legs into her body. 'How you'd seduced my nephew in the boardroom.' Obligingly she took her knees in her hands and drew her legs back, thrusting her softly furred and glistening pubis up from the seat. 'I was thinking about you dancing on the table for him. And how you fucked him where Miranda sat. And it turned me on.'

'I'll dance for you one day,' she murmured, spreading her gleaming divide for him and welcoming his swollen member deep into her butter-soft folds. 'If you'd like that.'

He didn't reply, he let his rejuvenated cock do the talking and fucked her like a teenager.

Basil's car had good suspension. It was just as well.

35

The morning after the dinner party Percy did not wake up till ten. This was extraordinary. Nobody in a household containing three children under six sleeps till ten – unless they have help. As Percy blinked at the digital clock on Felicity's – empty – side of the bed, he remembered they did indeed have help. And he remembered precisely the kind of help that had been given to him on this bed the evening before.

He was instantly struck by guilt. To have made love to Carol-Anne here on the marital bed while his wife and children were in the same house filled him with remorse. How foul and bestial his nature was! Though he had been unfaithful on holiday, that had been far away and under extraordinary circumstances – in researching a book an author was surely allowed some artistic licence.

But that was then and things were different now. For all the talk last night of persuading Carol-Anne and Brendan to stay, it must not be allowed to happen. It would be grossly unfair to Felicity. The moral fall from grace of the previous evening must never ever be allowed to take place again.

The door opened and Carol-Anne came in, bearing a tea tray.

'Morning, Percy,' she said, placing the tray on the bedside table and drawing the curtains. 'Felicity reckoned you'd be surfacing about now. I hope I didn't wake you.'

'No,' he said, quite devastated by the sight of her. She poured his tea and sat companionably on the side of the bed. Her face was in shadow but her big eyes gleamed and her white teeth shone as she smiled at him. The pale winter sun behind her lit up her hair in a golden halo. 'You're such a beautiful girl,' he said, his voice mournful with his impending loss.

'Thanks. I guess you'd like to see a bit more of me in that case.' And without waiting for an answer she pulled her top over her head and reached behind her back to unfasten her bra.

'No, no!' cried Percy – in his mind. From his mouth there issued just a feeble croak of surprise. And lust.

Carol-Anne maintained her pose, both hands behind her back, thrusting forward her full round bosom which was encased in a white semi-transparent bra. 'Here's the big moment,' she said. 'Perhaps I should make you wait until you've drunk your tea.'

'Carol-Anne, I . . .'

'Yeah, I know. You want to do it yourself, don't you?' And she leaned forward and rested her forearms on his shoulders, her little snub nose pressing on his large one, her hair falling around his face. In disobedience of all resolutions his hands rose to span her narrow waist and slide upwards along the firm glowing flesh of her back to find the flimsy strap of her brassiere. She chuckled, her breath blowing directly into his mouth, as he discovered only warm skin.

'I undid it anyway, figured you were out of practice,' she murmured as his hands travelled round her ribcage to close on the hanging fruits of her breasts, each globe filling his palm with a soft and precious weight.

'Oh,' he grunted with the thrill of holding her tits and the sudden sensation of her tongue corkscrewing between his lips.

She slipped one arm round his neck and her other burrowed beneath the bedclothes.

'Oh yeah,' she murmured as her fingers closed on his burning erection. 'I think I'm gonna bring you breakfast in bed every morning. Move over, Percy, I'm getting in.'

'But, Carol-Anne, you can't. We mustn't. What about—?'

'Felicity?' She sat back on the bed and looked at him for a

moment. Her brassiere had slipped down one arm and her round pneumatic breasts pointed at him, the nipples swollen and pink. Her hand ringed the base of his cock which thrust up from his belly like an extra limb.

'Felicity and Brendan have taken Crispin to a swimming lesson. Then they're going to the park.'

'Oh.' Relief flooded over him. He couldn't help thinking that at least he'd have the morning in bed with Carol-Anne before saying goodbye for good.

'So,' she continued, moving her hand up and down his shaft in a slow delicious wanking motion. 'Don't tell me we can't because we can. Don't say you don't want to because I can see you do. But if you think it's unprofessional to fuck your live-in nanny and housekeeper say so right now.'

'What do you mean?'

'Gee, Perce, I thought you knew. Felicity said you discussed it last night. She's offered us the job and we've said yes.'

'Both of you?'

'Yeah – I think it's fantastic. You won't regret it, I promise, and neither will this guy here.' She dipped her head and took his knob into her mouth for a second. A flame of desire licked up his belly.

Her head came up, eyes blazing and lips smiling. She jumped off the bed and unzipped her skirt. 'As I say, Perce, if you have any objection to fucking your employees ...' She stepped out of the skirt and yanked her panties to mid-thigh. 'I mean, if you're uncomfortable having my tits and arse available to you at any time, day or night ...' She straddled his hips and reclaimed his shaft with one hand. The other delved between her thighs to spread her labia, revealing to him the coral pink of her succulent interior. '... You've only got to say so.'

She spread juice from her pussy onto the head of his tool and poised herself over it.

'Well?' she said.

'No,' said Percy, his emotional U-turn completed by the

inflammatory sight of his cock disappearing into the hairless mouth of her vagina, 'I've no objection at all.'

'Ohhh Brendan, that feels glorious,' moaned Felicity as his hands manipulated her back. 'You know all the right spots, don't you?'

That I do, Brendan thought to himself as he looked down at the nude woman spread out beneath him, his to treat as he wished. Felicity lay face down on the bed with a pillow under her loins, thrusting her glorious white buttocks high and wide. He too was naked, kneeling up between her spread thighs, his tool half embedded in the back-thrust purse of her vagina. It was a highly pleasurable position for both parties.

Brendan pushed his thumbs into the creamy dimpled flesh on either side of her spine and heard the sharp intake of breath as the discomfort bit. He butted his pelvis forward a fraction and noted with satisfaction her answering sigh of pleasure as his penis slid deeper inside her. She was putty in his hands.

They'd had a very successful morning playing with Crispin, now it was Carol-Anne's turn to give the toddler lunch and put him to bed for a nap. Which gave Brendan the opportunity to continue his treatment of Felicity's aches and pains. He was determined to give his new employer unparalleled service.

'Oh! Oh! Oh!' she cried as his hands worked on her back and his cock thrust back and forth in the greedy mouth of her yearning pussy.

He finished massaging her neck and leaned back to savour the sight of her abundant flesh. From the waist up she was relaxed and de-stressed, her head pillowed on her arms, the luscious white undercurve of her breast bulging out from beneath her. But from the waist down she was a mass of jangling nerve-ends. Her incredible buttocks were jumping and quivering, her glistening pink pussy lips were gorging on his shaft and even the brown star of her anus appeared to wink with desire. Felicity vocalised the need that was so evident – 'Fuck me, Brendan, please! Stuff it up me hard.'

'Anything you say, Mrs Carmichael,' the Irishman replied and slammed his tool all the way home. Felicity groaned with pleasure. And when, a few minutes later, he transferred his cock to her arsehole and his magic fingers began to tickle her clit, she howled loud enough to be heard across the street.

One floor down, Percy Carmichael sat in his study, doodling on a foolscap pad. He didn't seem to be able to get his thoughts around the tedious history of Stamp & Mame just at present. He was thinking of sex. Of the absence of it for years, of the wonder of it in sudden abundance. Of the golden limbs of Carol-Anne twined around his own, her hot mouth on his and her velvet cunt kissing his cock. The smell of her pussy was on his fingers as he absent-mindedly scratched his nose.

From above came the sound of Felicity moaning. Her back must be really bad, poor thing. How fortunate that Brendan was a skilled masseur. Felicity cried out again, with a rising note that recalled to Percy more intimate times with his wife. He tried to shake the thought from his head. He seemed to have sex on the brain at present. In which case ...

He turned to a fresh page on his pad and wrote: 'Max Daventree's penis swelled beneath the thin fabric of his swimming trunks as he contemplated the swollen halves of his wife's sumptuous bikini-clad bottom. How he longed to rip the wet panties from her flesh and explore the line that divided her pouting rear cheeks.' Yes! Inspiration had struck. He'd dash off another sexy novel for Lucian Swan and stuff Stamp & bloody Mame. It would be about the dirty deals that must be struck to keep a marriage alive. He could call it *The Bottom Line* ...

As he scribbled feverishly, images of pulsing cocks and wobbling breasts scudding like fast-moving clouds across his mind's eye, he silently acknowledged his debt to Brendan. The Irishman had turned up the day before with the idea of helping Percy with a new book – 'I've done tons more research,' he'd said –

and Percy had laughed at the notion. Yet here he was, a few hours later, actually writing it. Brendan was a miracle-worker, no doubt about it. Perhaps when he had fixed Flick's back he could give her a game of tennis, squire her around the local antique fairs and escort her to a matinee or two – activities that Percy never had time for. And if Brendan could help Felicity relax a little then maybe husband and wife could put some real love back into their marriage. Now that *would* be a proper miracle.

'Oh God! Oh, sweet Jesus! Oh, oh yes!' howled Felicity from above as Percy's pen flew across the page.

36

It was only the second time Miranda Lynch had had a man's cock in her mouth and, as she shifted uncomfortably on her knees on the floor of Basil Swan's office, she swore it would be her last. Some twelve years had spanned the two events and, in her opinion, time had not improved the experience. The first occasion had been at university, with a rugger-bugger boyfriend who had insisted she fellate him on pain of chucking her the night before the May ball. After she had allowed him to maul her hair and jab his thin dick in and out of her face for what seemed like hours, she had done the chucking. She had counted that as her first act as an independent woman.

Perhaps that was what was so galling about sucking Basil's prick – the memory of being subjugated by a man. Miranda did not have a high opinion of the trousered sex. Most of them were fawning little boys, blinded by their own self-importance and too scared to take hard decisions. At bottom, all they wanted was to squirt their juices into a woman and take the applause.

'Ouch!' yelled Basil as Miranda's jaw closed on the bursting flesh in her mouth.

'Sorry,' she said, lifting her lips from the bobbing shaft, 'I'm a bit out of practice.'

'I'll say you are, my sweet. Why don't you kiss it there? Mmm, that's it. Now lick gently all the way up to the tip and open those pretty pink lips of yours. Oh yes, that's lovely!'

Miranda forced herself to comply. Much as she wanted to

wrench this throbbing broom-handle of flesh from her lips and squeeze the big hairy balls in her hand until his pips burst, she kept herself under control. She wasn't doing this for the fun of it. She mustn't spoil it now.

Basil had opened the door to her at eleven sharp that morning and ushered her graciously into a book-lined room overlooking a sumptuous back garden, flecked with winter frost. He had offered her coffee and made her welcome in a manner that suggested she were the person he most wanted to see in the whole world at that moment. Miranda wasn't to be deflected from her purpose, however – she'd gone straight for the jugular.

'We've turned up some discrepancies in the accounts from your time at Whimsical. Signature advances paid out on books that were never published and the money never repaid.'

'How annoying, darling,' Basil said, crunching into a biscuit. 'Fact of publishing life. Happens all the time.'

'It's still unacceptable. Particularly something like this,' and from her briefcase she produced a legal-looking document. 'This is the contract for "*My Lucky Lucky Life*, a memoir of an East End childhood by Adeline Summer". Fifteen thousand pounds was paid on signature eight years ago. Since then, no typescript has been delivered and no money refunded. Am I right in thinking that Adeline Summer is your aunt?'

'Indeed. Dear Aunty Adeline had a rare talent as a writer. Unfortunately she died before she could complete the book. A reasonable excuse, I'm sure you'll agree.'

'What about this one? Eighteen thousand pounds paid on signature for a biography of Tania Tingle by Georgina Swan. It's the same story – no delivery and no refund of the advance. Georgina's your daughter, isn't she?'

'And a freelance journalist of some repute. Unfortunately Tania Tingle overdosed before she could give Georgina the access she needed to write the book.'

'Don't you find this a little embarrassing, Basil – over thirty thousand pounds missing from our accounts and paid to members of your family? It's not something I can overlook.'

'What's your point, exactly, Miranda? And what's this deal you mentioned to me last night?'

Miranda's perfect pink lips flirted with a smile. At last she was getting somewhere.

'Let me tell you about a sensational novel we will be publishing next spring. I believe the author would be the ideal recipient of the Baxendale Prize.'

'Ah.'

So there it was, out in the open. The mention of the most coveted literary award in the publishing calendar clarified the picture for both parties.

'Why do you assume I have any say in the matter?' said Basil.

'Because you're the chairman of the panel of judges. Don't deny it.'

'What's the book?'

'*A Novelist's Wife* by Karen Hastings. The lead title in our new imprint, Blue Desire.'

'One of Lucian's porno books! You can't be serious.'

'I am, Basil. It's a magnificent, ground-breaking novel which validates one woman's emotional needs through the language of sex. It's going to be a sensation anyway but the Baxendale would give it just that aura of literary respectability which would make it a bestselling phenomenon. It might be possible to write off the thirty-three thousand pounds you owe us from the publishing profit.'

Basil thought for a moment. He looked grave.

'The panel is made up of five people. One voice won't carry it.'

'You'll find a way. I've seen you in action. You're a very clever manipulator of events.'

Basil's pale eyes focused on the white silk hillocks pushing against the ash grey of Miranda's business suit.

'You feel passionately about this book, don't you?'

'I do indeed.'

'I'd like a demonstration of that passion. How about taking your clothes off.'

'What?'

'As I remember from last night, Miranda, you said that sex was one way to get my attention. Right now I'm all yours.'

'You slimeball.'

'We *are* discussing a sex book, aren't we? The *Sturm und Drang* of fuck and suck in which, I assume, women show their naked bodies to men. Let me have a look at yours.'

Miranda crashed her fist onto the contracts lying on the desk. 'Your family owes us a significant sum of money. You have a week to pay or I'll start proceedings.'

Basil grinned at this display of indignation. 'Come off it, Miranda. Thirty grand is not the issue.' He pointed to a glass-panelled bookcase on the opposite wall. 'A handful of first editions from my collection would raise that money in no time. If you want me to use my influence in your cause you'll have to come up with something unique. Like your beautiful body.'

Miranda pursed her lips. This was the moment of truth. Despite her blatant approach to Basil the night before, she did not find him in the least desirable. But she had not lied about her feelings for Karen's book and, what's more, she saw it as the salvation of The Whimsical Press. How she would enjoy flaunting its success before her be-jowelled and be-suited competitors! But first she must bring home the Baxendale.

She stood and shrugged off her jacket. As her fingers slipped the tiny pearl buttons of her blouse through the eyelets she thought of Karen Hastings debasing herself in the name of artistic expression. She even remembered, as she stepped out of her skirt to display her remarkable dancer's legs, Lucian's sacrifice as he tongued the vagina of a buxom journalist beneath a restaurant table to clinch a serial deal. If author and editor were prepared to give their all, then she should be too.

'Faabulous!' drawled Basil as Miranda stood before him stark-naked. 'You're even more beautiful than I imagined.' He pushed his chair away from his desk and leaned back, his hands clasped behind his head. Miranda's eyes were drawn to the bulge in his trousers. It was immense.

'Now, darling, walk around the room for me. I want to admire your movable parts.'

Miranda walked – what else could she do? As she did so, she could feel her sizable breasts in motion with each step and her bottom cheeks, small and boyish as they were, flexing and undulating. She shivered under Basil's lecherous gaze, her nipples puckering. She blushed. Basil's lewd commentary did nothing to alleviate her discomfort.

'Well, well, Miranda, you *are* a sight for sore eyes. Come closer and stand in front of my chair. What big bouncy tits you've got for such a slim girl. And I just adore the blonde curls on your pussy. Open up so I can get a good look. Come on, use your fingers. It's a bit late to be shy.'

To her shame she did as he requested, standing with legs apart and spreading her labia to show him the pink stripe of her split. Then he commanded her to perform sundry small salacious acts for his pleasure. Like fluffing out her bush and pulling back the hood of her clit, putting her finger inside herself and wetting the length of her crack with it.

Then, at his bidding, she turned round and bent forward to thrust her bottom back into his face. He made her spread apart her buttocks and show him the dimple of her most secret hole and while she did that he leant and put his face into the fissure of her gaping cheeks. His hands came round to grasp the weight of her hanging breasts and he squeezed them like a farmer milking a cow as his tongue flickered over the lips of her quim, setting her nerves aflame. And just when she was at the brink of the ultimate humiliation, an orgasm on his loathsome tongue, he stopped and ordered her to suck his penis.

And now she was gorging herself on his fleshy stalk, caressing the plum of his glans with tongue and palate and working her hand up and down his shaft. It was thick and firm in her face, harder and stronger than she could ever have imagined it would be. And big. Bigger than most male equipment though, if truth be told, she had had no dealings with erect cocks in many years. The thought of it invading any of her other orifices was terrifying. If only she could make him come then she might avoid that fate.

'Ugh!' he cried suddenly, then 'Ugh, ugh!' again as his hands, wrapped in her hair, jerked her head into his steaming crotch and his mighty erection shot gouts of salty come deep into her mouth. She tried to pull away but he held her fast, thrusting and pumping his tool into her face until his balls were empty. Then he slumped back in his chair.

She was on her feet in a flash and scrabbling for her clothes. He seemed to have deposited a pint of semen over her. It was in her hair and running down her chest and the taste was thick in her mouth. As she pulled on her knickers they stuck to her thighs.

'Don't run off, darling,' he drawled. 'Give me ten minutes and I'll be ready again, wait and see.'

'I've got to go Basil. I'm late.'

'But *I've* only just come. Ha-ha!' His laugh was revolting to her. She wanted only the drumming of hot water in her ears and the feel of soft soap on her skin as she cleansed herself of Basil Swan.

'Before you go, sweetheart, I've just remembered something. It came to me while you were gobbling my tool with such vigour. Not the best blow-job I've ever had, to be candid, but not bad for someone so obviously rusty. We'll have to work on your technique.'

'Cut it out, Basil. That's all you're getting and you know it. That's the bargain.'

'Well, actually . . .' He looked at her with such self-satisfaction that her fingers stopped in the act of buttoning her blouse. 'That's what I wanted to tell you. I remembered that we salvaged what there was of Aunt Adeline's memoirs and put them out as *I've Never Seen a Straight Banana* under the pseudonym of A Cockney Sparrow – you probably didn't look under that title. And we cancelled the Tania Tingle book when she died because the market was flooded. We agreed Georgina could keep the proportion of signature money she'd invested on travel and research. Which was – I came across the correspondence recently, yes, here it is – seventeen thousand four hundred pounds. She sent back the six hundred as you can see.'

Basil offered Miranda a piece of paper which she snatched from his hand. It was a letter signed by the former financial director of Whimsical, a Basil puppet as she well knew, which confirmed what he had just said.

'Our agreement still stands,' she insisted.

Basil shrugged. 'It's hard to see how.'

'Stick to it, you bastard, or I'll tell the press what you've been up to.'

'What! That you attempted to bribe me by showing me your minge and putting my cock in your mouth? Go ahead, my dear, it will do my reputation a world of good.'

'I'll tell your wife!' she screamed but the threat was hollow and they both knew it. Sophie Swan had no illusions about Basil.

'I'll tell you what you can do, darling. Come round the same time next week – it's Lorna's morning off, you see. Dress up a little bit, I'm sure Whimsical will foot the bill for some sexy stockings and suspenders. You can economise on knickers. Then we'll discuss the matter further.'

'Never!'

'But I've a meeting with my Baxendale colleagues in the interim. Very hush-hush. Whisper not on pain of death etcetera. But I might whisper to you if you bend over my desk and let me put my willy up your pretty arse.'

The door slammed behind Miranda with enough force to rattle the glass on all the bookcases.

37

As Miranda strode in fury down the drive of Basil's house she realised she was stranded. Basil lived deep in the heart of London's leafy western suburbs, some distance from the nearest railway station. She had arrived by cab and had intended to ask Basil to call another before departure. In the circumstances she could hardly return and request the favour.

As she stood at the end of the drive, with the winter wind blowing flecks of snow into her face, the poop of a car horn made her look over her shoulder. A woman with shoulder-length russet hair was smiling at her through the open window of a smart navy convertible. It took her a moment to realise who it was – Sophie Swan, Basil's wife.

'You must be Basil's eleven o'clock,' she said. 'Can I give you a lift?'

Miranda hesitated, her thoughts in turmoil. She'd only met Sophie once or twice and obviously the woman hadn't recognised her. Considering that her clothes were in disarray and she was covered in Basil's spunk, it might be best to find her own way out of this salubrious wilderness.

'Good Lord,' said Sophie, 'it's Miranda Lynch. Hop in.'

So that solved that problem.

In the car Miranda began to shiver violently. Sophie was suggesting that, as she was going into town, she could drop Miranda near her office when she noticed her passenger's condition.

'I'm OK,' said Miranda.

'You're not. You've either got flu—'

'No, no. I'm fine.'

'—or you've been tussling with Basil. Did he – touch you?'

'It's OK, Sophie, honestly. It's just a reaction to – I mean—'

'Don't say a thing, Miranda. I understand how you feel. And I'm going to make you feel a damn sight better.'

Sophie Swan was as good as her word. She parked in a private bay behind a large house on the embankment and led Miranda into what looked like a hotel.

'We're going upstairs, Mathilde,' she said to a pretty flaxen-haired girl behind a reception desk and scribbled something in a leather-bound book.

'Number ten, madam,' said the girl and handed over a key with a smile. It occurred to Miranda that Sophie was well known in this place.

She watched in a daze as Sophie led her into a high-ceilinged bedroom which looked across the river, the water a silver grey in the winter sun. Sophie left her to admire the view and bustled through another door – a bathroom – from whence came the sound of running water.

Miranda lay in the bath and bubbles popped beneath her chin. She tried to take stock of her situation and failed. For once she was not in control. She had a moment of panic.

Sophie appeared with a crystal glass full of a bubbling gin and tonic. Miranda, a one-unit-a-week girl, sank it in two gulps and sucked the lemon. Sophie brought her another. With an alcoholic glow in her stomach, Miranda allowed the other woman to wash her hair.

'Mathilde will fix it for you later,' she said as she wrapped Miranda in a towelling robe and ushered her to a sofa by the window where a lunch of steaming soup and smoked salmon sandwiches was waiting. They ate in silence and, for the first time

239

in recent memory, Miranda was hungry. She devoured all before her but refused Sophie's offer of further refreshment.

'So,' said Sophie, 'do you want to talk about it?'

It hadn't occurred to Miranda that she could possibly confide in Sophie. Apart from anything else, she would probably have to commit adultery with the woman's husband to get what she really wanted. To be precise, she might have to bend over Basil's desk wearing suspenders and stockings and allow him to plunder her arse. The image had been haunting her in the bath. So too the knowledge that, if it came to it, she would let him. Just so long as she got what she wanted in the end.

Sophie was talking. 'I imagine he propositioned you. He's always been susceptible to pretty women but it's got much worse since the operation.'

'The operation?'

'Yes. We went on this continental cruise but that was really a cover for the medical treatment they offered on board. Not everyone went in for it, of course, but there were lots of middle-aged men like Basil who'd lost their oomph, as it were.'

'Really?' Miranda was all ears.

'I know I shouldn't be telling you because Basil's very secretive about it. But I can see he's given you a bit of a shock and I'm trying to explain. He probably showed you that great big willy of his, didn't he?'

Miranda fought back the urge to say he had hosed her down with it as well and simply nodded.

'He's immensely proud of it but I can't say I'm thrilled. The damn thing never goes down these days. I was glad when he hired that girl who used to work for you.'

'Lorna.'

'She earns her wages. Some days, I swear, she's positively boss-eyed with bonking.'

A peal of merriment split the air. Miranda was amazed to find it came from her.

Sophie made a face. 'Sorry – that was a bit crude.'

'That's OK,' said Miranda. 'He can screw another hole in the little bitch for all I care. Oops, that's a bit crude too.'

'The funny thing is,' continued Sophie, 'when it wouldn't go hard, I felt insulted. Now it's hard all the time, I just lock the bedroom door. Frankly there are worse things than having a husband who can't do it.'

'Did he really have a lot of trouble before the, er, treatment?'

'My dear, I've got some wonderful stories. And so have other women too. He never stopped imagining he was Casanova even when he had a week-old stick of celery between his legs.'

'I'd like to hear some of those stories,' said Miranda, wheels turning in her mind.

There was a gentle tap on the door.

'Maybe later,' said Sophie. 'Here's Mathilde to do your hair.'

It was the flaxen-haired girl from downstairs. She carried with her a case full of accoutrements for female beautification. As she laid out her things on the table, Miranda became aware that Sophie was watching her every movement with rapt attention.

'Lovely, isn't she?' she said as Miranda caught her eye.

Miranda couldn't deny it. In the glow of the pale sunlight by the window, Mathilde's complexion was as flawless as glass and the blonde plait of her hair gleamed like silver rope.

The girl looked up, her eyes a startling turquoise. 'Would you like me to undress, madam?'

'Of course, Thilde. Do what you always do. My friend will enjoy it, I'm sure.'

Miranda was bemused but she watched closely nevertheless as Mathilde slipped out of her uniform jacket and began to unbutton her high-necked blouse. Underneath she wore a little cream camisole top which she pulled over her head and dropped on a chair. She wore no bra – she didn't need to. Her breasts were gently curving bowls which swelled into little peaks, the nipples cherry ripe and mouthwatering even to Miranda.

For ten years Miranda had fought shy of sexual contact with other human beings. It had been a decision she had never regretted. That way she avoided sticky patches on the sheets and someone else's laundry in her machine, not to mention heartache and the career-wrecking threat of children. She was never short of escorts or companions or – most important of all – time. She could work an eighty-hour week if she wanted to and she often did. And if she required the fleeting pleasures of an orgasm she could give herself one of those, too – not that she often did these days.

So, to find herself within the space of a few hours parading naked for a man, sucking his cock and, now, ogling another woman's breasts was a hammer blow to her system. Particularly the knowledge that she wanted those breasts in her hands.

Sophie had beaten her to it. She was stroking the creamy hillocks of flesh and pinching the tiny red points to hardness. Mathilde had stopped in the act of unfastening her skirt and now leaned against the older woman, her eyes closed and cheeks flushed, allowing her mistress to do with her as she pleased.

'This is all Basil's fault,' Sophie murmured as she bent to plant a kiss on the white tulip stem of the girl's neck. 'I can't stand any more of that jabbing, thrusting maleness. Men are so hard and coarse and hairy. Girls are soft and tender and sensual. Especially girls like Mathilde. Aren't you, darling?'

Mathilde didn't reply, she just raised Sophie's head with her hands and their lips met. Miranda watched in shock, a pulse hammering in her temple, as the two women kissed for a long, long minute.

Lights were dancing in Sophie's toffee-brown eyes as she turned to Miranda. She reached for the publisher's hand and placed it on the girl's right breast. The flesh was warm and pliant and the hard little nipple burned into her palm. The girl moaned as Miranda's fingers began to explore. She slumped onto the sofa next to Miranda and pulled her other hand to her bosom. Miranda looked into the girl's eyes. The blue depths were smoky with desire.

'You're very beautiful,' the girl murmured. 'May I make love to you?'

'I don't think—'

'Yes,' said Sophie firmly.

Mathilde drew Miranda's head down to her warm white breast.

'Show me how,' said Miranda as a cherry-sweet nipple invaded her mouth.

Within seconds Miranda's surrender was complete. Her robe was pulled off, she was laid naked on the bed and held fast in the kind of embrace she had never dared to dream of. She and Matilda rolled on the bed, slippery with juices from mouth and pussy, their compliant flesh on fire as they hugged and squeezed and probed. Mathilde was very skilled, her little fingers dancing across Miranda's body, her mouth skimming and caressing then biting, sending a current of excitement flaring along the publisher's nerves, awakening long-neglected circuits of pleasure.

'No, no, you mustn't,' she cried as the girl's lips skittered across her belly and small hands pried apart her knees. But her thighs spread and her pelvis lifted and her vagina opened like a blooming rose to the girl's caress and she came with indecent haste on Mathilde's pretty face. Then the girl did it to her again, each strange and wonderful orgasm like a present of new life.

Miranda swiftly passed from uncertain compliance to greedy assertion. The mysterious white body in her arms was delicious. It was like discovering a new taste and she couldn't get enough. She wanted to devour Mathilde whole and she did so – tonguing the velvet-lipped vagina and slaking her thirst on the girl's love juice till her jaw ached. And Mathilde shook and shivered in turn, twining her fingers in Miranda's hair, calling out in ecstasy as the woman rimmed her clitoris with the tip of her tongue.

At some point in this sensual storm, Miranda wondered how Mathilde could pleasure her in so many places at once, but with her head buried between the girl's legs and her senses ablaze she was in

243

no position to discover. And when the truth dawned on her, as a different perfume mingled in the air and heavier flesh pressed against her own, Miranda was past caring. A string of orgasms rippled through her body, bursting like stars in her head and she heard herself keening with delight in a way she had never done before. If Sophie Swan could do this to her then Miranda had no complaints.

Later, after Mathilde had gone, Miranda squeezed Sophie's hand and said, 'You seduced me. You're as bad as your husband.'

Sophie turned on her side and looked into Miranda's eyes. 'But I succeeded, didn't I? And he failed.'

'I'd like to know more about Basil's failures. You were going to tell me.'

'So I was.'

'Well then? Tell me about his limp celery days – and the operation.'

Sophie studied Miranda's face. 'Are you just out for revenge?'

'No. Leverage. To save my bottom.'

Sophie's brown eyes darkened. 'From Basil?'

'Yes.'

She chuckled. 'Can *I* have it instead?' and Miranda felt a hand slide down from her hip to cup the curve of her buttock.

Miranda shifted forward in the bed until her belly met Sophie's furry mound. 'It's all yours.'

Sophie smiled and her fingers began to play across the proffered cheeks. 'Well, then,' she said. 'Let me tell you all about our summer cruise on the *SS Augmentia* ...'

38

While his wife was introducing Miranda Lynch to a new world of sensual delight, Basil Swan was pondering the publisher's visit to his study that morning. It had given him much satisfaction to have her at his command and he looked forward to continuing this new relationship with barely containable excitement. So much so that his cock was already chafing uncomfortably in his pants. He was going to relish corking Miss Mealy Mouth's arse on this desk. In the meantime, he needed some relief.

'Lorna,' he yelled. The girl had only turned up ten minutes before, still looking sleepy-headed. What was the matter with youngsters these days? He had an idea how to wake her up.

'Yes, Basil,' she said, appearing obediently in the doorway. She looked ridiculously tempting in a tiny skirt over long black leggings, like a coltish ballet dancer.

'Come here,' he said, getting up from his seat and unbuckling his trousers.

'No, Basil,' she said as she noted the wolfish gleam in his eye. 'I'm not feeling in the mood today.'

'What's up, my darling? Come over here.'

She walked towards him with her eyes downcast. As Basil drew her into his arms he noticed the red marks on her neck.

'You little tart,' he murmured with delight. 'You've spent the morning bonking, haven't you?'

'Well, I – Charlie came back from his trip early. I hadn't seen him for ages.'

'You slut.' His hand was under her skirt, worming a way into the waistband of her leggings.

'He's my partner, Basil, and you're a married man. We both agreed that our friendship was something extra in our lives.'

'It is, darling.' He had stripped her leggings down her thighs now, her knickers too. Her bush was wet under his fingers. 'My, he must have been pleased to see you. You're dripping with spunk.'

'Basil, please! And don't denigrate my relationship with Charlie. I'm an independent woman and I'll have as many lovers as I like.'

'Absolutely, darling. Now, turn round and bend over the desk.'

'Not now, Basil. I don't want to.'

'Why are you rubbing my cock then?'

Lorna looked down. It was true, somehow her fingers were twined round Basil's brutish member, tugging the foreskin back and forth across the blazing scarlet head.

'God, Basil, I swear it's stiffer than ever. I don't know where you get your energy from.'

'Considering my age, eh? Well, that's my secret. Now bend over and stick your pretty bottom out, my dear. I need to cogitate.'

'What do you mean—OH! Basil, for God's sake!'

Lorna was quivering with indignation, her pale bottom cheeks too, as Basil's great club of a penis breached the divide of her arse. She squirmed and wriggled and tried to rise but his strong arms pinned her to the desk top.

'Just relax, sweetie, and let me get – ooh, that's it.'

'Aah!' squealed Lorna as Basil pushed his tool up her bottom like forcing a cork into a bottle.

'Mmm, delicious,' he muttered as he contemplated her skewered rear, the peachy pale moons of her buttocks cushioning his belly, the mouth of her rosehole sucking on the embedded shaft of his tool. He squirmed a hand beneath her body and began to finger her moist pussy slit. There was no longer any need to hold her down.

'Oh gosh,' she muttered as he found her twitching clit. 'Sometimes, Basil, your behaviour is impossible.'

'Lorna, you're beginning to sound like my wife. Now, shut up. You can imagine you're with Charlie or whoever you like but I've got something important to think about.'

It was Basil's habit to address knotty problems while engaged in leisurely sexual activity. During his reign at Whimsical many an ambitious editorial assistant had spent time on her knees beneath his desk or half undressed on the office sofa while he contemplated the business dilemmas of the day. It required a willing woman, of course, but Basil had always been wily enough to have one of those at his beck and call.

Now, as his right brain savoured the aesthetics of Lorna's well-plugged bottom, his left brain picked at the puzzle Miranda had posed: could he fix the Baxendale jury? Unlike other literary prizes, no unanimity of opinion was required. Three votes out of five would swing the decision. Which made the task a sight easier – if he were to take it on. Not that there was much doubt about that. Even apart from the pleasure of shafting Miranda on a regular basis, it was the kind of challenge Basil could not resist.

Beneath him Lorna was moaning in wordless pleasure, her head pillowed on her arms, her face hidden in a mass of red curls. Basil removed his hand from her crotch and replaced it with one of hers. Let her diddle her own pussy, his fingers were getting tired.

This year the Baxendale judging panel comprised of: a former publisher (himself); a liberal bishop; a youthful Yorkshire MP; an actress with a reputation; and an Irish poet. None of them, including himself, were likely to vote for a porno novel without some sort of inducement. The best kind, of course, would be that they adored the book. He imagined that that would not be likely. *The Novelist's Wife* wasn't bad – Miranda had left him a set of proofs and a quick perusal was one of the reasons Lorna's services had been required.

However, neither the bishop (for professional reasons) nor the poet (who was philosophically opposed to the entire reproductive process) could be expected to vote for a sex novel under any circumstances.

Which left the MP and the actress. In former times, Basil could simply have promised them huge advances for their memoirs or bottom-drawer novels. That would be more tricky now as he no longer controlled a publishing company. But there were other things he did control. Like people.

Lorna's arse was flexing and rippling on his rock-hard pole as she played with herself. He admired the hollowing of her cheeks as she strained to get more of him inside her bum and then the swelling of her pretty moons as she buffeted the globes back into his belly – faster and faster until –

He allowed the wails of her orgasm to subside before picking up the phone and punching in the number of The Whimsical Press. By the time he had his nephew on the line, Lorna had lapsed once more into a gentle gyration on his rigid penis.

'What can I do for you, Uncle Basil?' said Lucian.

'It's what I can do for you, dear boy. How would you like to meet Henrietta Suckling?'

'The nympho actress? You're not handling her autobiography, are you?'

'Not at present but who knows? I take it you like her.'

'I had her picture on my locker at school. She used to be a stunner.'

'She still is. As you will discover for yourself.'

'Sounds good, uncle. I say, what's that funny noise at your end?'

'That's next door's dog – they've shut him in the garden. I'll be in touch about Henrietta, dear boy,' and he replaced the phone just as Lorna howled her way to another climax.

'God, you've got a bloody cheek,' she protested when she'd caught her breath. 'No one's ever made a phone call while fucking me before. And that remark about the dog ...'

Basil pulled his cock from her bottom and watched with interest as the pink fissure of her anus slowly shrank into a tidy little pucker. How remarkable the female body was.

'What are your politics, my dear?'

'My *politics*!' She looked at him over her shoulder in astonishment. He stood behind her, his gleaming cock still as stiff as a post.

'Put it another way – what do you think of Hartley Smythe?'

'The MP with the blond hair? The one who's on all the smart-aleck quiz shows?'

'Do you fancy him?'

Her eyes narrowed as she thought about it.

Basil took a large handkerchief and began to wipe his cock.

'Your silence speaks volumes,' he said. 'How would you like to add him to your list of admirers?'

'He's got a wife. She's gorgeous – I've seen pictures.'

'But she's in Yorkshire with four children. No, don't get up, my dear, that position really suits you. The thing is, Smythe is in town and so are you.'

'Are you pimping for me, Basil?.'

'Don't be vulgar, darling. I'm planning a little publishing intrigue. And, looking at you now, I can tell you'll be perfect for what I have in mind. You really have the most delicious bottom.'

'Basil, you're wicked.'

'So you're interested?'

'Of course I am – he's a dish. But, Basil, are you going to stand there all day polishing your cock while I lie here with my fanny on offer?'

Basil chuckled and ran a hand over her out-thrust posterior. The fascinating divide between her cheeks promised a feast of delights and, indeed, his appetite was far from assuaged. He ran a finger down her split to the dark-fringed mouth of her neglected vagina.

'Ooh, yes!' she breathed and wriggled at his touch as if she were trying to capture his digit between the pouting lips. 'Put it in me,

Basil, please. Put that big thing up my pussy and tell me what obscene and filthy things I'm going to have to do!'

As Basil felt the kiss of her quim on the glowing plum of his tool he sighed with satisfaction, his faith in the younger generation restored. For an independent woman, Lorna really was extremely obliging.

Basil's good humour evaporated that evening when he took a call from Miranda Lynch.

'My precious, how delightful to hear from you so soon. My loins have been desolate since you left.'

'Spare me your oily witticisms, Basil. I've just discovered a few things about you that deserve a wider audience —'

'What things?'

'—and I shan't hesitate to broadcast them unless I can count on your support in that matter we discussed this morning.'

'You can indeed, Miranda. I have plans afoot. I was intending to fill you in on them when we had our next little tryst.'

'There won't be any trysting between us. And if you ever lay a finger on me again I shall take great pleasure in talking to the press about your summer cruise on the *SS Augmentia*.'

'Are you threatening me?'

'Call it what you like, Basil, but I have chapter and verse on the operation to revive your fading virility, not to mention the names and numbers of several women who personally witnessed the need to have it carried out.'

'That's outrageous. It's true that I had a medical condition which required some attention but I am fully recovered now – as you can testify.'

'Please yourself, Basil. I'm lunching the gossip columnist of the *Daily Dog* tomorrow and I'm sure she'll be fascinated by the antics of a respected elder statesman of our industry. Not to say highly amused. Particularly by the account I've heard of your trip to Paris last Easter with a secretary called Mandy Proffit. I'm told she felt very let down by your performance. Fancy trailing her in and out of all the sex clubs on the rue St Denis and still not being able to maintain an erection.'

'That's a lie. She's a vicious little tart who'll say anything to make money.'

'Probably. She's spent the grand you gave her to keep quiet about it and I imagine she'd love to talk to the *Dog* if there's any way it could help reduce her credit-card bills. As would Fenella Fleetwood or Mitzi Playfair or Brenda George—'

'Hang on, Miranda. Please don't rush into anything. These are entirely scurrilous accusations and there's really no need to make them public. I can assure you that I am pursuing the, er, business we discussed this morning as a matter of priority.'

'I see.'

'And the remarks about you wearing suspenders and stockings were, of course, just a little joke.'

'As was the threat to sodomise me on your desk?'

'*Yes!* Honestly.'

'I see. In that case I can probably postpone my lunch with the *Dog* for a week or two. Let's say until the New Year. Would that give you enough time to move things along?'

'Oh definitely. In fact I was planning a New Year's Eve party at which matters might come to a head. You will attend, won't you?'

'Maybe. If your wife invites me.'

Now what the hell does she mean by that? wondered Basil as he replaced the phone.

Suddenly this Karen Hastings' book was no longer an amusing diversion. He'd better make damn sure New Year's Eve went with a swing.

39

As he munched the last mince pie, Percy's eyes were drawn to the sprig of mistletoe hanging from the sitting-room ceiling. After six hours on the motorway, returning from the annual Christmas sojourn with Felicity's mother, he was knackered. But the mistletoe jogged his memory and one part of him at least suddenly became frisky.

In the week before Christmas, with the kids on holiday, Percy had not had a chance to get Carol-Anne on her own. Except once – on the night before the trip up north when the children were in bed and Brendan was treating Felicity's back. Percy had whisked Carol-Anne beneath the dangling white berries and wished her the happiest of Christmases.

She had returned the sentiment. Not in words as such, her lips and tongue being busy with the traditional mistletoe greeting, but in the way she pulled his Yule log from his trousers and caressed it with her two small hands. Percy had explored beneath her loose cotton shirt, liberating her breasts from their push-up prison and rolling the berry-red pips of her nipples between his fingers.

It was two days before Christmas and Percy's spirits were so festive that he had spunked off into Carol-Anne's hand even as he was planning to remove her tights and adjourn the celebrations to the sofa. In the event, he still took her tights off and, kneeling in a little pool of his own making, tongued her vagina till her knees gave way.

At least I come more often than Christmas these days, he said to

252

himself as Felicity entered the room. Had she noticed the stain on the carpet yet? he wondered. He intended to blame it on a child's mishap with a glass of milk.

'I bet I know what you're muttering, Percy.'

'What's that?'

'What you always say when we get home from my mother's – thank Christ we don't have to do that again for another year.'

'Do I really, Flick? I thought we all had a good time.'

It was true. It had gone much more sweetly than usual. The old girl had been in fine fettle, the rest of the in-laws had been a good laugh and the kids had been delightful. More to the point, Felicity had been in sunny spirits the entire time. It made all the difference – especially to the way she looked. Even now, after the long journey, she looked quite scrumptious in her tight grey sweater with her hair flowing loose. Percy eyed her firm rounded thighs, exposed beneath her skirt as she sat curled up on the easy chair, and a nostalgic shudder ran through him. Time was, before they had children, they would screw like rabbits throughout the entire holiday.

He raised his gaze from her legs. She was looking at him, her eyes glistening like green stones. How was it he had slept in the same bed as this woman for the past three years and not laid a lustful finger on her?

'Flick—' he began, his throat unaccountably dry.

From the hall came the scrape of the front door and Felicity was on her feet.

'They're back!' she cried, rushing from the room.

His thoughts – whatever they might have been – remained unspoken.

Percy couldn't deny it was good to see Carol-Anne and Brendan. They'd returned from a riotous few days in London, so they announced, and Brendan muttered, 'Got some good stuff for the book,' to Percy as drinks were poured.

The four of them clinked glasses and raised a toast to the season and then set about the cognac seriously. Carol-Anne warmed her bum in front of the open fire, claiming she was cold.

'That's because you never wear enough clothes,' said Felicity – rather sharply, Percy thought.

'She's all for easy access, aren't you, Annie Fannie?' said Brendan.

'Don't call me that, you Irish lout.'

'Aussie tart,' he replied cheerfully.

'I see you're getting on as well as ever,' said Felicity, holding her glass out for a refill. 'We'd better separate you before there's a fight,' and she pulled Brendan away from Carol-Anne into the centre of the room.

He did not resist her but said, looking up, 'Fancy that, we're standing right under the mistletoe.'

Percy watched spellbound as Brendan kissed his wife. It was a rude, open-mouthed snog. A teeth-and-tonsils affair. And, to Percy's amazement, Felicity did not resist the assault. On the contrary, she hugged Brendan's tall frame with urgency as she surrendered her lips.

Carol-Anne was grinning at Percy. She took the hem of her dress and, for a split second, raised it to her waist. The sight of her nude pussy-split framed by black suspenders almost had Percy coming in his pants.

Felicity and Brendan broke their clinch. She was still clutching her brandy glass and she drained it in one.

'Let's have some music, Percy,' cried Brendan. 'I bet the ladies would like a dance.'

It transpired that they would. Felicity unearthed a smoochy jazz record and Carol-Anne dimmed the lights. Brendan circulated the brandy and Percy stood glued to the spot, his cock twitching and his mind racing. Would he be able to control himself once he was dancing with Carol-Anne? What would Felicity do if he dared to kiss the Australian girl the way she had kissed Brendan? Would this end in pain or pleasure? Whichever it was to be, right now he didn't care.

The room was L-shaped, acting as a lounge and a dining room. Brendan was pushing the furniture back against the walls to give them space. In a trance, Percy helped move the table and chairs. Then Billie Holiday was in his ears and Carol-Anne was in his arms.

He wondered why they hadn't at least begun with their proper partners. But Felicity had turned to Brendan without a glance in her husband's direction and now was circling the room in the Irishman's embrace. The pair were whispering and giggling and Brendan's hand was in the small of her back, buried somehow beneath her sweater. Percy was still in shock.

'Hey, loosen up, Perce,' Carol-Anne said softly. 'This is fun.'

He bent his head to hers. 'Yes, but I'm worried about Felicity.'

'There's no need – she's having a great time. Why don't you give my bum a little rub?'

'What if she sees?'

'What if she does? I know Brendan. He'll be rubbing more than your wife's back in a minute. Just tell me, do I feel good to you?'

It was a stupid question, of course. The satin of her naked buttocks beneath the silk of her frock felt like heaven – hard-on heaven. She squirmed the taut delta of her belly against his swollen cock and moaned. Percy steered her beneath the mistletoe and shut her up in the traditional fashion. He could at least justify the embrace if challenged.

But there was no challenge. As he kissed Carol-Anne, he turned their bodies, his eyes searching the gloom for Felicity and Brendan. They were out of sight, presumably in the other part of the room. He unbuttoned her bodice.

'Yes,' she whispered. 'Take my boobs out, Percy. I want them squeezed and sucked. Quick!'

The instructions were unnecessary but thrilling. As he carried out her bidding, baring her breasts and cupping the warm flesh, she kept up a stream of titillating commands.

'Ooh, that's nice. Now kiss my tits. Suck my nipples. Do it softly. Now do it hard. Oh yes! Say you'll fuck me soon, Perce.'

He raised his head from her flushed and glistening bosom.

'What about the others?' he whispered. 'We can't – I mean, what if Felicity – ?'

She took him by the arm and tugged him towards the fork of the room.

'See for yourself,' she whispered.

At first Percy couldn't see a thing – the light in this area had been turned off completely. Then he made out a shape in the corner, half on and half off an upholstered dining chair. The shape was pale and indistinct and moved in a steady rhythm. Above the music, Percy could hear whispers and grunts. Then the shape came into focus and he was staring at the ovals of Brendan's bare buttocks as they thrust backwards and forwards, the cheeks hollowing and filling, the dark stripe of his rear division pointing down to the hairy plums of his dangling balls.

It was incredible! Brendan was fucking Felicity!

They crept closer. She was on her knees pillowing her head and shoulders on the seat of the chair as he knelt between her splayed thighs. The big white cheeks of her arse were bare, her skirt pushed up to her waist. As Brendan ploughed into her from the rear, his hands were beneath her body, playing with the glories of her great breasts which hung down and overflowed his palms.

Percy watched in disbelief. It was the most exciting thing he had ever seen. But he also acknowledged the bubble of anxiety rising in his gullet as his gaze settled on his wife's face. Framed by the wild tangle of her hair, resting on her forearm, her visage was serene and glowing. Her eyes were closed and her lips were moving gently. Gone were the lines of anxiety and furrows of discontent. She looked about twenty.

A tug on his hand jerked him back to the present. He'd have to sort his feelings out later. For the moment other, more pressing, matters required attention.

'God, I feel horny,' Carol-Anne said as Percy led her to the sofa in the main room and pulled her skirt to her waist. 'Did it turn you on, seeing your wife getting her arse screwed off?'

'I was turned on anyway,' said Percy, spreading the girl's legs to look at her hairless pouting pussy.

'She's a gorgeous woman,' whispered Carol-Anne, her eyes gleaming. 'I bet you do it lots.'

Percy didn't reply. The music had stopped and from the other side of the room came the cries of Felicity letting her hair down. The sights and sounds of sex were in the air. The succulent orifice of Carol-Anne's quim beckoned him and he bent to kiss it.

'No, Percy,' she said, grabbing him by the hair and pulling him away. 'You can suck me later. Fuck me now. I want it like she's getting it.' And she got on her knees and wiggled her bare arse at him.

'Stick it up me, Percy. Fuck me like he's fucking her. Make me come off like your wife.'

And so he did.

40

Lucian arrived at Basil's New Year's party all of a fluster – and not just because of his appointment with Henrietta Suckling.

As he'd been getting ready for the party, he'd made the mistake of looking out of his window in the hope of seeing the delectable Nicole also getting dressed. He had not been disappointed – though, in point of fact, Nicole's clothes were being doffed not donned. Celebrations were obviously starting early across the street and Lucian was surprised to see that king-sized Freddy Cameron was already in the thick of things.

The pair of them were embracing enthusiastically. Freddy had obviously just arrived for he still had his jacket on and he was holding an unopened bottle of champagne in one hand. The other was sliding the pencil-thin strap of Nicole's camisole over a golden-brown shoulder. In turn, her hand was busy below his waist and, when they broke their kiss and she stepped aside, Lucian could see his long pole of a cock protruding obscenely from his pinstriped trousers.

It was an extraordinary sight: the diminutive African smartly dressed in his business suit with his big brown banana curving up from his fly. Nicole, now bared to the waist, slipped to her knees in a flurry of swaying tit-flesh and began to peel back Freddy's foreskin. From the way she stuffed the cock into her mouth, Lucian could tell that Nicole was very fond of bananas.

But it wasn't just this licentious display that had shaken Lucian to the core – he had after all witnessed Nicole entertain Freddy before. It was the appearance of a third party in the window across the street: a sandy-haired man with a bulge in his jeans and a camera round his neck.

'Good God, it's Hugh,' said Lucian out loud.

As Nicole warmed to her task, supporting herself on one hand while the other fed Freddy's shaft into her mouth, Lucian revised all his sympathetic thoughts about his tennis partner. He watched as Hugh gleefully pulled Nicole's tiny black panties from her milky-white rear and then framed his wife in the viewfinder of his camera. Obviously Hugh was a consenting party to Nicole's frolics with Freddy. *Flash!* went the camera. And *flash!* again as Hugh moved in for a close-up of his wife's hollowed cheek and glittering eye as she gorged on Freddy's tumescence. For all Lucian knew, Hugh might have been present when he had seen Nicole fucking the African before, hidden from Lucian's sight in another part of the room.

Hugh put down the camera and extracted his own wand of virility. Though not of Freddy proportions, it was hardly insignificant and it looked eager for the fray. Lucian knew the feeling. As Hugh sank to his knees behind his wife's gyrating bottom and pressed his swollen tool to her proffered pussy purse, Lucian fought the urge to ease the pressure in his own loins. God, how he desired that woman across the road! How he longed to have his cock between her lips like Freddy or up her cunt doggy-fashion, like Hugh, with her curvaceous buttocks buffing his belly and his hands on the dangling weight of her glorious tits!

The trio across the street were moving swiftly to their crisis, it was plain to see. But Freddy had one more trick up his sleeve and, as his mighty organ shot off into Nicole's mouth and Hugh erupted into her loins, the cork jetted from the champagne and a fountain of fizz splattered the happy threesome.

Lucian had turned from the window with envy in his heart and a hard-on of stone between his legs. His only consolation, as he splashed his loins with cold water in a vain attempt to cool his ardour, was to wonder whether the trio would have anything left to give by the time midnight arrived.

At the party, Basil met him in the hall and took his coat. 'All set, dear boy?' he whispered. 'Now, don't drink too much and don't you dare look at any woman other than La Suckling. Men are swarming around her already so you'd better get cracking. Follow me and I'll introduce you. And don't forget – I'm counting on you!'

Basil gave almost the same pep-talk to Lorna ten minutes later.

'I can't believe you're prepared to prostitute me like this,' she muttered as he led her into the party throng.

'Get you, dearie. You were singing a different song last night. I defy you to tell me you've gone off Hartley Smythe so quickly.'

'Oh my God, Basil—'

The dark-haired Member of Parliament for the North Grinding was approaching.

'—he's fucking gorgeous!'

'Just make sure you fuck him then. I say, Hartley! May I present my invaluable assistant, Lorna Prentice ...'

'Miranda – you came!'

'Not yet, Sophie, but the night is young.'

'Very droll, darling. How you've changed since I rescued you from Basil's clutches a few weeks ago.'

'I wouldn't call it a rescue, Sophie. You simply captured me for your own purposes.'

'Are you complaining?'

'Hardly. Is that Mathilde over there?'

'It is. She's helping with the refreshments so you can't lure her upstairs until the wee hours. Then she's booked, I'm afraid. Of course, you're welcome to join us.'

'I'll see. This is a working night for me. I've got to keep my eyes open.'

'Really? Don't tell me – it's something to do with Basil and who's going to win the—'

'Shh! You're not supposed to say it. It's an absolute bloody secret, Sophie, so don't breathe a word. *Please*.'

'This is a jolly significant occasion you know, er – Heather, isn't it?'

'Harriet. And you're the famous Rodney Branscombe.'

'I wouldn't say famous, actually.'

'A brilliant young publisher on the way up, then. A shit-hot acquiring editor destined to be an industry mover-and-shaker. A name on the lips of every writer and agent who counts.'

'Gosh. I thought you said you didn't know anything about publishing.'

'I just know the obvious things. Like who counts.'

'Crikey. You're quite a girl, Harriet, and stunningly attractive, if I may say so.'

'You may, Rodney. I value your opinion. You were telling me what a significant gathering this is. Why is that?'

'You're sure you don't work in publishing? Or for a newspaper?'

'Oh no. I'm sort of a librarian. In the country.'

'I see. Well, you've heard of the Baxendale Prize?'

'Vaguely. It's some kind of book award worth pots of money.'

'And with bloody funny rules. Like no one's meant to know who the judges are. But I can tell you, Harriet, and don't mention it to a soul – all five of them are here tonight.'

'No!'

'It's absolutely true. Our host, Basil Swan, is the chairman and I'd give him a wide berth if I were you because he's the biggest lech in the business. Unless you want to go home with fingerprints on your knickers.'

'Who says I'm wearing any, Rodney?'

'Really? Oh golly, aren't you?'

'I might show you later. Just tell me who else is on this panel.'

'Oh yes, well . . . That tall bloke over there with the fair hair—'

'I recognise him. He lives in my television set.'

'Hartley Smythe, MP. Smarmy bugger.'

'He's a hunk. Who else?'

'The bald chap with glasses and a big grin. Bishop Desmond Handcock. He's talking to another one, that little squirt in leather with the hair. God alone knows what they've got to say to each other.'

'Well, God *would* know, wouldn't he? Since he's a bishop. Who's the hairy one?'

'Garnet O'Dread the poet.'

'He looks like a rock singer. One of those heavy-metal guys who hasn't changed his wardrobe in twenty years. Aren't there any women judges?'

'Only one. Mind you, she counts for about six. I can't see her.'

'Who is she?'

'Henrietta Suckling.'

'That old tart!'

'I think she's fabulous.'

'She's coming into the room now. Perhaps you'd better go and pay homage.'

'Actually, I wouldn't mind a word with her. Why don't you and I meet up a little later? Don't forget you promised to show me whether you're wearing any, er . . .'

'Run along, Rodney. Henrietta's got a queue forming around her already. I expect it's because she *never* wears underwear at parties. They say it slows her down.'

But Rodney didn't hear, he was forging through the crowd towards the actress.

'Creep,' said Harriet to herself as she watched him go. She wasn't displeased, however. He had marked her card most effectively. She had promised Monty Hastings she would help him win the one literary prize he coveted above all others. If she brought home the Baxendale she had no doubt Monty would realise she was more than just a leg-over with the elevenses. Then it would be Bye-bye Karen and Hello Harriet on a permanent basis. Harriet Hastings sounded so much better, in her opinion, than Harriet Pugh.

She fumbled in her cocktail purse, hoping that amongst the make-up and contact lens fluid she might find – yes, it was there: the little crucifix she carried for luck. She fastened the thin gold chain around her neck and carefully adjusted the tiny cross in the valley of her intoxicating bosom. Tugging the scooped neckline of her clinging peacock-blue dress just a little lower, she aimed her 36DD cleavage in the direction of the bishop and the poet. Now was her chance to bring her real influence to bear on the events of the literary world.

41

'It's one of the ironies of life that I should be conversing with a bishop at an occasion of such spiritual bankruptcy. I smell the stink of depravity beneath this roof.'

Desmond Handcock, Bishop of Burlap, beamed at Garnet O'Dread and nodded his head. He always did this when he didn't understand what someone was talking about. And he hadn't understood much of what Garnet had said during the past five minutes. But the young man was a poet, which probably explained it.

'Here we gather,' continued Garnet in his dull monotone, 'to sound the death knell of a bitch of a year expiring in the vomit of its own corruption. And, wearing the mask of merriment to conceal the impurity of our neglected souls, we prepare to celebrate the birth of a new whelp of immorality.'

The bishop nodded more vigorously and drained the glass of orange juice that Basil Swan had given him. A young man with piercing blue eyes and tight trousers immediately replaced it. This gathering was certainly full of handsome youths!

'In the eyes of a holy man such as yourself,' Garnet droned on, 'the follies and pretensions of the literary world at play must be redolent of purgatory here on earth. Wouldn't you agree, bishop?'

'Er, I think it's rather a nice party myself. So much gaiety and laughter. So many attractive young persons having fun.'

Garnet barked a dry mirthless laugh, his stock-in-trade. 'You put me in my place, bishop. Unfortunately a poet cannot afford to rise above his sense of disgust. And mine is highly attuned, God help me.'

'He will, don't worry,' cried the bishop heartily, relieved to be on home ground. 'There's no need to address me as bishop, you know. Call me Des. Everyone does. And may I call you Garnet? You know, you remind of a someone in a pop group I used to admire when I was a student.'

'My father says I look like the singer in The Lace Banana.'

'That's it! How I used to enjoy their songs! They were so much more wholesome than all the others. 'The Hubble-Bubble Hymn', 'In Hippy Heaven', 'Roll Another One, Sweet Jesus' – how it all comes back!'

'I hope not, Des. Those are all drug songs.'

'Really?' The bishop finished his second orange juice and another waiter replaced it. As he pressed the glass into Desmond's hand he winked. He had a blond ponytail and the torso of a Michelangelo statue. The man of the cloth felt a sudden surge of gaiety and he laughed into Garnet's wryly smiling face. With that softly curling hair and his smooth cheeks, the poet too looked like a Renaissance youth.

'Don't look so gloomy, my young friend,' cried the light-headed bishop as he caught sight of a statuesque blonde heading in their direction. 'Why, here's a pretty maiden come to cheer you up.'

'She's a painted whore, Des. And she's showing all her chest!'

'Ah, but she bears the cross on her bosom, Garnet. She must be on the side of the angels.'

'Of course I am, bishop,' said Harriet Pugh as she introduced herself. 'I've been dying to know what you two have been talking about. Let me guess – modern literature!'

'No,' snapped Garnet, jerking his arm away from the be-ringed hand which had somehow alighted there.

'Really? On a night like this, surrounded by the stars of the publishing firmament, how could you not? Did you know that *everybody* here is talking about *Refulgent Ennui*, the brilliant new book by Montgomery Hastings. It's the most spiritually uplifting and poetically inspiring novel I've ever read in my life! It's just perfect for you two!'

Lorna was trying hard to impress Hartley Smythe, if not with her insider's gossip – thanks to Basil she had plenty of that – then with her slender model's figure, artfully displayed in a dress from a salon in South Molton Street. Even she, a girl who had regularly blown her stepfather's monthly allowance on designer frippery, had been staggered by the cost.

The green silk was a perfect match for her red hair which she wore piled elaborately on her head, her long white neck circled by a smart modern necklace in white gold. Though she'd sat for hours in the hairdresser's chair she did not begrudge it. The hairdo was something that could not be repossessed – the rest of her outfit was going back on the morrow. She felt like Cinderella. On the stroke of midnight, however, this part-time princess was meant to be dancing on Hartley Smythe's cock. Perhaps she should be bolder.

'I've spent all day in bed,' she said, 'with the most fabulous book.'

'Really?' A flicker of interest stirred in his brooding brown eyes. 'Tell me more.'

'Oh no. I'd be embarrassed. It's made me incredibly horny.' And she giggled, hoping her act wasn't too transparent. Not that it was an act really. Dressed in just a whisper of silk, standing in a dark corner close to a man of power and influence and film-star looks – well, she *was* incredibly horny.

'It's about a woman's revenge on her unfaithful husband. She decides to sleep around to get her own back and, frankly, she leaves him standing.'

'I didn't know women read books like that,' he said.

'Of course they do. We all like to fantasise. Escapist reading is basically a masturbatory activity.'

'I see.' When he smiled his teeth gleamed in the shadows. 'And is that what you were doing in bed all day – masturbating?'

Lorna gulped her champagne. She hadn't meant to make this kind of confession. On the other hand, she *had* decided to be bolder.

'I couldn't help it. *The Novelist's Wife* is a very exciting book.'

'I'd like to see for myself.'

'I'll send you a copy.' *You bet! I'm winning, Basil.*

'OK but it's the effect on you I'm interested in.' His eyes, those swirling umber pools, travelled slowly down her body until his gaze came to rest on her thighs, their pale bare length almost entirely on view beneath the wispy hem of her dress.

'Show me, Lorna,' he said in a voice like molten chocolate.

The sound caressed her, sweet and seductive. So he *was* a lecher after all and she would accomplish her mission. The knowledge made the moment all the more delicious.

'What do you want me to do?' she whispered.

'You know very well, you little tease.'

'I want to hear you say it, Hartley.'

'Pull up your dress and take down your panties. Show me your pussy. Yes, just like that.'

She obeyed him as he spoke, baring the fork of her long lean body for his satyr's gaze, and opening up her secret treasure.

'What a little jewel you have there,' he breathed. 'Let me see how you give yourself a thrill.'

'It's my pleasure,' she gasped, two fingers now embedded deep in the syrup-slick folds of her cunt.

Henrietta Suckling was everything Lucian had expected her to be: elegant, alluring, witty – and popular. It was now approaching midnight and he hadn't yet managed to get her on her own. Men buzzed about her like bees round a honeypot and the chief drone, to Lucian's chagrin, was Rodney Branscombe. For ten minutes he had flattered her shamelessly, proclaiming that her acting in a new sitcom could not have been bettered by a youthful Maggie Smith and going on to extol the virtues of her latest chocolate commercial.

'I swear, my darling, that when I first saw it I dashed out and bought a box – even though I hate mints. Your performance was so utterly hypnotic I was simply brainwashed!'

What hogwash, thought Lucian, though he wasn't so stupid as to say so. Nevertheless he seethed inwardly as La Suckling exclaimed, 'How sweet!' and kissed Rodney on the cheek. So it was inevitable that when Branscombe began to boast about the fabulous books he had recently acquired for GrabCo, Lucian felt the urge to compete.

'You can kiss goodbye to the number one spot in the bestseller list from April onwards,' he said. 'I've got the hottest property of the year.'

'How fascinating,' said Henrietta. 'What is it?'

'A story of betrayal and vengeance and the burning flame of erotic passion. It will create a scandal and capture the imagination of the nation.'

'Pooh!' sneered Rodney. 'It's only Monty Hastings' wife's dirty book. Too tacky for words, if you ask me.'

'As it happens, Branscombe,' said Lucian, 'I *wasn't* asking you. You'd publish this book like a shot – if you were allowed to!'

'Now, now, boys,' breathed the actress, placing a placatory hand on both their knees as they sat on either side of her.

At that moment the lights went out and the sound of chanting voices reverberated throughout the house.

'Ten – nine – eight . . .' they cried but Lucian was aware that his two companions were not counting – why not?

'Five – four – three . . .'

He leaned towards Henry, conscious of her warmth and musky perfume and the pressure of her hand still on his knee. Beneath the hubbub he thought he heard a sticky, lip-smacking kind of sound. Surely she wasn't snogging that twit Rodney?

'Happy New Year!' The cry went up and corks popped and the chimes of Big Ben rang out.

Despite the gloom Lucian could plainly see Henrietta's face pressed to Rodney's, her mouth parted as he probed with his tongue. Yet the flash of jealousy and thwarted purpose that shot through him was swallowed up in the lightning bolt of emotion which followed – as the hand on Lucian's knee thrust upwards to close on his crotch.

The horny slut, thought Lucian as nimble fingers unzipped him and burrowed into his underclothes, closing with practised intent on the rock-solid barrel of his cock.

'Oh Henry!' he heard Rodney whisper in the darkness. 'You're fabulous, gorgeous, I want to—' The voice was cut off as Henrietta kissed him again, her fingers still busy on Lucian's penis. He slid his hand onto her hip and up to her well-rounded bosom. Slipping into the opening of her décolletage, he felt for her nipple. It was big in his fingers, like a nut. As he squeezed the engorged nub of flesh she shivered and applied an answering pressure to the head of his rampant tool.

Lucian lifted her big right breast out of her bodice. The white flesh glowed in the dark and he lowered his lips to the dark bud at its centre. The hand in his lap was tickling his prick, tormenting and teasing. Across the hillock of flesh in his face he could see her other arm and the dark shape of Rodney. From his rival's moaning and writhing Lucian had no doubt that Henry had charge of his cock too. And when Lucian lifted her dress to her waist to explore the thrilling territory of her loins he found that Rodney was there ahead of him.

How thoroughly obscene this was, Lucian thought as his lips and hands sucked and fondled and roved all over the actress's lush body, taking turn with the other man in a bizarre act of lustful cooperation. He had his tongue in her mouth now, as Rodney yielded the upper ground to drop to his knees and raise Henrietta's skirt to her waist. Lucian held her quivering body tight as the other man spread her legs and thrust himself into the welcoming fissure between her alabaster thighs.

As his rival began to pump, Lucian was mesmerised by the sight, now clearly visible in the half-light. Rodney's cock was a dark gleaming weapon stabbing into the open purse of the woman's blonde-bushed sex. Her bared white body undulated with each lunge and the swollen orbs of her breasts rolled and shivered in a spectacular display.

The two of them began to pant and moan and Lucian realised that the harsh grunting that mingled with their voices was his own. Her hand on his cock speeded up and suddenly the three of them were moving together. Lucian pushed his fingers into the fur of Henry's pussy to find the tiny peg of her clit and the three of them came like that, Lucian with his hand trapped between their jumping bodies, his penis spurting gouts of spunk all over his trousers.

As euphoria faded and Rodney collapsed into Henry's arms, covering her nude and glorious flesh, Lucian realised that his arch-rival had got there ahead of him once again.

42

'How are you getting on, Lorna?'

She was standing with her back to Basil and the touch of his hand on her shoulder made her jump.

'For Christ's sake,' she hissed. 'Oh, it's you.'

Basil grinned. 'Where's Smythe?'

'In there.' She pointed to the conservatory door, which was closed.

'Why aren't you in there too? It's the perfect place to nail him.'

'Because—' Lorna didn't want to go into the matter in detail. It was more than embarrassing to admit that she had had her prey eating out of her hand and lost him. That she had shamelessly pulled her knickers down, hiked her skirt to her waist and wanked her pussy till the juice had run down her thighs. Then, at the point when the MP was surely about to throw himself upon her and give her what she needed with his doubtless mighty cock, another woman had turned up. The blonde in the too-tight pink suit had materialised out of the shadows and stood by his side as Lorna had taken herself over the hill and come off like a fire-cracker in front of the pair of them. Lorna had never felt so humiliated. Particularly when the blonde had said in a snotty voice, 'How very edifying,' and led the gorgeous Hartley off by the arm without a backward glance.

'—he's in there with another woman,' she said simply. 'And don't ask.'

'Well, I've got to know who she is.'

'I haven't a clue. She's a short, brassy blonde with too much on top and a voice like vinegar. He must like that kind of thing.'

Basil grinned. 'Come on, let's have a look. If we catch him with his pants down with her it's as good as him doing it with you.'

Lorna wasn't sure she agreed but she followed Basil out of the back door all the same. It was a trifle chilly in the garden, bearing in mind how she was dressed, but she soon forgot about that.

'Brilliant!' exclaimed Basil as he led her across the paved patio and pointed to the conservatory windows. The interior was dimly lit and tall spiky plants in tubs offered a degree of cover to the occupants. Nevertheless it was obvious at first glance that they were furthering an already intimate acquaintance.

'Just look at that,' said Basil. 'The Opposition Spokesman on Family Values making the beast with two backs.'

Lorna refrained from adding that he was actually making the beast with two backs and one pair of legs – Basil was always telling her not to be pedantic. But whatever the nature of the carnal creature before them its activities were undoubtedly fascinating.

The blonde had discarded her skirt and Hartley his trousers. She clung to his torso like a koala up a gum tree, her arms wrapped around his chest and her loins impaled on the branch of flesh that thrust rudely from his crotch. Lorna stared with wonder at the taut lines of his bare legs, sinuous and golden with hair, that rose up to support the top-heavy tower of grunting, grappling flesh.

'Mmm, I like the bum,' muttered Basil in her ear, a comforting arm around her waist.

'How could you?' said Lorna. 'It makes mine look undernourished.'

'Possibly.' He slipped a hand beneath her dress to test the assertion. Lorna made no objection, she was riveted by the sight of Hartley's broad hands supporting the woman's buttocks. Though sizable, Lorna had to admit the woman's arse was shapely and, in this position, displayed to obscene perfection. It was undoubtedly arousing to see the white flesh billowing over Hartley's fingers, the furrow splayed to reveal the dimple of her rosehole and the black-fringed mouth of a quim stuffed to the hilt.

Basil's hand had ceased its preliminary investigations and now burrowed between Lorna's legs. Lorna leaned her hip against him and allowed him to probe her tingling pussy, her attention still captured by the erotic spectacle.

'We've got him now,' crowed Basil. 'Two witnesses to an adulterous encounter in the conservatory. I wonder who she is?'

'Some PR tart, I expect.'

Now Hartley was jiggling the woman up and down on his cock, waltzing her around the room as he did so.

'Cocky bastard,' said Basil.

'I'll say.'

'He'd better watch out – if he falls on the glass table he might end up a cockless bastard. Oh Christ!'

Hartley managed to avoid the table but his legs buckled following an ambitious step and the pair of them crashed to the floor. The onlookers heard the shriek from within, followed at once by a gale of laughter.

'At least they're not hurt,' said Basil. 'Oh my, look at that.'

Lorna *was* looking and her elation at tricking Hartley Smythe vanished in an instant. 'I knew she wasn't a natural blonde,' she muttered.

'So what?' Basil's finger in Lorna's knickers had ceased its gentle frotting of her clit and he stood stock-still, trying hard to make sense of the scene before him.

On the conservatory floor, some distance from the sprawling lovers, lay a mass of brass-blonde curls. The woman, who now knelt to grasp Hartley's still-rampant member and re-insert it into her dark-haired pussy, was a born-again brunette.

'You've lost out, Basil. You can't blackmail Hartley Smythe.'

'Why not?'

'I recognise her now without the wig. That woman he's fucking is his wife.'

'You know, Garnet, I'm beginning to think you're right. This *is* turning into a celebration of lax moral behaviour. There are an *awful* lot of young women who don't appear to be wearing many clothes.'

'That's not the half of it, Des. Have you seen those two on the sofa over there.'

'You mean the woman with the décolletage and that handsome boy. But, Garnet, she's old enough to be his mother. They're just having a convivial chat, surely?'

'Have you seen where her hand is? Come a little closer, over here behind this screen.'

'Dear me! Saints preserve us! She's holding his – his penis!'

'His cock, Des. His foul and bestial organ of generation.'

'It's not foul in itself, Garnet. I have to say that, in purely visual terms, it's rather pretty. And jolly long. I don't think I've ever see one that size.'

'Well, you probably don't come across many erect dicks in your line of work.'

'Alas, no. That is, er, as a senior churchman I am somewhat removed from the more earthy side of pastoral care – oh my gosh, what is she going to do with it?'

'Put it in her mouth, Des.'

'But it won't fit! Oh, it does. The way she crams it all in is really most skilful. I imagine that the sensation is pleasurable for both parties?'

'Like silk on velvet. The throb of excitement in the pulsing stem, the gush of seed on the palate —'

'Ah, I can tell you are a true poet, my handsome Irish boy.'

'You're not so bad yourself, Des. If you weren't a holy man I'd be tempted to call you devilish good-looking. Oh look, he's having an orgasm.'

'I say!'

'Fountaining the milk of his desire into the generosity of her embrace.'

'How beautiful! Thoroughly reprehensible, of course, but aesthetically pleasing nonetheless.'

'Absolutely. Now I suggest we slip away quickly before that blonde whore with big breasts tries to molest us again. She's looking this way. Quick – follow me!'

Harriet regarded their departure with regret. There was a fierce glow in her loins and a romp upstairs with two men would have dampened the flames – *and* she would have killed two birds with one stone. But the Baxendale judges were proving an elusive lot. She'd frightened off the bishop and the poet, the MP was nowhere to be seen (she'd searched) and Henrietta Suckling only had eyes for cock – the one significant sexual appendage Harriet was lacking. Which just left the chairman of the panel and host of this gathering: Basil Swan. Before she succumbed to the allure of one of the many other young men who were roaming the party, she'd have a final attempt to bring home the Baxendale bacon for Monty.

'So, Basil, how is your master plan proceeding?'

'There've been one or two hitches, Miranda, but the night is still young.'

'No it's not. People are dropping like flies. There's a disgusting orgy going on in the front room but none of your fellow judges are involved.'

'There's Henrietta.'

'She doesn't count. If she doesn't lay half a dozen men at a do like this it's bad for her image. You'll never pressurise her into voting for *The Novelist's Wife*. You'd have more luck if you could say she spent New Year's Eve at home alone with a cup of cocoa. Now that *would* be bad for business.'

'I suppose you're right but—'

'Forget it, Basil. Your wife has offered me the use of her room and I'm going up there now to get away from this repellent fiasco. And I tell you this, if you can't guarantee me the Baxendale tomorrow then I'm going public about the rhino horn or whatever it was they injected into your horrible little prick.'

Basil watched her mount the stairs with malice in his eyes and despair in his heart. 'It's not little,' he muttered, 'at least not any more.'

'Talking to yourself, Mr Swan?' said a husky voice behind him. He turned to confront the smoothest, deepest cleavage he had seen that night. Encased in constricting peacock blue, decorated with a tiny glistening crucifix of gold, it set the tiger in his tank purring with desire.

'I just wanted to say what a truly fascinating evening this has been for someone like me who knows nothing of the world of books. Thank you so much.'

'How kind of you ... I'm sorry, I've forgotten your name.'

'Harriet. I came with a man from the GrabCo publicity department but he's gone.'

'So you're on your own and without a drink?' said Basil, taking her arm. 'Why don't we just slip into my study? There's a bottle of champagne I've been saving.'

Sod that bitch Miranda Lynch. Sod the Upstanding Member Hartley Smythe and Henrietta No Knickers Suckling and that silly slut Lorna Prentice and his useless floppy-haired nephew, Lucian. Sod the lot of them.

What Basil needed was a soft pillow to rest his head on for the night. Two soft pillows would be even better. Encased in peacock blue.

43

By the time she was halfway up the stairs, Miranda had banished
the altercation with Basil from her mind. She never cried over spilt
milk. If Basil's schemes came to nothing then she'd find another
way of getting what she wanted. Right now her thoughts dwelt
elsewhere – on the comfortable bosom of Sophie Swan and the
youthful white flesh of their mutual playmate, Mathilde.

But Miranda never reached Sophie's boudoir. Barring her
way, sitting on the step of the second-floor landing with her head
in her hands, was a young woman in tears. Miranda's face was
level with a pair of neatly turned knees when the sobbing figure
looked up.

'Lorna,' said Miranda, surprised.

The girl stared at her in anguish and suddenly Miranda found
herself bending over her, an arm around those slim shaking
shoulders. She'd never got on with Lorna but she could not ignore
her distress.

'What's the matter? Can I help?'

'It's B-Basil,' moaned Lorna, wiping the tears from her face with
her fingers and spreading mascara across her cheeks.

Miranda produced a handkerchief and began to wipe. 'What
about him?' she said.

'He's a bastard.'

'So you've finally found out. I thought you were in love with
him.'

'I hate him.'

'In my observation that's often the same thing. There, that's better.'

'God, I must look a fright.'

'Actually, my dear, you look how you always look – young and beautiful.'

Miranda didn't know why she said that or why, on impulse, she gave the girl a hug. Lorna hugged her back, her slender body still quivering with emotion. Miranda was conscious that, in their party finery, neither of them was wearing a great deal. Their bare arms and shoulders rubbed together in pleasant intimacy.

Lorna giggled. 'This is pretty funny, us sitting here like this. You kicked me out six months ago. And now Basil's chucked me. I must be the least-wanted editorial assistant in London.'

'What! Basil's fired you?'

'As of today. I guess that makes you feel good.'

'You think I'm pretty hard-hearted, don't you?'

'Until two minutes ago, Miranda, I thought you didn't have a heart at all.'

They sat in silence for a moment. Then Miranda took Lorna's hand and pressed it into the low, square-cut neck of her dress. The girl's fingers slipped between silk and flesh, moulding to the curve of Miranda's left breast.

'Can you feel my heart?' said Miranda.

'It's beating very fast.'

'I've changed recently, Lorna.'

The girl looked at Miranda, astonishment and fear in her big dark eyes. *And something else*, thought Miranda, as her nipple swelled in Lorna's palm. *How delightful.*

Desire.

'Do you think we're safe now?'

'Should be, Des. If we lock the door they'll think we're just a randy couple who've commandeered a spare bedroom for a bonk.'

The bishop sighed as he sat beside the poet on the bed. 'Don't misunderstand me, my boy, but if I have to listen to another hysterically enthusiastic young person telling me about an exquisite new novel I shall ask to meet my Maker ahead of schedule. Are all publishing parties like this?'

Garnet grinned and, from a zipped pocket in his leather jacket, produced a vodka bottle. He poured generously into two tooth glasses taken from above the washbasin in the corner.

'Not for me, please,' said the bishop hastily. 'I never partake.'

'Oh yes, you do.' The poet flourished a bottle of orange juice taken from some other compartment in his clothing and added it. 'Basil's little tarts have been spiking your drinks all evening.'

'Really!' The bishop was flabbergasted. So flabbergasted he took a mouthful without thinking. 'I've often wondered what it must be like to be under the influence.'

'And how is it?'

Des giggled. 'I feel like one of those novels everyone was going on about. You know – "ecstatically informed".'

Garnet smirked. '"Meticulously wrought".'

'"Mythically charged".'

'"Erotically inspired".'

'Oh yes indeed.'

'Really, Des?'

'Well, by that boy with the golden ponytail and—'

'The lollipop in his pants?'

'It was *huge*, wasn't it? I didn't *mean* to stare but – Garnet, what are you doing?'

'I think you ought to satisfy your curiosity about a few things, Des. You need a lollipop of your own to lick. How do you like the look of mine?'

The bishop gulped at the sight of his young poet friend who had continued the unzipping process and now stood with his tumescent wand of virility jutting from his leather loins.

'Well?' demanded Garnet.

The bishop opened his mouth but no sound ensued. The poet plugged the orifice in the appropriate fashion. With his lollipop.

In other rooms of the house, other orifices were being similarly filled. In the study, for example.

After the stroppy and disobliging behaviour of most of his female guests it was a relief for Basil to encounter Harriet Pugh. She had administered the first instalment of that relief while his glass of champagne fizzed merrily on the mantelpiece – Harriet being on her knees on the hearth rug with her plush lips stretched in a scarlet ring around his veiny cock.

She rose to gulp greedily from her own glass, a hand still petting his momentarily satisfied member.

'Mmm,' she breathed in thrillingly affected tones, 'it's the best kind of cocktail. I call it White Velvet.'

'You do?' Basil was at a loss.

'The taste of champagne and spunk. If you could bottle it, you'd make a fortune.'

Basil topped up her glass. 'Do you drink it often?'

'Whenever I get the chance. Why, Mr Swan, I do believe you're getting hard again. That's *most* impressive.'

'I'm impressed by you, my dear. What is it that you do – apart from giving the most delicious head?'

By way of reply Harriet slipped the straps of her dress over her shoulders and pulled the peacock blue veil to her waist.

'Oh I say!' exclaimed Basil as her two heavy-slung melons met his sight, the flesh quivering, the nipples blood-red with need.

'I cater to men of letters,' said Harriet as her dress hit the floor in a rustle of excitement, revealing her naked but for stockings and suspenders. 'It's appropriate we're in your study because, in fact, I also give very good office.'

She walked away from him, her broad curving buttocks creamy in the dim light.

'How would you like me, Mr Swan? Over your desk?' And she

bent over the table, unconsciously adopting the position favoured by Lorna in her former role of personal assistant.

Basil approached the magnificent rear, the twin globes out-thrust and spread wide for his personal entertainment. In the groove of her secret divide the split peach of her pussy, lightly dusted with brown fur, gaped in invitation. Above was the pink dimple of her anus and all around was the strawberry-and-cream marvel of her nude arse. It was twice the size of Lorna's boyish rear. Basil was sure it would afford twice the pleasure.

He anointed the scarlet head of his penis with juice from her sticky quim. As he filled the vacancy between her legs he was of half a mind to ask her to take up her current position permanently.

On the top floor, Lorna Prentice probed with her tongue, savouring the honey-sweet tang of the first pussy she'd pleasured since boarding school. Between her own slim legs the rapacious mouth of Miranda Lynch brought her to a shuddering gasping orgasm that had to be the best so far. What a way to start the New Year, she thought, to be locked in a passionate sixty-nine with a woman. A woman, what's more, whom she loathed.

'I loathe you, I loathe you,' she whispered into Miranda's sweet musky centre.

Miranda's hand stroked her slender flanks. 'I love you too, darling,' she whispered and began the happy business of bringing her off yet again.

On the first floor, Bishop Desmond stared at his reflection in the mirror above the sink. Was this the face of a man who had sinned? If so, why couldn't he get the silly drunken grin off his face?

Over his shoulder he could see Garnet lying on the bed, naked, with a similar soppy smile on his usually dour countenance. How beautiful he looked. And how irresistible.

'Come back to bed,' called the poet, 'and put your big cock up my arse.'

It wasn't poetry but it was the sweetest sound the bishop had heard in years. He did not resist the call.

On the ground floor, Basil straddled the succulent torso of his newfound admirer as she wrapped her big hot teats around the barrel of his tool. She'd done everything he asked and more until they'd both moaned and babbled and spread their juices all over the study furniture. He had only discerned one peculiarity about her – she had a tendency to bang on about some novel by that creep Monty Hastings when she got excited.

'Mmm yes, yes please,' she murmured, 'fuck me there, do. Promise you'll finish off on my tits. I love a man to spunk on my breasts. It reminds me of a passage in *Refulgent Ennui* when . . .'

But Basil wasn't listening. There was only one passage on his mind – the soft slick thoroughfare between her juddering titty globes that housed his throbbing prick.

The entire house reverberated with fucking. Throughout it all, Lucian spent the night alone on the front-room sofa. When he closed his eyes, his mind replayed delicious moments on the same sofa when Henrietta Suckling had manipulated his aching penis to orgasm. He could also see once more the galling moment when the actress had risen to her feet and dragged a smug-faced Rodney Branscombe upstairs – where he was doubtless still buried to the hilt between her juicy thighs even as he spouted bollocks about the marvellous books on his spring list.

Now Lucian lay with an enormous erection on his belly and the ashes of failure in his mouth. He could still feel the teasing touch of La Suckling's fingers on his tool and sleep was a distant prospect. And he was not looking forward to facing his Uncle Basil once this cursed night was over.

44

Basil strode through the debris of the party like a bear with a sore head. The hangover didn't help, of course, but that was to be expected at eight o'clock in the morning on New Year's Day. What wasn't, was the absence of his usual cure – to whit, a willing woman. Basil swore by cunt as solace for a thick head and this morning his head was very thick. Like his cock.

So the first irritation of the day had been when he reached for the hot and supple body that had pleasured him in the early hours on the study couch. But Harriet had disappeared. No trace of her remained apart from the lipstick stains on his prick, her pussy-musk on his fingers and the memory of her magnificent rounded arse rubbing against his belly. How he longed to bury his cock in that wide and welcoming divide! The angry tumescence thrusting from his loins wanted it too. The purple cap of his penis stared at him in reproach.

There were times, incredible though it was to contemplate, that Basil regretted the remarkable success of his rejuvenation treatment. On mornings like this, when there were weighty matters to consider, he resented being a slave to his libido.

The scene that greeted him in the kitchen had not eased his ill-humour. Sophie, in a fluffy blue dressing-gown carelessly draped over her ample charms, sat sipping coffee. Basil had not been slow to see an opportunity.

'Happy New Year, my darling,' he had whispered as he bent to kiss her mouth, at the same time slipping his hand into her gaping

283

neckline with the intention of dandling the big loose breasts he knew so well.

'Go away, Basil,' said Sophie, turning her head so he kissed only toast crumbs on her chin and grasping his hand before it made significant advances. 'You smell of last night's booze and last night's woman.'

Before Basil could open his mouth to protest – his transgressions were never openly acknowledged – Sophie continued.

'I've made a New Year resolution, Basil. No more dishonesty in our relationship. I want things out in the open.'

Basil took a step back. 'What do you mean?'

'I mean, meet Mathilde.'

On cue, a flaxen-haired girl advanced on the table with a pot of coffee in her hand. She was wearing a baby-pink T-shirt which barely covered her pussy mound and revealed thighs as white and breathtaking as a Nordic snowscape. Basil's cock twitched impatiently and his head throbbed.

'We've met already,' he said, taking Mathilde's free hand and gazing into her ice-blue eyes. 'You're by far the prettiest waitress we've ever had.'

'She's also my lover,' said Sophie.

'What!'

'You heard, Basil. I'm off men and it's all your fault. I prefer Mathilde. I'm sure you can see why.'

'Well, Sophie, I'm a liberal-minded fellow as you know and Mathilde *is* a most bewitching creature.'

'So let go of her.'

Somehow Basil was still clutching Mathilde's slim white fingers. He released them with reluctance, protesting, 'Sophie, please! What kind of a man do you think I am?'

His wife grinned at him and placed a proprietorial hand on Mathilde's rump. 'Surely you don't want me to tell you, do you, Basil?'

The girl pushed her bum back against Sophie in a small

movement that twitched the bottom of her shirt provocatively north. Basil stared at the bulge of her mons outlined against the pink material. Good God! He could even see some fine hairs, glinting like spun silver, below the pink hem.

He cleared his throat. 'I'm very happy for you both. And as a broad-minded man I can see no objection to your, er, friendship. There's just one thing...'

'Yes, Basil?'

'Can I watch?'

Basil saw the movement of Mathilde's hand fractionally before a pint of coffee was launched over his trousers. Fortunately the liquid was not piping hot but Basil nevertheless retreated to the hall in some discomfort. There he met Henrietta Suckling donning a leopardskin fun fur, looking as bright as a button.

'Basil, sweetheart, what a marvellous do! Such wonderful company! The best New Year's Eve party I've been to all year. Are you all right, darling? You've wet your pants.'

'I spilt some coffee. Won't you stay and have some?'

The actress shot him a wicked grin. 'No thanks. I've got a sexy young publisher lined up to drive me home and give me breakfast in bed. Now, where is he?'

Basil's spirits soared. 'You mean Lucian? I'll find him for you.'

'Is that his name? I forgot. Oh here he is. Come on, dear heart, take me home and ravish me instantly!'

Basil's sky-bound spirits crash-landed as Rodney Branscombe appeared from the downstairs loo. It was all he could do to mutter a civil farewell as the actress bundled her captive out of the door. Not that Rodney noticed. His eyes were hollow with fatigue and his face was as pale as paper. Basil doubted there was much ravishing left in him and wished that he himself could replace the whey-faced editor in the actress's bed. His obstinately erect cock throbbed in agreement.

Basil surveyed the damage in the front room, wincing at the wine stains on the Axminster and the stiletto marks on the mahogany table. From the chandelier drooped a pair of knickers and two used condoms. Thank God the help were returning at noon to clear up

A snore from a far corner led his gaze to the slumbering form of Lucian, stretched out on the sofa in the rear alcove. With malicious glee Basil tipped his nephew onto the floor where he lay in a dishevelled heap, quite disoriented.

'Get up, you useless boy. I knew I shouldn't have relied on you You've ballsed everything up.'

Lucian looked up from the ash-stained carpet. 'And a Happy New Year to you too, Uncle Basil.'

'What's the matter with you, Lucian? Wasn't Henrietta hot enough? While you've been having a first-class kip Rodney Branscombe's been shagging her arse off.'

Lucian struggled to his knees. 'Actually, uncle, I've only just dropped off to sleep. I've had a terrible night. By the way, do you know you've wet your trousers?'

Basil was about to make a suitably withering retort when a voice summoned him from the doorway.

'Goodbye, Basil.'

'Lorna, my dear!'

Basil's spirits lifted. Here might be a solution to one of his problems – the pressing one in his pants. And though Lorna looked a little delicate in the morning light there was no denying her basic fuckability. He advanced on her with intent.

'Before you go, darling, would you mind just popping into my study? Something urgent has come up and it can't wait til tomorrow.'

Her reply took him by surprise.

'I'm not going anywhere with you, you slimy sod.'

'Steady on, Lorna.'

'Have you forgotten what you said to me last night? You were rude and vile and you sacked me.'

'Did I? I recall I lost my temper—'

'You called me a brainless little tart who had outlived her usefulness in your employment.'

'Lorna, I can't apologise enough. I was distraught, I was drunk, I didn't mean it – look I'm on my knees.' And so he was. In Basil's experience, it was a necessary quality of a successful publisher to be able to grovel. 'Mea *mea* culpa, my angel. I abase myself before you. I kiss your heavenly feet.'

'Don't do this to me, Basil,' Lorna wailed. 'Don't try and get round me —'

'Hush, Lorna. Let me deal with this.' A different voice assailed Basil's ear. He looked up from his position at Lorna's feet to see Miranda Lynch approaching – from the rear. She took two athletic steps forward and launched her right foot.

'OH!' yelled Basil as Miranda's pointed patent-leather party shoe caught him squarely in the crack of his temptingly presented posterior. He pitched forward onto his nose and rolled over onto his back, whimpering with pain.

Miranda bent over him. 'I enjoyed that, Basil. And I'm going to enjoy kicking your reputation all over the newspapers if you don't deliver what you promised. You've got till tonight, remember.'

'My God, Miranda,' stuttered Basil, 'there's no need to resort to personal violence. Business is business.'

Miranda smiled and hooked an arm round Lorna's waist. 'That boot up the bum was for Lorna, Basil, because she wouldn't have the nerve to do it herself. Not yet. Just you wait till I've finished training her as my new personal assistant.

'And this is lesson number one, Lorna. When you've got an opponent on his knees, kick him where it hurts.'

What a ball-breaker, thought Basil as she pushed Lorna out of the door. *Literally*.

45

The year was not half a day old and already it was turning into an annus total fiascus for Basil Swan.

'Take that smirk off your face,' he yelled at Lucian in the wake of Miranda and Lorna's departure.

'Now, now, uncle,' said Lucian, making no attempt to hide his amusement. 'You're not my boss any more. I work for Miranda, don't forget.'

Basil hobbled towards the sofa and sat down next to his nephew. 'I'm sorry, Lucian,' he said. 'This morning is full of painful truths. I feel like a useless old fart well past his sell-by date.'

Lucian put a reassuring hand on his uncle's knee. It was still damp from the spilt coffee.

'Look, why don't you go and change. You'll feel much better.'

Basil sighed. 'I ought to check the rooms upstairs. See what's broken. Find out who's drowned in vomit in the attic. The usual drill after a party.'

'I'll do that. Then I'll meet you in the kitchen. Would egg and bacon suit you?'

Basil covered Lucian's hand with his own. 'Perhaps you're not such a useless boy after all.'

Basil cleaned the last dollop of egg yolk from his plate with a scrap of bread and poured himself another cup of coffee. He was showered and shaved, fed and watered. Physically he felt a hundred per cent better, mentally he was still shaken by the setbacks of the party and its aftermath. If only he could get Miranda off his back! She'd relish turning him into the laughing-stock of the publishing trade.

Lucian was reporting on his inspection of the house and Basil was barely listening. The fact that there was an upturned poinsettia on the second-floor landing and a pair of torn tights blocking the loo was not of significance in the greater scheme of things.

'Aren't there any publicity nymphets wandering around still angling for a plug?' he asked, mindful of his needy loins.

'Sorry, uncle, everyone's gone. Apart from the two guys in that little room opposite the airing cupboard.'

'What two guys?'

'They were asleep when I went in so I left them to it. I had to borrow a key from the next room because the door was locked.'

'But who are they?'

'I don't know. One's a lot older than the other and the young one has long hair.'

'Good God!' Basil was on his feet, a glint in his eye. 'Were they wearing anything?'

'I don't know. I mean, they were under the bedclothes. Though I did notice some leather trousers on the floor.'

'Fantastic!' Basil was grinning from ear to ear. 'Come on, Lucian, follow me.'

'What are you going to do?'

'Pull my nuts out of the fire and, incidentally, show you what it takes to be a great publisher.'

'Eh?' Lucian was bumbling along in Basil's wake as his uncle dashed into his study and flung open a corner cupboard.

'Aha! Got it!' Basil pulled a camcorder from behind a pile of typescripts. He thumbed the On button which at once glowed red.

'What's that got to do with it, uncle? Surely being a great publisher is all about finding unique and brilliant books that shape people's lives.'

'No, it's not, Lucian.' Basil was halfway up the stairs now. At the top he turned to his nephew. 'Being a great publisher is about not looking a gift-horse in the mouth – even if you first have to shoot it in the balls. Just watch.'

Desmond Handcock, Bishop of Burlap, dedicated churchman and lifelong celibate, woke in the arms of a hairy young poet. As the silver sunlight of a crisp New Year's day stole across the pillow, Des opened his eyes and gazed at the pale and beautiful face lying next to his.

'Good morning,' said Garnet O'Dread.

'Oh my God,' said the bishop.

'He moves in mysterious ways,' said the poet and kissed him.

It was not in Desmond's power to resist and, anyway, it was a little late for resistance. So when Garnet stripped the bedclothes from the bishop's nude body and kissed his way down to the straining sceptre that rose trembling from the holy man's loins, well – Desmond would have died rather than forego these miraculous new earthly pleasures. Garnet swung his body round so that his own tumescent treasure was temptingly displayed, and then sucked the head of Desmond's cock deep into his throat.

'Oh heavens,' breathed Desmond and slicked the poet's milk-white foreskin back over the ruby-red cap of his tool. So these were the rank and corrupting pleasures of the flesh. How dissolute, how terrible – how utterly intoxicating they were! As he closed his eyes and opened his mouth, Desmond resolved that from henceforth he would give redoubled sympathy to those sinners who sought solace for sexual transgressions.

Lucian reflected that the two lovers weren't so much caught red-handed as scarlet-cocked. When he and Basil stepped into the room the pair of them were side by side in a graphic sixty-nine which admitted of no innocent explanation. And, as the bemused pair drew apart, Basil's camera captured in explicit detail two puce and glistening male organs sawing the air in thwarted desire.

'Just a little fun, my dears,' said Basil as he zoomed in on Desmond's fingers ringing Garnet's leaping tool.

The poet scrambled from the bed and made for the publisher, murder in his outraged face. But Basil was prepared for that and pushed Lucian into his path. The pair ended up on the floor in a tangle and Basil shot that too, making sure to capture the onlooking Bishop of Burlap as he sprawled on the bed, naked and horrified and divinely erect.

Miranda and Lorna watched the video later at Miranda's flat.

'So that bugger Basil pulled it off after all,' said Lorna.

'He did,' replied Miranda. 'And you can be sure that these two buggers will now vote for *The Novelist's Wife*. With Basil's own vote that means the Baxendale's in the bag.'

Lorna peered closely at the television screen and the sight of the two men caught *in flagrante*. She giggled. 'You have to take your hat off to Basil, though I can't say I approve of his methods. Thank God I don't have to answer to him any more.'

'Indeed. You do have to answer to me, however.'

'Meaning?'

'That if you take your hat off for Basil, you can take your knickers off for me. Right now.'

'Yes, boss,' said a weary Lorna. Was there no end to the dedication required to get on in publishing?

POSTSCRIPT

46

As Montgomery Hastings took his seat at the Baxendale prize-giving dinner, he said a silent prayer to the ghost of the mad old lady herself. Gwendoline Baxendale had left her vast fortune to the establishment of a prize for 'the year's most exceptional and unpretentious work of fiction'. It was worth a cool £50,000 pounds to the winner and a matching sum to the lucky publisher, dwarfing all similar awards. Naturally, it had been highjacked by the literary brigade – pretension, like beauty, being purely in the eye of the beholder. So the Baxendale was not only the richest but the most prestigious prize an author could win – and Monty wanted it. He wanted it more than health or happiness or sex. And more than his marriage.

Which was why by his side sat his very personal assistant, the angel of his muse and the woman who had promised him the Baxendale – Harriet Pugh. She looked splendid, with pearls shining in her ears and lying in a glistening rope above the deep décolletage of her bosom. She caught his glance and, under the tablecloth, gave him a reassuring squeeze.

'Why, Monty,' she whispered, 'you've got a hard-on. How can you think of sex at a moment like this?'

'I can't help it,' he replied. 'If I win, I know I'm going to come in my pants.'

'You'll win, Monty, don't worry. Perhaps I can start the celebrations early.' And she slipped her fingers into his fly.

Monty savoured the sensation of her frotting fingers on his tool, allowing his gaze to wander round the vast gathering in the Costermongers Hall. The dinner itself was a naff affair – hastily served chicken in wallpaper sauce followed by jam tart – but the company was luminous. All the big fishes among publishing houses were represented and many of the minnows too. Because there was no official shortlist for the prize – as opposed to the many unofficial ones promoted by the book chains – everybody thought they had a chance. And now, before disappointment set in, was the time to make the most of the occasion. Conversation was at fever pitch and the Chardonnay was disappearing like best bitter at a stag night.

As Monty surveyed the throng, smiling at the great and the good and the downright wicked, he thought he caught sight of a familiar dark-haired figure on the far side of the room. He stared but people were on their feet, table-hopping and rushing to the loo before the big announcement, obscuring his view. When his sight-line cleared the woman had gone. He must have been seeing things. This was the last place his wife was likely to be.

Thump! came the sound of a gavel and conversation died. There was a scramble for seats. The chairman of the Baxendale Prize committee, Basil Swan, was on his feet.

Twenty minutes into Basil's speech – the old trouper being in no hurry to relinquish the stage – he dropped his bombshell. Authors and agents, publishers and press turned to one another baffled and bemused.

'Who?'

'What's it called?'

'Never bloody heard of it!'

'Karen Hastings? Hey, Monty – any relation?'

At the podium the radiant figure of the winner clutched her cheque to her adorable breast and in a clear voice bubbling with emotion told the world how disbelieving, thrilled and grateful she was.

'I'd like to thank my agent, Marilyn Savage, and my editor, Lucian Swan, and all the wonderful people at The Whimsical Press without whom—'

At a table in the far corner, a cork popped and champagne sprayed into the air. A beaming Miranda Lynch could be seen shaking the hand of a floppy-haired young man while their colleagues whooped and embraced and generally luvvied it up to the acute displeasure of everyone else present.

'But most of all...' Karen's speech rolled on in the usual fashion. Up to this point most people had hardly taken in a word, though her serene face and elegant carriage had already made a lasting impression. '...I'd like to thank my husband, Montgomery Hastings, without whom, I assure you, my book would never have been written.'

Monty was on his feet, swaying, his mouth open but his voice – like his wits – had temporarily deserted him. All eyes were on him as his body began to jerk like a man on the end of a massive electric shock. His eyeballs swivelled up in his sockets and his features crumpled as if his face had been filleted. In slow motion, it seemed, he keeled over and lay unconscious on his back. Only his twitching penis, sticking out of his trousers like a brandished flag, indicated that there was still life within.

Pandemonium erupted. Sympathetic hands rushed to cover Monty's loins and to search for other vital signs. Karen was borne from the stage on the shoulders of excited Whimsical Pressers. Journalists reached for their mobile phones and the general throng reached for their glasses. The hubbub was intense. At this moment the side doors to the hall burst open and an assortment of bright young things, shepherded by Lorna Prentice, began to distribute piles of books amongst the tables.

'I say, this is it – *The Novelist's Wife* by Karen Hastings.'

'Christ, it's that porno book they're serialising in the *Badger*!'

'It's got "Baxendale Prize winner" printed on the cover. That's quick off the mark.'

'Fix! It's a bloody fix!'

'It's not a fix,' cried Miranda Lynch, triumph blazing in her storm-grey eyes. 'I gambled. I bound some books like this because I was convinced we'd pull it off – and I was right. That's why I'm a winner and you lot are also-rans!'

'Congratulations, Karen.'

'Thanks, Lucian. I can't believe it.'

'It's true. You've won the Baxendale. Aren't you glad now you came to the dinner?'

'Thanks for making me.'

'Have you heard about Monty? They've taken him to hospital.'

'What!'

'He collapsed after the announcement.'

'Oh no!'

'I'm told it's just a precaution.'

'God, Lucian, it's all my fault!'

Amid the chaos and excitement, one mind was icily calm, one heart beat with measured coolness. At the moment of the announcement Harriet Pugh had become instantly sober. Her emotions were such that they extended beyond rage and betrayal to – revenge. She abandoned the pathetic relic of her unconscious employer, other hands would see to him. She had different matters to attend to.

She found Basil Swan surrounded by a fawning group of his peers, middle-aged suits the lot of them. She displayed herself boldly before him and received, as she knew she would, the most syrupy of his smiles.

'Harriet, how delightful to see you!'

'Come with me, Basil. We must talk.'

'As you can see, I'm a little tied up and—'

'Now, please. I'll make it worth your while.'

'What *are* you talking about?'

She leaned in close to display to advantage the lush expanse of her cleavage. 'I'm talking about what I want to do to your cock, Basil.'

She led him into a telephone booth off the lobby. It was a tight squeeze but she knew he wouldn't mind that.

She unzipped him in a flash.

'My dear! What are you doing?' As if he didn't know.

'I've got to hold it, Basil—' his cock was in her hand, brutish and eager '—while I ask you something.'

'Yes?'

'Why did you do it?'

'What do you mean?'

'Go back on your word.'

'I'm sorry?'

'You remember our night together?'

'Of course, my darling. I searched for you afterwards. You don't know how I've pined for you—' His hand was full of tit, groping through her thin dress.

'Then you'll remember I let you fuck me in the mouth—'

'Mmm, yes.'

'And in the cunt—'

'Ooh, you were tight and juicy.'

'And up my bum—'

'Divine! It was fabulous!'

'On the understanding that you gave the Baxendale to Monty Hastings.'

'What?'

'You promised.'

'I never did, my darling.'

'But that's all we talked about, fucking and *Refulgent Ennui*.'

'Now, look here, Harriet, I think you've got the wrong end of the stick.'

'No, I haven't, Basil. I had the right end then and I've got it now.'

'Ouch – what are you doing?'

'You shafted me so I'm going to shaft you.'

'Ow! Ow! Let go!'

'I'm going to send you where poor Monty's gone. To hospital. But when he wakes up *he'll* still have something to shaft with.'

'AAH!'

47

'God, Percy, I didn't know you knew how to – ooh – massage like this.'

There were many things his wife didn't know about him, Percy reflected as he sat astride Felicity's hips and manipulated the flesh along the ridge of her spine. Chief among them was his knowledge of her affair with Brendan, the late-lamented inspiration to Percy's creative genius. He had been gone a week. The holiday season now being upon the land, Brendan and the honey-loined Carol-Anne had abandoned their winter career as house-helps to the Carmichaels in favour of the summer on a Greek island. They were sorely missed.

'How's this, Flick?' Percy turned his attention to his wife's neck.

'That's lovely,' she said and groaned a kind of you've-got-me-going noise that Percy knew well. Unfortunately his recent familiarity with it had been of a vicarious nature – while watching Brendan finger his wife's glowing flesh through the bedroom keyhole. This evening, Percy had decided, he was going to experience all of Felicity's sounds of sensual satisfaction firsthand.

Following the festive evening on which Percy had witnessed Brendan taking Felicity on her hands and knees, he had confronted the Irishman.

'I just got carried away,' said Brendan. 'Your missus is a powerfully attractive woman.'

'It's OK, Brendan. I mean, I'm not angry or anything. I'm grateful.'

'You are?'

'I thought Felicity had given up sex for good. At least I now know she's still got an appetite for it – even if I'm not on the menu.'

'Hey, Perce, don't get upset.'

'I tell you, I'm not. But I *am* curious. Tell me, have you had her before?'

And so it had all come out. The truth about Flick's back treatment, the hank-panky of the previous summer, the threesome with Henry ...

'Good God, she let you put it up her arse?'

'Actually, she let Henry. But since then I've had her up the bum lots. She really likes it.'

These words were on Percy's mind as he mumbled something about needing access to the base of Felicity's spine. He tugged her skirt off and stripped her tights and knickers down her legs. She did not protest. As he slid a pillow beneath her hips, raising her big white buttocks off the bed, she squirmed her loins into the softness below.

Percy pressed down on the small of her back as he had seen Brendan do. Brendan had given him lessons in massage. They had even practised together on the taut and resilient flesh of Carol-Anne.

'Oh that's good,' moaned Felicity, wriggling her bottom, the brown nest of her pussy now openly on display between her lower cheeks. What mysteries women were, Percy thought as he drank in the sight. This was his wife's cunt, which had borne him three children, yet it was as if he were seeing it for the first time. His hands slid lower and pulled apart the trembling rounds of her buttocks. He pushed a finger between the long pink frill of her labia and it was at once sucked in to the second joint. He inserted another finger.

He'd missed Carol-Anne badly this past week. Not that they

were soulmates but even when they weren't engaged in furthering their carnal relations her golden presence in the house had thrilled him. Already, however, he was falling under the spell of her replacement as a nanny – a willowy drop-out who lived locally. Vicky had discovered he wrote erotic novels, surprising him as he opened a set of page proofs from Blue Desire. 'If you need a woman's opinion,' she'd said, 'try me. I'm *very* broad-minded.' And she'd looked at him boldly with her big brown almond-shaped eyes.

Percy pulled his fingers from Felicity's sticky quim and replaced them with his cock. She was so wet his big tool glided all the way in as if greased.

'Oh Percy!' she murmured, her loins gripping him in a handshake of welcome.

He slipped his fingers beneath her satin-smooth hip and stole across her belly to her bush. The nub of her clit was swollen and firm. He rubbed it the way he used to do in days gone by and she came, her big soft arse shaking beneath him.

He waited till she had recovered before he spoke.

'Tell me, Flick, what do you think we should do with that empty room upstairs?'

'Good Lord, Percy, must we talk about it now?'

'Not if you don't want to, darling.' Percy grasped her hips and began to shuttle his cock in and out of her vagina in a slow rhythm. 'But now Brendan and Carol-Anne have gone, I wonder if we shouldn't let it out to a student or someone.'

'I hadn't thought about it. Mmm, this is nice, isn't it?'

'Oh yes. I've missed you, Felicity. You and your wonderful bottom.'

Percy spread her cheeks with his thumbs to see better as the white pole of his penis plundered her dark-fringed pussy mouth. Above it, in the heart of her secret furrow, the star of her anus pouted in invitation. Brendan had been up there. And Henry. Percy jabbed deep into her cunt and she groaned in response.

'Do you remember Martin, Flick? The Robinsons' lad.'

The Robinsons had lived across the road until two years previously, then they'd moved to Leeds.

'Of course I remember Martin.'

'He used to have a crush on you.'

'Silly boy.'

He'd been seventeen two summers back and ever-present around the Carmichaels' house. Felicity had been breastfeeding Crispin at the time.

'I met him in the High Street last week,' continued Percy, circling her rosehole with his finger. 'He can't stand Leeds. He's doing Information Technology at the college.'

Felicity looked at him over her shoulder. Her hair was wild and her cheek was flushed. 'So you want him to live upstairs?'

'He hates his digs. He'd be much happier here.' Percy pushed the finger into the tight knot of her rear.

'I wouldn't mind,' said Felicity, her eyes sparkling and her bottom undulating to his assault. 'What about you?'

'You're used to having a handsome young man around the place. I don't want you pining after Brendan.'

'That's very thoughtful of you, darling. Oh!'

Percy suddenly withdrew his cock from her quim and moved his slippery red glans to the dimpled fissure just above it.

'Oh, Percy, yesss!' she cried, the sound rushing out on a hiss of breath as her arse-hole yielded and the elastic circlet of flesh swallowed his knob.

Percy savoured the sensation. At last he was back in the driving seat. As his wife pushed the generous velvet moons of her buttocks back into his belly, he thrust his penis all the way home.

48

Lucian arrived home from Oxford in the early evening. He could have stayed on at Adele's wedding reception but, after his conversation with Karen, he hadn't the heart for it.

'I'm sorry, Lucian,' she'd said. 'I don't want to write another book.'

'But, Karen, you're mad. You've won the Baxendale, *The Novelist's Wife* is top of the bestseller list and we're offering you an incredible amount of money. You've single-handedly pushed back the frontiers of erotic literature. This is your moment – seize it!'

She laughed, a musical tinkle. Her black eyes twinkled as she shook her head. 'You're not going to talk me into it, you know. I've resisted Marilyn and I'm not going to cave in to you.'

'Oh hell.' Lucian's shoulders slumped as he accepted defeat. He swigged from the glass of champagne in his hand without tasting it. 'Just tell me why, Karen.'

In the marquee around them bright young things chortled and flirted and middle-aged family members guffawed in groups. Lucian heard only the soft lilt of Karen's voice as she took his arm and spoke into his ear.

'I've promised Monty.'

'What do you mean?'

'I thought he was going to die. I thought writing the book and winning the prize had given him a heart attack.'

'But he's OK, isn't he?'

'Yes. It was only shock. But it made me realise I had done a dreadful thing.'

'Come on, Karen. It's a bit late for remorse. Besides, he deserved it – that's what you said.'

'Maybe. The point is, Lucian, when he was in hospital we talked. We realised we had both made a mess of our marriage. And we came to an arrangement.'

'You give up writing. It's a bit one-sided, isn't it?'

'No. We're going to have children. At least, we're going to try. And if we can't have them, we'll adopt. I'm giving up books for babies.'

'For God's sake, Karen, what kind of message does that send to women?'

'I don't want to send any messages,' she replied. 'I've got the rest of my life to write books, I haven't got long to have babies.'

There was nothing to say to that. As Karen was claimed by a knot of admirers eager to speak to the notorious novelist and 'friend' of the bride and groom, Lucian moved outside to contemplate the failure of his mission. It was two-edged. One of the reasons he had responded to Adele's unexpected invitation was to further his relationship with Karen. They had enjoyed a close professional understanding and Lucian had nursed hopes of expanding it into a more intimate sphere. Obviously that was now out of the question. Which was something of a disappointment – especially in these circumstances.

It had always struck Lucian that there was nothing like a wedding to set people's juices flowing. Maybe it was the prospect of what the bride and groom would be up to later or the effect of quickly-downed fizz at the reception but, in his experience, where there were nuptials, nookie was always in the offing.

This occasion was positively throbbing with sexual promise, he could tell. The warm May day was perfect for skimpy female finery and the grounds of the fancy hotel had plenty of leafy corners for those wishing to explore the extent of that skimpiness. Eyeing a breasty brunette with grass stains on her skirt, Lucian had had the urge to do some exploring himself. But he had no partner – they seemed hard to come by these days – and so he had returned to London.

As he entered the flat he discovered a postcard on his doormat. It was from Tania Pilgrim in East Marimba.

Lucian stripped off his tie and reached for the last beer in the empty fridge. The cold bubbles hit the back of his throat and he thought of bubbly Tania. How he longed for her now. For her big brown breasts and dirty laugh and slick strong thighs wrapped around his own.

Her card asked for an extension on the delivery of her next book – her research was proving so exhausting. She promised to make it up to Lucian in whatever manner he chose. Lucian intended to grant her request – and to extract every last ounce of repayment from her delicious body when she returned.

But that was a far-off prospect and didn't fill the void of his empty evening or assuage the ache in his balls.

The message light flickered on the answerphone. He rewound the tape and found himself listening to the husky tones of Marilyn Savage as she wished him luck in persuading Karen to sign a new deal.

'If you pull it off, dear boy, you can roger me senseless every night for a month but I tell you now you haven't a prayer. You must turn your mind to fresh pastures. Actually, I have a new proposal that could earn you a special bonus. Give me a call, darling.'

The thought of Marilyn's heart-shaped face ministering to his cock had his organ jumping in his pants. Lucian dialled her number. A recorded message clicked in at once. He hung up. He'd try later but he didn't fancy his chances. Marilyn was not a woman to be idle on a Saturday night.

A pile of paper in the tray beneath the fax machine caught his eye. It was from Caroline. A stab of guilt shot through him. He'd hardly given Caroline a thought in recent months. Then he smiled to himself, at least that was one demon he had laid. The smile turned to a grin. The way she had begged to be laid the last time they had met still gave him a thrill.

'Lucian,' said the top page of the fax, 'here's my new story idea. It's about a beautiful TV journalist who has a dark and turbulent affair with a waiter. As her media star rises so she becomes more debauched in her private life – but she can't live without the kinky sex! I'd really welcome your input. I do hope you like it and that we can work on it like last time. I attach the first chapter. Love, Caro. PS Can I have more money this time?'

Lucian took the accompanying pages and lay down on his bed to read. In the opening sequence the heroine allowed herself to be picked up in a nightclub by a slim and brooding Italian who dared her to make him a present of her underwear. With her knickers in his pocket, they took to the dance floor and he fingered her pussy through a slit in her dress until she came. At his apartment she protested when he sat her on his cock and pushed a thin dildo between the trembling cheeks of her bottom – but the double insertion gave her the kind of shattering orgasm she had never experienced before . . .

Lucian unzipped his trousers and freed his palpitating prick. It wasn't so much what he was reading that excited him, it was the thought of the snobbish and uptight Caroline dreaming it up and writing it down. As she did so, he knew, her pretty blonde-downed pussy would have been weeping into her panties – if she was wearing any at the time, of course. Did she masturbate as she wrote? That was an interesting question and one he would put to her at their first editorial conference.

He was looking forward to that occasion. Particularly the point when he would sit Caro on his cock and put a dildo to her glorious derrière. He would have rung her at once and suggested they get started if it had not been for a scribbled PPS which said she was out of the country for a week.

Lucian grasped the barrel of his tool and gently stroked – he couldn't help himself.

The ring of the phone diverted his attention just as matters were reaching boiling point. His member seemed to hiss with frustration as he reached for the phone.

'Hi, Lucian.' It was Hugh, his tennis partner. 'Are you busy tonight?'

'No.'

'Well, why don't you take a look out of the window?'

'What do you mean?'

'You *know* what I mean. Take a look. Right now.'

With a hammering heart, Lucian craned his neck and looked through the angled window across the street. Nicole was standing there gazing directly at him. She was wearing a tight blue T-shirt and cut-off denim shorts.

Lucian still had the phone to his ear.

'Are you watching?' said Hugh.

'Yes.'

Nicole took the hem of the vest and lifted it over her head. She shook her mane of dark curls free and tossed the garment onto the floor. She wore no bra. Her incredible breasts thrust out full and proud, swaying with her movements. She unzipped her shorts and bent forward, her tits hanging in mouthwatering invitation as she shucked the denim down her thighs.

Lucian was rigid with shock. As rigid as Hugh who now appeared by Nicole's side, one arm circling the honeyed sheen of her waist, the phone in his other hand. Both of them were stark-naked.

'As you can see, Lucian, we've got nothing on. So if you've got nothing on either why don't you join us?'

'Christ, Hugh, I mean—'

At the base of Nicole's belly, her chestnut fleece shone in the late evening sun. Her hand was on her husband's cock, slicking the foreskin gently back and forth across the bulging glans.

'Come on, Lucian. Nicole's dying to meet you properly. She needs your advice.'

'Yes?'

'Didn't I tell you? She's going to write a book.'

Of course.

As Lucian hurriedly pulled on his clothes and ran down the stairs it occurred to him that editing erotic material certainly took its toll.

He gave so much to the world of books. In so many ways.

A Message from the Publisher

Headline Delta is a unique list of erotic fiction, covering many different styles and periods and appealing to a broad readership. As such, we would be most interested to hear from you.

Did you enjoy this book? Did it turn you on – or off? Did you like the story, the characters, the setting? What did you think of the cover presentation? How did this novel compare with others you have read? In short, what's your opinion? If you care to offer it, please write to:

The Editor
Headline Delta
338 Euston Road
London NW1 3BH

Or maybe you think you could write a better erotic novel yourself. We are always looking for new authors. If you'd like to try your hand at writing a book for possible inclusion in the Delta list, here are our basic guidelines: we are looking for novels of approximately 75,000 words whose purpose is to inspire the sexual imagination of the reader. The erotic content should not describe illegal sexual activity (pedophilia, for example). The novel should contain sympathetic and interesting characters, pace, atmosphere and an intriguing storyline.

If you would like to have a go, please submit to the Editor a sample of at least 10,000 words, clearly typed in double-lined spacing on one side of the paper only, together with a short outline of the plot. Should you wish your material returned to you, please include a stamped addressed envelope. If we like it sufficiently, we will offer you a contract for publication.

TABOO

IN A WORLD OF NAKED INDULGENCE,
NOTHING IS FORBIDDEN . . .

Maria Caprio

BARBARA – the blonde aristocrat, long since addicted to the lazy colonial life and its myriad opportunities for sexual adventure.

ZOE – her young protégée, a shy brunette unused to the indolent ways of those who have nothing better to do than seek new conquests.

Together they experience the inexhaustible delights that East Africa has to offer. And as one refines her talent for erotic intrigue, so the other's undernourished capacity for pleasure expands to encompass a whole new world of sensual delights . . .

FICTION / EROTICA 0 7472 4552 5

A selection of Erotica from Headline

BLUE HEAVENS	Nick Bancroft	£4.99 ☐
MAID	Dagmar Brand	£4.99 ☐
EROS IN AUTUMN	Anonymous	£4.99 ☐
EROTICON THRILLS	Anonymous	£4.99 ☐
IN THE GROOVE	Lesley Asquith	£4.99 ☐
THE CALL OF THE FLESH	Faye Rossignol	£4.99 ☐
SWEET VIBRATIONS	Jeff Charles	£4.99 ☐
UNDER THE WHIP	Nick Aymes	£4.99 ☐
RETURN TO THE CASTING COUCH	Becky Bell	£4.99 ☐
MAIDS IN HEAVEN	Samantha Austen	£4.99 ☐
CLOSE UP	Felice Ash	£4.99 ☐
TOUCH ME, FEEL ME	Rosanna Challis	£4.99 ☐

All Headline books are available at your local bookshop or newsagent, or can be ordered direct from the publisher. Just tick the titles you want and fill in the form below. Prices and availability subject to change without notice.

Headline Book Publishing, Cash Sales Department, Bookpoint, 39 Milton Park, Abingdon, OXON, OX14 4TD, UK. If you have a credit card you may order by telephone – 01235 400400.

Please enclose a cheque or postal order made payable to Bookpoint Ltd to the value of the cover price and allow the following for postage and packing:

UK & BFPO: £1.00 for the first book, 50p for the second book and 30p for each additional book ordered up to a maximum charge of £3.00.

OVERSEAS & EIRE: £2.00 for the first book, £1.00 for the second book and 50p for each additional book.

Name ....

Address ....

....

....

If you would prefer to pay by credit card, please complete:
Please debit my Visa/Access/Diner's Card/American Express (delete as applicable) card no:

Signature .... Expiry Date ....